CARRY ON

CELIA LAKE

ALSO BY CELIA LAKE

The Mysterious Powers Series

Carry On

The Mysterious Charm Series

Outcrossing

Goblin Fruit

Magician's Hoard

Wards of the Roses

In The Cards

On The Bias

Seven Sisters

Charms of Albion

Pastiche

Learn more about the world of Albion and future books at my
website, celialake.com.

Sign up for my newsletter to be the first to hear about future
books and learn about fascinating bits of research. Happy
reading!

ABOUT CARRY ON

Can two war wounded learn how to carry on after life-changing injuries?

No one has told Roland anything useful since he awoke in the Temple of Healing following the battle of Ypres. Muzzy-headed from the potions he's forced to take and with no word from his family or friends, he is entirely alone. He's only allowed out of his room for command performances, talking about his experience of the War to people who refuse to listen to reality.

When Elen is assigned as his new nurse, Roland assumes she will be gone in a week or two like all the others. She's still there in a month, stubbornly insisting on doing everything she can to help him recover.

Elen has been sent back from the front after a head injury. She used to know the Temple of Healing well, back during her apprenticeship. Now, nothing works like it used to and she can't figure out what to do about the fact Roland's healer is entirely absent from his care. Except, that is, for baffling directives that are not at all in her patient's best interest.

Together, they must confront Elen's fear of questioning authority and find out why Roland has been isolated from everyone he knows.

Carry On is set during the Great War in Albion, the magical community of England, Wales, and Scotland. First in the Mysterious Power series, it has a happily-ever-after ending full of knitting, compassion, and romance.

CHAPTER 1

MARCH 15TH, 1915, IN TRELLECH

E len looked up at the footsteps coming down the hall. The sound of the hard heels on the marble floor indicated it was some secretary or aide, not a nurse or healer. She had been waiting on the administrative floor of the Healing Temple for at least an hour now. The waiting room was dull, with no windows, and had no clock, so Elen had only been able to tell the passing of time by the chime of the temple bells and the amount of knitting she'd done. Given how far she'd gotten past the heel of the sock, she thought it had been three-quarters of an hour.

"Therapeutes Morris? The Archiater will see you now." He was an older man, too old to join up, though he walked easily enough. She tucked her knitting into her bag and stood up, automatically smoothing her skirts.

She had dressed with care, wanting to look entirely ready for a new assignment. She wore her best mid-grey uniform dress with the matching half-cape. Her crisp white collar and cuffs were freshly bleached and ironed. A matching white linen cap covered the tight bun at the back of her head and she had attached the plain black bands on her forearms that indicated she was currently without an assignment. She was not on duty, so she was not wearing the apron or the sleeve covers, but they were tucked into the satchel over her shoulder along with her portfolio and her knitting.

The assistant walked to the centre of the hallway, and Elen worked at keeping up with his pace, to make it seem even, rather than be left scurrying after him. He turned abruptly into a side room, on the right. Elen entered behind him and caught a glimpse, through the windows, of the Temple gardens laid out below.

The spring flowers were beginning to bloom, mostly tulips, she thought. Before she could be sure, she was briskly escorted into the main office. She found herself standing with her back to the large windows there, feeling bereft of the view, and facing the chief administrator of the Temple.

"Archiater, Therapeutes Morris." This man, she knew, was Roderick Hudson. His dark hair was going silver, in a manner she was sure had been magically aided to be dignified rather than chaotic. His natural facial expression seemed firmly set on dour.

He had been Archiater, chief administrator of the Temple, for some ten years. It had given him plenty of time to be well established, and he had served in the Boer War as a healer, so he was at least moderately familiar with wartime needs. He stood, momentarily, the kind of bob upwards that men of his social class gave as a bare gesture to women like her, who were rather beneath them socially. "Therapeutes Morris."

No chair for her, then. She hoped it wouldn't be too long a meeting. "Good morning, Archiater. I'm reporting for reassignment."

He nodded, glancing at a manilla folder on his desk. She

assumed it must have her files in it. There would be positive comments in it, about her work. Also the negative ones about her own infirmities. She'd been told, with strips torn out of her, that there was no time for nurses to have a sit down because they were feeling woozy. Or worse, because their head was splitting and they were seeing lights and all manner of distractions that were not actually there.

No amount of arguing had worked, and she'd been sent back to Albion from the hospitals in France, in the hopes they might find something for her.

"Your records." The Archiater glanced up. "What do you have to say for yourself?"

She had practised this, repeatedly, in the mirror of the dressing table in her lodgings, stained and tarnished as it was. "I wish to serve, sir, and continue to use my skills, even if I am not able to do so at the front."

"You refused one of the country hospitals, rehabilitation work. Surely that would be better suited to your needs? Meaningful work, but a slower pace."

Elen took a breath, steadying herself. "I may need quiet sometimes, sir, when I have an attack, but I feel I have a lot to offer here, where there are more varied needs." Her healer had encouraged her to find something else to do, but Elen had no idea who she'd be if she weren't nursing. She certainly didn't want to find out.

After a moment's hesitation, she added, truthfully enough. "The attacks are much less common now, and quite brief, most often in the evenings after I'd be off duty." It helped to be away from the artillery, for all sorts of reasons. Brief also covered a multitude of options. Three hours was certainly more brief than eight.

She continued, keeping her voice even. "The duties in one of the care homes, the patients are generally more stable." They needed care, certainly, but she could do more than they needed. She wanted to do more than that. She considered, not for the first time, whether to bring up the other part, the reason she was here now.

He was sharp, the Archiater was, and he looked at her, narrowing his eyes. "And?"

Caught out, she swallowed. "I would prefer to serve in a temple, sir. I'm Therapeutes to Sirona. At the front, we just had the little shrines, but the auxiliary hospitals often don't have anything other than the personal ones in quarters."

Archiater Hudson snorted, and she was sure then that she had been slotted into a tidy restricted category: middle-aged spinster, overly religious. So long as the label included 'still useful' she could cope. There was a long silence as he flicked through her file.

"Specialities?" Which was in the file, but he seemed the type to want to prod at the information. Honestly, it wasn't hard to guess, once she'd spelled out the devotion to Sirona.

"The process of healing, sir, especially arranging for the best long-term results. Before the War, I served at the Temple of Youth, with young people who needed additional support recovering. Tuberculosis, poliomyelitis, scarlet fever, mumps, and so on if the illnesses were particularly debilitating or lengthy. But I have the training, sir, to assist a wide range of rehabilitative healing. They do not currently need additional staff." The letter she had from colleagues there made it clear they were cutting down on beds, to aid the war effort elsewhere.

He frowned at her. "Not in your current condition, certainly." Blast, he was one of those men who thought a nurse was nothing more than a source of additional magical power. And that was a bit tricky right now, she would admit, at least in her own mind. Certainly she would not say such a thing out loud.

She looked down at the floor, to avoid doing anything else to upset him, and heard him turning the pages again, flipping. "We have a patient," he said, finally.

"Sir?" Elen looked up again, just long enough to show her interest deliberately.

"Major Roland Gospatrick. Excellent family, well-liked. Aiding in recruitment efforts, as his recovery allows."

Elen considered. The name seemed familiar, but she couldn't immediately place it. "And his healing needs, sir?"

"He suffers from physical ailments, most of which are responding well to treatment. But not all of his concerns are physical. He hears things, has unexpected reactions. It is possible there are hexes, or curses, or something of the kind that we have not yet identified."

That suggested rather an unusual history of injury. "The physical injuries, sir?"

"Several deep wounds, healing well, but he fatigues easily, sometimes he cannot bear light. We would prefer not to leave him alone." He looked her up and down. "He has not become violent, you understand. If he had, we would be handling his case differently. But he has become - disturbed. Unmoored in time and place."

Elen had heard something about these cases cropping up, though this seemed worse than those she'd heard about. "And you wish someone to be with him, see to his recuperation..." She decided to take the risk. "Be alert if there is something that would affect the recruiting?"

That earned her a beaming smile. "Ah, you are as quick as your letters of recommendation made you sound." He clearly hadn't believed them. "Exactly. He will need someone for at least a month or two. Perhaps by then we will have another task for you."

It wasn't as if she could turn it down. It was this or a country hospital, likely dingy and out of the way. "Thank you, sir. I would be delighted to serve."

He made a few marks on a form with his pen, then lit a stick of sealing wax. He let it drip onto the paper before stamping the page with the formal seal from his signet ring. "You have rooms nearby?"

Elen bobbed her head. "Down the street, sir, nurses' lodgings."

"You may be expected to spend the night, on a cot, if he has a relapse." He glanced over at a clock on a shelf. "It is two, now. Report tomorrow morning, at nine, for your orientation and introduction." His eyes flicked to the black bars on her sleeves. "Deep green for your uniform." Long-term care, of course.

"Of course, sir. I'll see to it promptly."

"And any other little things you need to tend to. I expect you will be working long hours. We can't spare anyone else to attend to his needs." Which meant, depending on how badly off he was, that she could only go to bed when he was settled for the night, and she would have to be back well before breakfast and the morning rounds. She scarcely needed reminding to take advantage of the time she had, as she had been a working nurse for nearly fifteen years now.

"Good afternoon, Therapeutes." He rang a bell, and his aide reappeared, taking the form the Archiater held out. The aide cleared his throat. "Let me show you out, Therapeutes."

She had hoped to see her new patient's file, but clearly that would have to wait. Perhaps the ward sister had it. For now, she would retreat back to her soulless little room on a dim side street, and arrange things properly for the coming challenge.

The rooming house was not as awful as it could be; the roof did not leak, the hot water rarely ran out. However, their landlady certainly did not encourage anyone to sit around in the public rooms chatting. The public rooms were spare and spartan, not like the far more homey rooming house she'd lived in during her later apprenticeship with its piano and tea sets.

For the moment, though, it was where she would live. And from what the Archiater said, she expected she would not have much time awake in that room in the future.

CHAPTER 2

TUESDAY, MARCH 16TH, AT THE TEMPLE OF HEALING

E len felt like she was being towed along by an ocean tug boat. She had reported promptly at quarter to nine, then signed what seemed like interminable forms addressing every possible detail.

She finally finished at ten, enough time for the nurses to get through the usual morning routine without worrying about someone new tagging along. Her uniform was tidy. She'd sewn the dark green stripes on the sleeves, her fob watch was clipped in place, and she had fully stocked her personal supplies in her bag. Handkerchiefs, a few small packaged biscuits for a snack, her knitting, two books. She had no idea what to expect.

She had, of course, served in the Temple of Healing during her training, all nurses did. But they had rearranged the long-term care wards since then. There were four, at least right now, on the ground floor of two of the buildings at the back of the complex, forming a small courtyard between them. There were other wards above, but she didn't remember what those were at the moment.

She approved of keeping the long-term wards on the

ground floor. It would be easier to bring the residents outside on a pleasant day, or at least a little closer to the goings-on of the temple. Isolation, disconnection, those were nearly as dangerous as infection in a long-term patient.

The gardens, at least, had not changed in the past decade. The flowers were beginning to bloom, and she felt more alive than she had in months walking past the scents of the herbs from the apothecary plants. It certainly would be more pleasant than the grey and endless dust and mud in France.

Elen took a breath, on the broad paving stones outside the entrance, glancing back over her shoulder at the Temple, and the gardens spread out in front of it. Then she squared her shoulders and followed the little sign placards leading her to the ward nurse's office.

Sister Almeda, in charge of this ward, took her firmly in hand. "Therapeutes to Asclepius, of course." Most of the heads of wards were, there were biases in every system, including the hierarchy of deities honoured and served here. Sirona, to whom Elen had given her hands quite a long time ago, was respectable, but not the most influential of healing deities. "I expect all nurses on my ward to do their turn at temple duties without complaint."

"That is why I asked to be posted here, Sister, the chance to spend time in the shrines, properly."

There followed a string of questions about her qualifications, her best and worst skills, and why she was not at the front. Under Sister Almeda's unyielding gaze, Elen had been honest about the limitations, and also noted that her migraines had been much better since she'd returned from France a month ago. She did not directly offer her healer's report, and Sister Almeda seemed content with what Elen passed along, or at least indifferent. Elen had no idea what to do with that.

"Well. We need someone with Major Gospatrick, and we shall see if you will do." She considered, and unbent enough to say, "We can't otherwise spare someone for him all the time, and you, on the other hand, will need to demonstrate your skills and usefulness." Sister Almeda stood, abruptly, escorting Elen out of the office and locking up. The ward sister walked briskly down the stairs, then across to the next building, with Elen trotting behind.

This, at least, Elen had expected. She hadn't served in the Healing Temple proper since her apprenticeship, and most of the people who'd known her well were elsewhere, now. She'd never been skilled at coming to the notice of the influential people, so she didn't have notable nurses or healers vouching for her. She had known she'd have to prove that she was calm and competent, and all the more so since she'd been sent home from useful work at the front.

When they were in the next ward, there was a little sharp nod, a hint of approval. "The wards are all on the same basic layout. Supply closet there. Staff room there. The ward facing is the same plan, reversed, of course. The bell there will summon any nurse on call to the proper room. You won't answer those. You are to be with him from before morning rounds through supper, with only brief breaks for the necessities and your shrine duties. There is an orderly at night, and to assist as needed with bathing and rehabilitation exercises." She gestured at the hallway. Elen took the hint

"You may have a book or knitting, or some other appropriate quiet occupation with you. He dozes much of the time. We have bandages to roll, of course, as well, you'll be expected to do your quota."

"Yes, sister. May I ask more about his treatments? Or condition? I haven't seen his file yet."

"That is classified, Ministry orders." That came out tight and clipped. "You are to ignore anything he tells you when he is non compos mentis." Elen got the sense, suddenly, that Sister Almeda did not approve at all, but was not going to permit herself to so much as hint openly at that. She could see no way to ask about it, though, not without seeming difficult.

"His healer, Senior Healer Cole, has prescribed a regimen of potions. One of his juniors will come by on rounds." That was a little unusual, though perhaps Major Gospatrick had been here for long enough to become uninteresting to his healer. Elen didn't approve. Junior healers needed to learn, but she didn't think much of a senior healer who didn't check in regularly. There had been a senior healer at the Temple of Youth who'd spent his days in his posh office, or out chatting with the better-off families, and Elen had little patience for that kind of sloth.

"Has Healer Cole placed any limitations on rehabilitative approaches?" Some did, and it always made her work more difficult. Worse, too many healers thought they knew that side of the work better than the nurses who'd trained in it.

"Ordinary rehabilitative practices are permitted, exercises and walks, taking him to the courtyard if you think it appropriate. His prior nurses have agreed with Healer Cole that this seemed unlikely to have much benefit. No magical work other than the first and second codex." Warming and relaxing charms, the variants any Alethorpe healing student learned by their second year, if not earlier.

Elen frowned. "May I ask why a nurse is with him at all times?" She also didn't think much of the fact Major

Gospatrick appeared to have been stuck in the same room for weeks at a time, but it would not do to say so.

"He becomes disorientated. It is thought better to have someone who can reorient him." Sister Almeda made the kind of delicate pause that Elen had learned to pay close attention to. "The Ministry and Army officials have been insistent on his participation in recruitment efforts, and it would benefit the Temple for him to be able to take on more of that work."

Elen nodded. She could hear the unstated command there, that it was up to her to build his strength and stamina. "Yes, Sister." Elen thought anyone who'd been invalided out with serious and mysterious injuries at the rank of Major had already done rather a lot for the war effort. But she knew to keep that opinion to herself.

"He may ask you to read to him, from books of his choice, but we do not generally make newspapers available to patients at this time." Given how little of the news seemed good these days, Elen could not quite argue. One never knew when some particular report might strike like elf-shot for a given person, either, tangling up their magic and their healing and their sense of self.

"Does Major Gospatrick have a particular routine?" Back at the Temple of Youth, she'd have been presented with a properly formatted schedule, the best ways to contact the primary Healer, and half a dozen necessary documents. Here, there had been none of that.

"A bath in the afternoon, meals as provided by the orderlies." Sister Almeda's voice was increasingly crisp.

"No visitors, then, Sister?" Elen could not help but be puzzled by several things here. The isolation of someone who was supposed to be of interest seemed quite odd, but also, no one seemed to be considering the implications. On one hand, the Major rated a nurse of his own. But that sort of person usually had influential family or friends checking in.

"One, early on, a woman about his age, no one since, other than the Ministry and Army gentlemen. Here we are." Elen wondered why only the one. Perhaps he did not have family, or they were elsewhere in the Empire. Sister Almeda walked briskly down the hallway to a room at the furthest possible corner, tucked away in the back of the complex.

Elen considered where they must be. The wall and tunnels must be right beyond this end of the building, the network that separated the laundries and storerooms and kitchens from the Temple itself. It would be very quiet back here, with little to interrupt rest - but also little to engage the mind or the eye. She did not like that at all, but she had no idea how to ask if it were deliberate or an accident of which room opened up at which time.

Sister Almeda rapped twice on the door frame of the last door on the right, and there was a faint noise from inside, a grumbling. The light was dim, just a bedside lamp, that cast a dull golden light that didn't really illuminate much at all.

"Good morning, Major Gospatrick. Let's get you more light, and a bit of fresh air." Sister Almeda's voice was now the false brightness many nurses put on with patients, rather than the sharper clipped tones she'd been using with Elen.

The man in the bed made another noise, working up a protest, that Sister Almeda thoroughly ignored.

"Therapeutes Morris has been assigned to attend to your healing, Major Gospatrick. She served here in the temple some years ago, during her training, and elsewhere,

since. I'm sure she has some new stories for you." The
window open, she adjusted the overhead light to shine more
brightly.

It let Elen get her first proper look at her new patient.
Blonde, very much in the heroic mode, she thought. He was
squinting slightly, the kind of furrow in his brow that she
got when her migraines made all the light too much. The
Archiater, at least, had been informative when he'd
mentioned Major Gospatrick was light sensitive. She'd fix
that, as soon as she could. His injuries, whatever they were,
were not too obvious. Both hands, unscarred. Both feet,
beneath the blankets and sheets, one knee slightly bent.

He was wearing silk pyjamas, so he was a man of some
money, then, and not so ill they worried about him spoiling
them. His face, now, that was interesting. He had the broad
forehead and sharp chin of Albion's finest young men,
though she thought he was not too much younger than she
was. Early thirties, perhaps. The lines in his face, the darker
spots under his eyes, made that harder to read.

She had been cued by the Archiater's comments, of
course, but she felt some slight sense of miasma there. As a
concept for physical health, the idea was ridiculous, of
course, but nurses were trained to look for the slight signs of
a disruption in someone's magic or essence. In this case, it
was as if there were a murky fog around him, faint but
enough to fade everything. Or perhaps more like a whiff of
mold or damp. Soggy was the adjective that came to mind,
or maybe it was more like something silted up.

The room itself, as she got a chance to look, showed all
the signs of a long-term resident. There was a comfortable
easy chair by the bed, so she would at least not be straining
herself to spend hours there. It was not the sort of thing you
had on a surgical ward, or infectious disease where cleanli-

ness was the greatest concern. A second chair, this one wooden, stood on the other side of the window. A dressing gown hung on a hook on the wall, and there was a small bookshelf, with a dozen volumes. On top, there were some simple yellow flowers in a vase, likely from the temple maidens, as a token of cheeriness.

A narrow table, facing the bed, held the usual array of necessary items, a pitcher for water, a cloth laid out with a thermometer and various other small nursing tools. Good, she wouldn't need to go search those out. A folding table for meals was leaning beside it.

However, there were no photographs, nor any other personal effects in evidence, though the bookshelf had a larger scrapbook that might be relevant. There was a small wardrobe in the corner, and the room was big enough it didn't feel too crowded. The door cracked open to one side led to a tiled room. A lavatory, possibly also a private bath.

"Sister." His voice sounded tired. "Would you tell Healer Cole I would like a word, when he comes round?" There was a quiet resignation there, as if he'd asked the same thing a dozen times before with the same non-answer.

"I will note it on your chart." Then there was a little chime, like a portable version of a clock, from Sister Almeda's own watchfob. She glanced at it. "Pardon, I'm needed elsewhere. Therapeutes, an orderly will be by with luncheon at noon, and to help with Major Gospatrick's bath at two. During his bath, come report to my office."

"Yes, Sister." Elen refrained from bobbing, but stood at attention, waiting a moment. Then she peered out into the hallway, making sure Sister Almeda was indeed on her way out of the ward, before she turned back. "I agree that it's stuffy in here, but I think you would prefer a bit less light, am I right?"

CHAPTER 3

ROLAND'S ROOM, THE SAME DAY

Roland blinked at the figure at the window. She was lit from behind, putting her face in shadow. Another healer. No. His head ached already, still. Therapeutes. Nurse. Whatever.

"Less light?" Her voice was crisp, practised, but she was expecting an answer of some kind.

He nodded and regretted it immediately. He'd woken up with a splitting headache. It wasn't caused by his evening potion, though that left him feeling awful in entirely different ways. Not that that got him out of taking it. He'd tried arguing. Once he'd even tried fighting, and he'd gotten pinned down. A pair of orderlies had appeared from nowhere, then he'd been pinned by magic, and they'd used something to force him to drink.

Roland was smart enough not to try that again. And it was potions, so tucking the pill in his cheek and spitting it out later was out. He hadn't figured out a way around that, so far, especially as weak as he was, and as unpredictable as his magic seemed to be. Not that he'd been permitted to sort that out either. He'd even been told he couldn't try the most basic magical exercises he'd been taught as a child.

He realised suddenly that she was still standing there, patiently. Finally, grudgingly, he said, careful not to move his head more than he had to. "Less light, please."

She pulled the curtains closed, all the way, not leaving the narrow strip that was almost worse than having them fully open. "They are quite thick. Perhaps I could arrange a lighter layer, to filter, without being so much? It is a bright day out today, after all that rain."

Merlin's beard, she seemed like a chatterer, if that was how she started. He hated that. He said nothing, watching as she went to close the door fully, then set down her bag beside the easy chair that faced his bed. He wondered what she had in there. Knitting, probably, or something to be darned. She seemed the sort.

He got a better look at her now. She was nondescript, that was the best way to put it. Mid-thirties, maybe early forties, it was hard to tell in the dimmer light.

She had dark hair, pulled back into the tight knot at the back of her head that he always thought looked rather painful. Any hint of a loose strand was shellacked back with whatever magic women used for that sort of thing. A starched nurse's cap covered most of her hair except the bun and a line at the forehead.

She seemed sturdy, not the slender willowy sort of woman more common in his social circles, certainly not a fashionable sort of body. Not that it was easy to tell through the layers of uniform that all of them wore like armour. And she moved with a tight precision and efficiency of movement that seemed as regimented as his own comrades in the army.

She looked him up and down, like she was weighing him up. Then she went to the pitcher and glasses on the table at the far end of the room, filled one of them, and brought it back for him. "Water?"

Roland blinked at her. He was thirsty, but how was she to know? He nodded, very slightly, and took the glass. His hands weren't shaking too badly today, but he held the glass with both hands, just to be sure. Then he reached to set it down, and she let him. Other people would have taken it, immediately, as if a shattered glass were the worst thing that could happen. He couldn't tell if she didn't know or if she didn't care, and it gave him no hint of what to do.

"I am Therapeutes Morris. Nurse Morris, if you prefer."

He wet his lips. "Roland Gospatrick. Major Gospatrick." Well, he had been, and they wouldn't take his rank from him, even if he were invalided out now.

She nodded again, briskly. "Now. My previous work has largely been with children, or at least young people. You are neither a schoolboy, nor recovering from a childhood illness. I haven't served in the Temple here since my apprenticeship, so I'll be picking up a lot as we go." There was a pause, as if she were trying to decide how to phrase something. "The healers have charge of your care, but if there is something that is bothering you, please tell me, if you would. I can see if I can ease it, at least."

Curious phrasing. And at least she didn't seem like she wanted to be a martinet for the sake of it. He didn't respond, and she stood, looking at him for a long moment. "If I may, I would like to take your vitals. Get a sense of things."

It seemed harmless enough, not that he could stop her. Though she at least asked his permission rather than just grabbing for his wrist. He almost nodded, instead shifting his hand so she could reach the pulse there. She stood, in the universal posture he had come to know and loathe, of having someone obliged to touch him, and someone he was obliged to allow.

Pulse, then she counted his breaths, and he had to keep himself from the instinctive desire to hold his breath and mess up her count. Then she went to the table and brought back a thermometer, popping it in his mouth. She stood back, glancing at her fob watch, then, when she removed it from his mouth, asked briskly, "Pain? And how does your magic feel?"

The first was something they asked occasionally, but not, he thought, often enough. That didn't mean he wanted to tell her. He couldn't obscure the other signs, but he could lie about the pain. And his magic.

He didn't say anything. She let the silence be, then nodded once, as if not answering her were the answer she expected. She turned, and went to the back table, doing something to clean the thermometer before writing down half a dozen figures in a little notebook she'd produced from nowhere. When he still didn't answer, she settled down in the chair by his bed, and said, "I am glad to read to you, if you prefer."

Roland closed his eyes, and let himself sink back against the pillows, trying to find an angle that made his head pound less. He counted ticks of the clock for half a minute, then heard her take something out of her bag. A few moments later, he could hear the softest clickety-tap of knitting needles.

He must have dozed for a time, because the next thing he knew was a hand resting on his, very lightly. "Major

Gospatrick? Your luncheon will be delivered in a few minutes." He could faintly hear the rattle of the trolley in the hallway outside, muffled by thick walls, but she had silently cracked the door open just a hair. "May I open the blinds? Sister Almeda will ask about it, I'm sure."

Roland tried to parse that, then waved a hand, weakly. She took it as permission, and went to draw the curtains open, closing the window to a narrow gap, just enough to keep fresh air moving. The sun had moved enough that it fell at about his knees, rather than too near his face, at least. He watched her movements, squinting against the light. She turned back, and asked, "May I help you sit up?"

"I - I can." His voice cracked, and he coughed, but then he began to work his way around to sitting up, squashing the pillow behind him into place.

Instead of fussing at him, she turned to go and refill his water glass, bringing it back over to him when it was full. He had managed to get himself settled, and he felt it wasn't too poor a showing. She let him drink, again, not demanding she take the glass back, but he gestured at her with it, wordlessly, when he'd drunk about half of it.

He could hear the orderly at the next door, now, and Nurse Morris straightened, sitting down in the chair, or rather perching. When the orderly opened the door, there was a nod at her. "Table in the corner, nurse, if you would." It was polite enough, if in a rough accent. Harry tended to be less brusque than a number of them.

She brought over the bed table, setting it across his lap with quick practised gestures that made it clear she had done that particular task thousands of times. Not just someone who had volunteered because of the War. No, she'd said she'd served in the Temple some years ago.

His brain went flying off, wondering what she'd done since, and then whether he cared or not. By the time he'd managed to bring his focus back, there was a bowl of soup, and a meat pie, or rather a slice of one. It was cut up so he didn't have to manoeuvre through a thick and unyielding crust. He was never sure whether to feel insulted that they had, or grateful that he didn't need to fumble through doing it himself.

His nurse waited until he'd started, and then asked the orderly, "A word?"

They withdrew to the doorway, and he caught snatches of her voice, and of Harry responding, in a low bass rumble. He couldn't make all of it out, but she appeared to be asking about the routine, the process for his bathing, other schedules for the day. Harry seemed cordial enough, but distant. Not smiling, or teasing, like he did with some of the other nurses. It must have been a dozen exchanges, back and forth, before she said, a little more loudly, "Thank you. We'll see you at two, then."

She waited for Harry to leave, then closed the door again. The others hadn't done that, they'd always wanted to have the door open. In case - in case he did something. He didn't know if she hadn't been warned or if she didn't care. Maybe she was like him, and she didn't care much about anything, anymore, here in this exile.

"Would you like me to read, while you eat?"

He'd like her to read a newspaper, but he had learned quickly not to ask for one. He gestured slightly, with his empty fork. "Top shelf. Any book." They were all much of a muchness, the sort of adventure story that wouldn't cause any comment by anyone who glanced at his bookshelf. He'd learned a long time ago not to give the sort of people who wanted to pry anything to pry into. Here in the hospital, that was only more true.

She drew out one he'd read and had read to him before, about finding lost temples in the Egyptian desert, but that was fine. He knew how it went, it would give him a chance to get a sense of her voice without dealing with prattle.

CHAPTER 4

ROLAND'S ROOM, THE SAME DAY

When he was done eating, Nurse Morris stopped reading aloud long enough to clear his tray, and leave it and the dishes on the cart outside. Her voice turned out to be pleasant enough to listen to that he'd managed to be distracted from his food. She didn't attempt to chatter again, or to ask him more questions.

As it drew on for two, he said, "You are reporting to Sister's office?"

Nurse Morris glanced up, startled, looking rather more like a doe than something human. "Yes, Major." Then she inhaled, and said, "Did you have a request?"

He waved his hand. Having a request would mean wanting things, and wanting things was complicated. He mostly didn't. He considered if he had any real interest in asking about her background. He thought about asking her to find out about when Healer Cole would come by, but every other time he'd asked that, it had come to nothing. This would be no different.

Besides, chances were she'd be on duty with him for

perhaps a week, and then something would happen. She would disappear, to be replaced with a combination of orderlies and overworked nurses, never the same one two days in a row. Then they'd find someone else willing to be stuck with him. The previous nurse would never be talked about again.

Before he could make a firm decision, there was a knock on the door, and a "Harry, sir."

She gathered up her bag, and said, "Come in."

"We'll be half an hour, sister." Harry was being unusually deferential, which was curious enough to make Roland pay a little attention. "Do you know how to get to Matron's office?"

"Yes, thank you. Half an hour, then." She nodded, then set off briskly.

"Sir, can you sit up for me?" The obligatory intimacies, and the cajoling required, the dance of someone of less status and rank, making him do things he did not care about, but was obliged to do. It had the bones of a comic opera, somewhere, lost underneath the muck and mud and awfulness.

Harry went to start the bath in the next room, and Roland pushed himself fully upright, then swung his legs over the edge of the bed. They felt particularly sodden today. When he tried to stand, he immediately lost his balance, and sat down with a thump on the bed. There were days when he could make it to the loo or the bath and back on his own, and days when it was like this.

Harry sighed, softly. "Let me get Walter, sir." The other orderly on this ward. Harry went out, coming back a minute later with Walter, an older man, but sturdy.

"Heard you had a new one. What's she like then?" Oh, they were going to gossip. He usually hated it, they talked over him like he wasn't there, but this time it might be useful, if there was anything different about this one.

Harry grunted, going off to check the bath, then coming back, and taking up his place on Roland's right side, as Walter did on his left. With his arms over their shoulders, and their arms around his back, he could manage well enough. First to the toilet, while they retreated to the bedroom, and he could overhear. His ears still worked quite well, at least.

"Gather she got sent back from the front."

"Disgrace, or something else?" They sounded like they were doing the sort of rudimentary tidying up that put everything out of place.

"Dunno. Not going to serve there again. Maybe she's not brave enough." Roland thought that not being at the front was entirely sensible. Orderlies working in the safe and ordered hallways of the Temple of Healing didn't have any room to throw stones. At least Nurse Morris had made the effort.

"So no idea why she got sent here?"

"My Allie's best friend, May, she said Nurse Morris saw the Archiater." Walter sounded like that wasn't a usual sort of thing. Some sort of administrator, Roland believed, not someone he'd ever met.

"Huh." Harry was quiet for a moment, leaving Roland to listen to the sounds. "And assigned here?"

"Guess she did something, one of the other places? Sanitaria or somewhat. Before."

"Anyone know her?" Harry sounded slightly intrigued. "She got anyone?"

"Don't know anything about her, yeah? Though she wasn't wearing a ring, I guess. Just the uniform."

"Strict, then." Many of the nurses here had more

personal touches than were technically permitted, a brooch or ring or some other decoration.

Walter passed by the crack in the door, and Roland could see him shrug. "What was she like, then?"

"Polite enough. Didn't make me do all the set-up, like that Margaret Smith, upstairs." Margaret was, he gathered, snobbish and rather nasty, from the comments both Harry and Walter had made over the past few months. Also, apparently, with friends in high places, because she kept a position with a light caseload.

"Out of your class, man. Alethorpe, Allie thought. Her friend got a glimpse of the pendant, yeah?" Then there was a sound, like Walter clapping Harry on the back. "Come out with me Friday night, yeah? Allie's got a friend."

"Allie's always got a friend." That was good-natured grumbling, and at that point, Roland shifted to flush, and then called out "Ready."

It took a few moments to get him settled in the bath. "There you are, sir. We'll be making up the bed now, you give a shout if you need us."

Roland nodded. "Ta," he said. "Don't mind a bit of a soak." The water was restorative, the bathtub was charmed to keep it warm - it was part of his therapy, that, though not every day. And if they took the chance for a bit of a break and maybe a smoke while he was in the bath, he didn't mind.

He leaned his head back against the cooler cast iron and enamel, letting his eyes close again. Alethorpe, he knew a number of the healers went there. His mind seemed to want to wander down this thread of information, and he had no particular reason to stop it. He'd be here for fifteen minutes or so, then scrubbed, then popped back into bed.

He wondered if she'd wanted to be a healer, or if that

was something people made a decision about. There were female healers, he'd met some of them, though most of them were rather terrifyingly devoted to their particular healing deities and arts.

He'd not had much experience of healers before this, male or female, other than a few bumps and minor injuries at school and in Army training. It wasn't something his family ran to. It wasn't the hard work and commitment - they were good at that. But it was a different way of life, a sameness, that he thought his parents would never tolerate.

He'd known a bookbinder who'd gone to Alethorpe. A few other crafters, including the gunsmith he preferred for work and repair before the shooting season began.

He supposed he was going to have to think about some sort of new occupation for his time, since the thought of the guns going off made him shiver. Rather worse if he dwelled on it. Books, perhaps. Maybe working on regimental histories, or military history. His father would approve of that, perhaps.

He wasn't sure what to expect from his father now, he'd not heard anything from his family since he'd ended up here. Just that one fleeting visit from his former fiancee, early enough in his stay he'd have thought it a fever dream except for the letter she'd sent afterwards. He had no idea what to make of that, and it made his head hurt to think about it. His head and his heart.

He yanked his train of thought back to something else. Books, he'd been thinking about books. Of course, the book idea would only work if his eyes wouldn't start blurring after only twenty minutes. It had been ten, last month, so at least that was some progress.

He heard the orderlies again; perhaps they had popped out to the courtyard for a smoke, on the side no one would spot. They weren't supposed to leave him entirely alone, out of earshot, in the bath. He'd heard their orders. Well, he wasn't supposed to be left alone, period. If a nurse wasn't with him, his door was open, and there was a charmed device that alerted them to anything unusual.

Or, well. Or he'd taken his evening potion, been made to take it, and the next ten hours, he suspected he barely moved at all, the way he ached in the morning. More like a dozen hours. The blasted thing took a while to wear off, and whenever the healers did come round, he always felt muzzy-headed and unable to make the words come out to ask questions.

It was always one of the junior healers. They would inspect him, asking him a series of precisely defined questions as sharp as an interrogation. They talked about the senior healer, Healer Cole, but Roland couldn't remember ever meeting him. The juniors never listened to Roland, never gave him space to talk about anything that he was feeling that he hadn't been asked about. He wasn't sure he could tell them - or would - but never to have the chance made him want to retreat into a dark hole and never come out.

No one told him anything. Not how long he might be here, or when he could go somewhere else. Or even what was wrong with him. He'd heard murmurs, on and off, he gathered what was broken in him wasn't something they were terribly familiar with, even here. But they wouldn't explain to him what they knew, or what the potions did.

Sometimes he woke, and something had been shattered, a pitcher or a glass. Once, terrifyingly, it had been the rocking chair beside the bed, like something had cleaved it in two. That nurse, he'd never seen again, and the orderlies had only talked about her in hushed voices, glancing around to make sure no one overheard.

They started talking again, picking up a conversation. "You see the notice, about the, the aus..."

"Austerity." Harry had, he gathered, a larger vocabulary than Walter. "Yeah. Them wanting to save money."

"Well, there is a war on. But we work plenty long, and plenty hard, why should we pay for it that way too?"

"Dunno." They were making the bed now, the snap of clean sheets and the cedar from the storage closet filtering through into the bathroom. "Dunno how we can argue, though. And it's better than a mine, or the front, or a farm." Harry had clung to this job, saw it as a step up for his family.

"Farm's not so bad. Bloody hard work, but some rewards." They had this argument on and off. "And people always need food. Get yourself a bit of a specialty, cheese, cider, jams, somewhat, you can make a bit beyond the usual."

"Pah. You can keep a farm. Too many bloody animals." Then a grunt, and the sounds of the blankets being tucked under, hospital corners that pinned him down. "Besides. There's a war on. And not like to end too quick, despite what everyone said. Home by Christmas, they said."

Roland thought that whatever else, neither of these men had been touched too directly by it. They hadn't gone to fight, and he didn't think they had brothers or sons who had. Maybe he was wrong.

He knew the people making the decisions expected the war to go on. That's why they dragged him out, and propped him up. Why they wound him up like a clockwork toy, to encourage other men to go and fight. They weren't the ones who'd been down in the trenches, and seeing their men blown to bits, or killed by a sniper. Roland had taken shelter in the trenches here and there, in the course of his own duties. He'd seen the way the officers - the good ones - had taken that blow again and again.

He wasn't out there with the guns and the mud and the blood, not any more, but at least he'd done his bit. Maybe he could find some small favour in that.

CHAPTER 5

ROLAND'S ROOM, THE SAME DAY

len halted, once she cleared the doorway from the central ward where Sister Almeda had her office. There were four long-term wards, all on the ground floor, and Sister had taken a large room facing the Temple gardens in one of the middle buildings as her office. It enabled her to keep an eye on much of the coming and going, certainly anyone of particular note.

The side door, however, was not in her direct line of sight. Elen stopped, checked the angles of the windows, and then stepped onto one of the stone paths. There was a smaller garden here, a courtyard with plants at least, between the buildings. She took a deep breath, wanting to gather her thoughts before going back to her duties.

Some of the meeting had been a help, at least. She had finally been presented with a daily schedule, to be modified as required by others. She had been warned she would likely need to stay late after the Major had a recruiting event. The next one was in three weeks, barely enough time for her to begin to establish a proper understanding of his usual routine and condition and make a start on improving it.

Sister Almeda had not explained the actual events themselves, or their particular demands, and Elen wondered if she even knew. Elen was to accompany him there, wait outside, and accompany him back, without drawing attention to herself or to his needs. From what Sister Almeda hadn't said, she gathered these were a particular challenge, but Elen could not tell why. No one gave her a chance to ask. Perhaps Major Gospatrick would choose to tell her, given a little time.

The schedule itself was more or less what she'd expected. A half-day off a week. She'd expected that, though she had been strongly encouraged not to take one for a few weeks, to align herself with his schedule and treatments. The implication had been that there was a day in the cycle of treatment where her services were needed a great deal less than the others. And of course she would bend to that. It wasn't as if Elen had much choice.

Sister Almeda, despite being responsible for oversight of at least a few dozen nurses, had made it clear she'd be observing closely. Elen couldn't tell the reason for that. Elen was an unknown, of course. Major Gospatrick was an important patient, so they kept saying. Or perhaps Sister Almeda was just like that with everyone.

Mind, questioning the omniscience of a ward sister never ended well. At least not if they got the suspicion you'd so much as thought they were anything less than fully perfect. Or less than entirely in charge of even the tiniest detail of their wards. Elen was quite clear about the hierarchy here.

Elen couldn't shake a nagging thought that something was not quite right. It was impossible to tell exactly what.

She had been too long away to know how things were normally done. It might just be the expected difficulties of taking in many more with injuries, or different kinds of injuries, of not yet having sorted out the best practices.

What Elen knew was that Sister Almeda seemed both curiously interested in Elen's work, and entirely distanced from it. She'd been pleasant enough when answering a few practical questions about how this item or that was handled now, but she made no suggestions about treatments or approaches. Except she seemed, in glimpses, fragments, to be glad Elen was suggesting a few new things.

She had picked up all the small tidbits she could. Sister Almeda had been here quite a long time, and she intended to stay even longer. There had been the twenty and thirty year plaques. The latter had the slight veneer of tarnish that made it clear that the forty year clock was right around the corner.

That did not help her patient. Nor did it help Elen herself. Whatever was peculiar here was more odd than the usual disarray of standards and common procedures that the War had caused. Sister Almeda had been particularly unforthcoming about her patient. He had a set regimen of potions, he would take them as ordered. She was to observe, and to report any concerns immediately.

When she had inquired what sort of concerns, whether it was fever or tremors or infection, Sister Almeda said, "You claim to be an experienced nurse. Anything unexpected. We trust you will not report the usual run of minor needs."

That placed her firmly on the horns of a dilemma. If she did not report something and it was determined later that it should have been reported, she would be out on her ear.

At best, she would be hired on as a private duty nurse to

fuss over some older man or woman who needed minimal care. Or sent off to be the visiting nurse on a gruelling set of rounds, seeing all the worst bits of humanity in between the tedium of ear aches, colds, and minor injuries. And at worst, she'd have to take up a position with someone who pinched bottoms or groped or leered, or the sort of elderly woman who thought the nurse was there to fetch and carry every other second.

On the other hand, if she reported trivial things, she would also be out on her ear, and nearly as promptly. She would have to make those decisions without being given proper access to his file, so she could determine what his symptoms were, what the diagnosis was, or what the side effects of his potion regimen were. It was forcing her into shoddy nursing work, and for no reason that she could see.

He had not been inclined to tell her, either. Some patients, especially when they had been in hospital a while, wanted to talk to anyone who would listen. Major Gospatrick, instead, had thus far been near silent. Not quite sullen, that had a different feel to it, but there was a wall of reserve, as if the prospect of getting to know her was just too much effort for him to take. She had been honestly surprised when he asked her about the meeting.

She heard the bells begin to chime on the top of the Temple bell tower. It was indeed the pattern for the half hour, and she hurried inside the ward, turning down the hall to her patient's room. She would have to do this the hard way, by observation and perhaps an occasional well-timed question.

As she came up to the door, it opened, and the second orderly on the ward, came out, with a bob of his head. "Nurse." The other one, Harry, heard this, and opened the door a little wider. "That is Walter, nurse. And it's Ed and

Arnold, on the night shift. Major Gospatrick has had his bath and a shave, all ready for the afternoon. We bring supper around at six." For her to supervise before she left at half-seven, then.

She nodded. "Thank you. Appreciated. Do let me know if there's anything I can do to be a help?"

He looked her up and down, then shrugged wordlessly, and turned away to his next set of duties. She slipped into the room, closing the door behind her, and took in her patient. He was on his back in bed again, slightly propped up, staring at the ceiling. It was a particularly boring ceiling, even by hospital standards, there was not even much in the way of a pattern.

She considered very cautiously, "Major, would you - would you like something to look at? On the ceiling?" She'd done it for the children in the Temple of Youth, with some sort of image, constellations, sometimes she'd gotten someone to do an illusion charm with characters from their favourite story.

Major Gospatrick lifted his head, gave her the sort of quelling look that made her take a full step back. He didn't say anything. He didn't have to. She swallowed, then turned away, to check over the various items on the back table, the sort of check one did automatically and that could fill as much time as was needed.

"You may continue reading."

His voice sounded a little raw, and Elen was completely unable to get a sense of the emotion in it. She took a breath, then turned to look at him. His expression was entirely neutral, she couldn't read that either. Instead, she nodded. "Of course. What is the last thing you remember?"

Major Gospatrick coughed. "They were in the city, the bazaar, talking about hiring a boat to go downriver."

He'd dozed through a chapter then. Not one of her favourite bits of this book, but she'd have to read it again. Nothing much happened, and it rather bogged down in descriptions of the river boat and the bargaining. However, she had been asked to do far worse things in the course of her work.

"Let me get a glass of water. May I pour one for you?"

There was a hesitation. "I have not been permitted my own."

Of course Sister Almeda hadn't said anything about that. Sister Almeda hadn't said anything about much, really. "May I ask why?"

"They get broken." He didn't explain, and she wasn't sure how to ask.

"I'm a fine hand with a dustpan. Or I could get you a metal one?"

He tilted his chin to peer at her, down his nose, entirely dubious. "Water, please, thank you." The mixture of the expression and his automatic, instinctive gesture at manners infuriated her all of a sudden and she wanted to stomp away. But that wasn't the done thing. People who needed care got like this. People like him, even more so. He'd been an active man, with power and influence and control, and he certainly had far less of all three now.

It was why she'd preferred working with younger people. Oh, a boy of ten could be presumptuous and demanding, but that was far easier to manage than a man, particularly a man like this, fallen from whatever position he once held. She had no desire to insult her current patient, it would make everything harder.

Instead, she just poured a glass for him. "I'll bring along something metal tomorrow. Here." She waited for him to get a decent grip, took her own glass with her, and set it down within easy reach. Then she flicked through the book, back a chapter, and began reading again.

They got through three and a half chapters, with occasional points where he asked her to read a section again, or stop. He didn't explain himself, of course, but she went along with it. At six, precisely, his meal was delivered. Elen arranged the bed table again, and accepted her own plate. Apparently she was to eat with him, or at least at the same time, which meant no choice in her food.

It wasn't bad, mind. The evening brought her a simple curry, nothing fancy, but with a little bit of a bite to it, and a cooling yoghurt to smooth things out. And the portion was reasonable. She'd have to make sure to have a solid breakfast, though, as she had this morning.

When the meal was cleared, she coughed. "Sir, may I ask your preferred routine for the evening?" She was trying to cover for the fact she'd been given the barest schedule, and she had no idea about medications or potions or anything else.

He sounded almost bored. "At seven, they'll bring my potion. Twenty minutes later, I won't know or care what you do until the next morning." Something strong, then. Notably strong. She wondered why, but she couldn't ask. It would immediately reveal her ignorance.

"Of course. Well, let's see if we can finish this chapter, then, and pick up with the next in the morning."

CHAPTER 6

Roland hated these days. Bath in the morning as soon as breakfast was cleared, but everything still felt sodden and slow. Then he had to sit stock still so he could be shaved and his hair combed until his scalp hurt.

Putting on his uniform felt like insult added to injury. Everything fit wrong, now. The collar choked him, the jacket pinned his arms down, the weight of the fabric exhausted him. He'd worn his uniform with pride, before, and now it felt more like chains and shame.

Then he had to deal with the combined indignity of being bundled into a chair. It wasn't just that he couldn't walk on his own, though that was bad enough, but also the discomfort of going from indoors to sunlight, and back indoors. It left his head pounding, and of course there was nothing to be done about it and saying anything would make everything subtly worse. It wasn't far to the meeting room, at least, but it was more time outside than he'd had since the last time he'd been dragged out to one of these meetings.

Nurse Morris at least did not flit around fussing. He was, frankly, a bit startled she was still here, but she turned up every morning on time. She read to him, and knitted or rolled bandages when he dozed. She saw to each of his potions and needs with meticulous care, including making sure he always had a glass of water handy. He didn't always trust himself to hold it safely, but that was a different problem.

He still had no real sense of her, however. She didn't talk about herself or what else she'd done. Roland still had no more idea why she'd been sent home from the front than he had the first time Harry had talked about her.

He had no idea if she hated reading the adventure stories. When one of the helpful women had come round with a cart with reading material, he'd picked what felt safe. Unrevealing. A few times, Nurse Morris made a comment that suggested she'd read them before, about a future scene, so perhaps like him, she actually sort of enjoyed them. Or perhaps she'd just read them to other patients, long before him.

Now, she trotted along slightly behind them, carrying her ever-present satchel. And, in this case, the canes he needed to walk the short distance from where they parked his chair to where he was put on display.

It made him feel like a circus elephant, or a monkey in a zoo, as if he were entirely a show, not to be consulted, just performing on demand. He wasn't sure what good it did, since most of the time he wasn't even talking to people who might enlist, but instead the people who might talk to the people who might enlist.

This time was no different. He was wheeled into a side room, just a door or two down the hall from one of the bigger lecture rooms that were sometimes used for healer demonstrations and classes. "His canes, Nurse Morris?"

She promptly handed over the canes, and then came to steady the chair while Harry helped him up. It was worse than usual today, he could feel it. Not just sodden, but downright limp, neither ankle wanted to flex much, and his knees felt like they'd give out any minute. "I'll need a chair." He hated admitting it, but it would be worse if he fell down. For him, but also for Harry and Nurse Morris, he suspected.

"The basket chair?" He heard her voice behind him, and didn't risk turning around.

Harry tsked. "No, miss. He has to walk in, or they'll - well. I'll go see there's a chair ready, sir. You sit for a minute."

Roland let himself drop back into the chair. It creaked alarmingly, the woven basketwork was not nearly as sturdy as it should be. He finally permitted himself to glance over his shoulder. Nurse Morris looked like she wanted to say several things, and was restraining herself. Curious. Had they not told her about his dog and pony show? He suspected not. They probably imagined she wouldn't last more than one or two, too, so it hardly mattered.

It was only a minute before Harry came back. "Right big crowd there. Let me help you up, sir. Got the chair for you, and Nurse, one for you at the side, so you can be handy just in case. Also, looks proper, having a nurse there."

Roland caught her nod out of the corner of his eye, before all his attention had to go to the supposedly simple process of standing up and not falling down. He leaned on the canes heavily, and he could feel the sharp ache in his wrists start up almost immediately. Then, step by awkward step, he made his way out through the door that Nurse Morris held, with Harry right beside him in case he toppled.

It was one of the bigger lecture halls, enough to seat a hundred, at least. He'd never been able to decide which was easier. In small groups, they asked far more probing questions, as if the intimacy made them friends. It didn't, of course. In the larger hall, the questions were more distant, more general.

But there were more people, and the weight of their attention ground him down far more quickly. It was worse when they were mostly Army, the people who knew him, knew his father. Sometimes, knew his mother; he had long since stopped being surprised at who his mother had come into contact with in the course of her work. He could manage better when it was a faceless horde.

This hall had a low stage, and they had come in through the stage door, so at least he didn't have to manage stairs. There was a single chair in splendid isolation at the front. He didn't go to it yet, instead propping himself against the wall at the side of the hall. Nurse Morris glanced at him, then he could see a moment of decision. Before he could stop her, she had stepped out on the stage, picking up a small table that had been set out of the way as she did so. "You should have some water."

Roland could feel his eyes widen, and he willed himself not to react further. He permitted himself the nod of an officer, telling someone to do something she was going to do anyway, but that was a decent idea. She put the table on the far side, next to the chair, then bustled off, out of the hall through the stage door. A minute later, she came back with with a solid drinking glass, two thirds full of water.

Just having it there felt like a gift, even if he wouldn't dare touch it in front of all these people. And by now, there were quite a few of them, the rumbling of a hundred people or so talking quietly, catching up. It was these moments that made him feel most alone. They all were chatting away, easy with each other, and he was beginning to forget what that felt like entirely.

He heard the tower bells, and someone came out of the crowd as they settled down, the seats squeaking. His introduction, then. This time it was a brigadier, by the insignia, but not one he knew. The man was in his fifties, the kind of portly middle age that suggested he got plenty of rich food and almost no exercise, and had not been near the front himself. There was the predictable speech about brave men, and the service of the nation, and how to encourage more people to go fight.

He knew his cue, and he made his way out along the stage, awkwardly, leaning on both canes. The brigadier had the grace to step aside and give him space, not all of them managed that, but Roland thought he looked a little annoyed at how long the process took. There was a final nod as Roland sat, ungracefully, and then he was alone on the stage.

Now, all he could do was throw himself into the challenge of talking to a horde of nameless people, mostly men, who were looking at him with that mix of pity and fear. He could almost smell it on them, the fear, at least. He couldn't let them realise how badly this war had broken him. What little use he had now was people like these coming to hear him, see him. No one listened to him at any other time, he wasn't good for anything else.

So instead, he gathered himself up, and made himself shine. All the wit and the charm and the way he remembered being, in the past before the mist and pain and loss. "So sorry not to be standing here before you all, but I'm still recovering, you see, and I'm not supposed to overdo it. The nurses - isn't she lovely, there? - they do excellent work, now, but it's not nice to worry them so. But here I am, to tell you a bit of why I volunteered, what made me want to serve King and Council."

That had a story, a patter, that he'd worked out through grinding repetition. It was a thing to think about when he was flat on his bed with nothing to look at, those times when every hour felt like a week. There was the story about how he decided to join up, a conversation in a pub with three of his yearmates. How he'd been brought up to service and courage, a family that had served in the army, in the navy, over the generations. Doing the right thing, for the right reason, how he'd been sorry to miss out on the Boer War, the stories his older cousins had told.

Now, of course, he was sure they'd been lying through their teeth. He'd heard a few things from older men he'd served with, about how brutal the fighting had been there, or in the Sudan, or half a dozen other places. They all told lies, and here he was keeping to that loathsome and obligatory tradition.

He pressed on, into the stories about his training, about learning proper form, the marching that he'd not needed since he'd been sent overseas. Running, yes. Ducking, certainly. But if they had put a tenth the time into how to dig efficiently as they had into parade manoeuvres and cavalry charges, it would have gone much better. Or for that matter, shooting, though he'd been a good shot from a boy. Country living did that for you.

Roland moved onto the next set piece, about having charge of men, having to decide who got which task. This was always tricky, because of course, as soon as he thought of people, he thought of specific people, too many of them ghosts now. That wouldn't do, he couldn't permit that.

Instead, he talked about being part of something larger than himself, understanding that each of them played a part.

The bitterness was for later, all the poison deep inside him that had bubbled over when he realised the officers sending him off to fight were sacrificing his men for no good reason. Doing the same thing, over and over again, with horrific results.

He didn't talk about what he'd seen at Mons. He'd heard the stories, in the first hospital he'd been taken to. A few times, from his men. Ghostly images. Some had called them angels, some the ghosts of the bowmen of Agincourt, come to defend their fellow countrymen. All he knew is that he was alive and broken, and too many were dead, all to hold off the Germans for a mere two days. Heroic, successful, a miracle, that's what they said, and none of it was right.

Whatever salvation that might have been, there had been none at Ypres, in the long slog of a battle, on and off for weeks, with the cavalry shifting and harrying. He'd lost two good horses before the enchantments snared him and brought him down too. The horses had been lucky, he thought.

Somehow, he managed to get through the final stages, about what he hoped these distinguished folks would take away. He commended the treatment he'd gotten along the way, entirely aware that there were a row of healers in the back, their red robes and badges of rank marking them out. He wondered if Healer Cole were among them, and then how he'd know if he were. What would it mean, anyway, if the man came to this dog and pony show, but couldn't be bothered to consult with his patient directly.

This lot, mercifully, did not have many questions, and the ones they had were the predictable ones. Comments on his bravery, praise for his eloquence, questions about if he would speak to newly enlisted men and inspire them. He knew he'd say yes, in the end, but deferred with the expected phrases. "As I am available, of course. My Healers arrange all that sort of thing, sir."

Finally, after what felt like a full day march, the room finally began to empty. He could not force himself to stand, nor even to pay attention to what was going on around him. When he heard the voice beside him, he startled, almost lashing out before he somehow managed to stop himself.

"Harry's gone to get your chair, since they're all gone. Just a minute, Major."

CHAPTER 7

ROLAND'S ROOM, LATER THAT EVENING

Ellen glanced up from the letter she'd just finished to peer at the clock on the bedside table. They had gotten Major Gospatrick back, after that awful presentation, and he'd dropped into bed like a rock. He was running a slight fever, she thought, from where she'd checked his pulse earlier, but for the moment she was waiting and seeing. If he woke, she could ask what he'd find soothing.

She'd drawn the blinds, and had been sitting all afternoon and into the evening, with just the bedside lamp. She hadn't wanted to leave him. There was no reason she couldn't stay, she had said, and she could see to a late supper and his evening potion when he woke up. Harry had looked pleased, somehow, saying how it'd make things easier for the night staff.

Making friends with the night staff, or at least being seen as easy to work with, doing her fair share, was very much in her interest. Even if it had meant knitting until her hands ached, and then trading her needles for a book. Then a letter. Then bandage rolling. Then the book again. Then finally allowing herself the letter she'd been saving.

That had been a mixed blessing, because it was one from her best friend, and it made her heart ache. It had been one thing when she'd been at the Temple of Youth. She had been busy there. Sometimes the work was heartbreaking, children, young men and women, who wouldn't get the lives they should have. But she had felt like she was doing something useful, and she had been busy. Her friends from Lavender House, her home while she was at school, were all doing useful things.

This letter from Amet was another sharp reminder of how useless she felt. Her friend was working on a project with the apothecary, packaging up medicinal potions in different ways. She'd stayed on with the master she'd apprenticed to, because, as she pointed out, he had a tremendous amount more to teach her.

Elen knew it wasn't just that, that Master Luther had treated her like his own daughter, given her roots when she'd changed in ways her family couldn't understand. But Amet was very busy, and though Elen had been in Trellech a fortnight already, she hadn't been able to get free to see her.

Elen paused, thinking about families. She hadn't been so lucky either. Her family didn't complain that she'd gone into the Healing Temple. But her mother was baffled that she hadn't chosen midwifery, and her father muttered about how a healer would be proper useful, he wasn't sure what a nurse did besides pat people on the hand.

They loved her, she knew that, but they didn't understand her. And she didn't understand them. Her father had worked his way up to overseeing the Dolaucothi gold mine from being a miner. It was much safer for him now, and gold had always been safer to mine than coal. Though safe was a relative term.

Once she'd gone to school, she'd done her best to stay out of their way when she was home on holidays. She'd help her mother with the garden, run messages around for her father. Mostly, she'd holed up in Uncle Dewi's workshop, where she wouldn't bother anyone.

When he had time, he'd teach her how to work the locks - part of his trade, as the mine's locksmith. Or she'd watch him mend watches and clocks, though she'd never had the dexterity for that herself. Otherwise she'd knit, or read. All those habits had continued, until now she wasn't sure what else to do with herself when she wasn't working. She missed even that somewhat tenuous space, though, a place where there weren't so many expectations.

No matter. Amet was happy, that was good. She could write back, when she got a chance. It felt ridiculous, to be in the same city, and not have seen her yet, but her life had been her own recovery and healer appointments before she'd gotten her assignment. Now, there were a few snatched hours to deal with darning and laundry and her own personal needs. She doubted she'd be back before the lodging house curfew tonight.

It was at that moment that she heard the Major begin to stir. "Major Gospatrick?"

He grimaced, making a face like his mouth tasted foul, and she immediately reached for the glass of water she had ready. "Water, Major?" He pushed himself upright enough to drink, then took the glass from her, his hand shaking with a tremor, but not enough, she judged, for him to spill it down his front. He got a good half the glass down, before thrusting it at her blindly. Then he was pushing himself out of bed, aiming at the lavatory, and she almost stopped him.

She must have made some noise, because he growled over his shoulder "Don't." He didn't fall, but he almost toppled, taking a step or two, catching himself on the door frame, then staggering inside, closing the door behind him.

Elen knew she should go for one of the orderlies. Even if they were understaffed, even if there was a difficult newly admitted patient on the ward. She glanced at the door, then decided she'd wait, see if she heard anything worrisome. There were only the faint ordinary sounds of someone making use of the facilities. That was a good sign, perhaps. No sound of vomiting, or worse, of a body hitting the hard floor.

She'd make use of the time she had. She pulled back the sheets, gathered her magic into her hands, then spread it, cleansing and freshening the bedding, so that it had the faint tint of lavender and rosemary, rather than the stale smell of sickness and sweat. She refilled the glass, charming the water cool, and went to make sure the covered supper tray was ready.

Then, she considered her reserves, and tried one last enchantment, one she couldn't always manage, but that would make the bed feel far more comfortable, like one of the most plush woollen mattresses from her childhood. Then she gathered what she knew she'd need, the thermometer and a clean cloth for it.

It took several minutes, nearly five, by the clock, but then the door cracked open, and he made his way back to the bed. He was looking pale, even in the uncertain light of the charm lamp. She could see sweat beading on his forehead, too. A decided fever. He glanced at the bed, frowned, as if he couldn't place what she'd done, then he sank into it, then pulled his legs under the covers.

"May I take your temperature, Major? If you're running a fever, I can help with that."

He considered, looking for all the world as if he'd deny her. She was asking out of politeness. First, he could barely stand up, he couldn't do much to dissuade her. And second, she'd learned her early skills on donkeys and mine ponies and guard dogs. The day she couldn't get a creature to sit still and be dosed was the day she'd hang up her nurse's cap. Grudgingly, he nodded, and she pulled out the thermometer.

"A fever. I have your evening potion for you, but I'd like to give you something for the fever first, and your evening meal."

He grunted, then yielded enough to say, "Sure."

Elen got up and found the potion she'd set aside on the table, bringing the bottle over. Harry had said he could have one, chosen from the standard options, any of them she saw fit. Whatever he was taking, the regular evening potion, his other treatments, it didn't seem to be susceptible to interference.

She'd chosen one of her favourites for fever, one that didn't suppress it, so much as eased the course of it. Fevers had a purpose in the body, burning out infection, and she'd not get in the way unless it were actually necessary.

He blinked at the bottle, then glanced at her. "Why this?" His voice cracked, still dry, and she moved to pour more water, then to settle the bed tray over his lap, before bringing over the plates of food. They'd had a keep-warm plate, and the simple stew of chicken, potato, and carrots looked hearty enough, and largely easy on an unsettled stomach. Easy to eat with a spoon, too.

"Better for you than the others." She settled down in the chair, so as not to loom over him. He drank the bottle, handed the empty back silently, and then peered at his plate, beginning to pick at it. She'd noticed he didn't seem to have too much of an appetite. She let him eat without interruption, until he put his spoon down.

"May I ask something, sir?" She cleared her throat. "Two things."

He waved a hand, irritably. "Go ahead."

"Are your - presentations always like that?"

"Like what?" He sounded more than a bit annoyed.

Elen tried to figure out how to put into words what she'd seen. It was like he'd put on a completely different body. Still hurt, still unsteady, but his eyes had been bright and sharp, his attention focused, and oh, he'd been charming and smiling. There was something she'd seen in there, that reminded her of the tales of dragons with their hoards, the things that lit them up from inside, and gave them fire. Only, she'd also seen flickers that suggested the reality was rather more complicated, starting with how completely he'd collapsed afterwards.

"You shone, sir. Near glowed with it. Your focus, your intensity."

"Paying for it now. For days." His voice cracked again, and she instinctively reached to move the water where he could reach it more comfortably. He took it, then drained the glass. She stood to go refill it, then brought it back.

"You notice the water." It was one of the only times he hadn't seemed irritated at her.

"Water is life, one of my teachers said. And you look..." She tried to figure out how to explain this best. "There's a look, to people who haven't had enough. Pinched and dry. You have that. It's getting better. And it might help other things."

"Like what?" That had the tone of someone who was

suddenly quite interested in the answer, but trying not to show it.

She sat down again, and let out a puff of air, looking at him for a long moment. "Look. They won't tell me much about your treatment. I'm just supposed to do what I'm told, keep an eye on you." She suddenly hoped no one was about to come through the door and check on him. "I'd like to help you more, but that is tricky, when I don't know what you're taking,"

"Potion in the morning. Potion at night. That one - I don't like."

She glanced at the table at the far wall, with the small bottle on it. "May I fetch it? Get a good look at it? I won't make you take it yet. Not until we are completely certain you're done with dinner." She hadn't had a chance, previously, since Harry brought it in when it was time to be taken, and she had been sure he'd tell someone if she lingered over giving the proper dose.

Major Gospatrick peered at her for a moment, then at his plate, and then it clicked for him. "Oh, yes. I might have a few more bites, leave it there, please."

It made her smile, an honest smile, for what felt like the first time in days. "Exactly, Major." He might be slow due to his injuries or his potions, but she was - after that day's performance - now quite sure he was a naturally quick-witted man. She got up to fetch the evening potion dose, and when she brought it back, he was looking at her with a queer expression.

"Must you call me that?" Not at all what she had expected from him, the way he'd been treating her.

"Major, sir?"

"That, Major Gospatrick. Are you permitted to call me something else?"

"We are advised, sir, to use your rank and surname." Also, she had been firmly instructed in what to say if asked.

"Where were you a nurse before."

"The front, sir. Several locations in France."

"And before that?"

It was the first time he'd been interested. "The Temple of Youth, sir. Working with younger patients who were recovering from long-term illnesses."

"And what did you call them?"

She had to smile, he had been like a terrier with the logic. "It depended. Their age, their illness."

"My name is Roland. Roland Arthur Gospatrick."

"Sir." It didn't seem like enough, so then she ventured what should be a fairly neutral observation. "Your family seems to have been interested in famous heroes, then."

He snorted. "Yes. A long history of it. I've rather let the side down."

Elen was not at all sure what to do with that. Instead, she took the potion bottle, taking the chance to peer at it, then she drew out her notebook, sketching the bottle shape, noting the odd deep purple colour, not terribly common, and the wax on the cap.

"One of these every night? Do they all look like this?" She didn't have anything to take a sample away, and with the war on, getting glass vials would be complicated.

He nodded, and she looked up to see him focused on her. "They do. I think. I haven't much paid attention."

"May I see what I can find out about it?"

Major Gospatrick blinked at her. "I can scarcely stop you, now."

"If you told Sister Almeda, she would, I rather suspect, send me away and be done with it."

There was a long silence before he said, "I prefer your

reading voice." It came out more clipped. When he spoke again, his voice was muted. "I should take that."

Silently, she handed him the bottle, and a few minutes after he had drained it, he was well on his way into a deep sleep. She tidied things up, and then gathered her bag, letting the night orderly know she was leaving to go get her own rest.

CHAPTER 8

Two days later, Roland was startled when Nurse Morris asked, "Would you like to go outside for a while? It's pleasantly warm, and I found a spot that's not in the sun."

"Outside?" He hadn't been outside since he'd been brought here. "Are, am I allowed?"

"In your chair, yes." She fell silent and he caught the way her gaze landed on his face, then darted away. A decided tell that she was nervous about something, but he had no idea what.

"Will it cause you trouble if I don't go? Or if I do?" He pushed himself more upright, considering the question of clothing.

She coughed. "I suggested it might help your recovery, if you had a bit of time out in fresh air. Sister Almeda approves of fresh air." She glanced at the window.

"Do I have to keep calling you Nurse Morris?" He grimaced, feeling a twinge in his back. "And what am I supposed to wear out there, then?"

"Robe over your pyjamas, socks, and slippers, and a

proper lap blanket to keep you warm. You needn't get dressed, sir, if you'd rather not."

"I'd like for it not to be a difficult decision, but that's not on offer, is it?" He grumbled, but he glanced at her, and offered a slight smile. She'd been remarkably steady since their conversation in the late evening after his performance, professional and sharp, but he'd sensed something had changed. Perhaps getting him outside was part of it.

Nurse Morris smiled. "We can discuss alternate names outside, sir."

That was offered as a bargain, and it intrigued him enough he gave himself over to the impulse. "Outside, then. You'll need to help with the socks."

Sorting all of that out took a few minutes, including the time for her to go and claim a flask of tea and a few biscuits. When she came back pushing the basket chair, he managed to get himself into it with a minimum of fumbling. She was stronger than she looked, because once she started pushing, he was moving nearly as quickly as when Harry was steering him along.

She navigated through the hall, out onto the stone-paved path. Then she took a turn, aiming not for the small courtyard outside his ward he'd expected, but into the main gardens of the Temple. It was still rather early for many flowers, the only ones coming up were the early bulbs, crocuses, a few primroses.

He found being outside distracting, though he had to close his eyes against the sunlight. Logically, he knew it was spring, and not terribly strong, but compared to his room, it was far too bright and too sharp. It meant he had to rely on scent and the feel of the chair moving over the paving stones.

There were softer smells, some kind of not very

potent floral scent, but also what he thought must be medicinal plants or herbs. He couldn't name them beyond the mint, herb lore had never been his strength, but he knew some of their scents from the kitchen gardens growing up.

She pushed him rather far into the gardens, before she turned right. She finally slowed as she came to a paved stone area, and he could hear water burbling from what sounded like a small fountain. He could tell that he was in the shade now, and when he opened his eyes, he found that he was in a small grotto. A shrine was set into the wall and stone benches curved around the sides of the enclosure. She had parked him in the corner, where he could look to his left and see the shrine, or look out and see if anyone was coming.

The shrine, though, that was more curious. There was a goddess depicted, not one he knew. She was wearing Roman robes, a snake coiled around her arm, a basket of eggs in her arms, and a small dog stretched out at her feet, looking up. He tilted his head, distracted by the image, trying to parse it.

Nurse Morris asked, "Are you comfortable, sir?"

Roland considered, and decided he was, rather surprisingly. She'd put a cushion or something in the chair, he hadn't noticed. The blanket was soft under his hands, and not too warm, and she'd parked him in the shade. The grotto walls meant he could look up, and not catch the sun. He nodded. "Thank you, yes."

"Just a moment, then, and we can have some tea and biscuits." Without any other comment, she moved to the shrine. She put something in a small offering dish mounted by the fountain. Then she ran her hands through the water, cupping them together to catch some in her palms, then letting it flow again. She came back to take a seat on the bench, enough to be looking at him.

"May I ask?" Roland gestured at the statue.

"Sirona. I'm a Therapeutes of Sirona." She said it as that should make many things clear to him, and it did not.

"I'm sorry. I'm afraid I don't understand. They put me in a room, they didn't exactly explain how the place works, beyond what I've sorted out by myself." It came out rather testy, but she didn't seem to take insult.

"Oh." She took a breath. "Let me pour the tea, then I'll explain." He got the sense she was putting him off for a minute, to gather her thoughts. But he was scarcely going to argue with having tea and biscuits, rather than healthy healing foods and plain water. Mind, he'd sell his soul for a bit of beer. She handed him a small metal cup with a wee handle, but easy enough for him to hold steadily. "Let me know when you want more."

He nodded, and inhaled the scent. Strong and black, bracingly refreshing. The few times he'd gotten tea with his meals, it had mostly been rather weak. He took a sip, then held it in his lap to cool a little. "When you're ready." He did his best to avoid making it an order.

She let out a little sigh. "I trained here, but I haven't served here for a decade or so. Healers and nurses, we make our vows by one of the healing deities. Which one depends on the person. I'm sure my da would have preferred I keep to chapel ways, and swear to Christ, but I've my mother's line running stronger in me. Sirona's a Gaulish healing goddess, Gaul and Brittany. But she's got a care, particularly, for the slow healing. Recovery that takes time. The kind that takes food and patience, exercises and a bit of encouragement." Then she unbent enough to add, "I always liked the dogs she's shown with."

That at least made some sense to him. "And there are little shrines like these all over the place, then? If people swear their oaths by different ones?"

Nurse Morris nodded. "There's a chapel inside with shrines, and ones in the gardens, here, and then special rooms in the temple. There are healing springs, a whole set of rooms, different shrines, to soak in."

The thought of that sounded almost interesting, but he had no idea how you asked to go to them. His baths in the large bathtub were one of the only things he looked forward to right now. But he had no idea if one could take the healing waters, or how it was arranged.

She reached out, before she drew her hand back, as if it were overstepping. "Perhaps in a few weeks, if you'd like. You'll need to be able to get yourself down into it, and I'd have to find someone to help you. Male."

He didn't think he'd been nearly so transparent at all that, and he blinked up at her for a moment, trying to gather his composure. Instead, he went back to the earlier question. "Your name? Names?"

"No one can overhear us out here. We can see anyone coming." He realised, with a start, she was right. They had an excellent view of the path, and the grotto walls were solid. "I am Elen Morris. My da's a supervisor at the Dolacauthi Mines. My ma runs the household, teaches a bit of village school."

"Roland, as I said. If you can bring yourself to it." He felt himself leaning into the charm, and wondered why. In his life before, he might have admired a pretty woman of her background, but not offered so much as his name.

She let out a breath. "Roland." Hearing his first name made him feel somehow seen. For far too long, he'd been sir and major and someone distant and foreign. He'd spent far

too many weeks being held at arm's length. It felt like a
tremendous gift, but the next heartbeat later, he realised
he'd erred. When she left, when Elen left, he'd be missing
someone in particular, not a nameless nurse in uniform.

He shied away from thinking about that further, it felt
entirely too raw. Instead, Roland tried to figure out what to
offer her in turn. "You still haven't had a chance at my
records, have you?" She shook her head silently. "My family
are, plenty of them, military. Even my mother serves, in her
way, she is a defensive magics specialist. She was posted in
Egypt for a while, and India. Fortifications and protections,
for people going out to war." Talking about his family like
that felt safe enough. Distant and busy, which they must be,
they always were.

Nurse Morris - Elen - cocked her head. "She must be
very good, then."

He laughed. "Mother is utterly terrifying, and utterly
unyielding in pursuit of her goals. I am quite sure the idea
that someone might want to stop her never entered her
mind." He waved a hand. "Father and grandfather, that
tradition I at least understood a bit. I went to tutoring
school, went to Schola, served in the Army a few places, and
when this mess happened, I knew I'd be going."

Elen nodded. "May I ask how you were injured?"

He shrugged, slightly. "Cavalry. A small unit of magi-
cians, assigned to accompany the 2nd Dragoons. The King's
Bays."

She frowned at that. "A regular army unit? May I ask
how that works?"

"Officers, the usual sorts of duties, they assumed we
existed for messages. And looking handsome when needed.
We did - oh, shoring things up, protection cantrips, a dozen
different things." He hesitated and took a breath. "Half of

my specific lot, they're still fighting. The other half, besides me... still in France, six feet under." He'd been the only one to take a serious injury and survive it, and it made him feel even more alone.

"I'm sorry for your losses." She said it softly, simply, but it didn't seem to be a pat response. "And your family?"

"I've cousins fighting a dozen places, but I'm the only child to make it to adulthood in the direct line." He shrugged, not wanting to mention his younger sister, who'd died of a sudden illness when he was six and she was two. "I was engaged, when the War started. When I came back, she made it clear she had no interest. I don't remember what all she said, I was in and out, but I remember that much. That she thought I was done for." He looked up, deliberately, and saw half a dozen expressions slide across her face. She was no card player, he was sure.

"I am sure you'll prove her wrong."

He shrugged. He wasn't paralysed, but he'd had no glimmerings of interest of any kind since he'd been injured. He tried not to think on it, because dwelling on it made him particularly grumpy, and to absolutely no useful purpose at all.

She considered, then visibly made a choice. "They won't tell me about your case. I've written to ask a friend, in confidence, about your evening potion, and about other things, but..." She shrugged. "Without a sample, I don't know if she can do much. And it's hard to get a sample. there are protections on the vials to ensure it's all drunk."

Roland considered that, the implications of it. "But we can come out here?"

"This is therapeutic. Traditionally therapeutic. They'd have to argue against a millenia or two of good healing practice to deny it." He heard a hint of humour, there, and something like pride. Perhaps she was pleased she'd come up with an argument they couldn't argue with.

Roland considered this. He was used to thinking of things in terms of hierarchy, all his family did. She was, by observation, quite low in it, unable to pull rank she didn't have. And yet, like the best of the privates he'd known, she had the gift for using whatever she was permitted as well as she could. Making do.

"And you think it might help?"

That made her snort. "Look at you. Tea and biscuits and enough privacy for a conversation that's about more than your adventure books. I thought it might do something."

Roland had to admit she had a point, then he asked. "Do you mind the reading?"

Elen shook her head. "You enjoy it. And they're better than some things I've had to read. I've had more than my fill of the moralistic improving literature of our grandparents. Mind, I'm not sure they actually liked it either, they just thought it was improving."

"Who were you reading to that asked for that?" He wasn't sure why someone would.

"I was at the Temple of Youth, remember? Children, recovering from long-term illness. Some tuberculosis, some poliomyelitis. Some who'd had a run of other contagious diseases. There was one poor boy who'd gotten over mumps. He'd gone out for the first time in weeks and weeks, and picked up whooping cough. He was six months building his strength up again." Then she added, much more quietly, "Not all of them recovered, of course."

It hit him then, that she was not new to the kind of losses he'd been facing. It made him wonder what she thought of him, of being assigned to him. "And you were - the War?"

"Western front. There was an explosion, it knocked me out, a concussion. The others I was with, they bounced back, but I started getting awful headaches, migraines, if you know them." Her voice had become clipped, the kind of squashing of emotion that he recognised in himself.

"And so you had to come back here?" She nodded, looking somehow relieved that she hadn't had to say it. "And you're here for - how long?"

She shrugged slightly. "I don't know, honestly. But seeing to you, that's where I was assigned."

"And the headaches?"

Another shrug. "I'm making sure they are not a problem."

Roland tried to figure out how to make sense of that, but had not gotten anywhere with it before she said, "I shouldn't keep you out here long. If I overtire you, we can't do this again. Finish the tea, and we'll go back." Whatever passing openness had been there had slammed shut, and he had no idea why.

CHAPTER 9

FRIDAY, APRIL 9TH, ROLAND'S ROOM

Roland found himself annoyingly restless. Someone, not a Sister he knew, had come and pulled Nurse Morris away, unexpectedly. It had happened while he was still groggy from his potion, fumbling his way through the tail end of breakfast. Nurse Morris had made an apologetic face at him, but she had gone.

He expected people to leave, that wasn't precisely the problem. Or rather, it was a problem, but one that had become endemic in his life. His parents were both admirable people, but they were tremendously busy. They popped in and out of his life, over and over, between their other duties, important ones, leaving him with Nanny.

It was curious he'd not heard anything from them, mind. They might not be present, but they were usually regular correspondents. Surely by now they'd have had word of where he'd ended up, even if the letters had taken a while to catch up with him from the Front.

On the other hand, he hadn't written either. It wasn't only that he didn't trust himself to hold a pen steady, but he had no idea what he could possibly say. He had no idea if he'd be good for anything, ever again, and it wasn't as if anyone had given him any hope he might be. In a family anchored by duty and service, what good was he if he couldn't serve in some form? Perhaps that was why they never visited, or wrote. He must be a tremendous disappointment, to be sidelined like this.

His fiancee, Admantine, had come to see him early on, and then she had left after fifteen minutes. Three days later, a letter had shown up, with her ridiculous rose-pink shimmering wax, smelling faintly of lilies. He thought it was lily, anyway, something creamy, and with a hint of clove. Not carnation.

The letter had been brief, cold, and he had not been able to shake the few words from his mind. She thought it better that he were free to focus on his recovery, she was not suited for the care he would need, she hoped he wished her well. He did not wish her ill, exactly. But he could not wish her well.

He could not wish himself well, never mind anyone else. It had sent him spiralling down into the depths of his mind, unwilling to engage with the next nurse assigned to him. A nurse who had been there one day, and gone the next, after only a few weeks. Or the one after that.

Perhaps Nurse Morris was gone, too. Would be gone. Perhaps in a day or two, there would be some other chipper woman with an implausibly white pinafore. He had stopped caring. Except that Nurse Morris had done something he did not expect, taking him out to that little grotto in the garden. She'd told him her full name.

She was devout, in her way, he'd realised that as soon as she explained where they were. But unlike some of the nurses, she wasn't showy about it. It was in what she did, how she did it, what she did with her time, rather than in the public gestures.

His family weren't religious, not more than any military family were. Which is to say, every man he'd known prayed in the trenches, whatever their belief was, and he was sure it had been the same in South Africa, and the Sudan, and India, and hundreds of other places around the globe. As it was the same for people who were on the other side.

Roland was mired deep in thought, since he was not up for holding a book, never mind focusing on it, when there was a knock on his door. "Sir, a gentleman to see you, sir. May I help you into your dressing gown?"

Roland couldn't decide if that was better or worse, really. There was no dignity in talking to someone in a dressing gown, when they were in sharply tailored clothes.

With his mother, or his father, it made him feel as if he were about six. He had memories of having tea in the nursery when he hadn't been well, some childhood fever. His mother had come and peered from the door, and gone away again. Twenty minutes later, his father had done the same. They were not, as a family, particularly good with illness.

"Who is it?"

"A military gentleman, sir. A Brigadier Campbell."

"My dressing gown, please. And I suppose you'd better open the curtains a bit more." The obligatory fussing took only three or four minutes, but when Harry went to get the door, there were the sudden sounds of leather soles on stone floors. Harry retreated, with a "Call if you need me, sir," that did not specify if he was talking to Roland.

"Gospatrick." No rank, nothing other than his bare name.

He managed a passable salute. "Brigadier, sir. Please, have a seat."

"These presentations of yours. When will you be ready to do at least two a week?" As Roland had expected, the Brigadier remained standing.

That was not the question Roland had expected, though he wasn't sure what it was he'd anticipated. "That would be up to my Healers, sir. I am afraid they take quite a lot out of me."

"You've been taking your time recovering. You're not malingering, are you?"

Roland blessed the fact that Nurse Morris told him things. "I gather I ran a fair fever, after the last one. I would much rather do my part, sir, I assure you." He kept his voice even and brought out the clipped consonants and round vowels that made him this man's social peer, if not his equal in military rank.

"Untidy." It was said, largely to himself, but Roland was certain it was not a mistake. This was not the sort of man to be overheard accidentally. Then Brigadier Campbell peered down at him. "What do you have to say for yourself, then?"

"About what, sir?" Roland kept his voice pleasant.

"Your injuries. Why you are taking so long to recover. What you expect to do."

"I am no Healer, sir." He let out a breath. "They have said mine is a challenging case, but have not told me all of the specifics. I believe they feel I do not have the specialist knowledge to understand." He considered, for a moment, whether asking the Brigadier might shake loose something Elen could make sense of, but he could not at the moment see an opening that wouldn't put her at risk.

Roland considered how to put the next bit. "I know that

I am weak, some days I can barely walk across the room. I require a great deal of rest, and while I can make a public presentation every fortnight or so, more often than that would leave me entirely incapable. I am told I can have hope of improvement, but at some distant point."

"Hmph." Again, Roland was sure that was meant for his ears. "Don't you wish to return to your unit, son?"

Not your son. He might not be terribly close to his father, but his father would not do this. Or so he hoped. Then he realised with a sudden sickening certainty that his father was pushing other men like this. That his father had to know he was playing dice with other men's lives. "I'm not sure that will be possible, sir. Certainly not quickly. But I would like to do my part."

The Brigadier peered at him, eyebrows furrowed. Roland was saying all the right things, all the proper platitudes, but this man was sure there was something missing. "What do you see that as being?"

Roland shook his head. "That's impossible to say, sir, without more certainty about how much I might recover. I am quite willing to do presentations, to recruiting staff or recruits. Perhaps some sort of training position, if I recover enough, even if I cannot return to my unit or a similar one."

"You were assigned with the King's Bays, yes?"

"Yes. Messaging, some covert operations that required manoeuverability and charmwork. They did not know we were magical, of course."

"Rider, then?"

Roland nodded. "I was. Might be again, eventually. Quite sure I wouldn't trust my balance soon." He paused, then added, "Not sure the horses are that much use, sir, in this war. I lost two good geldings. One to foundering, one to a bullet."

The Brigadier waved his hand. "That's not your concern."

Roland rather thought that it was, if he might be on a horse in a similar situation again. But saying so would not improve anything. He'd learned well before he was injured that most of the ranking officers had no desire to hear how this war was different than the ones they'd fought and theoretically won.

The thing about growing up in a military family is that he'd not only heard those stories, any son of a man who'd fought might have heard those. But he'd also had the lectures about tactics, demonstrated with lead soldiers and sand tables, or in a pinch by the salt and pepper pots and a trail of crumbs from the tea cake. And he'd heard not just about the victories, but the awful bloody disastrous defeats.

The silence stretched out, until Roland remembered to say something. That was how a conversation went, and he was supposed to be making an effort. "It would be a help, sir, to know what the goal of the recruitment meetings was. So I could - could prepare properly."

Brigadier Campbell narrowed his eyes. This was not just thought, this was a deadly sort of calculation. Then he said, as if he hadn't done that at all, "Be persuasive about serving king and country, of course. You're well-built, you could be on the cover of any of the magazines for soldiers."

This was not wrong, but it was not at all reassuring to hear. He had not been injured in any of the visibly horrifying ways, so his function in this man's eyes was to serve as a pretty mannequin. Whatever was wrong with him, broken in him, was far more subtle. Possibly more devastating, but he'd scarcely had the chance to discuss that with anyone with a different kind of injury. They'd kept him well away from other patients. He wondered what Nurse Morris might say, when she returned.

There was a noise outside his room, and then a careful knock, and a "Sir, it's - pardon, Brigadier." That was Nurse Morris, in fact. "It's time for Major Gospatrick's afternoon dose, sir, if you don't mind?"

Roland opened his mouth to ask what afternoon dose she had in mind. Then he realised what she was up to, and nodded slightly.

Brigadier Campbell frowned. "Think about what I said, son, and recover quickly. Your country needs you."

Roland managed a slight nod. "Of course, sir, I take your advice most seriously." He waited until the Brigadier had pushed past Nurse Morris, out the door. She lingered in the doorway, once he'd gone.

"Talking to Harry." She said it quietly, for his ears only. "He said the Brigadier had been here a bit, and he wasn't sure why."

"Asking why I'm not able to do the dog and pony show three times a day. I did not care for him."

Nurse Morris blinked at him, and then made a curious sound that he realised a beat later was a strangled giggle. "I didn't either. Not at all. He loomed."

It was not a bad word. Roland felt like a rag that had been soaked and wrung out, and he was suddenly very glad he was not alone with that feeling.

CHAPTER 10

E len did not get a chance to discuss the outing with Major Gospatrick. Nor did she get a chance for another one as soon as she'd hoped.

The morning after their outing, there was an influx of new patients. Despite the fact she had been told she was assigned solely to Major Gospatrick's needs, one of the Healers came by and crossly demanded she come and assist.

There was no getting out of it. She was swept up into the maelstrom, trying to get the patients settled. And of course, ducking the glares from other nurses, when she didn't know where something was, or the current techniques for fresh injuries.

No one told her anything, of course, that would be far too easy. But she was able to piece things together, a bit. There were new injuries, ones that no one could make much sense out of, some sort of magic, or some sort of chemical. Men had died in the casualty clearing stations and field hospitals, and others had awful burns to their skin, blinding injuries, all manner of things. Quite different from her Major, she realised, whatever else there was.

The flurry of activity not only kept her busy, but it took her into wards she wasn't remotely familiar with. They had cleared out one of the buildings that was normally used for contagious illness quarantine. The orderlies and cleaners were going through with bleach and mops and charms to make sure everything was spotless.

The housekeeping staff followed with carts of blindingly white bedlinens. Behind them came the squeak of the gurneys, and the slow thumping of those men who could walk with the aid of cane or crutch.

The nurses who had largely accompanied them wore uniforms that Elen was not entirely familiar with and had to take a moment to place. Not nursing uniforms of the kind she knew, but rather pinafores over a dark dress. Voluntary Aid Detachments, then. She'd not had a chance to work with any of them previously, not more than very briefly in passing, before she'd been injured herself. Posh women, mostly. Like Major Gospatrick. She could hear it in their voices.

"Sister, pardon."

One of them was at her elbow. The woman who had caught her arm was perhaps a little younger, right around thirty, with the sharp and somewhat horsy features of one of the well-bred families.

"Yes?" She turned. Sister wasn't precisely the right term for her, but it wasn't completely wrong, either.

"Can you show me where we can get clean things? These men, it's been a very long trip for them. Towels, clean clothing for them."

Elen shook her head. "I don't know what they have." Then she straightened. "How many?"

The woman peered at her, and said, "Eighty. Twenty officers, sixty men. Are you new here?"

"Fairly, yes. But I know who to ask. I'll be back in a few minutes."

Elen went off, at a sharp pace, dodging through the hallways. Then she could cut down the back stair, and down to the front of the ward, and the nurses' lounge. There were several senior nurses in there, talking in undertones.

"Pardon, Sisters." She cleared her throat. "Therapeutes Morris, helping out for the moment. One of the V.A.D.s asked if there are clean pyjamas and towels and such for the men coming in."

The three of them turned as one, and the second, a sister had never seen before, peered at her over wire-rimmed glasses. "Morris." She said it as if she'd already heard half a dozen things, not to Elen's credit. "Which V.A.D.?"

Elen considered. "I didn't get a name, Sister. About thirty, dark hair, looked like one of the First Families, a country sort?"

"Huh." There was a little hum of the three sisters, the eldest nodded. "Come along. Where are you normally assigned?"

"Major Gospatrick, Sister, in Ward A. I've not been here long, though I apprenticed here."

"So if I send you to the laundries, you'll know where to go."

She bobbed her head. "Yes, Sister."

"Go find the V.A.D. who asked you, and show her where the laundries are. You may need to wait, but they'll be finishing linens and a start on clean clothing for our new patients. Get the things back, and then you can go back to your duties."

Elen bobbed again. "Yes, Sister."

There was an expectant pause, as Elen turned to go,

then the voice came behind her. "If your patient does not need you, come find me, I can give you a few tasks to help settle yourself in."

Elen turned back, a little startled. The eldest sister gestured at her throat, and the small charm, then at the one at her own throat with a pendant of a male face surrounded by the rays of the sun. "Blessings of Apollo Grannus on your work, Sister. Ask for Sister Pomona if you've time." She knew the imagery. He was often connected with her own beloved Sirona.

It earned her a sharp nod. "Go on. Plenty to be doing." While brisk, though, it felt like a companionship, rather than Sister Almeda's sharpness. There had not been much camaraderie for her, shut away in the corner with the Major, and the offer felt like sunlight and fresh water.

Part of her wanted to turn back and ask more, talk more, not be so alone, but the nurses had turned back to their conversation already. Elen turned and walked briskly back to the ward, looking around to find the V.A.D. who'd asked her earlier.

She was in one corner, helping someone move a bed, to a better location. "Miss? Sister asked if you'd come with me to the laundry. We can get the towels and some clean clothes there. If you come with me, then someone on this ward will know how to get there."

The V.A.D. looked up. "Oh. Me? Are you sure?"

Elen shrugged. She didn't particularly care, but she had her orders. "That's what Sister said. This way?" She gestured with her chin. "I'm Therapeutes Elen Morris."

"Aemilia Patrick-Lynes." The 'Patrick', so similar to Roland's last name, caught her for a moment, but it wasn't that close, even at first glance. A posh family, though, clearly, with a double-barrelled name. Her mum had always thought that a sign to mind your ps and qs and several other letters. Elen at least felt she had the upper hand here, in knowing the layout.

Elen nodded, and gestured with her left hand. "This way, then. The laundries are out past the back wall, I'll show you the fastest way there."

They went along at a good clip, dodging past people in the hallways, helping get things ready. It wasn't until they'd gotten downstairs and nearly to the back covered walkways that Elen could say anything. She turned into the covered hall that divided the temple proper from the essential but somewhat less obviously sacred spaces like the laundries and warehouses. "How many are coming in in all, do you know?"

"A hundred and fifty on the train arriving this afternoon. Another train in a few days, most likely." Miss Patrick-Lynes was keeping up with her, the nurse's pace that covered ground quickly, but was agile enough to stop suddenly if they came upon a patient. "Have you been here long?"

"I trained here, my apprenticeship, but I've been elsewhere. I was reassigned here two weeks ago. Long-term care."

"Is that your specialty?" Oh, she was a talker. Not that Elen minded, it might get her a bit more information, if she could figure out how to ask.

"Yes, I'm dedicated to Sirona. Long-term care and rehabilitation."

"Ah." There was a sort of wistfulness to her voice. "You're lucky, knowing what you want to do, to focus on. We have to do - well. A bit of everything. But you're not at the front."

That was rather more delicate. "I was, but I was hurt,

and they sent me back here. I can be quite a bit of use, of course. You?"

"They didn't let us close to the front. Just seeing to the canteen and rolling bandages, and such, until they needed extra hands for the train back. They've treated most of these men, best they could, but they need people seeing to them, don't they?" It was a rather earnest question.

"They do, and good nursing takes time. Changing a dressing properly takes a bit, or helping a man walk to the end of the room, or write a letter. The way I was trained, that's as much a part of recovery as the Healers."

The other woman was silent for a dozen steps, then Elen gestured. "Here, see the sign here, this is the way to the laundry. Storehouses that way, they're labelled by what they have, there'll be a clerk to help you."

"What sorts of things are in the stores?"

"Start with the laundry for linens and pyjamas and such. But if there are specific things needed, pitchers or tea canisters for the ward, vases, that sort of thing, the store rooms have it. Mostly, I suspect you'll want the bandages - that's the green storehouse - or items for the wards, those are in the yellow one."

"Green for bandages, yellow for ward supplies. Where are potions and such?"

"From the ward sister, they go through her inventory lists."

Elen glanced up, to catch a sharp look from Miss Patrick-Lynes, as if she knew something Elen didn't. Something about the nursing hierarchy that Elen had missed, perhaps. But then they were at the laundry. There were a good five minutes of figuring out what was needed right away, and what would be needed in a few hours. The

laundry supervisor piled things on carts, and grabbed orderlies to help bring them up.

They found themselves parading along back to the ward
with three full carts of supplies. When they got back, Elen
coughed. "I should get back to my ward. I hope everything
goes well with the transfers."

Miss Patrick-Lynes nodded once, precisely. "Perhaps I
will see you again, Nurse Morris." It was not a dismissal, but
there was a quality Elen couldn't place, something that felt
out of place.

Elen managed a smile and added, "Blessings of Sirona,
and all the healers," and fled back to her own ward. She did
not understand it, precisely, but at least she knew what her
role was there.

CHAPTER 11

FRIDAY EVENING, ROLAND'S ROOM

R oland didn't remember when he'd nodded off. Sometime before supper, he guessed, as he jerked awake, muzzy with sleep, and not sure what had woken him.

The first thing he realised was that the room was nearly dark, lit only by the bedside lamp. For a long moment, he thought he was alone, he couldn't see Elen or even her shadow.

Then he heard a gasp, from somewhere to his left, and he shifted, peering. The second thing he realised was that Elen was pressed tightly into the corner. Her hands were down against her thighs, as if she'd been willing herself to become one with the wall. Her breathing was shallow, he could hear it and see the way her shoulders were jerking.

Her chair had been pushed back by the wall against the window, almost a barrier between her and the rest of the room.

"Nur- Elen?" His voice cracked, as he spoke, and he couldn't make sense of that.

There was a shudder, then she straightened herself, in

what he recognised had to be a tremendous force of will. "Major."

"Are you all right?" He suddenly was terrified that she wasn't. That it would be like one of the men in the King's Bays. He was a man Roland had only nodded to in passing. He had looked fine, no injury to be seen. Then he'd died in Roland's arms, of a bullet wound that had been entirely hidden until they moved him. She had that same look, like those moments, the paleness and the stillness. Like some part of her knew any movement would be fatal.

She let out a shaky breath. "Are you?"

It came at him like a challenge, with a sharpness he didn't expect from her. Certainly not in this moment. He almost replied before he thought, wanting to defend himself, then he stopped. "Should I not be?"

Elen jerked her head, a tiny shake, a negative.

He tried again. "What happened?"

She gestured with one hand, and he could see the trembling, now, the shift of the light against her hand. She pointed at the table on the far wall. He blinked at her, then at the table, and he couldn't quite see. Something about the shape was different. Then she pointed at the chair. It was different than the usual, and he remembered they'd taken her padded chair for cleaning. He could see something on the seat, a shadow or a blotch.

"You'll have to help me. Please. What happened?"

There was another one of those uneven breaths, near a sob, something he'd never heard from her. "You - you were asleep, Major. And then something... You did something." Finally, she pushed herself away from the wall, and walked over to the far table. She picked an object up in her hands, and turned back toward him.

It was the metal pitcher, or what had been a pitcher.

Now, the metal was collapsed, twisted in upon itself, into a ball that had rested on a frail flat edge. It was as if some tremendous force had taken it up in a massive hand, and crushed it, as simply as he might crumple a piece of paper.

"May I?" Roland held out his hands to her.

Elen placed the metal in his hands, and he could feel a decided warmth to it, though perhaps fading. Roland turned it, one way, then the other, peering at the shadows in the lamplight. Everything was bent inwards.

Elen had moved to do something with the chair, he wasn't paying attention to that, until she let out a sudden squeak, and backed up several steps. She had moved it, pulling it back into place, and it had near enough split in half, as if it had been barely held together by splinters. As he watched, it tottered, and one half fell over, leaning against the wall, as Elen grabbed the other.

Roland set the twisted metal in his hand on the bed, and then asked, "I did that?"

Elen was wide-eyed, and she was barely breathing. He could see the little jerks of her shoulders at each breath. Then she nodded. "You." Her voice was a harsh whisper. "Your magic."

He took a breath, then risked a deeper one, before saying, as carefully as he could, "I'm awake now. It doesn't happen when I'm awake."

She blinked at him, but she didn't move. At least she wasn't fleeing out the door. Roland looked around, desperate to find some solution for the moment. "Will you trust me? Lean the chair, and sit on the end of the bed?"

It was forbidden to nurses, he suspected, the way her head turned, as if she'd been ignoring the fact the bed was there. Slowly, though, she moved, leaning the other half of the wooden chair against the wall. Then she perched on the bed, her feet braced on the floor right under her, as if she were a hare ready to spring away at the slightest hint of danger.

Roland swallowed. He desperately wanted a glass of water, but the pitcher was a ball of metal. And Elen certainly didn't want to come any closer to him than she had to. So he let out the breath he'd been holding. "I am sorry I scared you."

It didn't help much, but he hadn't expected it to. And on the other hand, apologising for something he had no control over, that happened only when he was a particular kind of exhausted, seemed wrong, too. But he was sorry she was scared. He had done the thing that scared her, and she was sensible to be scared.

She didn't say anything for a long moment, just looked at him. Then, carefully, as if the sound were as fragile as the chair, she nodded. "What do you know about it?"

Roland had to look away for a moment. He could have stood her yelling or crying or screaming much more readily than the way she looked. It was as if she had been betrayed, or had the rug yanked out from under her feet.

"When I have been upset..." Once he began, it poured out of him. "When I do one of the presentations. Or today, with the Brigadier, I assume. It - something feels wrong. Jagged, uneven, unstable. And it's happened before, that I've done things like that. It's why other nurses left."

He heard her inhale, and then she let out the breath, slowly, almost inaudibly. "Have you hurt anyone?"

Roland swallowed. "I - don't know. I don't know if they'd tell me. I'm sorry, you must be so scared. I understand if you want to leave." He fully expected her to nod, that sharp little nod, and walk out, close the door. For the orderlies to come back with a dose that would leave him senseless for a day or more.

Elen hesitated, then nodded. "It's not uncommon, with younger people, who are ill. Especially those right around the age to make the Pact. That the magic comes pouring out. Yours is a tad different, but - the same sort of thing." She tapped her thumb on her leg, a nervous tic. "Your evening potion?"

He blinked at her, at the end of the bed. "I assume it's meant to help that. Stop that, rather." He moved his hands, to resettle in the bed sitting up. He wasn't sure what to do, what he could offer. She wasn't leaving, she was still perched there.

"You don't like taking it, though." She was puzzling through something, he was sure now.

"I don't. It makes me feel awful. Why?" He wanted to work up the energy to be irritated, but being irritated at her was wrong, and the people he wanted to be upset at, throw things at, weren't coming near him.

"What sort of awful?" She was working through something, not that she was explaining herself.

"Muzzy headed, stupid, clumsy, not myself." He waved a hand. "I can't explain it better."

She let out another breath, more of a sigh this time, but dropped that line of questioning. "Right. Let me get a cloth so you can wash up a little. I'll figure out a way to sneak the pitcher and the chair out. Somehow."

They both looked at the window at the same time, having had the same thought. They were on the ground floor, he suspected there was a bush outside. Then she grinned, her teeth flashing. "I can probably drop it behind the bush. See if I can liberate something more comfortable to sit on from the nurse's lounge."

"What about when I destroy that one?" Then, he forged on. "Aren't you afraid?"

That got her standing, and brushing her hands off on her apron. "You haven't hurt anyone yet." It sounded stubborn, more than anything. "Do you think you'll hurt me?"

Roland had no idea how to answer that. "I wouldn't want to. But I don't know that I won't."

Of all things, that made her laugh. "Well. Let's see what we can do, then, about hiding the chair."

"And the pitcher."

"The pitcher will fit in my bag, that's easy. The chair..." She worked on getting the window open, then leaned out to look around, before she slipped half the chair through. He couldn't see all of what she did, but she must have lowered it down somehow, he didn't hear a thud or a scrape. "There. I'll go rescue it when I go home, and drop it on the refuse pile."

"Isn't this... shouldn't you report this?"

She turned back to him, looking fiercely resolute. "They don't tell me anything about your case. I am beginning to think I should return the compliment. If they want to know, they can ask."

CHAPTER 12

MONDAY, APRIL 12TH, THE GARDEN

The next day, Elen could not find time to talk further with Roland before his bath. After leaving his room, she had barely been able to sneak the broken chair out of the way, piece by piece, back to the rubbish, and bury it under other items to be taken away.

Explaining where a chair that had been halved had come from would be very tricky, but she'd managed to pull the legs out - they'd been screwed in, not glued, thankfully. It meant the individual pieces could be strewn through the compost and rubbish piles.

She'd barely made it back to her rooming house for the late curfew, scooting in under the entirely disapproving nose of her landlady. Then she'd been scolded over an early breakfast for coming in so late. The fact she'd been with her patient had saved her from worse, but only barely. The other nurses in the house had cordially ignored her, as if her disgrace were contagious. After that brief flash of companionship from Sister Pomona it felt all the worse.

Then the next two days had been one thing after another. There was a new nurse on the ward, tending to someone two doors down, who kept having questions about where things were stored. Half of them Elen knew, but the other half were things she'd not used here, such as the dressings for burn wounds.

The new nurse just kept asking for things, every few minutes. Elen finally excused herself and went and showed her the things someone more senior should have done, even if it meant leaving Roland alone. She certainly hadn't been able to talk privately with him.

And now here she was, exiled out of his room for another forty minutes, so he could have a haircut as well as the bath, they were bringing a barber round. She knew without being told that meant he was going to be trotted out on stage again, and sooner than later. Not tomorrow, probably, but by the end of the week, if she was guessing right.

Elen had curled up, settled sideways, on the bench in the grotto, and she looked up as she heard people come along the path. They likely couldn't see her, as she was well back in the shadows and the uniform tended to blend in. She'd left the apron for the laundry, to be cleaned, along with her sleeve covers, since she'd planned to put a clean one on when she went back on duty.

"I don't know, there's something not quite right." The woman who had spoken had a Welsh lilt to her words. It reminded Elen of her favourite aunt Margred, and she had the same dark hair with strands of silver, pinned up high on her head.

They walked by without noticing her, then must have turned into the next alcove, because a moment later, she could still hear them, remarkably clearly. "In the figures?"

They were speaking quietly, but rather urgently, the kind of conversation that made one want to listen more closely. They were both wearing the plain dresses of sensible dark fabric worn by the female staff who weren't nurses.

It was not quite a uniform, and yet effectively one, since visitors dressed quite differently. Not upper level administrators, she thought. Those usually had more obvious lockets or watch fobs or other adornments, or something like a cape. Something to set them off. No, these were likely mid-grade administrative staff.

"The figures, but also how people talk about the figures. You know how I notice that, Clarice."

"In any department in particular? Oh, let's pause here, Berth, the view is fine." Clarice had a precision to her voice, a sharpness. Elen wasn't entirely sure what it meant here.

"Long-term care, in particular. Several of Healer Cole's patients, but not just his. But then, the war injuries are all rather badly documented, on our end. Paperwork still catching up, they say, but they've said that for months." Berth sounded decidedly disapproving. Definitely from south Wales, though, with a name like that, and that kind of accent.

"Do you know anything about Cole? He's newly back here, isn't he? Been out somewhere in the Empire."

"Tilly, you know, she does the typing for the Healers, she said he's had letters from South Africa, and somewhere in India. Several of them. But he must have been there quite a long time, he doesn't spend much time with the Healers here. Even Healer Denby, you know how kind he is about including people who've moved back. And Healer Tipson usually has people around, wanting to know what they learned overseas. Even if what we do is best, of course." Berth sounded thoughtful, and as if she didn't know a lot of the healers directly.

"You're right, usually, we'd hear about suppers and

such. But then, Cole's on the long-term care cases, quite a few of them, and I suppose that keeps him busy."

Berth snorted. "That's what he says, anyway. But have you noticed he's always sending his juniors out? He's in his office, usually, doing important work I'm sure, but not the sort anyone sees the results of."

Then Clarice forged on. "Well, there's something a little off about anyone in long-term care, without the obvious sort of injury. Takes a sharp healer to spot that kind of problem and prevent malingering." That annoyed Elen, to be judging people on how they recovered from something awful.

"And we're getting more of those. The cases they won't talk about. I'm not sure what to think." Berth, at least, sounded a little more open.

"Well. It's hard to get any of them to say anything. I tried to ask Sister Almeda something the other day, and she almost took my head off." Clarice apparently thought that wasn't anything unusual. Elen was glad she wasn't the only one with difficulties there. That it wasn't solely her failing, anyway.

"You know Almeda's territorial. She always has been. Merlin and Nimue, I shared a house with her at school, and you couldn't leave a thing out in spaces she thought she had charge of without a ten minute telling off." Berth sounded deeply amused.

It made Elen wonder if they were talking about Alethorpe or about Schola. Most healers and nurses and midwives went to Alethorpe, but there were exceptions or people who came to their vocation later on.

"Even that young? My." That had an amused drawl to it. "Well. I suppose having different people here must have her on edge. She never has liked anyone coming near her authority. Why's she still only ward supervisor, that's what I want to know."

"You know the progression's slower on long-term care."

"Bah." Clarice snorted "That's no excuse. You know how their hierarchy works as well as I do. And she's been here near forty years. You think she'd want to finish her career a bit higher up the ladder."

"Not our hierarchy, dearheart." They were close, then, to have that kind of affection with each other. "Ours is sensible." Then Berth returned to her initial topic. "The figures, though."

"Oh, do tell me about it, Berth. If it's nagging at you."

"Clarice." She fell suddenly silent, as if she were looking around. Elen drew back against the edge of the bench, pressing herself out of the way even more. "There's half a dozen cases, now, that they don't talk about. Nurses assigned, outside the usual protocols."

"Anyone we know?"

"No." Bertha considered, as if she were ticking off on her fingers. "Someone who'd been at the children's home. Two women who'd been in France, sent home for compassionate reasons, elderly parents or some such. Two who'd been village nurses."

"Any trained here?"

"That's the thing. I can't get a look at the files. I can make some guesses, from the names, but no one who'd been here recently." Berth sounded utterly frustrated, as if normally it would be routine to check. It was the sound of a woman whose domain had been trampled on.

"The Temple of Youth, don't we know a few people there?" That was Clarice, now sounding thoughtful, her voice getting a bit softer.

"We do. I could write, but I'd have to tuck it in with some other questions."

"Perhaps ask about the knitting, swap some patterns? Or a few ideas for cakes, you had that carrot cake recipe, didn't you?"

There was a long interval, the sort of tutting murmur of a woman sorting through lists in her head. "I've enough to make a tin and send it along, I think. And that new pattern I've been working on. Easier heel than the one she'd sent me."

"Well, then. We might ask. And I sometimes run into Mallery, who's got one of the rooming houses."

Not Elen's, she knew that, but one of the ones nearby. "She might hear something, that's true. Or at least know where the new girls are being put."

"Do you think - is it the kind of thing we should report?"

That made Berth laugh, suddenly, a barking sound, unladylike. "Who to, Clarice? Who would we report it to? We can't send it up our chain, it's not like anyone listens to us. We just fill out the paperwork and the forms and the account slips. You know what happened last time we had to reconcile something larger than petty cash."

"Don't remind me. Half a dozen interviews from above, and with the Guard, and all because someone didn't file their own copies correctly. Discourages a person from pointing out the necessary, doesn't it?"

"Quite." Berth was clipped. "We'd need more than my vague feelings, certainly. And it's not as if we can get at patient records."

"No one's going to let us in the wards, or the sister's office. And it's not like you can lure Almeda out with any of the usual things. Or that Healer Cole would listen to the likes of us." Clarice's voice turned wry. "Even me. I'm not nearly posh enough for him."

"A devotion to duty is an admirable thing, but very tedious, yes. Well. Devotion to control, in her case. Less admirable, certainly more annoying. And Cole, well, I'm sure he's busy doing something, but he's awful about turning his paperwork in, so I've no idea what, or who to ask about him."

"Write your letter, I'll ask around, and we can see what happens, then." With that, they settled into rather less dangerous gossip.

Elen realised with a start that she would have to get back some other way, to avoid making obvious she had been listening, and so she waited until they had settled into far more routine gossip about a newspaper serial story and some bit of business about the Council and a recent proclamation. That wasn't anything she ever worried about. She ended up standing, slowly, to avoid the bench creaking, and then taking a sharp right out of the grotto, walking up the side of the main temple building.

The path was in deep shadow, between the height of the temple itself and the tall wall that divided the Healing Temple spaces from the rest of Trellech. She could barely hear the city beyond, carts and carriages on the street, people calling out, as if they were muffled by a great curtain.

She ended up having to go out the main gate, circle around on the street, folding her hands across her stomach and hurrying, since she only had her cap on, to duck into the tunnel at the back of the main grounds, then out into the small ward courtyard, scooting back into the ward just in time to grab a clean apron and slip it on.

A moment later, the new nurse came out of her room, and had yet another question.

CHAPTER 13

TUESDAY, APRIL 13TH, THE ADMINISTRATIVE OFFICES

"Nurse Morris?"

Elen was sitting on the long hallway again, waiting to be called in to one of the offices. Not the Archiater himself, this time, she gathered, but one of the people the next layer down. She still had not had time to talk to Roland. He had been washed and settled again when she got back, but they had had a constant stream of minor interruptions.

One had been a junior healer, coming to review his file, but he had refused to talk to Elen about any of it. The new nurse on the ward had been asking questions again. Harry had come by with a bit of broth for teatime. That one, at least, Elen had not disapproved of. She rather thought that a wider range of nourishing food wouldn't hurt.

And now she was here, and not at all sure why. She didn't think she'd messed up badly enough to be sent off to some gods-forsaken country house. She hoped. She stuck her knitting needles in the ball of yarn, nearly done with this set of wristlets. She hadn't been able to concentrate on shooter's gloves for a few days.

She kept thinking wistfully of the shawl she'd started last summer, just before the war started. It was set aside at the bottom of the knitting basket in her room. The pattern had been a gift, one she treasured. But she didn't dare try lace work right now, even without the guilt of working on something impractical.

"Coming." The clerk was waiting ten feet away, not rude enough to tap her toe impatiently, but the impatience was clear. On the other hand, no one could really argue with someone knitting for the troops, when they were waiting, and Elen traded on that.

She was shown into a smaller office, though still with a view out over the temple gardens, rather than the streets of Trellech. "Nurse Morris. Have a seat." The administrator, this time, was a somewhat mousy haired woman with her hair in a tight bun, and a severely plain dress of navy blue. A former nurse, possibly, but she thought not a healer. For all their faults, the demands of their training tended to shape them differently. This woman had a certain rigidity to her.

"Yes, ma'am?" Elen could be just as civil.

"You have been here for a month now, make your report."

A month already? It had scarcely felt like that, but she had been rehearsing what to say when someone asked her. If someone asked her. The trick, of course, was figuring out what they wanted to hear. She had kept a chart, the one that hung on his door, of doses given, but as far as she knew, no one ever checked it.

That gave her a moment's reflection. If no one was actually checking it, could she get away with giving him something other than that evening potion he hated so much? If she could get something suitable, anyway.

"I have been glad to see to Major Gospatrick's needs. I gather there has been some question about when he might be able to more fully step into recruiting duties?"

She got a sharp nod in reply. "Precisely, yes. When?"

That was trickier to navigate. Saying she'd not seen his file could be seen as an abrogation of duty, despite the fact she'd requested to see it, more than once. "Surely his healer would be better able to determine that, ma'am. I have been told I need not see his file."

"Ah." Most uninformative, not just the lack of words, but the neutral tone. "You have had care of other patients. Previously."

"Yes, ma'am." She gathered her thoughts. "My previous posting prior to the War was at the Temple of Youth. The conditions there are rather different, the ones treated, and the nurses are given quite a lot of leeway in determining treatments other than surgery or magical interventions. Tuberculosis cases were common, of course, and some cases of poliomyelitis, but the recovery process is different."

She considered how to continue. "Without knowing the specifics of the cause of Major Gospatrick's injuries, or his previous treatments, I can suggest strengthening routines, such as the visits to the garden. Perhaps some others, with permission, I believe some modest changes to his meals might be of help. I have seen some progress, but not as much as I would prefer."

"And his potion regimen?"

If she said nothing, and changed his potions, there would be a problem. If she spoke up, there could be a problem. In the end she thought about how much he hated the evening potion. "The day time potions he tolerates well, but he has developed something of an aversion to the evening potion, ma'am. Twice I have stayed into the evening, when he has slept for the afternoon, and he - he is obedient, ma'am, to his treatment, but a skilled nurse notices, of course, the reactions."

That got the woman leaning back and then saying. "And when he takes the potion?"

Elen marshalled her thoughts. "There are two aspects to consider, of course, ma'am. How well the potion achieves the desired effect, and his experience of it. The former is important, but in the past, I have found the latter makes a difference to the overall recovery. One can abide a number of unwanted side effects if the overall direction is toward meaningful healing."

"And you think this isn't."

"It is hard for me to tell, ma'am, without seeing his chart, at the very least." Not that that got her an offer of the chart. Elen hadn't expected it. "He complains of being muzzy-headed, finding it difficult to wake in the morning, or focus. From my observations, his pulse and respiration are slow until about twelve hours after the dose, he is lethargic, unwilling to talk."

"Consistently?"

"Consistently, ma'am. I have not been able to determine what happens if he does not take his evening potion, but I do know that if he's taken it late - because he slept after an afternoon presentation - the effects linger for half a day from when he takes it."

"I am sure that the healer in charge of his case has his reasons." She had a tone, though, that suggested she might be wondering about those reasons herself.

"Of course, ma'am. I can only report my observations." Elen shifted slightly. It was not entirely feigned, she was uncomfortable. But looking as if she had been scolded and was taking it seriously wouldn't hurt.

"If you were to discuss it with his healer, what would you say?" The question was almost idle, but Elen wasn't falling into that trap.

"If permitted, I would ask what the goals of the potion were, and if some alternate might be tried, for a few days. As it is, Major Gospatrick has limited time to rebuild strength and stamina. Once he is fully awake, it is nearly luncheon, once luncheon is cleared, it is his hour for his bath and shave. Once that is done, there is an hour or two before supper, and then we are into the evening."

"And if he were not so - slow - in the mornings, you believe he might regain his strength more quickly? Would you change his schedule?"

"I have, a few times, gotten him out into the garden. I was taught, and have found in my own previous positions, that being outside, when possible, contributes a great deal to long-term outcomes."

"In a chair?" The administrator leaned forward.

"Yes, ma'am. Though I would hope to have him walking a bit, in the garden, and then expand the distance."

"I will discuss the potion regimen with his healer." The decision was rapid, crisp. "It may be a reduced portion, or some other adjustment. You will be informed. Begin taking him out in the garden as much as possible. I will see about rearranging the schedule so his bath might be before lunch, so you might go out for an hour or two afterwards."

Elen inclined her head. "Ma'am." she agreed. "Should I make a further report to you?"

"A week, back here." The woman looked her up and down. "If anyone has questions, direct them to Sister Florinda."

"Ma'am." She stood, since that was clearly a dismissal.

"Nurse Morris," That had a warning note. "See to your

temple duties, in greater measure."

That wasn't mysterious, not at all. But Elen could only bob. "I'll stop by on my way back, ma'am." Of course, having said she would, she was then committed, and she had to take the long way down, through the side stairs, and off into the side of the main temple, along the long colonnade of pillars, into one of the side rooms.

She stopped at the pool fed by the healing spring deep underground, through some sort of ancient magic that no one had ever explained to her usefully. There, she washed her hands, ritually, using the wooden ladle to pour water over one, then the other, then splashing her face.

That done, she went and attended to the small tasks that any of them did as needed. She began by clearing the old candle stubs from the metal holders. Checking the small chalkboard tucked behind a curtain, she saw the offerings had not been changed today. She wrote in the date and time, doing her best to make sure the chalk did not squeak, and then replaced the eggs and wheat on the shrine from the small waiting bowl, putting the older offerings into a bucket that would go to the pigs.

Only then could she turn her attention to the actual shrine, and she knelt on one of the padded cushions. A more modern touch, the bare stone was likely more traditional. Closing her eyes, she did her best to calm her thoughts. She felt tossed around, pinned between competing needs, and not at all sure how to navigate. More than anything, she was frustrated by the constant inability to do her work.

The time in the shrine didn't improve anything, not meaningfully. There were no bolts of sunlight, or claps of thunder, or the roar of a hundred galloping horses. But she felt, as she stood, a new certainty that whatever else she did, helping Roland was worthwhile.

CHAPTER 14

Roland wasn't sure what had gotten into Elen in the past day. She had gone off for an appointment with only the barest excuse. He could read her well enough now to be sure she wasn't looking forward to it, the way she'd been tightlipped and tense. It created lines at the corner of her eyes that made him wince, the implications of the stress and pain there.

When she came back, nearly two hours later, she was different, but he could not for the life of him put a finger on how, never mind why. It was the why that mattered, of course, and he couldn't begin to guess. She might have been promised a way out of her work, for all he knew. It wasn't that, not precisely, he was clear by now that she cared deeply about her healing work, when she was permitted to do it.

Something had changed, though, and it wasn't just the schedule. The next day, Harry had come in to bathe him at eleven, the last slot before lunch. After the lunch tray had been cleared, she had brought out the basket chair, and said, "Come on, outside for us for a bit."

He blinked at her but didn't argue. It seemed quite a pleasant day out, from the glimpses he'd had from the window, and he'd caught a whiff of flowers here and there. "If that's what you wish?"

"I think it would be good for you." That was unyielding, to say the least. He was recovering enough to feel annoyed at people deciding what was good for him, even if he hadn't recovered enough to argue with them about it. He suffered the mild indignities of getting himself into the chair, clumsy again, and of her pushing him outside.

As he expected, they went down to the outdoor shrine for Sirona, and she settled him near the bubble of the fountain, where he could look out at the rest of the garden. "Let me know if anyone's coming, please?"

He blinked at her for a moment, then nodded. "I think I can do that." Then, a bit more daring, he asked, "For a particular reason?"

"I have a few things to talk to you about."

That didn't sound ominous at all. But all Roland could do was nod. "Go on, when you're ready?" Some part of him had that sense of being a junior officer, drawing out one of the enlisted men, the times he'd been in a position to do that. When one was homesick, during training, but terrified of admitting it. Or once they'd arrived in France, and he'd been posted with the Bays, of navigating the gaps in prestige and power.

It felt like the tables were turned, he certainly had almost no power here. But she didn't either. There was a moment where she clearly wanted to fiddle with the folds of her skirt or apron, and restrained herself.

"My meeting yesterday was with one of the administrators. Sister Florinda, she said her name was."

He nodded, not sure why Elen was starting there.

"She asked me what I thought about your recovery. I mentioned that I had noticed your evening potions seemed difficult. That you took them, but that there were the small indications, visible to any attentive healer, that you did not care for the effects. This morning, I received a note with permission to give you a half dose."

Roland blinked. "That's good. Isn't it?" He'd thought it was, he hated the leaden feeling it brought on. Even a half dose would be much better, he was sure of it.

"I still have not gotten permission to see your charts. Or even to talk directly to your healer. They send me away, when I ask. They don't even let me be there on rounds. They send his junior, who just checks your vitals and asks you a few questions to prove he's been there, and writes a few things down."

Roland had to laugh, that was quite an accurate description of every time the junior men had come by, even though Elen was normally sent out of the room to help roll bandages or whatever nurses did when they weren't needed for some other task. Or knitting. As if she read his thoughts, she pulled out her knitting bag, and set to work, with the needles clicking softly, without looking at it.

"Socks?" It came out a little cracked, and she blinked at him.

"A muffler. I don't have to think about a muffler at all. If i get distracted and it's a little longer than I'd meant, there's no problem."

He contemplated that for a long moment. Socks could be used in all weathers, even the wristlets could be useful on a chilly spring or summer morning. But a muffler. "You think the war's going to go on."

She tilted her head, as if he were catching up with her, and from rather a long distance behind him. "I suspect so, yes. If I'm wrong, I'm sure there's some poor soul in London or another of the cities who could use a muffler come winter. But I think it's going to the trenches."

Roland chewed on that. "Why?" Part of him hated asking, hating showing his weakness that way. If this were his tutoring house - filled with young and often merciless men from families with a long military history - he'd have been taunted.

At Schola, his head of house or one of the prefects would have led him with a brutal and rigid sternness, through the chain of thought that led to a thoughtless question. In his apprenticeship, his master would have raised an eyebrow, and that would have been a tonne of scorn, in one tidy package.

Elen did none of those things. Instead, she smiled, as if asking the question were the kindest thing anyone had done for her lately. Or the most thoughtful gift she'd been handed. And for him, her smiling hit him like a blow, the way she was open to it. Not rigid. Water, flowing around him, enveloping him.

She didn't rush into the answer, she took a breath, before she went on. "Most simply? They would not be so anxious for you to heal and recruit others, possibly train others, possibly go back yourself, if they thought the war would end soon."

That was another blow, and this time he felt himself shudder. He had to close his eyes against it. She was right, damnably right, and he hadn't put it together, not at all. He clenched his hands, and then forced them to relax.

When he could manage to look at her, there was a quirk to her lips. "They haven't given you a chance to see the whole picture, you know. With the drugging, and dragging you out to exhaust yourself whenever you begin to recover a little. As soon as you have a good day, they demand your time, your vitality, again."

"I want to serve. The country, the magic, whatever you call it. I always have." It came out of him in a rush.

She nodded once, as if she'd expected he'd say that. He didn't think he liked being so predictable. "They're relying on that."

"They?"

She shrugged, her shoulder twitching for a moment before she went back to the even clicking of the knitting. "The generals. The people in charge. The Archiater. Your healer. The Council, for all I know. I don't know, that's the point. People like me don't. We just know there are people, somewhere, making decisions they don't have to think about again, for people who'll be living with the costs for the rest of their lives. However long those were."

That was cheerful. Or rather the opposite. He couldn't argue with her, though, she remained damnably right. "Your meeting yesterday, it changed something?"

"Permission to bring you out here. More to the point, time to do so. That's why your bath was at eleven today, so we could take the whole afternoon. I've made arrangements for one of the healing baths in a couple of days. I had to trade a few favours, I'll need to leave you promptly after supper the next few nights."

He held up a hand, as if to slow her. "Trade favours?"

Elen shrugged, the click of the needles pausing again for a moment, like a song coming to a breath, before it started up again. "That's how things work. If you can't tell people what to do."

He supposed she divided the word into people who could tell you what to do, and people who did things. And he found himself uncomfortably straddling that line, in a way he hadn't felt since his Schola years, and a scolding he'd heard about how to treat the house staff. Not to him, thankfully, but to one of his housemates.

"What did you trade, then?"

She shrugged. "Evening bandage duties in one of the other wards. Not pleasant, but someone's got to do it, and I've a lighter touch than many. So that the person I'm trading with has something to trade with someone else, I'm not sure for what. But for that, we're on the schedule weeks earlier than you might be otherwise. They've been using a lot of the baths for the gas victims."

"And you think it will help?"

"It certainly won't hurt. And I do think it might help. I think." She frowned as if she'd dropped a stitch, because there was a long silence before she did something with the needles and started again. "I think there's something tangled in your magic. I don't know how to untangle it. But that's why there are prayers. Gods. For the things we can't figure out ourselves."

It seemed a very pragmatic view of religion and also rather outside his experience. "A pool for Sirona, or someone else? You said there were a number, didn't you?"

She glanced up, there was a flash of some expression he couldn't read on her face. "I'll be working that out. While you're having your bath tomorrow, actually."

Roland felt it would be best not to press her further. When he didn't speak, they fell into a silence that lasted a good twenty minutes, long enough for her to establish the muffler as more than a narrow strip. That done, she spent a good hour nagging him into alternating walking a few steps, then resting, over and over again, until he was sure his knees would not hold him more.

She did it fiercely, but with a kind of patience he hadn't

known since watching an older mare on the home farm breaking in a young and rambunctious youngster yoked with her on one of the carriages, just using her weight and skill to pin him when he misbehaved.

He wasn't sure what he thought of that at all. He was too tired.

"What's he like, your patient?" Elen had presented herself at the office that coordinated use of the healing pools promptly at eleven the next day. It was partly to make herself useful, and partly to figure out which of the rooms Roland might best use, of the available options.

The healer on duty was a short woman perhaps in her early fifties. She wore faded indigo linen robes, belted around a decidedly curvy and well-padded figure. They used the classical design that was little more than two lengths of fabric pinned and hemmed together, with a broad apron dyed in a medium blue to match around her waist. It was all very unlike the spaces above and the bright whites of their linens or the sharp points on the caps and collars. More practical around a pool, she supposed, and easy to change and hang to dry when it got wet.

The healer had introduced herself as Rhoe, the current healer seeing to the care of the pools and bathing spaces. They were in the lowest level of the temple, a labyrinth of stone rooms that had been there for centuries. Some people said they were Roman, though that didn't actually fit the history of the city very well. Certainly of Roman design, though, with smooth pale grey stones slotted into a series of rooms curling around the path of the central corridor.

At the core, she knew, was the ancient healing well. She'd been told the stories, during her apprenticeship, of how you would put a pebble in, and read the bubbles to determine how the healing would go. It was an art she didn't know, and she didn't think it was much done in the current Temple. The well itself had its own shrine, protecting it in a blanket of quiet reverence.

In the middle, lit by charms, was the great bathing pool, far more public. She'd been there only a few times, shy of being around so many people, and not knowing who was who. When people had clothes on, it was much easier to figure out how to talk to them. There were cues to tell whether she ought to talk to them like a healer or a fellow nurse or a patient, or someone from the city itself.

The office, staffed by those devoted to healing waters in particular, was just outside the entrance to the main baths, with stained glass separating it from the more public spaces. Elen could see figures through the opaque glass, just enough to guess male from female by height and the amount of curve, and she found the movements rather distracting. The healer on duty cleared her throat.

"Pardon, sorry." It came out automatically. "My patient doesn't have a particular patron, from what he's told me. I would have put him as a son of Mars, perhaps in one of his less aggressively martial forms, only..."

"Only?" The question seemed friendly enough. Elen certainly wasn't going to trust a stranger with her thoughts, that had never worked out well for her, but it was a little encouraging.

"When I explained what I was arranging, his first comments were about service. About wanting to continue to be of service."

"Perhaps not Mars, then." The older woman agreed, taking out a notepad with a sketched-in map. "Would he take well to a more distant deity? There are several pools dedicated to various of the Egyptian gods at the moment, or Mesopotamian. A few Hindu."

Elen blinked a little. She'd not known that, though she hadn't much asked. She'd always just gone to Sirona's pool, or the temple alcove or the outdoor shrine, depending on her needs and how busy things were. Looking at the map, though, she could see there were at least fifty small pools curving around the central main baths. Perhaps more than that, she didn't have time to count them.

"I don't think so? He seems very English, considering."

That earned her a grin. "Not Welsh, then, or Scottish?"

"Northumbria, I think, is where his family is from. So the Marches."

Rhoe nodded. "And his injuries?"

This was decidedly more delicate. "I have not been permitted to see his chart or to speak to the senior healer in charge of his case, but I have my own observations."

Rhoe raised an eyebrow. "Ah." It was a very disapproving sound, mild as it was. Elen could not figure out if the disapproval was aimed at her, or at the unnamed healer who'd made that decision. "And you are the sole nurse tending to him?"

Elen nodded. "I have been given permission - Sister Florinda, two days ago - to reduce his evening potion. It's a dull colour, sealed with purple wax, and it makes him lethargic. Muzzy-headed." It seemed an imprecise word for an imprecise state of being, but it was also accurate. "For about twelve hours after he takes it, he is hard to rouse."

"And have you reduced it?"

"The first time last night. This morning seemed a bit better, but it is hard to tell, given the variation day to day."

Rhoe nodded. "What else have you noticed?"

Elen let out a breath, wondering how far to go with this. "From what I can tell, again, solely from observation, he was injured in an attack that had a magical component as well as the physical. I have only been here, and tending to him, for a month, but his physical injuries have largely healed. Some scarring, some areas of tightness or restriction, but nothing that should be so limiting."

"What makes you think there is an injury to the magic?"

"Two things, ma'am." Politeness couldn't hurt. "First, that he is far more quickly exhausted than he should be. I am now permitted to take him out to the main garden, and we began yesterday beginning to rebuild his strength more deliberately, walking and resting, walking and resting."

"That is more your usual approach, then?"

Elen nodded. "My background is in recovery from long illness, but of course, one does not improve by staying in bed once one can move around a bit."

Rhoe laughed at that. "Certainly not. What else?"

This was the tricky part, then, but she'd known when she decided to arrange the pool for him, that it would come to this. She knew she'd need to explain at least some of it, with all the implications of poor care from others. "I feel there's something tangled in his magic. Both that he is not recovering as you would expect but also the way he has reacted."

She hesitated. Many nurses, the ones who had a different approach to their chosen deity than she did, scoffed at this, but she thought perhaps Healer Rhoe would understand.

Rhoe tilted her head, then gestured with one hand. Her magic nudged the door fully closed with a click, and a wave of her other hand lowered curtains from the top of the stained glass. The casual, easy use of that kind of magic made Elen realise there was a lot of power in this unassuming woman. "Something more confidential, then? I am a priestess before anything else, if that is a help."

It was and it wasn't. It was good Elen knew where she stood. "Priestess to whom, ma'am?"

The older woman laughed. "You are sharp. And careful. I approve. Belisama, the brightest one." Her eyes twinkled, and Elen could have sworn that the charm lamps burned a little brighter. "You sound as if you need someone to talk to, that is not above you in the formal hierarchy."

When Elen hesitated, there was a little gesture. "An open offer. But I owe my duty to the waters, and to the light. I care about those in between, but I am not beholden to them."

Elen had no idea how one could live like that, without taking the people around you, especially their demands, into account. But here Rhoe was, apparently unheeding of the ways other people could fence her in. "You understand, ma'am, that that is quite unusual?" Daft, but Elen could scarcely say that.

"I come from a good family, and they've backed me before, when it came to a power struggle. Probably will again." There was the kind of supreme confidence of the aristocracy in that, and for a moment, it reminded her of how Roland looked at the world. "Probably will need to again, honestly, because I do tend to have opinions. But yes. Quite unusual. Might as well take advantage of it."

Elen was certain there was a catch here somewhere, but she couldn't figure out what it was. And honestly, it was not as if she had many other options. She sucked in a breath and let it out. "I think something horrible happened to him, something he mostly doesn't remember. It damaged his magic, and it is continuing to. I think they've been drugging him so far because he's - damaged things with magic, in his sleep. Nightmares, maybe. I haven't pressed him, but when I was at the Temple of Youth I saw similar things in the children." It was accurate enough, and she had thought it a solid diversion from revealing what had happened.

After taking a breath to resettle herself, she remembered to add, "When I first was introduced to him, his magic felt odd. You know how things are easier to see, the first time? It was like something was blocked up, a stagnant pond instead of a flowing stream." Once she'd said that, she forced herself to look up and watch Healer Rhoe's reaction.

"Damaged things? Not people? Have you seen this yourself?" There was a great deal of sharpness there, as if a knife had come whistling across the room to land quivering beside Elen's ear. Only it didn't seem aimed at her. That kind of sharpness wouldn't miss its target.

"Once, ma'am." Elen tried to figure out how to explain, now she'd been caught out. "It scared me, but it didn't come near hurting me. He'd had a visitor, he's supposed to be helping with recruiting efforts. Encouraging others to do their part. He'd fallen asleep. I stayed, later than usual, since he hadn't had his potion for the evening yet."

"And?"

"He crushed one of the metal pitchers, for the rooms, like it was crumpling a piece of paper up. To about this big." She gestured with her hands, the shape of it, the size of a modest melon, perhaps. "And he split one of the wood chairs in half, like a lightning bolt hit it."

"Was there light?"

"There were - marks on the wood, ma'am. A bit like scorching, but nothing like actual fire." It felt better, much better, to say it. She was terrified that Healer Rhoe would turn, march her up to the Archiater, throw her out of the temple, but here, she felt, was finally a place she could speak the truth and be heard.

"And what happened then?" Rhoe leaned forward, considering. Watching, certainly, every little movement Elen made. It felt different than with the administrators, as if she were actively seeking out hints to help. Certainly, there was no sign she was upset. At least not at Elen.

"He woke up. I had, I had flung myself into the corner. He was fully aware when he woke, he apologised to me. We talked a little bit, he explained he'd done that before, he thought it was why the other nurses he'd had left. I wonder if it's why there's a nurse assigned to him, and just to him. Most of the time, he doesn't need someone there."

"That's most curious. I would like to do some research. I won't ask anyone about him, not without your permission. Just books. Notes." Rhoe leaned forward, as if eager to begin.

Elen let out a long breath. "That would be all right, ma'am. I have been doing my best, but I don't know what will help, or what will hurt. And if I go to the library, it would be rather obvious."

"What would you research if you could?" Rhoe's voice was quiet, but with a particular intensity now.

"These are new kinds of injuries. A new kind of war. But someone's magic getting tangled, aren't there cases of it from the Napoleonic wars? I half-remember reading something about cannon fire. It would take me time to track down, though, and people would make assumptions about him. I don't think it's that, precisely. But it might help find what helps with the healing."

Rhoe nodded, approvingly. "I was thinking along the same lines. Though care and kindness go a long way in those cases, we're still learning a great deal about them. I was also thinking about some of the pattern magics, but those would require his healer's permission." She shrugged. "Better to have the information when we can use it. No one's asked you about him having an outburst, then?"

Elen shook her head. It felt good and terrifying in equal measure to admit it. "No one asked me anything about it. No one warned me about it, either. But I'm fairly sure that's what happened to his other nurses."

"As a sensible nurse, you want to avoid what will hurt." Rhoe tapped her fingers, but she offered a warmer smile now. "You have excellent instincts, thank you." Then she turned all business and focus, like an animal stalking prey.

"I can see two directions, for a healing pool. One would be your own Sirona. You have a care for him, she is certainly suitable. But that would mean taking on a responsibility for him in that way, as well as your nursing. That is something no person should ask of you, it is something you might choose to offer."

Elen considered that. She agreed with that, that it had to be an offer. She had never done that before, though of course, the Temple of Youth had very different arrangements. "The other option, ma'am?"

"We've bathing rooms set up dedicated to both Apollo Borvo and Apollo Grannus at the moment. Complementary to your own commitments, but not so entangled. However, I am not sure if that will entirely suit, neither of them are particularly directly related to illness of magic. I am wondering whether Nodens might be a better choice on that front."

That suddenly reminded Elen of Sister Pomona, earlier. There was a sharpness in her chest, like she was caught out, and she couldn't begin to make sense of it, whether Apollo Grannus were the right choice, whether she should seek out Sister Pomona, why she hadn't.

After too long a pause, she asked about the last choice. "Nuada, in the Irish, the ... connections. What's the word. Cognate. And Nudd, for my own people." The way you sometimes couldn't be sure if three names meant three gods with similar interests, or one god using different names in different places.

Rhoe nodded. "Cognate, certainly. And Nuada is of interest, for an injury that destroyed sovereignty and rule, and yet was later reclaimed. I am thinking that might be particularly potent."

Elen was relieved that Rhoe hadn't asked why she paused. Part of her wanted someone to ask, like ground during a drought wants rain. The rest of her was sure she would freeze or run or scream if someone asked her the wrong way.

"And if that doesn't help?" She didn't say 'work'. Healing wasn't like lighting a lamp. It was a slow process, walking toward a goal with measured steps. Elen thought it rather like the trees going from bare branches to fully unfolded greenery in the spring, only not nearly as certain or regular in progress.

"Then we will try something else."

Part of her wondered what her own Sirona would make of the problem, but she found herself saying, "Nodens, please. When would be convenient?"

They worked out the details quickly enough. Elen found herself efficiently scheduled for a future conversation the following week. More than that, she was booked for a slot in Sirona's bathing room for herself the day after Roland's. Rhoe made it clear, with kind firmness, that she must be sure she tended her own needs as carefully as her patient's.

Elen found herself suspecting that this might be Rhoe's response to the complexities underlying her own responses, the things she had been so very bad at concealing. Perhaps it was also something else. She didn't argue, for all she wasn't sure it would do much good.

That done, Elen found herself gently escorted outside, into the garden, when Rhoe went to begin her research. She stood blinking at the sunlight and not at all sure what she had gotten herself into.

CHAPTER 16

MONDAY, APRIL 19TH, A SMALL MEETING ROOM

F ar too soon, Roland was trotted out again. This time, he had to go without Nurse Morris, who had not been permitted to accompany him. He wondered if that was because she'd been so present, with the glass of water, last time, or whether it was simply that they ignored the work of the nurses.

It had all been done in glances and two bare whispers. The last he'd seen of her, she had been standing at the doorway of his room. Her hands had been folded in front of her in the at-ease posture he had learned was as artificial to a nurse as it was to a fighting man.

This time, rather than one of the large lecture halls, he was wheeled along to a small meeting room. It was on the ground floor of an administrative building, to one side of the main Temple. He'd still barely been in the Temple, he realised, and he wondered why. Religious fervour was decidedly out of fashion among many folk with magic, at least beyond the necessary familial magics to keep house and home together. Still, he knew that the healers themselves made a commitment. He might ask Elen about that. As a religious woman she might know something.

Three minutes before the start of the meeting, half a dozen people trooped in, all senior officials. They chattered with each other, ignoring Roland entirely, until one more slipped in as a late arrival. That last was around Roland's age, dark haired, and he nodded to the others, but didn't even make an attempt to say anything.

One man in his seventies, perhaps, still hale, but decidedly the senior among them, cleared his throat when the temple bells stopped ringing, and everyone fell silent. He nodded at Roland. "Gospatrick." Again, the lack of any title. "We have some questions for you."

Not a presentation, then. It would be easier, not that anyone ever asked him, if they let him know in advance what kind of thing he was being asked to do. "Of course, sir, I will do my best."

There were no introductions, and they didn't offer any of their own names. One of the others, a blonde man with the sort of attentive focus of a skilled aide, began. He led the lot of them through a tour of Roland's experiences, his training, his postings, his battles. Roland had to force a pause for a moment to interject, because none of them had a clue how the cavalry units worked. Nor did they understand the implications for a supply train, and the need to care for the horses that overwhelmed everything else.

These were, he thought, the sort of men who rode, yes. But the sort who went out for a ride, came home, and turned the horse over to a stablehand until next time it was needed. Roland did not approve, he had not approved even before the War. A good rider tended to his mount himself, or at least checked in later. Horses were not machines, like men were not machines. Care and attention brought out the best in them all.

He listened to a series of questions, then had to stop to wrangle his mind and his words into something that would be remotely palatable. "Pardon, sir, but the difficulty on the battlefield is that the horses have a sense of self-preservation. They are loyal, and work hard, but even the best horse will falter if pressed into shooting, or a sea of mud. Even if they didn't, they—"

He swallowed, fighting down nausea at the memories. "They make very large targets. By the time I was injured, I was not at all sure a cavalry was any use in this war, at least in the battles we found ourselves in. Smaller sorties, outside the trenches, messenger duties, those things that require quick mobility away from roads or rail lines. For those things, the horses will serve, but not this new sort of battle."

They didn't listen. Well, most of them didn't. That one solitary man, the youngest, gave him a tiny nod, when everyone else was focused on Roland.

It didn't help, either. The questioning went on and on. They came around, as Roland had suspected they might, to his injuries, and he could only spread his hands. "My healers have not told me their particular theories. I only know that they do not have a current solution that might return me to duty. I've heard a few comments about different approaches to magic, experimental techniques, new munitions. How those are, naturally, much more difficult to undo or mend."

It frustrated his audience. Certainly, it frustrated Roland. The injuries themselves were bad enough. It was awful to be forever caught in the fuzziness of his thinking, the way everything in him responded too slowly, always a beat or two behind where he should be. As they kept asking, prying at him, he felt himself hardening against their questions. And not just against the questions, but against the small courtesies, another glass of water or a brief silence as they wrote down notes. He glanced down to find his hands clenching, nail digging into his palm, under the table.

He did not convince them. He didn't know how to. He did his best to do as he'd been trained from childhood, to give honest, forthright answers. To trust in the structure of the world. It didn't help. And in that moment, he wasn't sure if it had ever helped, ever been the right thing. He'd trusted those structures, the proper forms, to make things go well, and the War had made it clear they did no such thing. Too many people were already dead because of that trust, and there would be hordes more if nothing changed.

As things began to wind down, Roland felt they had found his answers unsatisfying. One of them tapped the table, and asked, "What do you think happened to you?" There was a slight hiss, as if that was the forbidden question.

It made Roland consider before he answered. "I don't know, sir. I don't remember the time in the field hospital. The potions they've had me on leave me foggy. And even when I was in school, my preference was for using magic. I was not one for the theory of how it worked, or why one might alter a charm or cantrip or what have you."

He was beginning to have theories, mind you, but he wouldn't tell them that. He had standards. To know who he was talking to, at a bare minimum. It was an abysmally low standard, but he had to start somewhere.

Eventually, they all stood, pushing back, all of them going out in a knot. He looked up, and was startled to find the younger man looking at him steadily. "Captain Deschamps. Thank you for your service, Major." Then that brief hesitation, that even Roland in his current state could see coming. "May I ask a few more questions?"

Roland inclined his head. The man had introduced himself, treated Roland like a fellow officer. That was better than it might be. "I'm glad to see what I can do." They both knew it was non-committal. Then he repeated the name. "Deschamps." He tried to place where he knew that from.

"You were year mates with my older brother. He was a Boar." There was a tiny hesitation and Roland feared he knew what was coming. "He was killed in action two months ago."

Roland let out a hiss. He remembered Deschamps. Allery, that was the name. He'd played on the house bohort team, he'd been skilled at solving puzzles, if with a tendency to go charging at the ones that might yield to force. "My condolences." It seemed useless to say, but the formalities meant something to him. "I remember, he was always cheerful."

The younger man nodded. "He was." Then he added, "I'm Cadwell, sir."

Roland nodded. "I remember he talked about you a few times. After matches, or in the salle. Hoping you'd do well. You started the year we left, didn't you?"

Cadwell nodded, then he cleared his throat. "Sir, what you said, what you didn't say. You think there was some new magic, you have some ideas, but nothing you'd venture in front of strangers. I agree with you about cavalry being a horrific idea, not that infantry is much better." It came out in a burst, of a man who'd hit his limits of patience.

Roland nodded slightly. "As you can see, no one wants to hear it. Certainly not from me."

"It would make the War impossible to win."

"At least as we have fought in the past," Roland agreed.

"I don't have a better answer, but doing the same thing that is not working, is killing so many young men, so many horses, so many others... I cannot see that that is any good either."

There was another pause. Cadwell was a man who measured his actions, Roland could tell this much. That was unlike his brother, who had tended to boldly go ahead, trusting to his excellent instincts. It was as if he were deciding between two different lines of question. There was a flicker in his eyes as he made the choice. "And your own injuries?"

Roland permitted himself a shrug. "They have not been forthcoming. My nurse has a few ideas she's being allowed to try out in the near future. I'm willing enough to see what happens with them."

"How can you be patient like that?" Ah, that was a younger man's complaint.

"I don't precisely have much choice. I have the situation I have. I can be patient with it, or impatient and waste what energy I have wailing and complaining. Frankly, patience is more challenging, but less exhausting." Which he desperately needed right now.

Cadwell's lips twitched at that. "True enough, I suppose." He glanced at the door, over his shoulder, as if to check the coast were clear. "There are some odd reports coming out of the hospital. People recovering more slowly than expected."

Roland contemplated the implications. "Not just me, then."

"No. I don't know who else, it's mostly rumours. Smoke, fog."

"Are you assigned to Trellech, or where?" The question was, would this man have a chance to investigate further.

"Here for another month, then getting sent across the Channel. France or Belgium."

Trenches and mud, then, wherever he was, most likely. "Your speciality?"

"I was still finishing my apprenticeship when I got assigned." Career Guard, then, or at least one of their kind. "Pattern magics. I'm not as good as I should be, but we need everyone we can get."

Roland tilted his head. "Not a field I know much about." Easier to admit it, even if it were harder on his pride.

"Everything from the supply chain management to how troops move in battle. Some of Mons made for very interesting data, if one could ignore the human costs." Cadwell couldn't, clearly. It made Roland relax a little more.

"And the temple, here?"

Cadwell shook his head. "I don't have many contacts. I'll keep my ears open. Who's your nurse? It might be easier to get a message in through her."

"Therapeutes Elen Morris. One L in Elen." Roland added one more thing. "Dedicant of Sirona, if that helps."

"That does, actually. Gives one a better sense of how to go about things."

There was a knock on the door then, and Harry. "Pardon, sir, but we should be getting back or we'll be off schedule. Oh, sir, I didn't know there was someone still here."

Roland shook his head. "Perhaps you might come call again, sometime, Captain Deschamps? A visitor is a pleasant change of pace."

Cadwell was quick enough to pick up the hint. "And I'm somewhat at loose ends until I'm posted. I'll see what I can do." He nodded at Harry. "Thank you, orderly. I won't keep the major further."

By the time Roland had been ferried back to his room,

he found he was exhausted. Elen had warmed the bed for him with some charm he was coming to rely on. By the time he was tucked into it, it was far too easy to give himself over to sleep. He was roused briefly for supper and his usual dose, before falling into deep sleep again.

CHAPTER 17

TUESDAY, APRIL 20TH, THE GARDEN SHRINE

"How bad was it, yesterday?" Elen had settled him in what had become their usual spot in the garden, even though the weather was rather overcast and grey.

They'd barely had time to talk. The new morning schedule had some benefits, but it meant that there was someone in or out of the room much of the morning. Breakfast, waiting for the healer's rounds to reach them, then the preparation for the bath, and the bathing, and then luncheon. And he'd been tired, both last night and this morning, even with the lower dose of his evening potion and a reasonable amount of sleep.

Now, here he was, in his chair, a light blanket tucked over his legs, and feeling very much the invalid he was. He'd also been feeling on edge all morning. The conversation with Cadwell had woken up something in him. It was as if he'd been on a narrow path between two tall walls, unable to look to either side, and now he was getting a glimpse of gates into gardens or estates.

"It wasn't one of the big presentations." He owed her an

explanation, at least. She was doing her best to help him, and she was still here, even after he'd terrified her. Or after his magic had terrified her, anyway, and surely they were essentially the same thing.

She had picked up her knitting again, as always. No longer the muffler, but a tube. Sock or wristlet. "Do you get bored knitting the same thing?" He'd been curious about this for some time, but at the moment he also wanted to do anything but discuss the meeting and Cadwell's comments.

Elen looked up at him, wide-eyed, as if he'd caught her out in something, then she looked down at her hands. The needles clicked for nearly a minute. When she spoke, her voice was so quiet he had to strain to hear. "We're not supposed to."

It made him suddenly angry. "Why not, you're human, aren't you? What would you be knitting if you could? Mind, you'll have to explain it to me, I don't know much about it." The anger startled him, the surge of feeling, and he tried his best to moderate it, to avoid scaring her. No need for both of them to be worried by what he was feeling.

She looked at him, and held up the needles. "Needles. Wool. This is going to be a sock." In case that weren't obvious, which it hadn't been, so he supposed he was glad she'd explained that.

She continued. "It's all the same thing, over and over, for a long time. There's a bit of shaping, turning the heel, but mostly, it's just the same stitches, over and over again. More complicated than a muffler, but I've knit a lot of socks now. There is something soothing about that, about not having to think about it at all. But it's also boring."

"I suppose so." Roland agreed. "There's more than one kind of stitch, then? I know nothing about the, about the art. And that's more than two needles, isn't it?"

That made her smile, and he liked that. "There are two basic stitches in knitting, knitting and purling." she said. "P-U-R-L. Not like the kind you put in jewellery." It had the air of someone who'd explained that to clueless men before. "You use three needles or maybe four to hold something that's circular. You work the last, and then you take the one you just freed up, and repeat the process."

"That seems easy to lose."

Elen shrugged. "It's how it's done. Been done for ages, honestly. And it's not as if they usually have minds of their own."

Her tone made him laugh, he began to suspect that knitters had their own superstitions about such things. "When do you use one stitch versus another?"

"You can combine them, to make different kinds of fabric. Like ribbing, that's a knit fabric that has more give to it. You can add stitches to a row, or knit them together, too. Shaping something, like the heel, or a helmet, to wear in the trenches." Roland nodded, he'd seen enough of the knit pieces that covered everything but the face, how they curved around the chin, the neck, tucking down under the jacket.

"Those are bloody useful in the cold." he agreed. "And square wouldn't do." He hadn't realised he'd sworn before he saw her grin again. Amused, not offended, at least. She didn't seem upset by his show of emotion, at least.

"They're somewhat interesting to knit, but I do need a pattern for them, to keep track of where I am. And they're bigger, so they take more space to carry around. Socks, now, you can stuff socks in your pocket, so long as they don't come off the needles."

He nodded, then leaned forward a little. "You haven't

answered my question." He hadn't answered hers either, but he was still thinking about that.

Elen ducked her chin, and when she met his eyes again, she was smiling again. "Of course you noticed. The first thing I miss is the colours. You can get quite a good range of colours in yarn these days, or at least you could, before." She gestured. "But for the Front, everything has to be muted. Khaki or grey. Nothing that will stand out." She considered. "Nothing that shows dirt badly."

"Or worse, no." It slipped out before Roland could stop himself.

She nodded. "Or worse." Then she was knitting again, doing a dozen stitches before she continued. "I like the deeper colours. My aunt dyes yarn with natural dyes, she can get quite a good purple out of logwood, or indigo's blue. The colours against each other, though, sometimes. An edging on something, to set it off."

"What sort of things did you knit? Before?"

Elen glanced up. "I've got a half-finished shawl in the basket in my room. It's been to France and back with me, now, and every so often I sneak it out, in the dead of night, and knit a row. But I shouldn't, I really shouldn't. And if anyone saw, they'd say I wasn't doing my bit."

Roland blinked at her. "Not doing your bit? Have they not noticed that you're here twelve hours a day, no time to yourself, keeping me together, and also knitting a fair number of things. Can't you have a half hour for yourself, in the quiet, to do something that brings you joy?"

Elen waved the needle she'd just freed. "I wouldn't be doing my bit. And I'm here, quite safe. I even have my own room, not a cot in a dormitory. I don't have to fight for a bath, much." She added, "Mind, that's mostly because I'm here late so often."

"Small favours, I suppose." Roland agreed. "What's the shawl like, then? Not the same thing over and over again, then? And what colour is it?"

"The shawl is lace, though I'm only a little way into that part." Elen smiled again, that more relaxed smile. "And it's a logwood purple. A darker purple. It doesn't go with much I wear right now, I suppose. Traditionally, it would be white, but..." She gave a little shrug.

"Lace is combining the stitches a different way?" Roland had certainly seen plenty of lace, though he thought perhaps some of it wasn't knit, but made by some other means. He vaguely thought there were machines for lace now.

It got him a laugh. "Yes." she said. "You can do an extra loop of the yarn, and then the next time you go over that stitch, you do something so it makes a hole in the fabric. Here, give me a minute, I'll do a row or two of that, and then take it out."

"Unproductive stitches? My. I won't tell of course." Teasing her felt unexpectedly good, and she grinned right back.

"Tell me about your meeting." There was a bit of steel in her voice now, as if this were the trade for her work. He supposed it was fair enough, for all he wished she'd asked about anything else.

"I met someone I didn't expect." It wasn't where he'd planned to start, but it seemed the most important piece.

"Who, may I ask?" Her needles were going quite quickly now, as if having a pattern and a goal were driving her on, or doing something interesting had freed her.

"The younger brother of someone I knew at school. His brother died, he told me. Deschamps. Allery Deschamps. This was Cadwell."

"Would it help to make an offering?" Elen's voice was softer now, but the comment was utterly unexpected.

"I'm not religious." His voice came quickly. "I mean, I don't want to give offence, and I suppose all men pray in the trenches or on the battlefield."

She looked back at him, and something about her was now extremely steady, as if she had a certainty to her that wouldn't be shaken. "You don't have to believe to make an offering. It's the act of making it that counts."

"But all the stories about hubris and doing things wrong, and whatever." He shook his head. "That made some sense to me. Consequences for doing the wrong thing, at least. I can make sense of that."

Elen snorted. "It does follow logic, doesn't it?" She considered. "But you're willing to do a bath in one of the shrine rooms? Were you raised in a faith?"

Roland closed his eyes. "Father is nominally Christian. Holidays and so on. Mother, I don't know. She never talks about it, but I'm fairly sure she believes something." He opened his eyes to catch a brief sharp nod.

"We're not priestesses, or priests, or ministers, or what-ever the term is. Clergy." Her voice was quiet now, even. "We're there to see to the work of whoever it is we're sworn to. That the offerings are made properly, that the temple's tended. That the work we do is an offering. I don't always believe, but I always do the work. It's soothing that way."

That comment about not always believing, he was suddenly sure there was a story there, and an important one, and he was just as sure she'd never tell him. She had no reason to. He shifted in his chair. "Do you make offerings, then? Here?"

She glanced at the shrine, over his shoulder, and nodded. "Nothing fancy, out here. There's a shrine in the temple. I tend that as part of my duties. We have a roster, it changes as people come and go, as well as a turn in the main temple. Candles burn down, they need to be replaced, the offerings have to go out."

Roland took a breath, finding himself fiddling with the blanket in his lap. "Will you show me? Sometime? The Temple? The shrine?"

There was a moment where he could have sworn she lit up, as if she were truly glowing, but then it disappeared, as quickly as it had come on. She nodded. "I will. And I'll explain the bathing, tonight. What the process is." Then she stopped knitting, and stood. "And here, here's some lace."

It didn't look complicated, at first, it looked like a series of evenly spaced holes in the knitting. Then, as he looked more closely, he could see there were careful, planned variations, the way music made patterns that were more than the individual notes. Without asking, he reached out, to touch the yarn, lightly, then drew his hand back.

"How complicated does it get?"

"Very." She was amused now. "I could bring a few photos, and show you. One of my aunts wearing one."

"Something you made?" It felt daring to ask, but he was suddenly curious.

There was a long hesitation, then she apparently remembered something. "I think so, yes. If I can find it."

"Thank you." Then, suddenly, he felt tired. "Could we go in? I'm starting to feel a chill."

That was enough to break the moment, and get her fussing over tucking in the blanket so it wouldn't catch in the wheels of his chair. He let her make all the tiny adjustments, thinking about how quickly and freely her fingers moved to their task.

CHAPTER 18

E len was, she admitted, fussing with making sure everything was tidy while Roland ate. She was still nervous about Roland taking the waters, in the most metaphorical and literal senses, both. Especially after he'd asked the questions about how the shrines worked. She had been immersed in the Healing Temple and in healing work in general for so long that she forgot most people didn't think of things like they did.

Oh, she was sure there was more than one shrine in the Guards. And in the crafting quarter, there must be quite a few. People certainly had their own devotions. She'd seen enough guild medallions with a stone or engraving or carving of the guild on one side, and some god or goddess or their symbol on the other. Often not the ones you'd most expect, either.

That always made her wonder. During her apprentice-ship, she'd helped more than one crushing injury from a hand that got caught in the looms. She'd half thought about doing a study of whether people who wore tokens of

Athena or Frigg or Saint Maurice were less likely to have bad injuries. But comparing the results against a control group, that would be a trick.

"You said you'd explain the bathing?" Roland was settled in bed, and he'd finished eating.

Elen turned back, and settled down, considering her knitting. She'd have to work back to before the lacework demonstration, and she wanted to do that in better light, if she could. First thing tomorrow, maybe. She settled on the chair she'd taken out of the nurses' lounge, in the hopes it would be sturdier. It was a rather battered upholstered number with a blanket over it to hide the worst of the fading, but she thought it would not be missed.

"The main Temple is on the ground floor. It's been rebuilt a few times, but there's a natural spring down there. When they rebuilt it after the Pact, in the late 1400s, they built in a number of rooms below the main temple. Several dozen, I think close to fifty."

Roland blinked at her. "How big are these rooms?"

Elen shrugged. "Most are just about, oh, this size. Eight foot square, ten foot. When I was an apprentice, I always thought they felt a bit like horse stalls, only they're not in straight lines, but in a sort of curve. In the centre, there's a, oh, egg shaped cavern, and that is the general bathing rooms. Designed like Roman baths, but all curved and tiled. Dark blue and living green and white."

Roland let out a small huffing noise. "And people can go there?"

Elen nodded. "The main rooms, whenever there's space. It has all the different temperature pools."

"Do you go?" His question seemed almost casual, he wasn't making a big point of it. She thought there was something there he was trying to avoid talking about, but she couldn't figure out what it was.

She shook her head. "Not very often." The question was, did she explain why. Emboldened by their conversation earlier today, she decided to see what he did. "I'm very aware of status. When it's the baths, it's impossible to tell who's who."

Roland almost said something, then he stopped and caught himself, cocking his head to one side and peering at her. "You're one of the most polite people I've met in my life. You can't be afraid you'd be rude."

That was better than it might be, and it almost made her smile for just a moment. "It makes me nervous."

He waited, letting the silence fill the room, as if he were deciding what to do. When he spoke, his voice was quiet. "Where are you from? I mean, Mother would ask who your people were. You told me your father oversees the Dolaucothi mine now, and your mother sometimes teaches, but that's, that's only part of it."

Elen nodded. "Dadi, he worked his way up. When I was very little, he was still going down the mines, and I remember how scary it was for Mami." She let herself use the Welsh forms, with a bit of the music to it. "And then he got promoted. I remember having to learn quick how to be polite when we met his bosses, the fancy people, when they were looking at the mines. Mind my manners, speak properly, all that. Once I was old enough, I spent a lot of time with Uncle Dewi, in his office, out of the way."

Roland blinked at her several times. "And you - took that to heart."

She nodded, and then she had to look down and away.

"Elen." His voice was very careful. "Is it particularly

hard for you, not knowing what the Healers are doing with me?"

She couldn't look up, but she nodded again, and she could feel her hands clenching at her apron. Good thing she hadn't been knitting, she might have snapped a needle. Without moving more than that, she added, "It is. Not knowing what's expected."

"Ah." His voice got gentle, and she hadn't expected that from him at all. "So. How do we fix that? On a practical level? What are our options? You know about how this place works, far more than I do. Do we have potential allies? Resources? Possible strategies?"

Elen blinked at him. Whatever she'd expected, it wasn't this. He was treating her like a peer. Not just in her nursing skills, she was confident about those, but other things. She gathered her thoughts, which was tricky, the way they were darting around. "Well, normally, your chart would be on the end of your bed. Or outside the room. And it's not."

"That's curious, isn't it? So who would have one? Sister Almeda?"

"I assume, but if it's in her office, I can't get into that."

"Why not?" He pushed himself up more in bed, so he could lean forward. Elen was startled to realise he was deeply engaged in this, more than he had been in anything since she'd met him. "Tell me about the set up. You've seen her office?"

"Yes. It's in the ward, there, across the way."

"It is much easier to build a strategy for something you've seen. Especially if it involves sneaking. Laid out like this one?" His tone was suddenly eager, a sharpness of desire to it she hadn't heard before. It was almost like something out of one of his adventure books, and she wasn't at all sure what to do with it, or how to dissuade him from something terribly foolish.

She nodded and kept to the basic facts. They were far safer. "You know where we go out the door? And there's another ward, the same length, on the other side?"

"Why are they split up like that?"

"Some of these used to be infectious disease wards. You wouldn't want people with different diseases mixing, that would be horrible. Separate doors, separate laundry chutes."

"What about food?"

She blinked at him, and he waved a hand. "Food has to come and go, so it can be a way to sneak in. Besides the laundry chutes. And what's upstairs, these are two floors, three?" Elen wondered all of a sudden what he'd done in the past that made him think about sneaking into buildings like that, and if this was a mark of something from the War.

Elen glanced out the window, looking across the way. "Patient rooms on the ground floor, and on the second, depending on how full things are. Which we will be, shortly, I'm pretty sure. The upstairs are usually less nice. Not private, either two to a room, or four, or a long ward with ten or twenty beds."

"The same kinds of conditions as the downstairs?"

Elen nodded. "Usually. Nurses assigned to a given floor. Not a single patient. You are quite unusual."

"Several ways round." he agreed, wryly. "Apparently. So the notes?"

"There's an office, for the ward sister, on every ward. Some of them are big, some of them are tiny. Here, it's not bad, they built the wards with that in mind. Ours is the lounge now, which is tiny, but it's not like we're ever in it for more than making a cup of tea."

"Where does the food come from, then, if there's no kitchen or whatever?"

"There's a massive kitchen behind the wall."

"Wall?" He blinked at her, several times.

"When we turn right, to go to the garden. there's a wall behind us. Facing the temple. About twelve feet high. There's a walled walkway, with an arched roof. It's paved, smooth, some special kind of stone, I don't know how they shape like that, so there are no ridges. All along the walkway are doors and ramps, where they can load bins of laundry, or bring trays of food. It's all very efficient, the orderlies go and fetch the cart for their wards right on time, there's a particular sequence, so that there's no waiting."

"Huh." Something in that had distracted him, but Elen was not at all sure if it was the design, or the scheduling, or something else. It wasn't as if Roland normally made a lot of sense to her. "So not something you could take advantage of easily. The orderlies are all male?"

Elen was suddenly not sure if he was actually feeling better. Certainly, he seemed rather more quick-witted. But now she worried this might be a sign of some mania she should report to someone. Not that she knew who to report such a thing to. That being part of the problem. "They are, yes. And dressing up like one would not be plausible."

He looked her up and down for a moment, and she felt suddenly rather rounder than usual, and also shorter. "No, quite. I'm not sure you could bind your chest enough." Then he went blithely on. "So. Some other solution. Do you know if there are times she leaves her office?"

She had no idea how to take that, so she kept to the practical question. "Her temple service. We all have to do it. Even the senior nursing staff and healers. Mind, they swap around a lot, but I could come up with a reason to see her, and keep trying until she's not there. And I'm sure she has some meetings she has to be at."

"In that case, we just have to get you into the room when she's not there. Much easier problem." He seemed positively cheerful at that. Elen wasn't sure about that at all, but arguing about it didn't seem worthwhile. When she'd been quiet for too long again, he continued. "And what about other people?"

That made her stop and think. "Sister Florinda took an interest, but I don't know if she could help." She hesitated. "There was a nurse, Sister Pomona. One of the other wards, when I was helping with the men coming in from the trains. She was more friendly."

"Do you think you could find her again? When she had time to talk a little?"

Elen frowned. She wasn't precisely sure how to figure that out, but at least she knew how to go about that problem, unlike the utter daftness of the idea of her playing spy. Find an excuse to go through the different wards and check the lists. "Probably? It might take me a little."

"Good." He seemed very pleased at that. "That's a way to move forward, then. I can see if I can get a message to Cadwell. Anyone else?"

"There was someone I overheard, but I don't know her last name. And she was in administration, I don't know how things work there. She wasn't sure about some of the records. But I just heard her called Berth. Welsh."

"Perhaps Sister Pomona might know." Elen nodded, though she wasn't sure how she'd bring that kind of thing up. Instead, she changed the subject. "The baths?" She wanted, suddenly and rather desperately, to get back onto safer territory. Or into safer waters, technically.

"The baths." At least he wasn't being difficult about

being redirected. She took a deeper breath, let it out, and began explaining about the preparations, and how long he'd be soaking. It was reassuring to just talk about something she knew, something she understood. Something she'd done hundreds of times. Rather than his absurd ideas of breaking into locked offices.

Roland found the entire process of this trip to the baths more than a little puzzling. It wasn't the idea of Roman-style baths he had a problem with, of course, he'd done those at school occasionally. One of the Gospatrick homes still had a functional hypocaust and bathing pools. That was of course the eldest home, where his grandparents still lived. But of course, whenever the family was there, the aunts and great-aunts took it over, and young boys weren't permitted, never mind young men.

This was different. Not only because he was going to be down in the crypts below the Healing Temple, or what would be crypts in any other temple. It made him suddenly wonder what happened to people who had died at the Healing Temple, what happened to the ones who didn't have family to take them away somewhere. The temple was right in the middle of Trellech, surely there wasn't a cemetery attached, too.

Now he was outside his room more regularly, he was increasingly aware of just how large the temple complex must be. He'd known about the temple itself, of course, the facade that faced the street, with the high walls and the administrative buildings behind them, on both sides.

He'd been to the gardens, more than once, for various events to raise funds for projects of the Temple or to renovate a ward. But of course, when there were a few hundred people milling around, it was hard to see the size of the space. People talking and drinking and commenting on other people's party frocks broke up the long lines of the garden.

What Elen had said, about there being a whole system for kitchens, to get the food to people promptly, that implied a wholly larger infrastructure than he'd imagined. There must be something similar for laundry, given that that went away in carts regularly, and someone changed his bed every three days or so. Less often now than when he'd been prone to fevers at the drop of a hat.

Being out in the open area of the gardens also made him feel quite queer. When Elen took him out, she kept to the side paths, where there was the comfort of the tall wall and its shade. Harry was taking them straight down the centre of the gardens, a broad path paved in smooth stones, a good fifteen feet wide.

He felt suddenly horribly exposed, and set himself to not letting it show on his face. Not too much, anyway. Passing someone else, going the other way, he caught the same frozen expression, the way the other man's hands were gripping the arms of the chair too tightly, and he forced himself to relax. He had to remind himself this wasn't the open battlefield, with snipers taking aim. This was nearly nearly the safest place in Albion.

As Harry pushed him along, Elen trotted with them, to one side, nodding occasionally to another nurse as they passed. He thought it was perhaps the automatic nod to a colleague, as he would to another officer in uniform, nothing personal. At least that's how it looked, from the glances he got when they stopped to wait for someone moving slowly with the aid of a cane to cross their path.

They went not to one of the great main doors of the temple facing the garden, but instead, off to the side, where a passage about nine feet wide gently sloped down below the ground, meeting a similar passage on the other side. Plenty of room to get people through, even if they were on a stretcher, rather than a chair, he realised, as they moved into a broad hallway.

"Healer Rhoe? This is Major Roland Gospatrick." Elen was standing up straighter. Roland peered up at the woman who had stood to greet them. Unlike so many of the people here, she was unhurried, as if she had all the time in the world. She carried herself with a self-possession he hadn't seen much of, as if she were utterly sure in what she was doing. Even more startling, she focused on him, rather than talking to Harry, or to Elen.

"Major, we're delighted to have you. Nurse Morris, I know you have some other tasks to see to, we'll be at least ninety minutes, probably closer to two hours. You're welcome to come back to my office if you finish whatever you're up to before then."

Elen bobbed her head, visibly deferential. "I'll see you then, Major." She took herself off, before Roland could say anything.

The Healer looked him up and down. "Along this way, please. You must be Harry. We'll be having one of our staff ready to help, once the Major is in the right room, I'm sure you have things to do as well."

Harry allowed as how he might, though Roland suspected that it involved an extended smoke break. The healer led the way down a curving hallway, lit by charm lights every ten feet or so, that gave the whole space a feeling rather like catacombs. Not that Roland had ever been in catacombs, but he'd read enough adventure novels.

The rooms didn't feel particularly damp and humid, either. There was a little of that, but it was comforting rather than stultifying. The charmwork and ventilation for that must be rather a trick. Instead, it felt peaceful and quiet.

After going past about twenty doors, she opened a door on the right and gestured Harry in. He couldn't see much at first, it was more dimly lit, not beyond seeing there was a changing area with a bench and a curtain. "Back here." The healer pulled the curtain back, and then nodded, precisely. "Thank you, Harry. We'll manage bringing Major Gospatrick out." Harry blinked at her, looking unsure. "Left out the door, follow the main passage until you're back at the desk, you can find your way from there."

Only after the wooden door of the room was closed did the Healer turn back to him. "So. I've had a chat with your healer of record, who, I note, thinks this is ridiculous, but who is not going to exert himself enough to argue with it. Bathing and therapeutic techniques are somewhat at the discretion of the nurse. Also, he's a lazy bastard. I am Healer Rhoe - that's my first name, not my last. Fidelius will be along in a minute to help you to the bath. Anything you want to tell me first?"

Roland didn't even know where to start, then he at least found a sentence. Two. "Can I do this wrong? And will it get E - Healer Morris - in trouble?"

"No and no. I mean, it's not making her better friends with your healer. But that wasn't likely anyway, so no loss there. There are several people interested in what happens if she's allowed to use her skills properly. Best thing you can do is do your best to let the waters do their work. Don't fight it."

Roland felt he was very mild when he replied. "I am not much good for fighting anything at the moment. That's rather the point." Then he considered the rest of what she said, the implication that Elen might have more resources than she'd realised.

It made Healer Rhoe laugh. "Ah, good, there's some spirit in you. More since she got you off that potion dose?"

"Noticeably better, yes." He considered. "I suppose that's another way she hasn't been making friends?"

"Exactly. So, I'm sure she explained the general process." She moved briskly along to the task at hand, and he liked that about her. "This is the pool dedicated to Nodens. You do not have to believe, you do not need to say any prayers, but again, this will work better if you don't fight it."

"I wouldn't have agreed if I couldn't be respectful."

"Good man. Fidelius is actually Christian, mind. But he's one of the sort who feels any healing has the touch of the divine in it. What form that takes, or who someone prays to is up to them. Mind, if he'll gladly talk your ear off about his own preferences if you ask him. But we have a wide range here."

"Nurse Morris mentioned. I'm afraid I don't know much about Nodens. Or why, why I'd be here, in specific?" He gestured. "I'm afraid after she talked to you I had another visit with various officials, I've been exhausted, since."

"Another reason you're not up for a fight, then. Well, Nodens is a Welsh god of healing. We choose which bath someone will be in through a combination of practicality -

what's available when - and thoughtful consultation of the gods. That is part of my role. I talked to Nurse Morris, and based on that conversation, Nodens seemed the best place to start. He was injured in fighting, and forced to cede his rule of the gods until that was resolved."

She paused before obviously making a decision to say more. "There were some challenges with that. Healing isn't a straightforward road, often. There are twists and turns and setbacks." He got the sense that wasn't something she laid out so clearly for everyone.

There seemed half a dozen places to argue with Nodens as a model for Roland's own life, but he settled on the simplest. "Start?"

She shrugged. "If this does not work, does not seem to help, we have other options to explore. And we can do that." She considered, then added, "If it does help, then an offering is considered appropriate. You've seen the Roman tablets, but these days we prefer some sort of improvement to the temple spaces that will be useful."

That, at least, was something Roland understood well enough. He nodded. "Do I, do I need to do anything?"

"Fidelius will be along in a minute, he will help you take off your gown. We have a linen robe to get you to the bath. You will soak in the waters, which have been blessed by a priest of Nodens. I will anoint you with a healing oil, pour water over you, and then I will dim the lights and you will soak for a period of time. Fidelius will be observing, through a charmed mirror, nearby. You can call out if you need help, or feel faint, and he'll see if you need help and can't ask for it. But mostly you will be alone for a bit."

"Is that safe?" They fussed so much about the bath, upstairs, though right now it felt that might as well have been a whole different world.

"With the precautions here, yes. In your bathtub in your room, no."

Roland inhaled, then nodded. "All right." At that point, there was a knock on the door, a sharp rap. Fidelius turned out to be a man about Roland's age, with bright ginger hair, who looked far more Irish than anything else, and sounded it too. He was amiable, brisk, and far better at letting Roland do things for himself than Harry usually was. It was a matter of minutes before Roland was guided to the sunken pool, making his way down shallow steps and ending up chest-deep in warm water.

He found himself sitting on a ledge, facing the shrine, which had candles flickering all over the flat surfaces. He couldn't make out all the objects on the shrine, other than a sizable silver hand, sitting in the middle of the space. Healer Rhoe made sure he was settled, and then murmured. "Thank you, Fidelius. When you're ready."

The man bowed, and withdrew. There was a click of the door, then Healer Rhoe began chanting, a prayer that Roland thought was in Greek, rather than Welsh. Though, as he spoke neither, he couldn't be certain. Then the language shifted, and he was more sure the new one was Welsh, it had a lilt to it a bit like Elen's voice.

That went on long enough that he had trouble concentrating, the light of the candles seeming to cast an almost fiery glow around the healer's form. It felt timeless, and as he'd been told, he didn't fight it, letting his eyes half close, letting the heat of the water relax him.

It felt amazing to be fully immersed, to be able to move and stretch his legs and hands. He was caught for long moments in just feeling the movements in the water, slow and gentle. It felt wonderful to have space to move, not the narrow line of the bathtub. To be able to have his elbows out, bend both knees without slipping under the water. He wondered at the way the resistance let him feel his body properly for the first time in months.

First, it was the pressure of the water on his skin. He'd barely looked at himself in the bright lights of the bath in his room. Here in the warm glow of the candles, it seemed possible. He stretched out his hand, looking at healed scars along his arms, smaller cuts from shrapnel.

There was a larger injury on his thigh, and he ran his fingers along the scar tissue, though it was healed now. Touching felt different, suddenly, like his attention to his body was releasing something that had been chained for months. Sensation flooded through him, the prickling of pins and needles as all his skin woke up.

He realised, suddenly, that the chanting had stopped, and he could see the shadow of Healer Rhoe now bending over him, a small jar of something in her hand. She poured a little over her fingers, then made a symbol on his forehead, saying something in yet another language. Then, she added in English, as if it were important he understood this, "May you be blessed, may you be healed, may you be restored." Finally, she took a large ladle and poured three scoops of water over his head, angled to drench him, but not make him splutter.

It was becoming harder for him to dismiss what he was feeling. And not just the way his body felt like it was coming back to life. There was something in the room, something gentle. It had a sense of pressure against his face, like the pressure of the water against his body, that was warm and reassuring. He took in a deep breath, then let it out, then another. By the time he opened his eyes again, there was another sound, like a door opening, and then there was the burble of water.

It was flowing down a channel in the rock, from the shrine, into his bathing pool, an arm's length away from where he sat. He leaned forward, and he could feel that it was colder water, not as warm as his pool, for the moments until it mixed and mingled. He could smell, too, something sharper and herbal, that made him feel refreshed. Not mint, not lavender, not the scents he knew and could name, but something that brought them to mind. Thyme, maybe, or bay leaf, he didn't know.

He was so distracted by the water that he didn't notice the Healer leaving until well after she'd gone. It left him alone in the dark with his thoughts and his hopes. Roland leaned back, letting the stone of the bath support him, finding a notch where the back of his skull fit perfectly. He closed his eyes again, letting the sensations wash over him.

It felt safe here. Not only that, it felt safe in a way he hadn't felt since he was ten or so, before all his formal schooling, before his apprenticeship, certainly before the war. There was nothing he was supposed to be doing differently now, no way in which he was failing to carry on his duties and his obligations, and his familial responsibilities.

The only thing was sitting in the water, in the dark, and letting it restore him, if he was indeed to be blessed.

CHAPTER 20

Elen had emerged from her own time in the baths uncertain. She hadn't known what she'd hoped for, precisely, but whatever she'd gotten wasn't what she'd expected. It wasn't as if she thought Sirona would descend from some high place, lay hands on her head, and take away the migraines. Or the sense of everything being wrong, which was, frankly, worse. The unending sense that she was always wrong-footed, too slow, too clumsy, missing important things. Or the times when she could barely convince herself that anything mattered.

The bath hadn't done any of that, not directly. She knew perfectly well that that wasn't how the gods worked things. Not for most people. Certainly not for someone like her, of little consequence. Miracles were for heroes, kings and queens, people out of legend. She certainly was none of that.

But she felt, in some way, cleaner. Not just physically, though the chance to relax in neck-deep water had worked kinks out of her back and shoulders, easing something she hadn't realised had been so tense. Instead, it was rather like someone cleaning accumulated dust and grime off a window. One could see through it before, but now things were clearer, brighter. Sharper.

She'd arranged to be away from Roland until supper time, just in case. Sister Almeda had been a bit grudging about it, but Elen's healer had been glad to sign off on the time. Frankly, she thought the woman had been glad Elen had an idea, since nothing the healer tried had made nearly as much difference as a quieter place to sleep and fewer blasts of artillery had.

It meant, though, that it was only half-three, and she had a good two hours before Roland was expecting her. She'd thought she might go sit by the shrine in the temple, or perhaps out in the garden, but she felt an undeniable push to go do something. Anything. To move forward.

She turned away from the Temple, walking back across the gardens with her hands folded under her apron, proper and tidy. She could still feel her hair, a little damp at the nape of her neck where it hadn't fully dried. She stood a decent chance of finding Sister Pomona, she thought, if she could figure out which ward to ask at. It was the middle of the afternoon, when nurses were often a little less busy than usual. A little more able to take a few minutes. And it wasn't as if Elen couldn't make herself useful somehow, rolling bandages or folding cloths or whatever was needed.

She started with the ward she'd found Sister Pomona in before. There was one junior nurse, in her twenties there, making tea with the nervous expectation of an imminent interruption. "Pardon, Nurse." Elen kept her voice even, polite. "I was hoping to find Sister Pomona. Do you know if she might be free for a word?"

That got a little bob - the nurse was clearly a bit intimi-dated by Elen, though why anyone would be, Elen had no idea. "She's upstairs in her office, Nurse." The younger woman didn't ask why, but nurses often wouldn't, if they were junior.

"Sorry to disturb you. Blessings." Elen managed a smile, a smile was the right thing here, to reassure, even if she had to deliberately remember to do it. Then she turned and went up the stairs, along to where the nurse's office was. It was the same place as Sister Almeda's was in her ward, looking out over the gardens. The door was ajar, and when Elen knocked, a voice promptly called out, "Come in."

Sister Pomona was seated at a small desk in front of the window. She swiveled her chair, and smiled. "Ah, I wondered if you were looking for me. I saw you, coming across the garden. Come in. Please, sit down, if you'd like." Elen edged into the room, glanced at the chairs along the wall, then back at Sister Pomona. The senior nurse waved a hand. "Sit, sit. I've a nice herbal tea, will that do?"

Sister Pomona then stood, and went over to close the door, then to a side table where a teapot waited in a cheerful red cozy, the colour of her namesake apples. She was a short round woman, not all height and angles like Sister Almeda, but she moved like it was a dance, efficient and effortless, closing the door on the way by.

Elen sat, crossing her ankles and folding her hands in her lap, wanting to do this right, even when she wasn't sure what that involved. Within a minute, she'd been presented with a cup of tea, something with a bit of orange and spices and orchard fruits, and two biscuits, plain shortbread. Sister Pomona sat down in the other chair, and then looked her over. "I do not think you are here simply to lend a hand for an hour or two."

"Um." Elen wasn't sure how to begin to answer that. Not when it was called out that bluntly.

"Let me tell you what I see. Nurse to nurse." Clearly, Sister Pomona was going to, unless Elen fled the room this moment. She wasn't sure she could bear to listen to someone name her flaws, but she wasn't sure how to go, either, not without tremendous insult. So she sat.

"You are in a new place. And you are assigned under Sister Almeda, who is skilled in many aspects of healing, but not, shall we say, necessarily as good with people's hearts as she might be. Excellent at critical care, excellent at running an efficient ward, but not always aware where a bit of kindness would make things so much better."

Elen couldn't argue with this, but agreeing with it seemed rather dangerous. "Sister." She kept her voice neutral, acknowledging it.

"And you, dear one, have been assigned here, following injury. You see a healer, you are getting..." Sister Pomona considered, looking her over. "Adequate care. But no great change."

This was a little easier to answer. "My healer said that if my headaches did not resolve, being here, they might - linger. That it would be a matter of learning what to avoid. What my, what my new capabilities were. That a nurse of my experience, my background, knew how to judge that as well as she could."

Sister Pomona inclined her head, and took a sip from her tea cup. "And yet, as nurses, we so often do not see ourselves as clearly as others can see us. I think you are doing better than you were, when I first saw you. But not yet well."

Elen could not argue with that evaluation. She nodded a little, echoing the last comment. "Not yet well, sister." Then, with some hint of bravery from the bath, she added,

"I took the baths, earlier. It helped but it didn't - it didn't fix things."

"Head injuries are often particularly tricky. I know you know this here..." Sister Pomona tapped her forehead. "But not, perhaps, here." She put her hand over her heart. "And it's different living it, certainly. That is not all of it, though, is it? You would not have come here just for yourself."

Put that way, Elen could only nod, a tiny movement. Then, gathering together the shattered shards of what bravery she'd once had, she cleared her throat. "You were kind, before. And I wondered if you could tell me about how things ought to be here."

Sister Pomona beamed at her. "That is a fine question, and of course I am delighted to help. Do try the biscuits, they're some of my aunt's shortbread."

Elen managed a weak smile. "I am assigned to a single patient. Major Gospatrick. I have been told I may not see his file. I have not met his senior healer, Healer Cole. The junior healers send me away when they come through on rounds."

She hadn't really thought about how to ask this, so what she ended with, faintly, was simple. "Is that how things are done here now, please?" Her stomach rolled, and she reached for a sip of the tea, and then carefully to nibble on the biscuit, hoping that would help.

Sister Pomona paused, looking at her. It was gentle, somehow, not judging. "It depends on the healer, but that is not the normal way of things, no. Not for most healers. Let me ask a few questions, then."

Elen nodded. The shortbread was delicious, and it had all the proper comforts. Sugar and butter and vanilla, unlike what she got at the boarding house. A treat, not just fuel to keep going for another day.

"Have you asked to speak to Healer Cole?" Elen nodded. "Seen him at all?" She shook her head no. "Had any information about whatever potions or other treatments are applied, other than your own?" A second shake no. "Been given any guidance on how you might best support that?" A third, and then Elen looked down at her hands.

"Well, that's no good then." Sister Pomona sounded peeved. "There's a man not upholding his oaths. Possibly the junior healers as well, but I can't tell. They might simply be deferring. Do you know their names?" Elen didn't, so she shook her head another time.

When Sister Pomona paused, Elen worked up the courage to ask. "His oaths, please?"

"You know, of course, that Healers make oaths, like nurses do. To avoid harm, first and foremost, but also they are to know their limits - not to take on the surgeon's role, or the nurse's, to let us do our work as it is needed. And we, here in the Temple, we've always felt that there is the harm of doing the wrong thing, but there is also the harm of not doing the necessary thing."

"Like surgery or debriding a wound. My teachers used those as examples." Elen knew that.

"Exactly." Sister Pomona's voice was warm, full of a praise that Elen wanted to cling to. "And you obviously want to do your best for your patient."

Elen ducked her chin, and blushed. "I do, of course." She drew in a breath. "Do you know more about Healer Cole, please? Or - what it would be like, if he'd broken his oath?" It seemed a ridiculous thing to suggest. Certainly if he had, someone else besides her should have noticed.

Sister Pomona leaned back, considering something for a moment. "Cole came back to the Temple from elsewhere in the Empire, quite recently. We are short of staff, healers are being called up to war service, of course, and those who are skilled at surgery or acute critical care, being sent there."

Elen frowned. "Surely someone who'd served elsewhere, they'd have some skills?"

"I don't know the whole story, but something about why he came back means he does not do surgery. The small things that require dexterity. It might be age, as much as anything else. Our great surgeons have only so many years to be great. It could be a touch of palsy, or some personal excess that's affected him."

Elen supposed age made some sort of sense, though she'd never really thought about it. The nursing magics weren't like that. For some things you needed energy or strength or stamina, but that was different than the delicate movements of a scalpel or finely honed magic. But many of the best nurses were older, people whose knowledge and efficiency of magic more than made up for any lack of strength due to age. "Which would explain why he was assigned to Major Gospatrick's case. His wounds have all healed, I know that."

"Quite." Sister Pomona was thinking through something. "Your Major Gospatrick, is he of a good family? Well-off?"

Elen nodded. "I gather so. He has silk pyjamas, he's used to having people around, staff, servants. And his voice, his manner." Which were probably the most telling of all.

"There are a few other patients, of similar background, under Healer Cole's care." Sister Pomona spoke more slowly, as if she were thinking through the implications. "And not making much progress, I gather. Not getting worse, but not improving as we would like. And it is unclear why. Is that true for your patient?"

Elen swallowed. "Yes. Getting him outside, walking

more, that has been helping. Sister Florinda, in the administration office, arranged for me to reduce the evening potion that seems to be the most significant problem. But it would need Healer Cole to change it, and ... " She shrugged, helplessly.

Sister Pomona paused, and Elen could tell that she was deciding to say something. "The things Cole is doing - those strike me not just as poor care, but as a broken oath, somewhere. Or one that no longer exists. He was still here as a healer when I started my training, and I remember someone saying he was sworn to Apollo Acestor."

"The arts of healing, but also protection from evil." Elen knew that as well as any of them.

"Precisely. And what he is doing - whether by design or by neglect - strikes me as a kind of evil. So now I find myself very curious about what I would see or feel or hear if I saw him. About whether he's ever in the Temple proper. I do not know how one might arrange those things, or find them out. But I am rather curious."

Elen sucked in a breath. She hadn't thought about it that clearly, but she supposed a priestess of Apollo Grannus would be inclined to shine light into dark places. Then she nodded. "Yes, Sister. I don't know how to find out those things either, though."

"You are doing very well keeping your own oaths, having a care for your patient. And, I hope, continuing care for yourself." Sister Pomona tapped her fingers. "Let me ask around a bit then, dear. See what the cases have in common in more detail. What else I can learn about Cole. I know who to ask, and more than a few people owe me a favour or two. Have you heard anything else, in passing, that might be a help?"

"There was - I didn't mean to eavesdrop, Sister, they

were near where I was sitting by the outside shrine." Elen hated to admit it, but Sister Pomona smiled at her.

"Anyone talking outside should know there might be someone at the shrines." That was true, but people got angry about that sort of thing. "Go on."

Elen took a breath. "One of them was talking about inconsistencies in the records. That more than one person wasn't turning things in properly. Healer Cole among them."

"Ah, that's a useful line. The administrative folk aren't nurses, but they spot entirely different sorts of issues. Did you hear a name, by chance?"

"Only the first. Berth and..." Elen frowned, calling it back to memory. "Clarice. Berth was Welsh, her accent was like where I'm from, the mines, South Wales. I got the impression they worked in the same tasks, but not perhaps always together?"

"That should give me plenty to be getting on with. Now..." Sister Pomona seemed about to say more, when there was a knock on her door.

Three minutes later, Elen found herself cheerfully bundled out the door with a small canister of tea, half a tin of shortbread, and a promise to be in touch. She turned to go back to Roland's room, feeling entirely turned about.

CHAPTER 21

R oland had been in no state to discuss anything after his visit to the healing baths. For one thing, he wasn't sure he remembered what had happened when he was alone in the dark. It certainly didn't fit tidily into sentences with nouns and verbs and adjectives. He just knew that it felt good. Right. Possible. Even hopeful.

He had kept turning 'hopeful' around in his head once he was settled back in his chair, tucked in, his hair dried with a charm. No one asked him if he'd seen anything, or felt anything. They just trusted, with a kind of trust he envied, that it had done what was needed. He might have managed something more, but Harry was already waiting with Elen when they brought him out. He certainly couldn't talk about it with both of them at once. Whatever this was, it felt fragile, like questions would shatter it.

He'd hoped for a chance to talk privately with Elen, but the rest of the afternoon and early evening were taking up with the usual quotidian needs. Harry was in and out with his supper, with his potion. Elen didn't ask him about the bath, instead settling down to read to him.

His dreams that night had been different. Sometimes, now, he dreamed of the War. Of the noises of the Front, particularly, the cracks of shots, the shouts and screams, the sounds of the mud. This time, he dreamed of noises, but they were utterly different. The night held hoofbeats in some meadow, a horse at full gallop. It was the sound of the sea beating on the shore, and a hint of baying hounds.

Roland had thought at first they were hunting him, they had that note to them that he knew, with certainty, was a pack who'd found their quarry and were running it to ground. A moment later, he realised they weren't hunting him. It was more like he was a part of the hunt, carried along, part of a community again.

He woke, on the edge of tears, from that sense of being included in something that mattered. The idea that he could be, that he was not so badly broken as to lose that forever, consumed him.

Fortunately, he had woken early, before Elen appeared, before Harry showed up with his breakfast. By the time anyone opened his door, he'd pulled himself together, and was sitting reading. Once again, he didn't have a chance to talk to Elen. She was called away for part of the morning. That afternoon, she had her own time in the baths, and wasn't back with him until nearly supper time. He wondered, looking at her, if her experience had been anything like his, what her dreams might be like, but he'd have to put that aside for another day.

The next morning had apparently been chaos. Elen had been called away to help with something again, and Harry had been in and out with various bits of laundry and someone came in to wash the windows and mop the floors.

It was hardly restful. Elen came back just in time to help with his lunch. As she was about to help him into his chair for the afternoon trip to the garden, there was a knock on the door.

"Pardon, Major. There's a Captain Deschamps, called to see you." Harry ducked his head. This was new, though Roland should have expected it, really. He'd thought Cadwell was at least somewhat likely to follow through.

Roland glanced up at Elen, and she considered. "Outside, do you think? Or would you rather in here?" Outside had more privacy, but greater complication. That won out, however, even if it would be awkward.

"Outside." Roland swallowed. "I - thank you. Harry, if you'd tell Captain Deschamps we'll be outside in a few minutes. Elen, I suppose I should manage a shirt and trousers, at least." That took longer than he liked, but inside of ten minutes, she was wheeling his chair out the door to the ward, and nodding to Cadwell.

"Just along here, Captain, there's a nice spot outside." Elen's voice was brisk and much more distant now. Roland wondered for a moment if he'd hurt her feelings, but she knew Cadwell had offered his help. When she had him settled in the usual shrine area, she stood. "I should let you talk. I'll be back in an hour, Major, to check on things." Before Roland could say anything further, she'd nodded briskly, and made her way off.

Cadwell perched on the edge of the bench. "Sir." A nod to Roland's rank. Then his face cracked into a smile. "Pardon, I didn't realise it would be quite such a production."

"Nurse Morris has very strong opinions about the power of being outside, and she's not wrong." He settled back. "I can see people coming close, from here. What brings you, then, Cadwell?"

"Several things." The use of his first name had relaxed the younger man, making it clear they were going at this as peers, not a superior officer issuing a command. "I'm assigned to London, starting next week, and overseas a fort-night or so after that. So I'm afraid what I've found is what I'm likely to find."

"The Front?" Roland was immediately worried about the implications.

"No, headquarters, in France. Some assignments in the field, but mostly analysis. I want to do my part, but - my brother."

Roland considered how to say what he wanted to say. "There's no sense wasting your life. No sense wasting anyone's life. Use your brains, see how many others you can save, that's an honourable fight. And a needed one."

Cadwell exhaled, and murmured. "Appreciated." Roland felt a rush of pride, all of a sudden, like he'd not felt in months. That he'd done something worth doing. Perhaps the bath had unlocked a door in him, made it possible to improve things for someone else. He'd thought he'd never feel like that again, that it would be endless days of not achieving much at all. But he could hear it in Cadwell's voice, that the man had needed someone to tell him it was all right not to charge heedless into the guns.

"So, what did you find out, then?" Roland kept his voice even. He'd always been good at this bit, steadying junior officers, encouraging them to share what they'd seen.

"There's a half dozen or so cases like yours, though none so prominent. Captains, one other Major, of good families, with money, who aren't recovering as they should be, what-ever that means to healers. You're the only one they're bringing out for presentations, though. The others aren't so well-spoken. Or even speaking much at all. Not very responsive."

Roland frowned. If they were on something like his evening dose all the time, he could well believe none of them wanted to do anything. Above and beyond whatever injuries they had themselves. "Do you have names?"

Cadwell nodded. "Safe to give you a list?" Ah, he was a clever man.

Roland frowned. "I don't suppose you have a book on you, you can leave here? I'd say write it into the margins, there. They don't - they have not been as diligent in searching my things as to suggest they'd find that."

"You feel that, then, that you're something of a captive in the Tower of London, as it were? Treated well, but - limited." Cadwell's voice was cautious now.

"I do, rather. It is rather a bother, not knowing who is doing what. I'm quite sure of Nurse Morris's good will, if you need to get something to me, but anything else..." Roland let his voice trail off.

"How about this. When we're done here, I'll go off to the bookshop, find a couple of books you might enjoy, and write the names starting on - hmm. Page 52 of the oldest of the books." Cadwell waved a hand. "I can come back and leave them with the orderly. I'll tuck the names into the gutter, so someone thumbing through shouldn't spot them."

"Suitably random." Roland approved. Especially not knowing what books might be handy and unlikely to draw attention in Roland's room. "Ta. That's more than we knew so far. I don't suppose you found out anything about why they keep trotting me out?"

"Nothing more than you knew already. You are articulate, you know how to give the right show about things."

Cadwell hesitated. "I've heard several people comment that you are your father's son. And your mother's."

Roland stiffened. "Ah." He couldn't quite hide his reaction, and he saw Cadwell take that information in. A man with that sort of knack for espionage wouldn't miss something like that twitch, unfortunately, and cursing him mentally seemed entirely unfair after he had been so usefully clever with the books.

"I saw your father briefly, when they called me in for assignment. I might do so again. Probably will, from what they said. Do you - may I pass on a message for you?" There was a brief moment, and Roland could see Cadwell doing the maths, that if people were keeping Roland isolated here, that his father, his parents, might play into that somehow.

Roland shrugged slightly. Anything he said would be wrong, entirely too revealing, or both. And while Cadwell might well be a suitable ally, he didn't know the man well enough to take a risk. "My father knows where I am and how to reach me."

Cadwell looked at him for a long moment, then nodded, changing the subject promptly. "Is there anything I can pick up for you besides the books? Newspaper? Do they permit you a paper?"

"No. Rather infantilising, honestly, though Nurse Morris passes along the essential news."

"Do you get to talk to other patients much?" Cadwell glanced around, taking in the larger gardens. There were two settled in the shade, perhaps fifty feet away, playing some sort of game. Chess, probably. There were a few other small groupings, but most were individuals with their uniformed nurses or orderlies.

"No. They've kept me quite separate. I gather the others on my ward are rather seriously injured, and there's nothing like a day room." Roland shrugged minutely. "One further mystery of the place."

"I admit I'm not clear on how the Temple - or any other hospital - is supposed to work. And there must be concerns about infection, or staffing, or people interfering with other people's treatments. But still even soldiers mingle from time to time."

Roland was about to say something again, when a nurse came by, inquiring whether Roland was all right, where was the nurse responsible for him, and he had to spend a good five minutes reassuring her that he was quite capable of sitting in a chair outside with Cadwell. By the time that was done, a nurse and her patient had parked themselves on the nearest benches, and by mutual agreement he and Cadwell turned to inane conversation about school, people they knew in common, and the current bohort tournament rankings.

CHAPTER 22

ELSEWHERE, THAT AFTERNOON

E len wasn't quite sure how she had gotten herself into this. She didn't know what had come over her, certainly. But once Roland had suggested she get a look at his files, she hadn't been able to let go of the idea. It seemed entirely mad, but even the time in the baths had not washed it away, had perhaps even lodged it more intractably in her mind.

Now he was off with Captain Deschamps. Certainly, it was good someone had called to see him. No one expected Elen to be anywhere in particular. And, best of all, this was the afternoon Sister Almeda had a longer meeting for senior staff. A good forty-five minutes, if all went well. Almost certainly half an hour.

She stuck her hand a little more in the pocket of her apron. There was her notebook. She'd have to trust on her personal shorthand to obscure it enough. But more importantly, there were the set of narrow lockpicks tucked into the small leather sewing kit she kept on her at all times.

She hadn't used the skills in years, not more than once

or twice. But every so often, at about the point she'd considered packing the lockpicks away, she'd need to unlock a wardrobe door or a trunk when the key wasn't handy. Once, at the Temple of Youth, when a small boy had locked himself in a closet. She could only hope that she remembered enough and enough of the charms that helped, or there would be no chance of getting at Roland's files.

Elen lurked at the end of the hallway for several minutes, waiting for Sister Almeda to leave for the meeting. Finally there was the sweep of skirts, the scolding "Nurse Williams, what do you think you're doing there, tidy this up immediately. Spic and span is a nurse's work."

Elen disagreed. Tidiness helped with their work, of course, knowing where things were, being able to lay hands on them in an emergency. And cleanliness avoided infection, and that mattered a lot. But tidiness was a means to the end, not the goal in and of itself. That, however, was for another time.

Two minutes later, the hallway was clear, as the nurses still on the hall disappeared into the lounge for a tea break. She sympathised, having Nurse Almeda right on top of them must be horribly difficult.

That left her to make her way down to the office doorway, getting the lockpicks into her hand, then beginning to work on the lock. As she'd hoped, it was not actually a difficult lock, though it needed one of the charms to ease it. She murmured the words under her breath, remembering how Uncle Dewi had explained it was like oil in the lock, helping the pins move freely.

The lock clicked under her fingers, and she eased the door open. It didn't make a sound, and Elen was grateful for a moment that Sister Almeda liked sneaking up on the nurses on her ward, and kept the door well oiled. Once inside, she closed it again, silently, and then looked around. There was a door in one wall, ajar enough for her to see that was a private lavatory. No use as a place to hide or escape through, then, not if Sister Almeda came back. Only short curtains, a few bare inches longer than the window sill.

The room was not large, either. The desk took up most of the space, a large wooden monstrosity that was far more for show than use. There were tidily arranged supplies on the top, an inkwell and dip pen, as well as pencils. A row of file cabinets stood along the back, and Elen went there immediately.

These were locked, and she suspected the locks were rather more particular. A number of people had some reason to enter the office itself, to leave a file or pick something up. There were certain medications and potions that had to be logged, those were in the cabinet by the door that most people would assume was a wardrobe. So the door itself would have to yield to a variety of keys, but the files, those would be more private.

The cabinets were labelled, in a way, but not with anything Elen found immediately sensible, like the alphabet. Instead, each had a symbol on them, something that would make sense to Sister Almeda, surely, Then she peered more closely, and frowned. Some of them were planetary symbols. She knew the one for the sun, there was Venus, there was Mars. There were others, too, that she suspected came from alchemical sources or something of the kind.

Perhaps that meant that the files were sorted by the cause of the illness, rather than by patient name. It was a ridiculous system, not least because it required knowing about the cause before you could file someone. For anyone else needing the file to know enough about the case, you'd need to look in the right place.

Elen wondered how someone would keep track of it. At the Temple of Youth, active files were kept alphabetically, and archived files by the date of arrival, with a ledger and a series of cards, ordered by last name. She couldn't see anything like a card system, but a ledger seemed plausible. She looked around, frowning at the desk.

Whatever index there was, it would need to be easy to get to, because you'd be consulting it all the time. She pulled a silk handkerchief out of her other apron pocket, and wrapped it around her fingers, to avoid leaving any smudges or marks that could be traced back to her. No sense being foolhardy.

The top drawer, at the right of the desk, was quite wide. When she opened it, there was a good size book of deep brown leather, worn darker on the corners where fingers must touch it frequently. She tugged another handkerchief, her regular cotton one, out of her skirt pocket, and used them to put the ledger on the desk, then thumbed through the front quickly.

That was promising. The first pages were a series of lists and columns that stretched across the facing page. There were spaces for the patient's name, where they were from, a symbol for where the file was located, the date of admission and discharge. Death, in some cases. Too many, she thought, glancing at the lists. They were in order by date of admission, and there was a brief diagnosis for many of the patients, though not all.

She thought hard, about when Roland must have been admitted. She carefully turned the pages to find the entries for last November, and then reading forward, until she found his name in a neat enough hand. Reading across the line, she copied the information down. There was a file identification number that must match up with records somewhere else, when he was admitted, and then the diagnosis line. *Magicis per contumeliam.*

Her Latin normally only extended to plant names and healing treatments, but she thought that was probably not terribly informative, even if she knew what contumeliam meant. Something by magic.

It did however give the symbol for where his file was. It was filed in the Mars cabinet, which she might have guessed. Since there was no further number, she could only assume it was alphabetical in there. She glanced at the watch pinned to her apron. Eight minutes gone. She didn't have long left. She carefully put the ledger back in the drawer, then turned to the cabinets.

Not only was the Mars cabinet locked, but she could get no leverage with the first lockpick she tried, or the second. There was something slippery about the pins, like they kept twisting out of her reach. Logic told her they were solid metal, and couldn't do that, but her fingers were sure there was something else going on. After two minutes she stopped, and took a breath.

Forcing something never helped. She'd learned that long ago in school, in training, even aside from Uncle Dewi. Instead, she stood, cupped her hands, and under her breath, terrified the noise would carry, she gave her heart to the petition.

"Blessed Sirona, Long-lived Sirona, Star-kissed Sirona, you who hold the tools of healing and renewal, bless me in my work, guide my hands. I seek only to know what my patient, Roland, needs, fearing I may do him harm without this knowledge. He is a good man, a steadfast man, a man who thinks of service and loyalty and duty.

Gift me with the knowledge I need, that I may guide his healing."

Her breath went out of her in a whoosh, and then she felt a rush of something. It was like the beating of wings, or a burst of wind, twining around her, ruffling her hair and her skirts, before it faded. The picks in her hand felt different now, a faint tingling of some presence or charm. She didn't know whether to call it power or magic or blessing, but she couldn't deny it was there.

There was nothing for it but to try the lock again. This time, the slipperiness eased, when she used the pick that was vibrating most strongly. She felt the pins fall into place, then she could turn the lock, and open the drawer. Inside were file after file, and they were blessedly in alphabetical order. Roland's was about a third of the way back, and she pulled it out, setting it on the desk as she checked the time again. Ten minutes to read, before she had to put everything back as it was.

The file was too thick to read in detail, but she opened it, praying for a summary sheet or something of the kind. On the top of the file, there was a brief record. She pulled out her notebook, scribbling down the information. It included his vitals when he was admitted. Finally, the expected scoring of the questions asked to see if he were aware of where he was, who he was, what was going on.

His scores had been quite poor, similar to someone who had suffered a traumatic injury or a high fever. The notes mentioned he said things that didn't make sense, That had to be febrile hallucinations, she'd have to look at the reports to see if there were more.

The summary also had half a dozen potions, only two of which he was listed as currently taking. She wrote as quickly as she could, the complete list and the dates he'd stopped taking them. She hoped Amet would be able to help her understand more about what they did, Amet at least had access to the standard formularies.

That done, she began turning pages, looking for a few specific things. Nothing in the summary gave a hint of the cause. Finally, she came to his intake record, about ten pages down. It had been placed after a whole set of routine and uninformative records of his movements and vitals every time he was moved to a new location or ward. She skimmed the text as quickly as she could, finding incoherent mentions of some sort of magical damage. The theory most frequently offered was that his magical self had been disarrayed by some unknown attack. It had left him unable to tolerate noises, light, or the presence of most people.

Elen honestly thought the latter was just good sense, given the attitude of most of the people who'd wanted to see him so far. There were a few mentions, vague unless you knew what they must refer to, about his magic reshaping metal, damaging wood, terrifying previous nurses. She flipped quickly to the back of the file, where previous records from nurses often were, but there was nothing there. That was decidedly unhelpful. Even knowing their names might have been a start.

The fact there were no reports from his direct nurses, however, was quite unusual. As she flipped through, there were brief reports, from the Healer, one Ozymandius Cole, and several of his juniors, and occasional notations from Sister Almeda. But it was becoming clear that it was the Healers controlling the information, or lack of it, not Sister Almeda herself. There was even a note to that effect, from a few weeks before Elen had started.

There was only the briefest notation about her own assignment, then the single sentence "Healer overruled by

Administrative Sister Florinda. Evening potion to be decreased at Nurse Morris's discretion. Healer Cole made formal petition, appeal denied by Archiater Hudson." That was most helpful, it strongly suggested a difference of opinion about treatment, and the fact the senior administrators were willing to use their influence even if they weren't willing to reassign Roland's care.

The problem was why. Elen could think of some good reasons, but also some horrifying ones. Perhaps the senior administrators wanted Roland out of the hospital one way or another, or to force him to be the puppet the Brigadier and other senior officers wanted to make him into. Without knowing more about Healer Cole or perhaps Archiater Hudson, she had no way to tell.

Another glance at her watch told her she was right at the limit of her time. She made sure the files were all as she'd found them, tucked the folder back into the cabinet, and then locked it, feeling the pins settle into place. Elen looked around one more time, making sure everything was as she'd found it, and then cracked the door open.

The way was clear, but as she closed the door, feeling it lock, she heard at least two women coming out of the lounge, still chattering away. She hastily pulled out a record she'd brought for the purpose, an excuse to leave something for Sister Almeda.

It was nothing more than a routine report of temperatures and his potion doses, just as she made them regularly. Where they went, she had no idea, since they hadn't seemed to be in his file, but it made a good excuse to be standing here. She slipped it into the wooden holder beside the door, then ducked her head at the other nurses.

"Didn't hear you come in, dear. Did you need Sister?"

"Oh, no, I was just dropping something off for her, my

regular report. Do you think it will clear up tomorrow? The gardens are coming out nicely, aren't they?" It was the classic combination of weather and flowers, and she hoped it would distract them long enough for her to be unremarkable. Parting from them, she decided to go make a further offering at Sirona's shrine before she went back to see how Roland had fared with the Captain.

The next afternoon, thankfully, was sunny again, and once Elen had wheeled him out to the shrine to Sirona, Roland looked her up and down. "You owe me a trip to the temple proper."

It wasn't what she was expecting. Frankly, it wasn't where he'd been expecting to start, so that was fair. She looked startled, for a moment, like a doe caught in the moment before she fled, but then there was a flash of a smile. "I suppose I do, yes. How was it, in the baths?"

"You didn't ask before." He couldn't decide if he was relieved she hadn't, or annoyed.

Elen shook her head. "I didn't. I wasn't." She stopped, then she looked up at him. "I'm sorry."

Roland pushed himself up a bit on his elbows, and then peered at her. Something was not quite right, and the hints of annoyance faded. "I'm not sure what you're apologising for?"

"For not asking you. And you were so careful about it. Not sure what you thought."

He waved a hand. "I was, but Harry was in and out.

And then Cadwell. And you were rather quiet. Are you all right?" He suddenly was more sure something was decidedly odd. Certainly, she seemed more than a little distracted.

Elen let out a long breath, then she stood, pacing to the end of the paved space and back, then again, looking around. "I, I did something that would get me thrown out, as a nurse. If anyone found out about it."

That was not at all what he was expecting, either the admission, or how serious it was. She had seemed, to him, entirely rule-abiding. The kind of woman, if she had been a man in his cohort, who could be relied upon absolutely to follow orders once given, even if she disagreed. Even when she'd disapproved of his treatment, she hadn't more than gestured at it, or offered to do more than hide a destroyed chair.

"I won't tell anyone." And then he added, "And I don't think I'm talking in my sleep anymore."

As he'd hoped, that made her turn back, and smile. She settled down on the bench again, closer to him. "Tell me if anyone's coming. Twenty feet away."

"Of course." He was entirely distracted now, from his own desire to talk about the bath. It was clear to him, though, this was gnawing at her, and in some complex way he couldn't sort out.

"I broke into Sister Almeda's office and looked at your file." When she said it, it took him a moment to realise what she meant. He hadn't expected her to take the suggestion that seriously. Certainly, he had no idea she'd risk everything for him. He wanted to take the blame, knew it was his.

What came out of his mouth though, was a question. "You - wait. You broke into Sister Almeda's office?"

"Yes." Elen glanced at him, and then looked down at the ground again.

"Did you see the file?" He was tremendously curious about the file, of course, but he was even more intrigued by the idea she'd broken in. "Wait. Wasn't the office locked?"

"Yes?" Her voice had gotten softer. "And the cabinet. I have lockpicks."

He didn't know what to say, then found himself repeating her. "You have lockpicks."

Elen nodded, a small movement.

"Well. That's surprisingly useful. Do you have other skills you've not mentioned?" He kept his tone light, wanting to settle her.

She blinked at him, several times. "Lockpicks, though I'm not very good at a safe. I can tell true gold from false. I can sing in harmony in chapel, if relevant. And I knit. But you knew about the knitting. I'm not bad at herbs, though I'm no herbalist or apothecary."

Roland could tell she was beginning to get shaky, and so he held his hand out. She hesitated again, but then put hers in it, and he could feel it was soft, and warm. Trembling, a bit too, so he squeezed once. "There we go," he said. "You were very brave. Also very clever. You must have had a plan that worked?"

Elen nodded. "I have an honorary uncle, the locksmith for the mines. He taught me how, gave me the picks. Usually just for getting a trunk open if the mechanism's jammed, that kind of thing."

"Still, it takes quite a bit of dexterity to do that. Adventure novels always have a bit of it. I tried, but I was never at all good at it. I got myself stuck a couple of times. And in trouble more than once."

She snorted, looking much more amused now. "It's not

something you just know. You have to learn. And then practice. Rather a lot, actually." Which also told him something about her life when she learned it.

Roland stretched slightly, looking for a way to further ease the tension. "A lot of time on your own, then?"

She nodded. "When I was home from school for the summers. I helped my mother out, of course, and there were things like herb gathering and gardening. But when it rained, I'd be with Uncle Dewi. He had space in his office, and he wasn't on at me to do things all the time."

Roland rather thought they had more in common than either of them had thought originally. "Lonely, and on your own, and for whatever reason, your parents weren't the solution."

Elen glanced up at him, meeting his eyes, then looking down. "They mean well. Just, I've always wanted things they didn't understand. And they're both very outgoing people, wanting to be in the middle of things. Doing things - quickly. I'm not so good at quickly. It got me in trouble, in France."

"It strikes me that battlefield medicine would require a lot of quick decisions," Roland said, as gently as he could. "Administrative trouble, or something else?"

Elen shrugged slightly. "A bit of wall collapsed. And I got caught under it, and I should have been faster. I get headaches, still, and." She looked away again.

"Hey." Roland waited until she looked back at him. "You were injured, doing your best to help people, putting yourself in harm's way, when you didn't need to. That's something to be proud of. You weren't trained to go off to a war, you weren't trained to be around artillery. And when they invalided you out, you wanted to be here, working, not somewhere quieter." Elen didn't say anything. Roland kept watching her, attentive to all the little movements, the set of her shoulders.

Finally she let out a little breath. "I suppose you'll win if I keep arguing." She didn't precisely sound defeated, more like she was trying to put something heavy and unwieldy down.

"Quite. Tell me about what you found out, instead."

That at least sparked her interest again. "Your file is bizarre." Then she reconsidered her terms. "Not at all the usual sort of things. Some of it was more or less what I expected. When you were first taken in care, you weren't making a lot of sense. It sounded like febrile hallucinations, talking about things that weren't there. They had you on half a dozen potions, rather than just the two now. I need to write to my friend and find out what they all are. I don't know a couple of them."

"Is there a library here? Or something like one?"

Elen twitched a shoulder. "In theory, yes. If I go looking for it, though, someone might comment. Especially given what I found in the rest of the file."

"That does sound unusual." Roland leaned forward a little, doing his best to ignore a new bloom of nerves. He wasn't given to collywobbles, but it felt like his stomach was trying to do loops. It was most unsettling.

"There should have been a lot more notes in your file. From your nurses before me, from me. It's not as if I haven't turned things in. Even if I didn't say much more than your vitals and that you took your potions, or that your appointments wore you out. None of that. What there was..."

She cleared her throat, visibly gathering her thoughts. "The basic theory is that your magic was damaged, somehow, when you were hurt. But they couldn't decide if it was because of what hurt you, or the nature of the injury."

Elen paused for a moment. "That happens, sometimes, at the Temple of Youth. Especially children on the verge of making the Pact, puberty. I wonder if they thought that's what the outbursts were, something like that, but with a grown man's strength."

She withdrew her hand, reaching into her apron pocket and pulling out a notebook. He clenched his fingers around the empty space, helplessly. He could scarcely ask her to put it back. "There's some notes from your senior healer, Ozymandias Cole. A few hints of theories, but there's no formal plan of treatment." She paused, then asked. "What do you remember, when you got hurt?"

"Not much." Roland shrugged his shoulders. "Being shot - my leg, the thigh. I fell, in the mud, but it wasn't just the physical, everything felt wrong. Boggy. Then I woke up, I think, in field hospital, but it's all a haze, until I was here. Had been here a while."

"But you felt it then, that it wasn't just the injury to your body. Right. We'll work from that principle."

"You said there were hints of theories?" Roland wanted to know that, suddenly, very much. He'd felt, from the first, that something had come unlaced in him, disconnected, but he had no idea how to say that. He wondered if it might be improving, between the garden and the bath and Elen's attentive care. But it might just be an overly-optimistic fantasy.

"Just vague references to magical injuries. I assume he has a full plan of care, in his own notes, but they're not in yours, which is, which is horribly wrong. Your file should be together, and accessible to the people providing care, all of us. All that's in the file is a sort of high level summary. Um. If it were a battle, it would be 'charge at the enemy, repeat until dead'."

Roland sucked in a breath. "That's not that far from some of the orders they're giving out. But not how it should be."

Elen shook her head. "Not at all. Not here. There should be a detailed plan, which potions when, under what circumstances to change them, a plan for increasing stamina and restoring magical vitality. All sorts of things. It's like..." She frowned. "It's the kind of thing an author who didn't know what the real thing looks like would put in a novel."

"Do you know anything about him? Cole?"

Elen shook her head. "No, though I - I did talk to Sister Pomona after my bath, and she had some ideas? She's much better positioned to find out if there's gossip than I am. I barely know anyone." Then she paused, and Roland wasn't sure what to make of the hesitation. "She brought up the question of his oaths. Whether he'd broken them. She thought - she was going to see if she could find out more - he'd been sworn to Apollo Acestor. Healing, but also defeating evil."

"And whatever's happening to me, there is a touch of evil in it, isn't there? Neglect is a particular kind of evil." Roland swallowed, not at all sure what he felt about being the target of something like that. "That was clever of you, talking to her. And brave. She's a senior nurse, then? Not on this ward, but she knows how things should be done?"

Elen nodded. "She said - she said there's some other patients like you. Slow to recover, where Healer Cole is responsible. She was going to find out who. But I don't know if she'll tell me. I can't just call round there on the off chance."

"We might beat her there. Cadwell - Captain Deschamps - brought me a list yesterday. Penciled into the books he brought. And he's going to find out more, if he can." Roland felt suddenly better about this. The fact that two different independent sources thought there was something weird, that was surprisingly reassuring.

Elen smiled a little. "That's also clever." She inhaled. "So. Healer Cole. The file did say he'd been overruled, about your evening potion, us changing the dose. Not just by the administrator I talked to, who gave me permission, but he apparently appealed it to the Archiater." He must have looked blank at the title, because she continued. "That's the administrator for the entire Temple of Healing. Like the First Minister, for all of the things going on here."

"Huh." Roland had to think about it. "Cole's not an uncommon name. I suppose it could be someone with a grudge against me or my parents or something. But it doesn't make sense."

"There's a lot that doesn't make sense. Surely they don't need you in specific for recruiting, or strategy, or whatever else they want to talk to you about. There are plenty of other people."

That made Roland grimace. As his mind was clearing, day by day, he had to admit she was right. A lot of things didn't quite add up. "And they haven't sent me off to some quiet country hospital, either. Which, if what I needed was rest and potions, you'd think would be easier than my taking up space here."

Elen nodded. "Your file mentioned some of the things with your magic. Like the pitcher and the chair. You've done it several times, but there wasn't any explanation for why they thought it was happening. I got the impression it was why the other nurses had left, but why wouldn't they warn us?" She sounded quite offended at that.

"That part bothers you?" He shifted slightly, then risked reaching out to touch her hand, on the arm of the bench.

Elen looked down at that, where his hand was resting on hers, then up at his face, meeting his eyes again.

"Nurses do all sorts of unpleasant things. We put ourselves at risk all the time. Patients lash out, with their bodies, with their words, when they're in pain, or so out of their minds they can't choose how they act. But we should have the information available about what's going on, what risks we're walking into, what precautions are possible. If they don't tell us, how can we figure out how to do our job properly?"

Her voice rose a little, at the end, in her annoyance. It struck him, suddenly, that that passion, that insistence on doing the thing right, that might be what was saving him. He hadn't expected it from her, not from any nurse he'd met, they'd seemed so fixed in their routines and patterns. But if the patterns let them make those choices, maybe that was something he hadn't understood.

Then, suddenly, he coughed. "Two nurses, coming this way. You're telling me about some of the herbs and medicinal plants that are about to show."

"The purple, there, just starting to come in? That's red clover, it makes a lovely tea. Useful for women's needs, but also good for the blood. Doesn't have a lot of flavour, though, not like mint or coriander or fennel." She picked up smoothly, continuing on. To Roland's annoyance, the nurses ended up standing in a shady corner of the garden too nearby to risk further conversation.

F ive days later, Elen could tell Roland was working himself up to saying something. They'd had limited chance to talk privately. It had rained every afternoon, when they might have gone outside. Instead, she had prodded him into first walking around the room, then down the hallway. Then she had lured him with the chance to peer into the nurse's lounge by the entrance. That was good for his recovery, but not for figuring anything out.

When the rain cleared after lunch, she immediately set things in motion. "Let's get outside for a bit, before it decides to be changeable again. Give you somewhere new to walk to, if it isn't too slick."

Something in that amused Roland, but he was obliging about the necessary fuss of dressing gown and shoes rather than slippers, this time. Elen pushed him out carefully, back to their usual spot. She eyed the bench before carefully placing her hands over it and chanting a short tune to dry off the remaining damp.

Roland was watching her when she turned around

again. "That's handy, isn't it. I don't think I've seen you do that before."

She shrugged. "My best skills are making light, and a few things like that. Comfort and ease. Cool hands for a fever, for example."

"Lighting candles? Like the baths?" His voice had a different note to it, suddenly. A little hesitant, but also with a depth that she hadn't heard from him much before.

Elen looked up. "What was Healer Rhoe like for you?" She didn't have a more elegant way to ask him, this would have to do.

"She was..." Roland stopped, visibly trying to find the right words. "She was something else. So confident, so sure of what she was doing? She did a chant, a prayer, I don't even know the language, never mind the words." Then his voice got so quiet Elen had to lean close to hear. "She told me not to fight it. Whatever was going to happen."

Elen nodded, then ventured to reach a hand out for his, resting her fingers on top of his hand. After a moment, he shifted, so her palm was against his, his fingers curled around the side of her hand. "That's good advice. Healing is like water. Letting it flow is better."

He let out a puff of breath. "Someone could have told me that months ago. Would have helped." Then he shrugged. "I didn't fight it. I listened," He stopped again. There was a long silence, nearly a minute, before he spoke again. "I felt safe, there. Like I haven't since I was a child. Before tutoring school."

"When you were young."

"When I was young. When I wasn't responsible for anything. When I hadn't done things wrong."

Elen looked up at that. "Do you think you've done things wrong? I mean, recently?"

Roland snorted. "Oh, all the time. I'm sure. Not just the petty things, like not recovering fast enough. But, whether I'm getting Cadwell in trouble. Or you. Whether I'm doing something else I shouldn't be doing. Or not be doing something I should."

"Sins of omission and sins of commission." Elen's voice turned dry.

"Not your sort of thing?" Roland leaned forward a little.

She shook her head. "The old gods, they didn't go in for that. Hubris, foolishness, bragging when you didn't have cause for your pride, oh yes. Those were problems. Still are, as far as I can tell. Certainly it's good to try to be a better person, not a worse one, however you define that. But the rigidity of omission and commission? Those have never appealed. There are too many times when it isn't that simple."

"Healing." Roland's voice had turned thoughtful, and she looked at him again to find his eye half-closed, his head cocked to one side. "The pool. I don't know if it was that."

"Tell me?" She kept her voice even. Even asking about this could be seen as rude, if not outright unethical.

"It's all right to?" He was looking back at her now.

Elen nodded. "If you choose. If it feels all right to you. If you weren't told not to. Not by a human person, by - something beyond us."

Roland smiled a little at that. Then he shifted his hand a bit more securely around hers. "It wasn't like anything I've felt before. Darkness and quiet and safety, like I said. Nothing obvious. Not like, I don't know. Some stories are burning bushes, or swans, or thunder, or lightning bolts from the sky, or earthquakes. None of that."

"I always thought those things must be awfully annoying to clean up after." It was certainly why Elen preferred Sirona, who wasn't inclined to anything so destructive.

Roland laughed. "I'm fairly sure gods don't clean up after things like that. But you have a point. You're a god, you appear like that. Well, people are so busy reacting to the earthquake or the giant serpents or the waves of light. They don't pay proper attention to what you're saying."

"There must be a line, between being impressive and being too much." Elen agreed, with the gesture at Sirona's shrine. "Maybe that's why I've always liked Sirona. Little touches that make it clear this isn't just someone wandering along, but nothing, well, earthshaking."

"This was, Nodens has things to do with the sea, yes?"

"The sea. Dogs. Hunting, the kind meant for food and need, not, you know, pure sport." Elen shifted a little, not letting his hand go. He went still for a moment.

"I think I heard the ocean. The way the waves go, the sound of it, even though the pool was quite still." There was a little hitch in his breath. "Is it normal to think of someone? A friend? I didn't even remember it until just now, but I must have thought of him then, or had it knocked loose." He hesitated, then softer, as if this were far more fragile, he added, "That night, I dreamed of horses and hounds and the ocean." As if that had mattered a great deal.

"There's nothing normal or not normal. Just what you felt and saw and knew." The automatic response came out without her thinking about it, it was what they said so often. There was no one way to heal or be healed. People came with their own needs, their own ways they put faces and labels on their experiences.

She heard him snort again. "Would you go see him? The person I remembered? For me? I'm fairly sure he's in Trellech."

"Not serving somewhere else?"

Roland shook his head. "He has a weak heart, has since we were younger. He has some sort of fiddly desk job, research, for the Ministry. Something about the banks, but he's not from a banking family."

Elen considered. "Would he see me? I'm a stranger. Someone like that, he's not going to see a strange nurse."

Roland waved his free hand. "I can send a note around, if you'll drop it in the message box. Could you get the time?"

She ran through her calendar for the next week or two in her head. "I have a half-day next week. Wednesday. The morning, not the afternoon."

Roland began to say something, then he stopped. "You must have something you had planned for it."

"Sleeping in, mostly. I am inclined to sloth, given a chance. And a few errands, things I need from the shops."

"More yarn? Needles?"

That made her laugh. "More hair pins, some more thread for my mending kit. Maybe a new book, if I have time."

Roland ducked his chin. "I shouldn't ask you to give up the book shop."

That amused her. "All right. I'll make your call for you, if you set it up, and he's free next Wednesday morning."

"I'll make it clear your availability is limited."

"Won't he want to come talk to you himself?" Elen was sure that was the more ordinary sort of thing.

"Merlin and Nimue, no. He hates healers. I mean, as a class, the collected number of them. Heart trouble, remember? He's been poked and prodded so many times. He won't come near. And besides, as I said, busy man. He can make time to talk to you on his morning tea break. But coming all the way over here, waiting for someone to sign him in, to be escorted here? He won't do all of that."

"And you assume he has a morning tea break?"

"My dear Elen, we do try to be civilised people." He said it in a remarkably dry deadpan, and managed to hold his expression steady for a good thirty seconds before it cracked and he started laughing. The sound was delightful, and seeing him relax like that made her increasingly sure the bath had been a good idea. "No, he usually takes a tea break. Quite strict with himself about keeping to a schedule."

"All right. I'm willing to try it."

"When we get back to the room I'll write a note, if you can drop it on your way back to your, your." He stopped. "Where do you live, anyway?"

"A lodging house for nurses. I have my own bedroom up in the attic, because of my headaches. And these days, because I keep odd hours, you're not on the standard shift schedule. Share the loo and the bath with five others." Elen tried not to make it sound horrible. It certainly wasn't the worst place she'd lived in, even if it wasn't the best.

"That seems a bit dire."

"Oh, better than some places. We've got plenty of hot water, I have a window that doesn't look out on a brick wall. I can see two trees. Well, parts of two trees."

Roland shook his head. "Well. Better than my view, I suppose. I envy whoever's got the view of the gardens, there." He pointed at the end of the ward.

"Nurse's offices, mostly. Sorry to disappoint. Well, one of those rooms is a particularly nice room, I think. But only one."

"Huh." Roland peered at them, thoughtfully. "So it's nurses, watching us stagger about out here?"

"It would be if the nurses weren't so busy the view's wasted on us. The light's good, though, and when there are lots of reports, that's a big help."

He let out a long breath. "I'm learning a lot more about how this place works from you than anyone else, I must say. You said there were laundry and cooking facilities?"

"And storehouses, for all sorts of different supplies, yes." Elen gestured toward them with her chin.

"And they don't have the sorts of things nurses need? Hairpins? Thread?"

"I suppose they could stock something like that, like a school shop. Did you have one of those?"

"The chatelaine had something like that. We all queued up to get our inks and pens and all that. In the upper years, we could go down into the village, and there were shops there. Mostly designed for the teachers, and the people on the island who weren't students, though there was a sweet shop. A rather stuffy bookshop, the sort of tea shop with too many flourishes for boys, three pubs. Two friendly to students, one for people who didn't want to see them."

Elen nodded. "The village near Alethorpe was the same. Anyway, I suppose they could do something like that, but why would they, when they can just send us off into the city to get what we need."

"That theory," Roland pointed out, "Only answers if you're not working the entire time the shops are open."

"I am fairly sure they did not take that into consideration." Realising she was falling into a quite easy banter with him, she cleared her throat. "We should give your walking a try. Come on, then. It's not too slick."

"**G**ood morning. I'm here to see Master Treeve Dixon." Elen tried not to make it sound like a question. She was dressed in one of her few good ordinary outfits, a creamy white blouse and a deep periwinkle blue skirt. It felt quite odd not to be wearing her uniform, she'd not left the rooming house without it for weeks. Her hat was pinned on her hair, a modest straw hat with a periwinkle and green ribbon that went with the skirt. Smart and well-chosen, without pretending to be anything she wasn't.

The woman at the desk was in Guard uniform, though without much in the way of insignia. An apprentice, perhaps. "Do you have an appointment?"

"Yes, for half-ten. Therapeutes Morris." It was twenty past now, she'd expected she'd need a little longer to find her way. This was one of the more curious Ministry buildings, tucked into the back of the quarter, a series of Georgian buildings that weren't quite like townhomes or houses.

Her title got a glance up from the Guard, considering her in a different light. "Ah, yes. Here you are. Go along here, take the hallway to the right. There are chairs at the end. His assistant will call you in when it's time."

"Thank you." Elen wasn't sure how she'd expected that to go, precisely, or for that matter why there was a Guard stationed here. It must be rather boring work. She went along, as instructed, and thought she caught the Guard glancing at her to make sure she went where she was told. There were only two choices, right and left. Her boots were leather soled, not her usual rubber, and quite audible on the marble floors. That marble seemed rather posh for offices, actually.

There were two wing back chairs that might have been more at home in one of Trellech's private clubs. Just the two, though, which suggested there were not too many people waiting for appointments ever.

Precisely nine minutes later, the bells of the Guard tower chimed, and the door nearest her opened. "Therapeutes Morris? Please come in." The speaker was an older man, well past his fighting years. "Master Dixon will see you now. This way."

They walked through the front office, decorated in a way Elen always thought of as the style of the man insisting on civilisation. Wood panelling everywhere, in some dark wood that didn't draw the eye, oxblood leather chair and fittings, rows of bookshelves. The inner office had a large window and a sepia-toned globe that took up much of the space before it. A large wooden desk faced the window from the far end of the room.

The man behind it was standing, polite and formal, as she came in. "Therapeutes Morris? Do come in, I have a few minutes. I'm Treeve Dixon. May I offer you tea?" There was a small tea service on a rolling cart. One empty cup was waiting, matching the teacup and saucer with precisely one digestive biscuit centred on Dixon's desk.

Dixon himself was slender, dark haired, pale skinned, and sharply featured, putting her in mind of a fox. He wore simple clothing of nearly pure black, with a long row of fussy buttons down the front, and sparkling white cuffs and collar peeping out. It gave him the air of a mediaeval clerk or scholar.

"Please, if it's no bother. A smidge of cream if you have it. Thank you for making the time." Now she was here, she wasn't sure how to begin. She and Roland had talked about this, in the time between sending the letter and getting his reply. The older man, the aide or personal secretary, whatever his role was, immediately moved to pour her a cup of tea.

Dixon gestured at the chair facing him, waiting for her to settle herself before he sat down. "I gather your schedule is rather busier, or at least less under your own control. Thank you for your service." She couldn't tell if he meant it as the casual phrasing that everyone seemed to come out with, in some variation, or something more sincere.

She nodded and gave the little half-smile of acknowledgement that one did. False modesty wasn't attractive, but neither was pointing out that it was awfully hard work. "I do appreciate you managing this on my morning off." There was a cup of tea in front of her, rather suddenly and efficiently, just an edge off black. And a chocolate digestive biscuit.

"Thank you, Roger. Let me know if we get too close to my next appointment, please." Roger withdrew, taking the tea cart with him, and once the door was closed, Dixon leaned forward. "How would you prefer to be addressed, first? And then, what is it that Roland wanted to know?"

"Nurse Morris is fine, sir, thank you." Elen took a deep breath. "You understand, sir, that I can't talk about Major Gospatrick's medical concerns or personal matters, but his note outlined his hopes, I believe." She didn't just believe, she knew, she'd read it after Roland wrote it.

"That he had a particular experience, I came to mind, and he would like my analytical mind applied to the problem." Dixon's eyes were a rather intense green. "And that he was giving you permission to speak freely about those matters, as your judgement permitted."

That, she had not seen, he must have added a postscript. "Sir." Elen gathered herself again. "He made it clear you are not at all fond of the Temple of Healing, and for good reason. Anyone who's had a chronic condition poked and prodded over, well it's about two out of three that sensible people respond that way."

"What do the less sensible do?"

"Go in for hypochondria, usually. Every little twinge must be some new crisis, for some of them. And yet, many of them do know there's something wrong with them, something not working as intended." His own amusement and the way he was utterly focused on her were rather like some sort of truth potion, if they existed outside the realms of adventure novels. She found herself saying rather a lot more than she'd expected.

It made him laugh. "I can see why Roland likes you. So, then, tell me, what are the circumstances that made him think of me? No, first, how is he doing, that you can share. And can I arrange anything besides this conversation that might be a help? I'm sure his family have all the basic comforts sorted, but anything I can do without actually visiting him, I'm glad to."

Elen rather thought his family hadn't seen to much at

all. Other than a few books there were few personal effects in Roland's room. Something of her thoughts must have been visible, because there was a snort. "Or, no. they did the other thing, where they're cordially ignoring him until he's better." He threw it out as if he were testing a theory.

"They've not visited. He had a short letter or two before my time as his nurse, but I'm not sure who from."

"And how long is that?"

"Nearing two months."

"So you've had some time to evaluate his progress. Is he recovering? And what is he recovering from, then?" Dixon leaned forward, took a sip of his tea, and set the cup down.

"To be honest, sir, that's part of the problem. To answer your first question, he is beginning to make some progress. I was able to encourage a modification of his potions regimen that is helping, and he took the waters, under the temple. That's part of what we wanted to talk to you about."

"The potions or the bath?" Now he was teasing, and she found herself responding to it, in a way she had no idea how to describe. There was something flattering in having this man's full attention.

"Both, sir. The bath is where he had a sudden image of your face, in particular."

"And that brought you here. Curious. Intriguing, in fact." He leaned back a little, looking at Elen steadily. She took another sip of her tea, nibbled at the biscuit, then set both down. "And the potions?"

That was the tricky part. "In brief, information about the cause of his condition has been very hard to come by. In the normal way of things, I would have had access to his file, regularly, and on request. In this case, I have not been permitted to see it at all, and I have not been permitted to ask questions about his treatment. His Healer has not only made no gesture toward consulting me, but I have never been in the same room. He normally sends his junior to check in, but even then I am usually sent out on some errand."

"Your previous experience at the Temple is otherwise?" The question was sharp, entirely keeping up.

"I have not been posted there since my apprenticeship, but it is quite different both from that and my more recent service. I am in fact kept rather isolated. I live in a rooming house with other nurses, but my schedule is sufficiently different from theirs that I rarely get much chance to talk to them." She hadn't quite realised that particular part before. "It's quite unusual for there to be a single nurse assigned to a patient for so many hours, with no relief. A senior healer on a different ward confirmed that's odd, still, too."

"A morning off, how often?"

"Every fortnight." Elen glanced up at him, and was startled to see he was offended, visibly so.

"You mean to say that in two months, you have worked every day, had a morning off every fortnight, no other time to yourself? How long are your hours?"

"I arrive at nine, and I am there until half-seven, sometimes later. It is not difficult work. And some of it, I am tending to the shrines at the Temple."

Dixon tapped his fingers on the table, and she had the sudden certainty that for this man, this lack of control was a sign of deep anger or discomfort. "You are being treated like less than the merest skivvy. And I presume you have significant training?"

"A full five years apprenticeship, and ten years since as a qualified nurse."

"And how long do others work?" He seemed fixated on that.

"A more usual schedule would be an eight or ten hour shift, five or six days a week. A full day off, but not necessarily any particular day consistently. Nursing's needed the week round."

"Quite." Dixon waved his hand. "So, you are in an exceedingly unusual position, without the sort of information or support you would normally rely on. Your usual channels - your superior nurses, whoever - are unresponsive."

"Yes, sir. Two have helped, where they could, but they have limited..." Her voice trailed off and she swallowed, then took the risk. "I - um. In confidence, sir?"

He waved a hand. "I am certainly not going to go telling apparent incompetents what you tell me. Go ahead."

"I was able to arrange, with some difficulty, a chance to look at R - Major Gospatrick's file." She hoped desperately he didn't notice the slip, while being sure he had.

Dixon leaned forward. "Oh, have you. What did you find out?"

"Not as much as I hoped!" The frustration came out in her voice, and she had to look away.

She heard a knock on the door, then, and Dixon quickly called out. "We'll be a few more minutes, Roger. Push back as needed." Once the door closed, Dixon returned his attention to her. "Tell me what you can, please."

"There's very little documentation. No theories about what caused his symptoms, other than thinking it was related to his magic. Not nearly enough in the way of reports from people who've seen him. One of the people I talked to, one of the administrators, she was able to overrule the healer in charge. They agreed to a change in the dose that was causing Major Gospatrick the most problems."

"The healer's name?"

"Healer Ozymandias Cole." Elen was glad enough to give it.

"Huh. Interesting." Dixon leaned back. "It would be helpful to me if you could put the word out, and find out what you know about him. Or if Roland can do so. What kind of person he is. I have a niggling idea I've heard the name recently, but I can't pin it down." Then, his attention shifting again, he said, "And what do you want me to do, precisely?"

Elen managed to look up and meet his eyes. "The, well, vision of your face. I think Major Gospatrick decided you would know where to look, what to pay attention to? He wasn't entirely sure what you do, mind." She offered the last like she'd make an offering to Sirona, hoping it pleased the ineffable power before her.

It made him laugh, full-throated. "I amuse myself with patterns. Also sometimes dragons, gold, double-entry record keeping, embezzlement, and other such matters." Then he tilted his head, peered at her, and said. "Morris. The Dolau-cothi mines."

Elen blinked, startled. "My father, sir."

"You have something of the look of him, and your delightful mother. A good man, and a good manager. Unlike this Healer Cole, clearly. Even if there are things you aren't being told, there must be better ways to handle it." Dixon waved a hand. "Go see what you can hear, if you get a chance. Write me a note. I'll do a little investigating myself, quietly. I'll let you know. Every other Wednesday is your morning off?"

"Usually, sir. Unless Major Gospatrick has a commitment that requires my presence. But those are usually in the afternoon now."

That got a nod. "Right. And I'll be sending around a package for him, some things he might like."

"I shouldn't, you must be very busy." She suddenly realised they must have been here for quite a lot longer than she'd expected.

"Roger will see you out, get the best way for me to send a private note round. Take care of yourself, Nurse Morris." And then softer. "And keep taking care of Roland. I know you will."

There was an earnestness there she had no idea how to answer, so she merely nodded, and stood up. "Thank you. For listening." Then the door opened, and Roger, whatever his last name was, was showing her out into the outer office. He asked her to wait while he cleared the tea cups and showed someone in, before the flurry of getting her particulars and walking her out took over.

CHAPTER 26

THAT AFTERNOON, ROLAND'S ROOM

"How did it go?" Roland had been on tenterhooks, waiting. The time before lunch had never been so long, it felt like a century. Nearly as long as waiting to go into battle.

Elen was wearing her uniform, her cap starched and pressed, looking utterly at ease with the day. She'd come in just before lunch, gotten everything settled, and then been pulled away to help with something on the ward. When she finally came back, Roland had finished his meal, and was feeling very much lacking in information.

It did not help that in the last half hour, it had picked up raining, and there was no chance they'd make it outside.

Elen settled in the chair, taking out her knitting. "No outside walk for you. We can do the hallway in a bit, they're still moving things around, someone new is settling in down the hall. Had a bad time of it, I gather."

Roland cleared his throat, pointedly. "The visit?"

Elen started her needles going. "Is it safe, do you think?"

"It's pouring out." There was a crack of thunder to

punctuate, and then the rain coming down harder. "No one's going to come and bother us."

She raised an eyebrow. "Those are dangerous words. Tempting the fates."

"The Fates weave the tapestry, so it's not tempting them, either they were already tempted or they aren't." It wasn't particularly good logic, but it made Elen smile.

"All right. Keep an eye and ear out, all right? Otherwise, we're talking about my cousin."

"Cousin Tristan?" Having a name would help.

"That is more an Irish name, not a Welsh one, ta."

"You pick something then." Roland settled back, pleased with the way she was responding. He'd been worried, once they arranged this, that Treeve wouldn't listen to her, that it would be five minutes of polite nothings, and no help for them.

"Tesni. It means warmth from the sun." That was promising, Roland thought, though there was a sudden stab of some less pleasant emotion than promise, all of a sudden.

"That will do. So, you had the meeting, as you planned? Did you have trouble finding it?"

"Oh, no, the directions were good. And his assistant, his personal secretary? He let me in promptly on time. Do you know why there's a Guard at the desk for the building?"

"Everyone in the building has particular skills. The Guard is there to make sure they don't get bothered unduly, and to keep out people who might get in the way. Or worse." Treeve had talked about the precautions, a few times, over drinks in one of their clubs. There had been more than one kidnapping attempt, and more than one attempt to coerce one of the research staff. "It really was all right?"

"It was. I got shown in, and offered tea. And a biscuit."

Roland grinned. "I did tell you he had a routine." He'd gotten very familiar with Treeve's need to have things arranged just so. The man was brilliant, capable of piecing together twenty different pieces of information into a singular whole in a few seconds. However, if you changed the time of his morning tea break, he was useless until lunch.

"We talked a little about what I had permission to say. I hadn't realised you'd added a postscript, you shouldn't trust me like that, you really shouldn't." She stopped, gathered herself. "And I said that I understood why he'd not care to be back in the Temple of Healing." She took a breath, the needles stopped clicking. "He's very compelling, isn't he?"

Roland sucked in a breath. Something in how she said that, the fact she'd stopped knitting to say that. He'd never particularly felt jealous before, but he was now certain. There was a surge of something. Treeve was a good man, a clever man, a thoughtful man. Certainly all things Elen had every right to be interested in and by. He let his breath out, inhaled again, and said, in as measured a tone as he could manage, "What kind of compelling?"

"Like he could get the truth out of you without a potion. Just by asking you a few questions. He was so focused, like there was nothing in the world but what I was telling him."

"And you told him what we've sorted out?"

She nodded silently. Then, deliberately, the needles started up again. "He asked some other things, first. Why you wanted me to come talk to him. What my training was like. He was really offended at how many hours I work."

Roland felt that surge again, and something else, something that wanted to be protective. To be a barrier between Elen and everything that would get in the way of her work.

She was sitting there, tidy and pressed and clean, and he could barely get out of bed without help.

For the first time since before he'd been wounded, though, he felt other urges stir. More than stir. He couldn't help a sharp inhale, and a quick glance down to see how obvious it was going to become. He could scarcely rearrange himself, not as they were. The blankets, he thought, might cover it in their folds.

Nothing for it but to ask, "And you don't think it's too many?"

Elen shrugged. "It's less than I did at the Front. A half day off, and usually a ten hour shift, not twelve. It's a bother to get things from the shops, but I don't need to do that often." She added, "He - um. Tesni, asked after your family, he assumed they'd been seeing to your comfort."

"Ah." That wasn't quite enough to deaden his response, but it was a near thing. "Not really their sort of thing. Apparently."

"He said he'd send some things round. I'm not sure what, I promise I didn't ask him to or anything."

Roland waved his hand, then put it back, when that rearranged the blanket folds alarmingly. Her worry about overstepping was also more powerful than he'd realised. "He is a man of his own plans and projects. We can expect something interesting to show up in a day or two, I'm sure. What next?"

"That's when we got along to your case." She glanced up, as if to make sure no one had appeared in the room without notice. "And your file. I told him what I'd found."

"Or not found, as the case may be." Roland pointed that out.

"Rather. And he listened." She looked at Roland and her expression was softer. "He listened. It's been a while since anyone listened." Before he could object, she added, "You have, since we started talking. And Healer Rhoe. But that's not so many."

It did not make his body react less, that was for certain, and he shifted, cupping his hands in his lap. Which was utterly distracting in a new way. Thankfully, she didn't look down, just went back to her knitting, if she'd admitted something new and damaging. It gave him a chance to gather his thoughts.

"Is there a reason people don't listen?"

"Oh, dozens." There was a sharpness there, not aimed at him, but instead something she was letting him see. "I'm Welsh. Of an ordinary sort of family. No powerful patron easing things. My parents didn't think I should be a nurse. I don't have the right connections. I focused on a strand of healing that is rarely showy, but the kind that is slow and patient. The kind people think anyone can do, that doesn't take skill. And here, they've funnelled me off, assuming I can't do much else." She grimaced, and then rubbed her head.

He said, promptly. "Headache?" He certainly knew what that felt like.

"They've been much better, here. But, the weather." She gestured vaguely outside.

"Is better that you have fewer of them, or that they are not as bad, or that you can hide them better?"

She looked up sharply at that, then there was a hint of a smile. "All three. Let me get a little tea. Would you like some?"

He didn't want her to leave, but if she needed the tea, he wasn't going to stop her. "If you're getting some for yourself." It would at least give him a chance to rearrange the blankets better, and get his thoughts in line. She nodded, and disappeared out the door.

Roland took a deep breath, trying to understand why his body had picked now, of all bloody awful times, to react like he had at Schola. It was embarrassing, and likely insulting to her, as well. She took her work, her vocation, seriously, and here he was, thinking about her body. Not just her body. He found her mind, her thoughts, attractive, more than her body, but he kept getting flashes of her movements.

The steady shifts of her hands, whether she was tending to something for him or back at her knitting. The quirk of her lips in a smile, or the way her right eyebrow arched. How she held his wrist when she took his pulse, steady but gentle. The way she stood, conserving her energy for a long day, but ready to move at a moment's notice. More than anything else, her patience and kindness that were somehow never about pity.

She'd clearly enjoyed the conversation with Treeve, too. It was no wonder. He was charming, when something caught his interest, and he had that intensity to him. Having that kind of sharp attention focused on her, when she'd been feeling no one listened to her, must have been near enough a drug. Certainly a burst of sunlight through the storm.

Roland swallowed. He didn't have much to offer her. He was bent and near-broken, not even able to walk twenty feet on his own, reliably. If he ever could, chances were good he'd be sent off to do something for the War effort, likely something unpleasant. He had some money, there was a great-aunt who'd been fond of him, but it might well not make up for going against his family's wishes. He was sure they'd not approve of someone of Elen's background. Or profession, for that matter.

What he could do, however, was pay attention to her, listen. She was doing her best to help him, after all. And he could do it without expectation of anything other than her professional best. He swore to himself he would not pressure her, he would not make things awkward, he would not jeopardise her position or professionalism. More than he had, anyway.

None of this made his increasingly intense desire for her any easier, of course. Just thinking about her, now, made him want her to come back, just so he could start listening to her again, have her full attention and give her his own. It was like the sun, or some other bright star was there, when she came closer, something that eased everything else.

He thought better. He felt better. He felt, period. Somehow, she had dragged him out of the murk and mud and fog of the War and his injuries, the way his body and mind weighed him down. Roland was certainly, utterly certain, that she didn't give herself enough credit there. He'd certainly seen other nurses, been tended by them, without anything like the same results.

Perhaps, if he were very lucky, he might make her believe she was worth listening to.

CHAPTER 27

THAT AFTERNOON, ROLAND'S ROOM

Elen took a moment once the tea was ready to remind herself that they were working on sorting things out. The discussion with Master Dixon, this morning, had been unsettling, in ways she still couldn't name. It had felt rather like being examined by a snake, even a dragon. She couldn't begin to parse what he'd meant about his work having to do with dragons and embezzlement. She hadn't dared to ask. He'd barely left her space to say what she'd needed to.

Then there was Roland, and the way he was reacting. He'd gone all squirrelly for a moment, in there. She had wondered if he'd begun to have feelings for her, of one kind or another. The way his shoulders had hunched gave certain impressions of a rather particular sort of discomfort.

Every nurse knew it happened sometimes, but it wasn't something she'd needed to deal with before. At the Temple of Youth, it was much more innocent. She would be deluged by drawings or pressed flowers or perhaps a bit of a sweet from a care package from a distant relative. That was quite easy to manage. And at the front, she'd not had too much time with any one patient. Enough to be sad, for the ones who died, and glad for those sent to other places to recover, but nothing more than that.

This was different, though. It was the first time since her apprenticeship where she'd tended to a single adult patient for an extended period. Even then, she rather thought there were not many times when she'd cared for an adult man who wasn't married or otherwise clearly attached. At least she was fairly sure he was unattached, there had been no sign of any lady sending notes, or flowers, or anything else like that.

Elen had come to enjoy her time with him. Not just in the manner of a patient who presented some interesting challenges, if not as many as might keep her properly busy. He was thoughtful. As she'd pointed out, just now, he listened, in a way that she wasn't at all used to from anyone except a few friends. Unlike many of the men of good families she'd been around in the course of her nursing, he didn't treat her like an invisible servant. Even in the beginning, when he had said little, he'd been polite, with please and thank you.

She could not begin to tell if that was his native politeness, or if that were something he did to her, in particular. From seeing him at his presentation, she was clear that he could turn on the charm, in an instant, even when his body was rebelling.

Whatever it was, she had to admit she found it intriguing, even enticing. He'd never even suggested turning that charm on her, and she wondered what that would be like, if ever did. If she'd be able to do the right thing.

At the moment, it was the fact that he listened to her. That was a thing to treasure. And he not only listened, he went along with her treatment ideas with only the sensible amount of questions and discussion. That was, in all honesty, far more enticing than his charm might be.

Elen took a breath. She'd have to figure that out later. Now it was time to pick up the saucers, balancing the teacups carefully, and bring them back. There was no one in the hallway to avoid, but she could hear low voices from the cracked doors of two rooms. She set down Roland's cup, and then came around the bed to set her own down, leaving the door a crack open.

"I hadn't asked, before." Roland's voice was quiet. "Do you have a fellow, or someone?"

It was such a close echo of her own thoughts that she startled, then blinked. "No, no."

"Not at all?" He seemed more than a little startled.

That made her ask her own question. "What about you? I've - pardon, I've assumed not." The way he stiffened, she knew she'd hit a nerve, and she immediately said, "Pardon."

Roland waved his hand, then reached for the tea, as if that would be reassuring. "I had a fiancee. She broke things off with me not long after I woke up here."

"That's not fair." The indignation flooded her before she could think better of it. Though it did explain part of why he'd been so alone.

He shook his head, just a twitch side to side. "It wouldn't be fair to hold her to the engagement when I'm a different man."

"She didn't give you much time to figure out what sort of man you are now." Elen fumed, then shook her head, and reached for her own tea cup. To ease the conversation a little, she said, "I suppose it's traditional for nurses to take up with healers, but that hasn't been on offer for me."

Roland tilted his head, following her into the distraction. "More fools them."

"I'm rather boring, you know. All work, little play." She shrugged. "My line of healing has never lent itself to much time to go to social things. All sorts of different shifts, sometimes changing day to day."

He just kept watching her. It wasn't an intense gaze, the way Master Dixon had looked at her. This was something softer, as if he were taking all of her in, the way you looked at a garden or landscape, not just one plant or one tree. He didn't say anything, and eventually she filled the silence. "What were you planning on doing? Before the War?"

Roland didn't answer her. Instead, he shifted, leaning toward her. She wasn't sure if he was about to do something, or say something. She thought, for a glancing moment, that it was the kind of way one hoped for a kiss. Before either of them could move further, there was an appalled bark from the door. "Nurse. On your feet."

She stood, almost knocking the chair behind her, her heart racing and a sudden stab of pain in her head. She forced her hands down to her sides, rather than grab for it, trying to make her eyes focus on the door. There was a tall man, well-fed, in the robes of a senior healer, the draping gown of scarlet red over a sharply tailored suit.

Roland gathered his wits much faster than she did. His voice was sharp. "Who are you?" It wasn't a request, it was a demand, certainly equal to equal, if not equal to inferior. All at once, she could hear in his voice all the years of breeding and security in his position, training and money, sharpened by a military manner.

"Nurse. Report to Sister Almeda's office, immediately. Wait for me there. Bring your things."

"Who. Are. You." Roland's voice was louder now, and properly fierce. Elen's head throbbed.

"Sir." She wasn't even sure who she was saying it to,

whether to Roland or this strange man, this senior healer. She bent, reaching for her bag. At least the knitting was tucked away, she hadn't taken it out yet.

"Nurse Morris. Stay." That was Roland, and Elen managed to stop. She blinked to get her eyes to focus long enough to see that he'd gone pale, in a way that couldn't be good for him.

"Nurses are employed by the Temple. They are not yours to bid to go or stay. Major." The last came out in a snarl, from the door.

Elen straightened up, and took a breath. "Sir, I'll be in Sister Almeda's office, or waiting outside."

"Tell her Senior Healer Cole will be along presently, relating to a serious matter."

Elen felt faint, but she nodded slightly and regretted it immediately. "Sir." She repeated it as if it would fix something, while knowing perfectly well it wouldn't. She couldn't bear to look at Roland, she knew if she did, she would burst out in sobs or fall to the ground. That would be useless and awful. She took one step, then another, focusing her eyes on the floor, five feet in front of her. First the worn boards of the room, then the healer's polished shoes.

He finally stepped aside and let her pass, though with the sort of tight disdain that made her feel lower than low. She got halfway down the hallway, before she heard Roland again. "Explain yourself." Then the door closed with an insistent and final click.

She'd left him alone. With that man. Who she did not trust one bit. Who Sister Pomona thought might be doing evil. And yet he could not go back. Even if she'd wanted to, she didn't know what she'd do. She could barely put one foot in front of the other.

There was at least no one in the hallway. She had a

minute or two, maybe no more, before Healer Cole came out of that room and came looking for her. By the time he did, she needed to be at Sister Almeda's office, no matter how much she wanted to flee.

She couldn't. She'd be thrown out of her room in the lodging house, and never able to work as a nurse again, anywhere in Albion. Even if she was going to be sent off to some tiny hamlet with nothing that really needed her skills, she might eventually find her way back to something worthwhile. Maybe.

She glanced behind her at the door, and then deeply regretted moving her head. But she thought she had enough time to drop a note in the message box. She found one of the slips, managing to scribble a barely legible note to Healer Rhoe, a brief line. "Healer Cole with Roland Gospatrick. Sent me away. 'serious matter.' Please check on him. Roland." It was entirely unprofessional, and not at all helpful, but she could not think of any other way to put it. She dropped it into the message box, where it would be whisked away, sorted, and delivered promptly enough.

Then it was time for her to put one foot in front of the other, stubbornly refusing to give up. She went slowly out the door, across the small courtyard, then up the stairs. Sister Almeda was not there, the door was locked, so she sat, feet pressed together tightly, head bowed, ignoring any conversation, her bag tucked in her lap.

CHAPTER 28

Roland lay back, his eyes barely open. Elen had been sent away, and not only had she not come back, everything had gotten much worse. Again.

It had been four days now. No, five. He was losing track of time again. The first day, after she'd been sent away, he'd been left entirely alone, except for the orderlies bringing food and seeing to his bath. But they wouldn't talk to him, not one word beyond what was needed to accomplish their assigned task. He thought, as much as he could think, that they had been scolded, reprimanded, even threatened, the way they treated him.

Healer Cole - Senior Healer Cole, as he insisted on - had torn strips off of Roland for the better part of an hour. It had gotten tangled and confused in his head. He wasn't sure if that was because of his illness, or if it was because Senior Healer Cole wasn't at all coherent.

The lecture, the scolding, had been designed for a schoolboy. It had been a mess of calling him out for taking advantage of her. There'd been more, about not having the moral fibre when she took advantage of him, blame for not having recovered, and scorn for Elen's approaches that had actually been helping. Complete with a flurry of moving red, from his eye-burningly scarlet gown.

Roland wasn't sure what to make of it. Each time he tried, it got tangled up in his head. Everything turned murky and hard to grasp. There was some thread of it that seemed wrong, a note out of tune. Someone driving a mule to a charger's gallop. But it wasn't like he'd been able to stop the man and ask. Or, as it turned out, ask anyone else.

At the end of it, punctuated by comments about how Roland was taking him away from critical war work, the man had left. He'd tossed a comment over his shoulder about how he was adjusting the dosage again.

He tried to remember what it had been like after the bath, when it felt like he could find safety and hope again. The tirade had shattered all of that, tangling his tongue and his courage up. The potions, back to the original doses, had made everything worse.

There had been no way out of taking them. One of the orderlies had stood over him, and Roland had realised that the healer must indeed have something over them. He wasn't sure what someone like Cole might have over them, except perhaps for threatening to send them overseas, into the worst of the War, but how would Cole have that kind of influence? It made his head hurt worse to think about it.

Tactically, drinking seemed the best of a bad lot of choices. He couldn't improve his situation, but he could at least not put the people assigned to tend him at greater risk. It was entirely too small a thing, but it was all he had.

Whatever he was taking seemed even more awful now. He slept longer, nearer fourteen hours, and the muzzy-headedness never really let up. He'd fallen into a sort of timeless incoherence far too quickly, with time only really anchored by whether the meal he was brought was break-fast or dinner. Even then, it was sometimes hard to tell, since his meals had become a procession of easy to swallow porridge or soup.

By the third day, they had dug up a new nurse to sit with him. She didn't talk to him, either. She hadn't intro-duced herself, though Harry had called her Nurse Eglinton once, when they thought he was asleep. She wouldn't even sit next to him, she had moved her chair to the far end of the room. She was perched next to the table where things were stored, with a small charm lantern. She didn't knit, either, she just sat.

Roland did not approve. Not of the food. Not of his treatment. Not of Elen's absence. Not of any of it. But he could not see what to do about it. He let out a long sigh. Nurse Elington didn't even look up. He wasn't sure what she was there for.

There was a knock on the door, and then the lights flicking up brightly, that made him wince and rub at his face. A man in uniform, that couldn't be good.

"Major Gospatrick." The man gave him a curt nod. "Nurse, if I could have a minute."

She didn't say anything to him, just stood, and went out, closing the door behind her. Roland pushed himself until he was sitting more upright. He'd make the attempt, anyway.

"We have had a further report from Healer Cole. He says you will be fit for a series of regular presentations beginning at the end of next week. Both here in Trellech, and one is being arranged in London, a discussion with several from their military about the options that magic can provide."

Roland blinked, several times. "Regular presentations, starting next week?"

The man gave another curt nod. "And others to follow, still being scheduled. You are expected to be ready, and do your duty. Healer Cole has made it clear to us we should consider anything else to be malingering. We do not wish to take steps toward a court-martial, but we will if it is necessary."

Roland managed to keep from swearing, letting out a long stream of invective. He only won that battle by driving his fingernails so tightly into his palms he was sure he was drawing blood. Even with Elen, that would have been too much to ask, and without her, he had no idea how he could possibly survive it.

Protesting, however, was going to get him nowhere. First things first, he had to get more information. He had to force his way through the sludge in his head and get a better sense of what they were demanding, and what he should expect. "So I can prepare, can you tell me more about the audience and goals for each meeting?"

"You may take no notes." The man still hadn't given his name. "But I am permitted to tell you a few things. The Trellech meeting will include senior Ministry officials, as well as representatives from the Guard, and two visitors from the Army. They are seeking to build up training capacity for those with magic to assist in various tasks without risking breaking the Pact."

Hence the Guard, who had more than a little experience with that. Albion, per se, as a magical community, didn't have a standing army. Before the Pact, everyone fought as they needed or chose to. The lines of feudal oaths and obligations held the magical as well as the non-magical, and so generally there were fighters with magic on both sides. Even more often, they had provided protective warding and the occasional miracle that permitted an evacuation in the nick of time.

Since the Pact, the magical community was separate, bound by their oaths not to reveal magic or their magic in specific. It made being part of a larger army rather complicated. Over the centuries, a bridge had formed, between those who fought for Albion and the British forces. Individuals might go and fight, using their talents as they could. In larger wars, small groups might be sent for warding, incursions into enemy territory, or other tasks where maneuverability, training, and specialised skills were relevant.

Roland knew the theory of all of that, certainly, he'd literally learned it at his father's knee. But he couldn't understand why he was the one under such pressure to explain it. He knew perfectly well there were people whose job it was, had been for years, to explain that, to bridge the gaps between the two communities. His father, for one.

If they needed him, had something happened to his father? Something no one had told him? He'd half expected someone to use that as a blunt weapon to enforce his obedience, but he found the utter lack of reference to his father decidedly more chilling. That thought distracted him, utterly. It would explain why no one had come to visit him. Or write. Or anything. Beyond them being ashamed of him, which was frankly also a possibility. Especially if he were being threatened with a court-martial.

He hadn't been able to sort it out even when he could think more clearly. This time, he took one particular way through. "Pardon, my current potions make some things more challenging. Why me? Why can't one of the Guards explain? They surely deal with such things more regularly."

The man waved. "They have other obligations. You..." There was a wave of his hand, his chin lifting, as he peered down at Roland. "You do not have other occupation. And your healer has approved."

Roland let out a puff of breath. "And the London event?"

"You are of good family, you are comfortable with people of authority." He gestured again. "You can be charming, when you wish to be, I gather." The man looked him up and down. "And dressed for the occasion." Then, dismissively. "I am told you still require canes."

Even if he'd been improving, enough to go a good fifty steps without them, yes, he would claim them. "I do, yes. And someone will have to accompany me."

There was a dismissive wave of the hand. "We will see to your transportation to and from. A room, in London, overnight, near the offices where the meeting will be held. There may be some questions for you once they have had a chance to discuss privately."

Roland could see that any protest would be dismissed as quickly. "I'll ask the orderlies to make sure my uniform is properly pressed."

"See to it." The man then nodded sharply. "In a week, Major. Do your duty and you won't have trouble with us."

Roland could do nothing else but nod. He couldn't see the man's insignia properly, the way the light was. "King, Council, and Country." It was the safe answer, the one that no one could argue with. There was a simple nod, a click of the heels, and then the man was striding out. The movement was rapid and forceful, especially compared to the slow pace that Roland had become used to. Nothing happened quickly in this corner of his world, not any more.

He let himself relax back into the pillows, exhaling, as much as relaxation was possible. He did not like this one bit. Someone was pulling strings, more than one person, and he didn't think it was just Senior Healer Cole. He hadn't liked the man at all.

Which made him stop and think again about why. His mind was as clear as it was going to get, it was an hour or so before supper, and his potion. The nurse wasn't here to stare at him. He needed to make the most of it.

Elen had been straightforward and practical. She wore the standard nurse's uniform, made of good quality cloth, but nothing remotely fancy. It was designed to hold up well, he thought, the way his country shirts were, or his breeches, so they could be laundered repeatedly. Given her work, presumably with stronger soaps, too.

She hadn't worn any particular adornments, other than her locket and her watch fob. The watch was clearly a working tool for her, given how often she used it when tending to him. She lived in a rooming house, with plenty of other nurses, but she didn't seem to have many luxuries.

Healer Rhoe, she'd been wearing good quality linen, a step up from Elen's dresses because it was less study for harder work. He seemed to remember hearing something about how that shade of indigo, the darker shade, was more expensive to dye, but other than that, she'd had no obvious adornments.

Her voice, now that was the accent of the people he'd grown up with, people with power and influence. She'd hidden it well, smoothing out the vowels and the way she said her R, but he could tell. Of course, she'd been educated, he expected that of any healer. But her confidence, her bearing, her comfort with decisions, those all suggested someone notably well-born.

He'd trained himself near enough the same way, to avoid problems when he was serving with others. He wanted to come across as educated, capable, certainly an officer, but not with the sort of affectation that some of the set he'd been born into preferred. He didn't see a point in affectation for fashion's sake, certainly.

Even Sister Almeda had been dressed practically, when he'd seen her. Her dress was of better cloth, though, he thought a wool silk blend, the way it moved. Her aprons had been the brilliant white that hadn't been bleached over and over. She'd had more jewellery, both the necklace she wore, and the watch. He was sure he'd seen tortoiseshell pins in her hair, and a ring with a quality emerald on her finger, more than once. Neither of those came cheap. Even if they were family pieces, that implied something about her background.

Senior Healer Cole, though, had been in an entirely different category. Now that he thought about it, he was sure the man had been wearing shot silk, two shades of red that gave it an uncanny depth, the liveliness of blood. And it wasn't just the sleeves, that was common enough among the better off sort, but it was the full robe.

Not an inexpensive outfit at all. Especially when you considered that silk tended to stain if you looked at it wrong, even with all the charms and magics at their disposal. Certainly that was not the dress of anyone who expected to be near the untidy parts of healing.

It made him wonder how much a senior healer made, or what the financial arrangements were. Did they have housing provided, for example, which would free up a fair bit of income? That kind of clothing not only implied money to buy it, but money to maintain it. More than just a valet in a flat, but a house with staff.

Cole was too common a name for him to be sure what kind of family the man came from, though the way he'd spoken suggested things. Actually, now he considered, there had been an odd note here or there. A choice of words that wasn't what Roland or his family would do, wasn't what Healer Rhoe would have chosen. He couldn't remember the tirade clearly enough to pin down which words it was, only a handful. But he'd had that feeling before, with someone who was making out he was something he wasn't.

That was a particular thing Roland disliked. He'd met men - and women - from all sorts of backgrounds, because of his parents, and because of his own work before the War. Elen, for example, obviously came from working class roots, but she was thoughtful, clever, hard working. There was no shame in that. Someone making such a point of being some-thing else, though, that made Roland curious. And perhaps a little suspicious. Not that he could do anything about it.

His thoughts were interrupted by Nurse Eglinton coming into the room. She had a small crate with her, and the lid had been opened, then set back loosely on top, with a gap. "This was delivered for you." She put it on the bed beside him, not even handing it to him.

Roland considered the box. He had not been expecting anything, and it didn't seem like something Elen would send. Then he shifted the label, and recognised Treeve's handwriting. Inside was a tin of tea, and a small box of marzipan in various shapes. A standard set, with the Schola house animals, and a selection of other such things, a few potion bottles, stacks of books, slender wands. They were a small touch of cheer, but not informative.

There was no note at all. Not that Treeve was good at notes, mind, but he'd expected something. "Was there any message with it, nurse?" He kept his voice polite.

"Not that I know of, sir." Her voice was crisp and rather forbidding. "You can keep one of the tins by you. The tea, I think." She wouldn't even permit him that choice. "Too much sugar, well." She cut off there. "You should tell whoever sent it to make better choices."

As if Treeve would be told about such things. Roland took the tea canister, and tucked it over by his bed. Nurse Eglinton promptly took the rest of the case off his lap, unpacking the marzipan. "You can have one piece a day, no more." As if he were a small child.

Roland didn't argue. He'd long since learned not to waste his energy on hopeless begging.

E len let out a long sigh, twitching slightly. Amet slid a fresh mortar and pestle and a bowl over to her. "Make yourself useful, you." They were tucked into the stillroom in the Tudor house that held both a workroom and home. Amet had, theoretically, moved out when she finished her apprenticeship, into a small flat two streets away. She still took most of her meals here, and spent long hours in the stillroom.

Elen had perched on the stool for guests. She leaned her elbows on the great central working table in the middle of the room. The space felt comforting, somehow, with the raw ingredients in jars down one side, and the smaller rack for ingredients that were ready to be mixed and blended on the other.

There was something satisfying about reducing the dried roots she'd been handed into dusty powder. This was the third batch Amet had handed her, the things that didn't take particular skill, just dogged stubbornness.

"What are you going to do, then?" Elen had been here long enough Amet was going to ask, then.

Elen shrugged. "I am on leave, with half-pay, while they investigate." Her voice sounded dull, thudding, even to her. It certainly didn't reassure Amet. It had been nearly ten days with no news at all, and she certainly didn't expect to hear anything now until at least next Tuesday.

"That is about what they are doing, which you'd already said. Not about what you are doing." Amet's voice was tart, as she stood to pull down a different large jar, this one of small dried berries. Juniper, she thought, from the whiff of sharp scent.

"I can't see him." Elen sucked in her breath. "And I'm worried about him."

"Could I get in to see him, do you think?" Amet settled down on her stool, matter of fact.

Elen considered that. "You sometimes make deliveries, don't you?"

"I have a pass and everything. Back to the storerooms." Amet sounded pleased with herself, and she should. Those weren't terribly easy to come by. It was much more common for one of the orderlies who managed the warehouses to meet a delivery at the back gate and take over from there. "I have to confirm proper storage of some things, and sign others over."

Elen worked on the roots, tapping the pestle on them several times to start breaking them apart. "Which ones?"

"Any of the poppy derivatives, those we have to sign over. Some of the other sedatives. A few things that are poisonous in any sizable dose. Could I get to his room, do you think?"

"Getting there, maybe. Doing any good - that's more of a question."

Amet frowned. "Well, that's no help. Do you have

anyone who could? Anyone who'd trust you, when you said there was something wrong?"

"I sent a note to the Healer who helped in the baths. She was, she was different. Not tangled up in the Temple politics. I thought, later, about sending one to Sister Pomona, but I don't know if it would reach her. Or if it would do any good. I don't think she has much influence? Knowledge, skill, but not influence."

Amet tapped the berries with her pestle tentatively, then went and got a different mortar and pestle set. "Tell me about that. The first one."

It took a few minutes of grinding before Elen had her thoughts in order. That was the relaxing thing about Amet, she'd never expected anyone to say anything quickly. She took things in their own time. It had been the only place Elen could imagine being right now. She needed to be somewhere no one would rush her. "I wasn't sure what to expect when I came back, not exactly. But things are different."

Amet nodded, patiently, the pinned up braids around the crown of her head shifting slightly as she tucked a wisp of hair behind an ear. "Not informative, El."

Elen grimaced. "It's hard to find words for. A lot of people aren't there, that used to be. I mean, most of the folks who are good at crisis healing, they're either on the Continent, or they're wrapped up in what they're doing at the Temple."

"And you're living in a rooming house, not one of the dormitories. So you don't have the, what was it, when you were apprenticing?"

"The refectory. No. And my schedule's been off from most of the rooming house. The landlady keeps giving me an awful time about coming in late, even though I always tell her when I'll be back late, which is usually."

"Long days."

Elen nodded, laying it out for Amet, the schedule. She'd been thinking about it, actually, since Master Dixon had been so offended about it, and she finished up asking about that. "I don't mind. There is a war on, I was doing twelve hour shifts, fourteen, at the front, every day, with barely time off to see about laundry."

Amet paused in her work, setting the pestle aside for a moment to stretch her hands out. "There is a war on. But you are not at the front, and is that the usual sort of schedule?"

"It's hard to tell what's usual right now." Elen admitted. "Especially since I don't have much contact with other nurses."

"Your rooming house?"

"People without connections in town. Most people who are at the Temple for years find a flat with another nurse or two. Maybe with a landlady in the building to see to deliveries and maybe some meals, but not the same way."

"Tsking when you come in late, like you're a schoolgirl. Not that you did that when you were actually a school girl, as I recall."

Elen ducked her chin. "Like that, yes."

"And the Temple itself? What's different there? You said that Healer Rhoe wasn't like the others."

"For one thing, she listened. Sister Pomona did, too. But they've both got - all sorts of other things they need to do. Why would they bother about me? Or even Major Gospatrick." Elen ground the roots with a few more aggressive twists of her wrist. "Sister Almeda must be very busy too. And once I saw the file, it was clear to me that they're not telling her half the things they should be. But I don't know if they have told her more than is in the file, of course."

"Mind-reading would be so difficult, and yet so helpful." Amet sounded resigned, like it was something she'd thought about rather a lot. "So the question is whether this is because of the War, the more ordinary changes since your apprenticeship, or something else. And if it's the last, what you do about it."

Elen prodded at the roots in her mortar a little, before passing it over to see how much more was needed. She said, carefully. "If it were the ordinary sort of change, the file would look different. It's just, just, wrong to not document things properly. Dangerous. Deadly, even."

Amet nodded at the mortar. "Do another batch like that, ta." Then she looked up, peering over her glasses at Elen. "You have good instincts, you always have. Remember back in our third year, when you were certain someone was sneaking things."

"Poor Gladys was starving, it turned out." The girl had come from a family who didn't approve of her education, and who'd done everything they could to make things horrible for her during their holidays.

When they were back in school, she'd stolen things, here and there, to hoard away. Mostly food, but occasionally a hair ribbon or a book someone had finished reading. Their housemother had been very gentle, when it had come out, as well as making sure Gladys didn't have to go off to her family again.

Amet nods. "And part of you wonders if there's actually a good reason now, like there was then."

Elen considered that, then she nodded slowly. "I guess

so." It felt odd to say it, but it was true enough. "But I keep coming back to the records."

"Do you know anything about that healer? Cole, I mean."

"No." Elen shook her head. "I wrote a note to Healer Rhoe, as I was leaving, I couldn't, I'm sure it didn't make sense. And maybe she can't help. The baths are, they're their own area. She might not know what to do."

"What made you talk to her in the first place?"

Elen shrugged. Talking about this felt odd. It wasn't forbidden, she knew that. But it wasn't a thing people talked about especially outside the Temple itself. "She's one of the Healers responsible for the baths. I thought one might help Ro - Major Gospatrick."

She realised she'd slipped as soon as the beginning of his name was out of her mouth. Amet, of course, caught it immediately. "First name, is it? Roger? Robert? Rohitabel?"

"That's not a name!" Elen was, despite herself, amused. Enough so that she added, after a moment. "Roland."

"Roland Gospatrick. Why do I..." Amet stood suddenly, and went off to a volume. "Oh, his mother's proper fierce. She's something quite high up in the Guard, some sort of research post. Not a Penelope, an analyst."

Elen didn't know much about what the Guard did, aside from the people in uniform. She had treated two of the Penelopes, specialists in dealing with unweaving magics, during her apprenticeship. An experiment had gone wrong, releasing a dangerous gas that had caused hallucinations. The rest of the Guard, she had no idea, though in this case, she could at least offer something. "He said she was a specialist in defensive magics, something like that. Posted to Egypt."

Amet, whose family had emigrated when she was only a

baby, nodded slightly. "I might ask Papa." She slid the volume closed. "Rather powerful family. They can't do anything?"

"None of them have been to see him since I was there. And I don't think they've written, though I suppose it's possible I missed that." Elen tapped the pestle once. "Master Dixon thought it was odd, I think. I think he expected they'd at least have sent packages."

"What does one normally send to a hospital?"

Elen waved a hand. "Books. Magazines. Ro - Roland could have sweets or biscuits, in moderation, if he wanted. Or better tea than we have. Flowers, or some cheerful plant."

"You have sweepings, is what you have. Remind me to send you off with some decent stuff." Amet's mother was from a merchant family, and she had the strongest opinions about tea of anyone Elen had ever met. Which was saying rather a lot in Albion. "Something is wrong there."

"With his family?"

"Maybe. Or maybe what his family has been told. Would that be a thing? Families like that, they'd see to the customary sort of thing. A weekly letter, a package, even if no one visited. And your Roland isn't contagious or anything, is he? He's able to have a conversation."

Elen could not avoid a slight flinch at 'your Roland'. She knew as soon as she reacted that Amet would catch it, no matter how quickly she repressed it.

Amet seemed about to say something else, then she set the mortar and pestle aside, leaning her elbows on the table. "Oh, like that, is it then?"

Elen couldn't look at her, but she nodded, very slightly. "I - I might have feelings for him. Beyond what I'm permitted. Reason enough to turn me out, for that alone. If they figure it out, which they probably will."

"You do realise that your profession and vocation is horribly manipulative and controlling, don't you? And don't you argue with me, I remember your apprenticeship stories, the ones you try not to remember these days."

Elen opened her mouth, then snapped it closed. Arguing wouldn't help.

"Right. Start at the beginning, tell me everything. Who you've talked to, who's been remotely helpful, this friend of his you mentioned. No, wait. Let me clear this up, and put the kettle on, we can go out in the garden for a break. I'm ahead of things today, thanks to your help."

When Amet took charge like that, there was no arguing. Not that Elen wanted to, it would be good to talk it out, all of it, without ducking around the uncomfortable feelings she knew she had for Roland.

CHAPTER 30

MONDAY, MAY 17TH, ROLAND'S ROOM

Roland had been feeling increasingly irritable all day. All of his clothing felt wrong. The sheets and blankets were too heavy, too itchy, too stiff, too flimsy, too cold, and too hot, sometimes second to second. His skin itched too, a dry feeling like sandpaper, only when he tried to scratch it didn't help. It didn't help even before Nurse Eglinton glared at him.

He had been shuffled off to a small meeting, today, in preparation for the one in the Ministry now scheduled for the following week. They had permitted him to be wheeled in the chair. It made him feel entirely put upon and it left him with a sense of pent-up energy, like a river building up behind a dam. He didn't like that feeling, one bit.

The discussion itself hadn't been horrible, not the way some of them were. No one asked him terribly difficult questions. It was more about telling him who would be there, and why they were important. He'd recognised a few names from house parties with his family, all before the War, but no one he knew well. That was probably a blessing. Roland still wasn't clear why they wanted to haul him, in particular, out.

One of the aides there had made a comment about how brilliantly he'd spoken at an earlier event, how inspiring his message was. How it evoked a desire to go forth and do likewise, in the men who listened. Roland had trouble believing that. Oh, he knew how to put things, well enough. And he did, truly, want the best for King and Council and Land. He just was sure, now, that this war wasn't the way to do that. At least not as it was currently being fought.

Of course, none of them ever asked him that. He had his script, near enough, the points he was supposed to make. Roland's job was to let his voice do the work, the way his accent, his bearing, his training as an officer made them sit up and take notice. Perhaps made them strive to be better. He was certain he wasn't the only person who could do it. Though he supposed, in his clearer moments, that having him do it might make more of an impression than someone who'd never been to the Front.

Roland grimaced to himself, liking the implications less and less. He didn't want to be convincing young men, or older men, for that matter, to go and throw their lives away. Something in him twinged, every time he thought about it.

It was one thing to be telling majors and colonels and generals what the conditions were like. Or doing his best to explain how this war was different than what they'd known in the Sudan, or fighting the Boers, or in all the other points in the Empire where fighting flared up. But encouraging ordinary men and women to fight, to go into the jaws of that fatal serpent? That was something different.

No one had asked him, though. He'd gotten his orders, and he could see no way to appeal them, or even to adjust them. No matter how much he thought about it, he couldn't bring himself to mutiny.

It wasn't death he feared, exactly. But he would bring shame on his family, on his fellows, anyone they thought he'd influenced. And he'd never get a chance to do anything meaningful, ever again. When it wasn't the fearful shame that stopped him from refusing, flat out, it was something else. He could never do anything good with his life, if they put him up in a court-martial and found him guilty.

Instead of being able to do anything useful, he had been brought briskly back to his room. Roland had been tucked back in bed, with the kind of brutal distant efficiency only an annoyed nurse and a cowed orderly could manage, afterwards. Harry had brought a mug of beef broth, which helped, and now he was here, waiting for it to be time for dinner. And then time for his potion. Not that he wanted his potion, he would much rather not have his potion, but no one had asked his opinion. Or given him space to share it.

There wasn't much to remember about his evening, but somewhere after his potion, he knew he had to have drifted off. Nurse Eglinton refused to read to him, so he was doomed to his own thoughts until the potion's effects overcame him.

The next thing he knew, there was screaming. Truly terrified screaming, this time, not Elen's startled yelp. It hadn't made sense to him at the time but now, some distant and analytical portion of his mind was measuring out the differences. Pitch, timbre, length. Then something shook the end of his bed, rattling his head and shoulders, and he drew a breath and managed to get his eyes open.

Someone flung the door open, with the bright light of the hallway pouring in and making him squint. He couldn't work out what was going on, at all, but there was someone bustling in, ignoring him utterly, and asking "What happened?"

There was a babble of sound, from the corner, and Roland could only make out bits of it. "He." Then a "Exploded. Just exploded," and the rattling of something.

Roland became rather sure he'd had one of his attacks, and a stronger one than usual. Certainly, Nurse Eglinton was making decidedly more objection to it than Elen had. He pushed himself a little more upright, then suddenly regretted it, as his head began to throb.

He was too far gone himself to make sense out of what happened after that. Someone bustled Nurse Eglinton out of the room eventually, he could hear her sobs receding into the distance. Someone propped his door open, somewhat cautiously. One of the night orderlies, he couldn't see which, perched in a chair outside. He eventually drifted back to sleep, without anyone ever bothering to check if he was all right.

If he had more energy, he'd be horribly offended. And throw a more productive fit.

He woke the next morning, to find Healer Rhoe sitting at the end of the bed. She was shaped entirely differently than Elen, and she was sewing something, rather than knitting, with quick neat little stitches. She glanced up, smiled at him, and slipped the needle into a fold of cloth. "Well, then. How do you feel?"

Roland blinked at her several times. She had the curtains drawn, so the light didn't attack him, just the lamp. Like Elen. He'd been sure she was a tremendously busy woman, from what he'd seen in the baths. Yet here she was, waiting for him to wake up.

"Um." It was not his most coherent. At all.

She set the sewing down, onto the top of something by her feet. "Water? Could you stomach something for breakfast?"

Roland could only blink at her again, trying to marshal his wits and failing utterly. "Healer Rhoe?"

She beamed at him. "Exactly. Tea? Let's start with tea."

Tea was generally a safe guess, he supposed, and he nodded. Then he regretted the movement immediately. She must have caught the flinch, because she said, "I have a pastille for you, it should help the headache."

He didn't try to nod or move, just made the sort of non-committal agreement noise. A moment later, she was handing him a solid mug full of tea, warm but not piping hot, which was good. Then the pastille.

"They don't have any idea why you keep doing that, you know." Healer Rhoe had settled back down in her chair, with an amiable grunt.

Roland focused on taking a sip of the tea, and when that didn't upset anything, he tried another. There was a good minute before he attempted to speak. "Do you know, ma'am?"

She beamed at him. "There we are. Such a polite young man, I keep saying so. And you haven't actually hurt anyone directly, have you? Though I'm afraid Nurse Eglinton might have nightmares for a bit."

"I, what did I do?"

Healer Rhoe shrugged slightly. "There is a lot we don't understand about magic. You're a Schola man, you had many of the same lectures I had, about ritual being the way we shape our magic, give it channels to run in."

"Professor Lollard, yes." Roland remembered those lectures reasonably well. Not the specifics, of course. He'd forgotten half of that after his exams. But the earnestness with which Professor Lollard had lectured about it had stuck, about why changing the proven rituals was dangerous. Then he blinked at her. "I thought healers went to Alethorpe?"

She laughed, cheerfully. "Well, there we are, sure your mind is coming back together properly. Not all of us are Alethorpe's. It's probably good. Now, how do you feel? Start at your head, tell me whatever you feel."

He'd done something like this before, though not quite put that way. "Headache, worse if I move my head. Aching, otherwise, a dull ache, like I used all my muscles entirely too much. And, and." He stopped and swallowed. "I'm starving. Much more than I expected."

"Right. I'm fairly sure I know some of what's going on. What I don't know is how to fix it. And Nurse Morris knew about your moving things around." It wasn't a question.

He nodded very slightly, then regretted it. Not just because of the movement, but because it gave things away. "Do you, wait, did she talk to you?" He felt like he was lurching for any hope.

"She sent me a note, I believe the day they sent her away. I wasn't able to do anything until this morning. It's very difficult to intrude on another healer's case, even after your bath. And it was not a very informative note." Roland bristled, and it must have been visible, because she held up her hands. "She was clearly in a state. Do you know where she went?"

Roland thought back. "She was in a lodging house, for nurses, not far away. She didn't say which one. Her family's Welsh, the Dolaucothi mines, but I don't know if she'd have gone back there. Is she in trouble, do you know? I mean, professionally?"

"Did she actually do anything that would be a problem?"

Roland swallowed hard, and looked away. "She - I was thinking about kissing her." He kept his voice low, barely audible.

When he looked up, Healer Rhoe was watching him, thoughtfully. "The question, my dear young man, is whether she was inclined to kiss you back."

There was a knock on the door, then, and she tsked slightly, before shrugging her shoulders. It changed her posture entirely, from a gentle-featured woman, all curves and softness, to something crisp and martial. That was despite the fact she was still wearing the simple unstructured robes he'd first seen her in.

By the time the door opened, he would have sworn she was done up in the equivalent of a full Victorian ballgown. She seemed armoured with stays and a hoop skirt that made everyone keep their distance and give due deference.

CHAPTER 31

E len waited on the front steps of the Temple of Healing as she'd been told to do. She was in her best uniform dress, a deep blue, but without any of the other pieces. Her token of Sirona was prominently pinned where her watch should be. She wanted to fuss with the apron she wasn't wearing, or the cap that wasn't pinned into her hair. Having her hair bare here felt utterly wrong, even though it was at least properly put up in a sturdy bun.

Elen had her other things with her, the apron and her watch and her cap. all the other pieces of her uniform. She'd been told to bring them. And she had her knitting, for all her fingers itched to be doing something. The letter had said for her to be here promptly at half-nine with all her things, dressed as she was, and so she was here.

As the bells struck the half-hour, with the distinctive pattern of chimes, Elen saw someone come out of the main doors. It took her a moment to figure out who it was, between the light from behind, and the clothing.

Healer Rhoe came forward, wearing a full healer's gown. It was a deeper red than Elen had usually seen, over a brilliant white tunic bordered with deep purple that came down to her ankles. Elen had never seen quite that combination before. She had her dark hair up formally, the kind of hairstyle one would wear to a party with the First Families. It was anchored with some sort of comb in back, and small red jewels pinned into the twists the comb held in place.

It made Elen think of the stories her mother had told her when she was little, about the fierce Celtic warrior women going into battle. Healer Rhoe strode over to her, and nodded once, precisely. "Excellent. Come along, then."

Elen blinked at her. "Pardon, Healer, where?"

"A small ordeal. Nothing actually dangerous." Rhoe's voice had a purring sound to it, something triumphant and even joyous, like she'd managed a particularly fine trick. "Come along."

Elen had no choice but to follow. Healer Rhoe didn't actually drag her along by a wrist, that would be undignified. But she cut through the crowds coming and going from the Temple smoothly, like one of the great ocean liners through the waves. Elen trailed along in her wake.

Their course led to the front of the Temple, by the central dais that served as altar and platform for the greater rituals. There was a small semicircle of senior Healers and administrators standing around the altar, formally dressed, dripping with the robes and decorations of their rank. She felt decidedly small and shabby, in comparison.

She recognised the Archiater, and Sister Almeda, and Healer Cole, but there were others she didn't know, wearing robes that marked them as senior nurses and healers. The Archiater seemed comfortable enough, but Sister Almeda looked strained, and Cole looked entirely ill-at-ease.

Someone came up behind them asking, "Your bag, Therapeutes?" She handed it over without complaint, when

Healer Rhoe nodded once. It gave her a chance to glance around at the rest of the temple, and realise that everyone else was giving the main altar plenty of space.

Not all of them were healers, though, or even from the Temple. One woman wore a tunic pinned together at the shoulders, a broad length of light cloth draping around her torso. Her hair was held up with a complex web of ribbons, dotted with the same sort of gilded pins that Healer Rhoe wore. She had a snake twining up one arm, a living snake, and she was holding a small goblet in her other hand. Elen glanced down, and found there was a small dog at her feet, and a basket, with things in it hidden by the folds of the woman's skirt.

Elen realised this must be one of the senior priestesses of Sirona. She instinctively bent her head. Then she made the small gestures of respectful devotion with her hands, as if cupping water and offering it. The woman was older, perhaps sixty, she had strands of white in her dark hair, but she smiled at Elen. It was a broad smile, as if they were sharing a joke no one other than perhaps Healer Rhoe knew about.

No one said anything to Elen, so she looked at the others more closely. One was a man, in his fifties, with senior insignia and a full Guard uniform. There was a woman who might be from the Ministry, she had the right sort of chain of office for someone from the courts.

There was another man, who looked like Healer Rhoe, especially around the eyes and nose, and the same curling dark hair. He was wearing formal robes of a deep purple velvet, that matched the band on Rhoe's tunic. A compass rose two inches across hung pinned on his chest. That must mean something specific, but Elen had no idea what. All powerful and important people, and she had no idea why they were here.

The Guard coughed. "Therapeutes Morris. Has anyone spoken with you about why you are here?" His voice was steady, a deep bass that rumbled slightly.

"Sir, no, other than the instructions I received by letter. I brought the items requested, nothing else." It had been a very clear and impersonal letter. She hadn't been able to read the name on the signature, but the Archiater's seal had been unmistakably real.

"And you have not spoken to Healer Rhoe, or to anyone else from the Temple of Healing since you were dismissed from service?"

Elen considered. "I was permitted to remain in my lodgings, sir, with the other nurses there. But I kept to myself, I did not talk with anyone there about why I was not serving, or anything else related to my work, only the household necessities." Also, she'd had a horrible headache for the first several days, the kind that had her head throbbing at the slightest movement or light. She'd barely been able to keep down weak tea and broth.

The man who looked like Healer Rhoe got a gleam in his eyes, but he didn't say anything. Elen had worded that as carefully as she could, but honesty compelled her to be clear that she might have talked to other people. Well, one other person, Amet. She hoped they wouldn't ask about that.

"How have you occupied your time?" That was the woman from the Ministry.

"Reading and knitting, mostly, ma'am." Elen kept her voice as clear as she could. "Walking in the park when the weather permitted." She glanced at the priestess, and added, "My personal devotions, as well." Again, leaving that narrow gap. "I took the opportunity to catch up on some of the professional literature, the journals I hadn't had a chance to read."

"Senior Healer Cole has made a demand for your dismissal. He said that you have broken your oaths, the ones you took as Therapeutes. How say you?" They were formal ritual words, from the woman again.

Elen took a breath, steadying herself as best she could. Part of her wanted to cry out at the unfairness, that Healer Cole had not kept his oaths, that she had done nothing wrong. But that would not do her any good here. "I have kept my oaths, ma'am."

That got a little twitch of the woman's chin. "This is not a court of law. Breaking your oath would not be a matter for the courts, unless you also committed a crime. We cannot invoke the magics of Justice here. However, Healer Rhoe has reminded us of an ancient option. Astrophella, here, has offered to provide a suitable ordeal. If you pass, you will be returned to your duties. If not, you will be barred from any further work in any place of healing. Do you understand?"

Elen took a deep breath, hanging onto the first part of that. "I believe so, ma'am. Am I correct that this - this method cannot be questioned further? Whatever the results might be?"

The woman nodded. "Exactly so. You may not appeal the decision - but neither can Cole." Elen began to get the sense this woman hadn't much cared for him, to be using his bare name, not his full title.

Elen straightened her shoulders. "What do I need to do, please?"

That made the man who looked like Healer Rhoe grin for just an instant, she caught the way his eyes danced, before he focused on the priestess, who stepped forward. "I am one of the priestesses of Sirona. The sister who made space for your oaths is, she regrets, unable to travel."

It seemed like there was more she wanted to say but instead the older woman held up the cup. "I will bless the cup. If your oaths hold properly, you will drink it easily. If you have broken your oaths, then you will not be able to swallow it."

That seemed more civilised than most of the ordeal methods Elen had heard of. "How will you know that Sirona has touched it?"

That made the priestess laugh, freely and with delight. "You are a sharp-minded woman, I like that. These fine people are here to observe what happens. We hope there will be an overt sign, the omens and divinations have been promising. If there is no obvious sign, we will have to see what we can discern together."

It wasn't a final answer, then, but still worth doing. If it did solve her problems, all the better, but it seemed like it wouldn't make things worse, unless she really had broken her oaths. In which case, she would deserve what she got.

She remembered making them. It had been in a ceremony here, with the rest of her nursing class, all of them turned out in their new uniforms for the first time. She remembered how the starched cap had felt precarious, compared to the simpler cap they wore in training, and the weight of the watch when her teacher had pinned it on her apron strap. Most of all, she remembered the light and the water, the way it had felt crystalline to her.

There had been a fair set of invocations, to each of the healing deities they were pledging. Hers had been a sizable class, and she had waited patiently for the more commonly made oaths. A few to the Christian trinity, half a dozen to Apollo, more to Asclepius, some to Hygeiea. Then it had come down to those powers who attracted fewer followers and less notice.

It had been perfect, though, with the priestess lifting up her hands, pouring water from one cup to another, then offering it. Elen still remembered the way that tasted, like the purest mountain water, with a sharpness like mint and lavender twisting around each other, but without anything like a flavour.

There was a slight cough, that drew her back to the present moment, and the priestess was smiling at her. "Ready?"

Elen nodded. "At your pleasure."

The answer apparently amused her, and certainly pleased Healer Rhoe, who was standing beside her. The priestess nodded and stepped forward, facing Elen across the altar. As she set the cup down, the dog moved to curl up at her feet again, and the snake slithered from her wrist to form a loose coil on the altar itself.

None of this seemed to bother the priestess at all. Instead, she held her hands over the cup, and began, first in Gallic, long rolling vowels, mingled with clipped consonants, the trilling W for the V. Elen didn't speak it, not more than enough to pronounce some of regular prayers respectfully, but she rarely even got the chance to hear it. However serious the moment was, she felt the sincerity of the priestess.

Nothing happened. Elen tried hard not to feel cheated, or worthless, but she could not quite restrain a flinch. Healer Cole certainly spotted it, his chin went up, and his chest puffed out, as if he was about to say something. The Guard glared at him, and he subsided, without the priestess paying the slightest attention.

Instead, the priestess began to speak, this time in plain

English. "Star-kissed Sirona, bringer of healing, cleanser of illness, you who restores health and wellness to those you touch. Here, in a place sacred to healing, here in a place of oaths, here in a place of the miraculous, we ask a boon. This therapeutes, sworn to you, has had her oath questioned. Grant us knowledge, by right of ordeal, right of the corsned. Fill this cup with your magic, great and gentle lady, and let us know the truth, that healing might be done."

It was a curious proclamation, but Elen's heart was beating faster now, and she couldn't begin to untangle the words. Again, there was no overt sign of anything changing, and again out of the corner of her eye she caught various of the witnesses shifting impatiently.

The priestess waited a moment, for something only she could see, then she lifted the cup, and beckoned to Elen. "Come, drink."

Elen had only one choice, really. She reached across the altar, taking the cup carefully in both her hands. It felt surprisingly heavy, for a small cup. The metal was cool against her fingers, like the waters of her original oath, too cool for the room. Then she closed her eyes, made her own wordless plea to the heavens, and lifted the cup.

It tasted the same. It held the same sharpness, the same refreshing coldness, that washed away everything that was dirty and charred. She didn't pause in the drinking, draining it down in five sizable swallows, before she lowered the cup, and offered it back. She felt no different, but she realised, as she opened her eyes, that several of them had stepped back, instinctively. Including Healer Cole.

Astrophella was beaming at her, reaching to take the cup. As their hands met, the snake shifted from the altar, by Elen's elbow, and twined up her arm, and she felt the smoothness against her wrist. It settled on her forearm, peering at her, tongue flicking out, before it reversed direction, and Astrophella held out her hand for it.

"I believe there is no question, then?" Healer Rhoe's voice was resonant, echoing in the large temple space, though Elen wasn't sure how to name the emotion there. Something Rhoe was suppressing, for the moment, at least.

There was a grumble from several of the witnesses, a wordless grudging agreement, and then several peeled away, and went, mostly separately, to different doors, mingling in with all the other people in the space, coming and going from tending the shrines or making their own personal pledges and prayers.

Healer Cole himself had vanished into the crowd of other people, and Elen could see the flash of his red robes for a moment. It was as if he was sure he did not want any part of the gods anywhere near him. It made her more certain something was wrong in his oaths, but she had no idea how to ask. The Archiater looked after him, considering, and Elen was not at all sure how to read his expression.

The woman from the Ministry inclined her head. "You may return to duty, Therapeutes. Healer Rhoe will explain further, if needed." Then, without saying anything further, she nodded and walked away.

It left Elen blinking, not sure what to do now, and she looked to Healer Rhoe for any help at all. She was whispering to the man beside her. Then she waved at him and said to Elen, "My brother, Cyrus." It was a very uninformative introduction.

He made a slight bow, and he was clearly amused by something, but she couldn't tell what. "Congratulations, Therapeutes." His voice had the measured ease of someone used to people doing what he said, and without argument.

"We should not keep you from your duty. Do you have somewhere you can change?"

Elen let out a breath. "I can find somewhere, sir." Suddenly, she wasn't sure if that were the proper form of address. She glanced around again, but the others had melted away, all except for Astrophella, who had gathered up her basket and settled the snake comfortably in it.

"Come visit us, sister, when you have the chance. At the country shrine. We would love to spend more time with you."

She didn't explain what had convinced everyone either. Astraphella simply turned, and made her way out, the dog trotting along at her side in her own elegant procession of one. Elen realised she was not going to get any answers, and so squared her shoulders, going off to find somewhere to change into her uniform, so she could see Roland again.

CHAPTER 32

LATER MONDAY MORNING, ROLAND'S ROOM

Roland had sunk back into the pillows in the dim room, feeling utterly awful. Whatever it was they had him on felt like it was draining him as the days went on. He had also been entirely alone, bar the meals and assistance from the orderlies, since Nurse Eglinton had been scared away. Since he had terrified her, not to put too fine a point on it.

It was getting on toward lunch, when he heard someone at the door. He turned his head, not really wanting to know who was going to bother him now. The door opened, with a faint creak, then it was closed.

"Well, you're in a fine state, you are."

Elen. Not only Elen, but she sounded surprisingly well. He turned, rolling his head back, and then stared. He didn't know how to describe it, not at all, but there was quite a glow about her.

It wasn't bright, precisely, and yet it was like shouting. It was the kind of light you saw in paintings of saints with halos, or some other divine touch, the way the light shimmered around a fire, how everything was just a little off-set, like looking through clear water. He pushed himself up on one elbow, his jaw dropping open.

"Roland. What's the matter?"

He waved a hand, still without words, just blinked at her. She took a step back, as if surveying him.

"Are you all right?"

That, at least, he could nod at. He was all right. Much better now, actually. He swallowed hard, then managed a sentence, a question. "Did you know you're glowing?"

Her eyes went wide, he could see that much, between her faint glow and the dim light. "Glowing?"

"All of you. Head to toe. Are you - are you all right?"

She didn't answer, instead she came and sat herself down on the end of his bed, as if going any further would mean she collapsed. "Oh. I suppose that's why they let me come back."

"Let you come back? Who let you come back? Why are you glowing? Do you know why?" The questions bubbled out of him.

Elen let out a long breath. Her voice was almost a whisper. "They put me through an ordeal."

Roland looked at her. She was neatly dressed, in her uniform, her hair and cap pinned in place by whatever arcane methods nurses used. If it had been an ordeal, it seemed to have been an unnaturally tidy and well-behaved one. "An ordeal?" Then he ventured, "Start from the beginning, perhaps? When they - I'm sorry, first. It's my fault that they sent you away."

"Your fault?" Her voice was uncertain now.

"I wanted to kiss you. I let it show. I shouldn't have. I should have known that wouldn't be, that I shouldn't."

She went entirely still for a moment, then she reached out a hand, groping for his. "I realised, when I was gone, that I'd wanted you to." Only then did she look up to meet his eyes.

Roland fumbled for her hand, then found it, squeezing it. "Right. Well. Right. I, we can talk about that. Can we talk about that? But not yet. Why are you glowing?"

It was desperately hard to yank his mind back to the essential questions right now, or at least the more immediate ones. And certainly, if he were going to talk about wanting to kiss her, they should do that only when lunch and the necessary interruptions were not looming.

Elen swallowed. "When they, when he sent me away." She was doing her best, Roland could tell.. "I managed to send a note to Healer Rhoe, asking her to check on you. I don't think it made much sense, but I only had a minute before I had to be at Sister Almeda's office."

"Was that awful?" Roland squeezed her hand again, because that was what he could do, and her hand was still in his. He could feel the strength in it, and the little bits of callus. Not like women he'd known before the War, whose hands were smooth, satiny. Who hadn't worked. That was another distraction, and he yanked his attention back to what she was beginning to say.

"Very. They both, they yelled, and they, they made me feel like nothing I'd ever done was right. That I'd failed as a nurse, that I'd failed as, as a person." She let out a long breath, looking down at her lap. "I don't want to talk about what they said. Ever." It came out as a whisper.

"Don't, then." Roland did his best to keep his own voice even. "They sent you away?"

"Suspended me from service, yes. They sent me back to the rooming house, and they said they'd tell me what to do. Only they didn't."

"What did you do, then? Besides knit." He was fairly

sure there had been knitting in there, even if much of it might have been angry knitting she had to redo later. He was rewarded by a little quirk of her lips, not a proper smile, but moving in the right direction.

"There was knitting. After a really awful headache. Eventually I went to see my friend Amet." She hesitated, shying away from something there, and Roland didn't press. "Then I got a letter from the Archiater. I think Healer Rhoe was the reason."

"She came to see me. Not for several days after you left, she said she'd had trouble. And they'd given me a new nurse." He flinched for a moment, at the memory of the scream.

This time, Elen was the one to squeeze. "Don't need to tell me. What happened?"

"I'd had another presentation. I have one, in London, next week. Less than a week, now. Is that why they sent you back?"

Elen shook her head. "I don't think so. I got a letter, telling me to come to the Temple at..." She reached with her free hand to lift the watch. "Half-nine. Two hours ago." She said it as if she wasn't quite sure where the time between had gone.

"They didn't tell you why?" Roland was not entirely sure he approved of that.

Elen shook her head. "Just to be there, out of uniform, what to bring. No warning. I guess, from what they said, that is part of the point."

"They?" Roland was sure he wasn't following this, what he wasn't sure about was whether he was confused, or the whole thing was a tangled mess of confusing points.

"There were a dozen people there. The Archiater. Healer Rhoe. Her brother, I'm not sure why? Healer Cole,

Sister Almeda. Someone from the Ministry, a woman, and someone from the Guard. Other healers, I didn't know them. And a priestess. Astraphella, her name is. A priestess of Sirona." Her eyes went wider, and the glow got a little stronger.

Roland watched her, watched that reaction. "Is that why you're glowing?"

Elen let out a breath. "I suppose so. Healer Rhoe said there was a form of an ordeal. Like the witch hunts, with water or fire or awful things. But this wasn't awful? The priestess, she had a snake and a dog and a basket, and I suppose the basket had eggs, but I didn't see." She cut off suddenly. "I'm babbling."

Roland squeezed her hand. "Tell it however you like. The priestess was there for a reason?"

"The ordeal was that she blessed something in a cup, and I had to drink it. If I'd broken my oaths, it would make me ill, I suppose. Be obvious, somehow."

"Clearly," Roland's voice was dry. "It was the other thing."

It made Elen laugh, and then she smiled and her eyes crinkled properly. She squeezed his hand again and shifted a little more comfortably onto the bed. "They were very firm about it being my oaths that mattered. Not professional ethics, or all the things Healer Cole was yelling about."

"What - um. Pardon, but it is a tad relevant. What precisely are the restrictions?"

"It's not proper to form an affection with your patient." Elen said. "But people do, especially in private nursing, when you're together for so much time. It's not considered appropriate to act on it, while someone is a patient. And certainly, it's a problem if we neglect our duties, or let the affection get in the way of our nursing. If we avoided a treatment that was necessary, but that hurt in the moment, for example. Debriding a wound, or a solution that burns when it's applied, that sort of thing."

"Other than disagreeing with my potion, you have been rather strict with my care. Plenty of making me walk further than I think I can." He wasn't trying to tease, but it came out a bit of one anyway.

She nodded. "I, um. Talking with Amet, she was clear I'd developed feelings for you. And I'll not deny it. But it's not proper to act on them, so can we put that aside, until you're not my patient anymore?"

"How are we defining that?" Roland didn't want to press her, but he did want a clear line to work with.

When Roland looked up at her, Elen was chewing her lip. "How about that you can see to your own basic daily needs - get yourself to the bath, have a manageable walk, a full circuit of the garden, and we've weaned you off the evening potion."

"With or without the canes?"

"Oh, with. But at that point, it would be rebuilding your strength and stamina, and you don't need a nurse for that. Maybe a valet or something with a little bit of specific training." She peered at him. "Do you have a man? A valet?"

It made Roland chuckle. "I did. Should again, sometime, but they wouldn't permit him here. Been with me five years, used to my foibles."

"Your valet, then. Is he, is he somewhere?"

"The family house, I presume. He didn't go to the War with me. He has an ankle brace. Steady as anything when he's wearing it, but wobbly without it, and not fast on his feet."

Elen said, distractedly, "Polio, then?" She used the

name he'd be most familiar with, he expected, rather than the more precise medical name.

"When he was a child, yes. Anyway, he's doing some clerking to free up others to go fight, that sort of thing. So, I will have a man when I need one. What do we do now?"

Elen let out a breath. "Well, I don't know what I'm permitted. Other than being here. They said Healer Rhoe would tell me, but she just sent me off?"

Somewhat predictably, that was when there was a rap on the door, and a "Sir?"

"Yes, Harry." Elen stood, immediately, dropping his hand, which Roland regretted.

"Sister Almeda would like a word with Nurse Morris in the lounge if it's convenient."

They looked at each other, and Elen let out a breath. "If I don't... if I don't come back, I'll find a way to get in touch. Promise."

Roland did not like that at all, but he could not argue. She nodded once, and turned to go out the door.

Elen let out a breath as she came back out of the lounge, and hurried back to Roland's room. To Roland's side, she couldn't fool herself about that anymore. She glanced down at her hands, and thought the glowing might be fading, now. Certainly, Sister Almeda had done her best to avoid looking, as if something about it made her feel uncomfortable.

She knocked on Roland's door. "Major Gospatrick?"

His voice was rather delighted. "Nurse, of course." When she came in, she found him sitting on the edge of his bed, as if he had been contemplating standing up. She tsked.

"Given a particular goal, I am the sort of man who gives his all, Nurse Morris." He was trying to sound relaxed about it. "Unless you have other instructions."

Elen considered, closing the door. "I have permission to guide your recovery as I see fit, consulting as appropriate. Healer Cole is still technically overseeing your care, but has been instructed not to interfere so long as you improve. No. No one's explaining why, I don't know why they aren't just removing him entirely. I can't add potions to your regimen easily, but I can decide you don't need them." She hesitated, and added. "I think they're not sure what to make of the ordeal, who knows what they'll decide next week? Or what that means for him."

"If I don't improve?"

"Then I'm not sure a bit of miracle will save me."

Roland settled more firmly on the bed. "Right. What do I need to do then? No,wait, what do you mean about Cole?"

"The ordeal unsettled him. I mean, Sister Pomona implied that she thought he might have broken his oaths? Only Sister Almeda didn't say they were investigating that, or anything. But she might not tell me. They might not tell her, I suppose. Healer business. Or the Archiater's business, anyway."

"Even though you have exceedingly relevant information." Roland frowned. "I suppose we can't fix that. What do you have in mind for me?"

Elen came around, settling into the chair, facing him, looking at him thoughtfully. "First of all, we're going to try you without that evening potion again. I want Amet to do an analysis of it, so we can figure out what you've been getting."

"Amet is your friend?"

Elen nodded. "We were at Alethorpe together, in the same house and year, and in complementary specialties. Either we were going to be best friends, or we were going to be each other's nemesis or whatever you want to call it."

It made Roland laugh, which was a relief. He'd been a bit intensely focused on her since she'd gotten back. "And she can help?"

"She's an apothecary, fully trained." She considered. "Would Master Dixon be willing to help? Would he know anyone who could do an analysis? The things she can't figure out?"

"Treeve would, yes. You might have to run it over there yourself, but you could leave it with Roger. Treeve, Treeve. He sent a basket along, while you were gone, but that nurse who replaced you didn't approve of the marzipan. And not actually much of the tea, now I think about it. That's there." He pointed at it.

Elen nodded, standing up. "How about we start with tea, then. And marzipan. And I will take your vitals, and get samples ready of your potions, and you will tell me how you've been sleeping and eating and such in detail. Then I'll come up with a plan."

The briskness obviously reassured Roland. "Since we have a mutually desired goal."

"Oh, quite." Elen moved to the table, rearranging things properly, before she picked up the tea canister, spooning it into the teapot before she went to fill it with boiling water. A sound that wasn't the tea against the metal drew her attention, and she peered inside the container. When she looked more closely, she could see an edge of paper was peeking out from among the leaves. "There's something in here."

"What sort of something?"

Elen brought him the canister, and then handed him the spoon she was still holding. "Let me go get the hot water." He nodded absently at her, distracted. By the time she came back, carefully holding the teapot so she wouldn't burn her hands, he had extracted a piece of paper, a small note, perhaps three inches by three. "What's that?"

"A note. Well, a blank piece of paper, but I am quite sure it's a note."

Elen set the teapot down. "How do you know?"

"We used to send each other notes in invisible ink. In school. By which I mean orange juice, mostly. They were easier to come by than lemons, Schola has an orangery." He flicked the paper with his finger. "Do you have a candle or a lamp or something?"

"Open flame is not a common thing in a hospital. Entirely too many flammable vapours."

"The tea pot? No, that won't be warm enough." Roland frowned. "I used to have the knack of it, but I don't know if..." His voice trailed off.

"What sort of knack?"

"Oh, making heat. With magic. Heat, light, solidness. Three great gifts on a battlefield, even if you have to be careful about the light. My father drilled me on them. Relentlessly."

"Your father?" Elen kept her voice careful, he hadn't said much about his family, but after Amet's comments, she had started to wonder precisely why. There were a number of possible reasons.

"He assumed I'd follow him into the military or into the Guard." Roland looked up. "In your professional estimation, may I make an attempt at some magic? Some deliberate magic, rather?"

"You haven't since, since you got here?" Elen had thought about this, since she'd started, but she hadn't been sure how to ask. Ordinarily, that was the healer's role. "Other than whatever it is you do in your sleep?"

Roland shook his head. "I was told it was forbidden."

"Well, that's no good, is it. Honestly, I don't know what they were thinking. That's the sort of thing the Healers are supposed to see to." She came and settled in the chair in front of him. "Let me take your vitals first."

He nodded but held up a hand. "What do you mean by that?"

"Well, your magic is something like water. It's supposed to flow within you. If it's blocked, then it can build up, and come out in unexpected ways. Or it can turn mucky, like a stagnant marsh."

"And that's what happened when I startled you? With the pitcher?"

Elen nodded. "Quite possibly, yes. Mind, since your Healer is supposed to see to that, it didn't occur to me, even though I knew he wasn't doing the proper things. The juniors should have seen to it, it's one of the first things they learn. I know the theory, but I'd want to do a bit more reading up. The question is, why did he want that?"

"And is that awful potion involved?" Roland's voice had turned thoughtful. "They've been so insistent about me taking it."

"Tell me." Elen tapped her fingers together, then drew out her notebook. "I know about the incident with me, there was one with the nurse who replaced me?"

"I rather terrified her. It was, um, Harry would know the date." Roland glanced at her, embarrassed. "I'm afraid I rather lost track of when today is."

Elen snorted. "It's the 20th of May. Thursday. I'll ask Harry. Was there some reason?"

"A presentation. I have another next week, in London."

"Sister Almeda said." That had not been an agreeable thing to hear. "She said she'd get me the travel arrangements by tomorrow, so we could plan appropriately. I suspect an overnight will be needed. I don't suppose you have any friends with a private home there, or something secure, on the magical side?"

"In case I do whatever it is I do." Roland shrugged. "I

wouldn't blame you for not wanting to be with me, after. Not knowing."

"None of that, you." Elen was firm about this. "I wouldn't abandon you to managing it alone. And I do note you haven't hurt anyone so far. Scared a few people, Sister Almeda admitted that's what happened to several other nurses." Getting that confirmation out of her had felt rather a victory, even if she would rather have had useful information.

"Do you think it's the presentations themselves having something to do with it, or the potion?"

Elen leaned back, watching Roland's hands now, the small movements of his body. "I think it might be the inter-action of the two. You're charming, when you're speaking. Charismatic, engaging. There's a theory that says that charm, that attention on you, that's you using your magic. If that's the case, and the presentation gets your magic flow-ing, and then you come back, and take a potion that silts it up again, that might be a cause for the outbursts, all by itself."

"There isn't precisely an easy way to test before London, though, is there?"

Elen shook her head. "And I know you hate the presen-tations. I suppose we could try some of the exercises, for replenishing and renewing your magic. At least now I can go consult the library without anyone getting too upset."

"More books?" Roland leaned back, stretching. "All right. Vitals, and then we see about something simple, is that the plan."

"It is. Do you need anything before we start? The lava-tory, a glass of water?"

He shook his head. "No, actually, I'd rather not put it off." He held out his wrist, for her to take his pulse.

Elen lifted her watch with one hand, settled the other on his wrist, feeling for a moment for his pulse, and waited for the second hand to reach 12. Then she counted, carefully and precisely for thirty seconds, and multiplied it. "Thermometer."

That took another minute or two, for the mercury to register properly, but once she'd done that, she said, "Nothing unusual there. Your pulse is a bit lower, that might be the potion. Did anyone take you out walking?"

Roland shook his head. "Harry did a little with me in the hallway, but only a few minutes. And the food's been awful pap."

"Well. For all they say they want you to get better, they're not doing a very good job of helping that happen."

Roland looked up at her, his eyebrows furrowing. "You wouldn't have said that before."

Elen shook her head. "I wouldn't have. I suspect it's partly the magic." She had to admit that, to herself, if not also to him. "I feel emboldened, is that the right word? And it was clear Sister Almeda's in an odd and uncomfortable position. She couldn't come out and say it, but I'm quite sure she hasn't been at ease with your treatment, either."

"I suppose that's something." Roland paused. "I've been thinking Cole might have something on the orderlies. Is it possible he's got some hold on Sister Almeda, too?"

"How would we know?" Elen let out a puff of breath, frustrated. "She's scarcely going to tell me, now is she? Though if she stops forbidding things, we stand a decent chance or sorting it out."

"Well, then. Magic? Do we try magic?" Then he considered the paper beside him on the bed.

"What does it take, to show this invisible ink, if that's what the note is?"

"Heat, like a candle flame, traditionally. You write the letter with something acidic, citrus or vinegar. There are some specialised recipes out there, but those will work well enough. Then you apply the heat to the back of the letter, and the letters appear."

"Isn't that awfully insecure? The sort of things you might want invisible ink for surely shouldn't be so easy to solve." Elen considered, and said, "Let me get a pitcher of water. Just in case. If you're going to be heating paper."

"That is probably not a bad idea." Roland admitted it with a wry grin. "Since I've no idea of my own strength or lack at the moment. And no, the ink by itself is not at all secure. There are charms and cantrips to hide it unless you also have a passcode. Something similar to the authorised signature prints they use on legal documents these days."

Elen came back from the bathroom, setting the pitcher down on the table, where she could grab it if needed. "And you know what Treeve would use."

"There are benefits to being schoolmates." Roland took a deep breath. "Are we ready?"

"As ready as I'm going to be. How do you plan to do this?"

"If you would take the letter, and be ready to hold it over my hands, not touching, like you would with a candle flame, that will do well. I will focus on calling heat and holding it, and we'll see what comes out. Your notebook is ready?"

Elen nodded. "In my lap." This would require some juggling from here.

Roland nodded one more time, straightening his shoulders. "Here we go." He half-closed his eyes, eyebrows narrowing, as he concentrated. At first, it seemed like nothing was happening, his face looked strained, all his muscles tensing, like he was trying to lift something heavy and failing. Then, suddenly, something shifted, a bit like watching a dam break. Or, Elen thought, with a moment of fear, like watching an avalanche on a mine tailings slope, the moment where everything gave way in a torrent of power and uncontrolled destruction.

That terror passed, though, as she saw Roland's face shift again. He was smiling now, truly smiling, as if something was uncoiling for him. Like he'd been after his bath. That was promising, very promising. He shifted his hands, cupping them together. "Here, try it now."

Elen moved to hold the paper over his hands, so he could read it, and then they both watched, leaning over it, as letters began to appear. Faint at first, they became more and more legible, a sort of odd sepia brown. But even reading upside down, Elen could tell the letters were all jumbled up, and didn't make much sense.

Roland took a breath, and lowered his hands, once the colour was as dark as it seemed to get, rubbing them together automatically. Elen would have suggested it if he hadn't, it was an excellent way to smooth out the magical energies. He took a breath, let it out, and then took the paper from her, holding it in the top corners, thumb on top, very precisely, before he muttered something under his breath. She could hear only a word or two, and it certainly wasn't in English.

As she watched, though, the letters shifted and reformed into words that had the right sort of shape, and certainly fewer Xs and Zeds and thorns in the mix. Roland read it, then turned it around so she could read it too.

"Challenge v. interesting. Send excellent nurse when you can to arrange visit. Must explain in person. T."

Elen blinked at that. "That's not very informative."

Roland waved a hand. "Given enough time, it's possible to break the cypher charm. Will you go round and talk to Roger? And find a time... I suppose he'll have to come here."

Elen considered, thinking about the practical aspects, before she let herself dwell on the implications of that note. "We could have an outing, if he has somewhere secure, somewhere we can get your chair into. Practice for London."

"Ah. Good point. Go round tomorrow, then, and see what he can arrange?"

Elen nodded, but before she could say anything further, there was a knock at the door. "It's Harry, sir. Time for your bath."

I t took them three days to arrange time to meet with Treeve, which was rather faster than Roland had anticipated. In the end, Treeve offered a meeting in the garden of his townhome late Monday morning. It was closer to the Temple, much more private, and an easy walk.

In the meantime, Elen had ruthlessly taken charge. She'd seen to it that he was getting plenty of nourishing food. She'd promptly removed the evening potion. Most of all, she both made him walk increasingly long distances with his canes and had him practising a particular regimen of rehabilitative magical exercises at least three times a day. He couldn't keep count, honestly.

What he knew was that it was working. Yesterday, he'd walked across the entire length of the garden, with just the canes, Elen pushing the chair beside him. He'd had to stop in the middle to rest, but he'd gone the whole way. It had felt like real progress, finally, like he was getting a sense of himself again at last.

Now, she had managed to push him, by herself, along the paved sidewalk toward Treeve's home. Standing outside, by the gate to the garden, was a woman, about Elen's age. She had a light shawl, covering her hair and looped around over her shoulders, as his mother did when she was working on certain contracts in Egypt. Her skin was a deep tan, the bits of hair he could see at the edges of the veil were a dark black.

"Amet!" Elen sounded delighted.

Roland coughed. "You hadn't mentioned?"

Elen leaned down to murmur, "Wasn't sure she'd have something for us yet. Master Dixon said it was all right."

Treeve's man was coming to the gate now, perhaps alerted by the voices. "Master Dixon is glad to receive you. Mistress, Nurse, Major." They made a little procession along the side path from the street to the back garden, moving into a beautiful walled garden that had not changed in all the time Roland had been coming here. Ivy grew up the walls, rose bushes were just beginning to consider budding, and a small fountain burbled at the back.

It was utterly quiet, as well, thanks to the charms and protections Treeve had installed. He was settled at a chair next to a circular table, with a small tray with drinks and cakes.

As he saw them come in, he stood up, waiting for them to be escorted over. Roland waved a hand at Elen, and pushed himself upright. "Treeve. Pleasure."

"It's good to see you, and thank you for coming here." Treeve was business as usual. "Nurse Morris, a pleasure, again. And you must be Mistress Salah."

Amet bobbed slightly. "Master Dixon."

He waved his hand. "Please, do call me Treeve, if we are conspiring together. First, the garden is warded to a fare-thee-well, professionally, by the Guard, and I ensure they haven't left any little ears. My man is entirely trustworthy.

Nurse Morris, I remember you like your tea with a little cream. Mistress Salah?"

"If you are to be Treeve, then Amet, please. And just lemon for me, if you don't mind."

Elen nodded. "And Elen, yes." She accepted the cup of tea. "I'm hoping that the fact Amet is here means there is news?"

Roland settled into his own chair, waiting for Treeve to pass him a cup.

Treeve nodded. "Both of us have some results for you. I am not quite sure what they mean, however." It wasn't like Treeve to be uncertain, which meant they were in deep waters indeed. Then he gestured. "Amet, if you would begin, that might be best."

Amet took a sip of her tea, then set it down precisely in the saucer, gathering herself before speaking. Roland was fascinated by watching her, the ways her manner was similar to Elen's, and the ways it was different. They both had a slight lull, before they did anything of importance, as if they'd been trained to take stock and not to rush.

When she spoke, her voice was clear and crisp. "The sample of the potion I received is rather curious, precisely because it is a blunt instrument. It is a mix of three herbs, at least."

Treeve added, quietly, "Six, but three in trace amounts."

Amet nodded, not offended by the additional information. "The three that I could discern in the time available are a particular type of tincture of poppy, an alchemical preparation of lemon balm, and a rather strong dose of valerian. By themselves, all preparations used regularly by healers, but the method and mechanisms of combination suggest they were thrown together, with some sort of alchemical layer, to produce a particular effect."

Roland followed that much, for all his alchemy and potion-making skills were minimal at best. "The goal being to drug me for the night, then, no matter how they went about that?"

"But aren't those all things that are used routinely? Common herbs, well. The poppy's more usual for pain, and there are concerns about the use, but it has a purpose." Elen was thinking out loud, and Roland was glad she wasn't too overawed by Treeve to do that.

Amet snorted. "Just because we can use herbs sensibly doesn't mean we do, you know that." She then inclined her head at Treeve. "Though I'm guessing there's a bit more to it than just the herbs."

Treeve nodded. "The thing I notice is that, on the whole, all of the ingredients are quite inexpensive. I don't claim to know all of the healing potions, or the apothecary standards, but the poppy is relatively easy to come by, widely used, as I understand it, and the other two grow abundantly in our climate."

"The other three ingredients, according to my analyst." He tapped a pile of papers by his right hand. "All alchemical distillations of similar status, heavy handed, but inexpensive to produce. Though two of them have some research attached to them that suggest they can have an effect of blocking one's magic, they're sometimes with prisoners awaiting trial for that purpose."

Roland tapped his fingers. "We'd wondered about the block on the magic." Then he considered further. "You think there's something in them being all inexpensive ingredients then?" He could follow Treeve's suggestion. "I don't know much about the usual sort of thing for the Healing Temple. Elen? I presume it's not that you give the least expensive dosage possible, even if it's not very effective. Or worse, damaging."

Elen shook her head and again, Roland noticed that small lull before she spoke. "No. The Temple of Healing is funded by a combination of the Ministry, various private donations such as the Garden Party every year, the winter gala, and so on. Bequests, and a certain percentage of money forfeited to the Ministry, I believe." Treeve nodded at that. "And then there are requested donations from families who can afford it, especially for more complex cases."

"For which I qualify. The family's not short of coin, and I've certainly been there a fair while. Would that ordinarily be in my file?"

Elen shook her head. "Only a brief notation, if that. Everyone is supposed to get the same quality of care. On the other hand, normally, I'd expect that you'd have better care, not worse. All those things in the potion, they're very blunt instruments, to keep you muzzy-headed and exhausted." She considered, then asked, "And the daytime potion?"

"That one is less sedating, and it seems to be a mix of more or less nutritive herbs." Treeve glanced at Amet, who nodded in agreement. "Much less damaging. I assume you are not taking the evening one at this point?"

Elen answered, quite promptly, and Roland let her share her expertise. "Entirely off it, and improving rapidly now."

Amet furrowed her forehead. "Elen, do you have your notes on what you found in his file?" Then she looked up, obviously worried she'd said too much.

Treeve waved his hand. "I gather that Elen has been most resourceful. Why would I tell them something they're apparently not bothering to notice or correct?"

Elen half-smiled at that, and then rummaged back in her notebook to the list, reading them out, one by one. Amet immediately grimaced as she got to the last name. "Those aren't the potions he's getting. The two that are listed as current, they're actually both quite expensive. One has saffron in, for example, and the other has a mushroom that's quite rare and difficult to harvest. A few other things like that, I'd have to check the formulary. It's not anything we make, mind."

Treeve had rather lit up, the way he always had, when he saw a particular puzzle forming before him. "Oh, now, that's quite my line of expertise. One of them. How much do you think the potions would go for, if they were being made for the Temple?"

Amet looked down, doing the maths in her head, Roland suspected. "A full dose, taken every night, that would be, well. Half a senior healer's salary for the day, or better. For each dose, and you've been there for months. I can check the numbers when I get back to our records."

Roland blinked. "And they'd be asking my family for that?" It wouldn't bankrupt them, certainly, but the family did not have that kind of money to be spending foolishly.

"For at least a portion of it, yes." Elen shook her head. "Is that why the Ministry is fussing so much about you getting back to fitness? Could they be asked for some of it? Since it was due to battlefield injuries?"

Roland contemplated that. "That gives me something concrete I can ask Cadwell, at least. He'd be able to figure out the usual process, I suspect. Mind, this war is quite different from our earlier ones, and I'm sure that's affecting the approved procedures." He tried to count the days and failed. "If he's still in the country, he was getting sent overseas sometime soon."

Treeve waved a hand. "I'll set Roger on it. Last name?"

"Cadwell Deschamps." Then he added, "You might not remember, his brother was our year. Died two months ago, nearly three now."

"A loss." It came out flatly, then he turned his attention to the practical, as Treeve generally did. "I will see about finding him. Who else do you think knows about a potion exchange?"

Elen chewed on her lip for a moment. "I think Sister Almeda must know, and I don't think she approves. But he might have some influence over her, somehow." She then flicked through her notebook.

"The administrator I saw, the one who gave me permission for adjustments, she might be worth speaking to. Sister Florinda." She paused. "Healer Rhoe and Sister Pomona were both helpful to me, but this isn't their area of specialty. There were two women who were talking about accounts, and maybe Sister Pomona figured out who they were?"

"And have you found out anything further about Healer Cole?" Treeve was making notes about both the names.

Elen shook her head. "Not much, but I asked the librarian, at the Temple, when I was checking on resources about what to try next a few days ago. Casually, you know, they keep profiles on all the healers." She had mentioned it to Roland, but they hadn't been able to decide what it meant.

Treeve leaned forward. "And?"

"Healer Cole was in South Africa and India, for a number of years, nearly forty. Long enough that not that many people here would remember him. The senior healers when he apprenticed would have retired."

"And other Healers he apprenticed with?"

"I couldn't find that out without being rather obvious about my questions, but they could just be spread out.

Anyone who could help with the War might well be focused there."

"What was his speciality, originally?"

"Healer Cole trained as a surgeon, but I gather he did a bit of everything overseas. And Sister Pomona pointed out that people may stop being surgeons, after a certain age. However..." Elen hesitated. "I didn't find anything that made sense of why he'd be assigned this case. No speciality in magical injury, or anything like that. Though the War is bringing in cases that don't fit tidily into our specialities all over the place."

Treeve frowned. "Indeed. I will see what I can find through my sources. You let me know if you learn any more." He tapped the book. "Roland, would you like to see your family, or would you rather not?"

That made Roland grimace. It was like Treeve to go to the heart of something complicated without noticing it was difficult. "They've not written. I don't even know if they're in the country right now." It sounded entirely feeble to him, and even if they were out of the country, he'd have expected to be hearing from Nanny. "One thing at a time. Let's take the mess in London first, maybe?" He asked Elen, as much as said it outright.

Elen nodded. "That might be fair." When Treeve looked puzzled, she added "Roland is being shipped off to London for a discussion or demonstration or whatever they want to call it. I'm to go with him, at least, and it's not far from the Bedford Square portal, I gather."

"Ah." Roland wasn't sure how to take that. "For next week or so, then. Right." There was a soft cough from about ten feet away, and all of them turned to see Roger waiting. "Sir, I'm afraid your next appointment will be waiting."

Treeve pushed himself up. "Take your time heading

out, if you would like. I'll be in touch. Amet, with you sooner than later, I suspect."

Amet nodded. "I should get back as well, if you both don't mind."

Elen shook her head. "Not at all. Send a note round."

Amet grinned. "Try and stop me." Then she reached for Roland's hand, to shake it, quite deliberate. "A pleasure to meet you, and I hope to have a chance to talk more soon."

Roland was pleased she approved, at least, but when he looked up at Elen, she had the kind of expression he suspected was universal when a good friend was perhaps amusingly predictable.

E len had worried, without ceasing, the last three days. She had been sure something awful was going to happen. But now here she was, through the London portal, with Roland. Harry was pushing his chair, and they had a short walk to the inn where they had rooms. Roland would have time to rest before the presentation this afternoon, and they would stay the night, so as not to do two portal trips in the same day.

Roland had taken one look at the inn, and snorted. "What I expected."

Elen asked him, once they were in their rooms, what he meant. The rooms themselves were entirely reasonable. They were panelled in wood and plaster. It was the sort of generic Tudor common in many buildings aiming at quaint rather than the heights of Georgian elegance.

They had two adjoining rooms with a door between them. Someone had arranged space for Harry in the attic, with a bell to summon him as needed. She had a rather broader bed than the one in her lodgings, and his was downright spacious.

Thinking about the size of his bed made her blush. It was as if being out of the hospital made it possible for her to think about what it might be like, to be intimate with him. What his interest - and hers - could lead to. He was a hand-some man, and more importantly a kind and thoughtful one. Why he was interested in her, she still wasn't sure, but she wanted, very much, to find out if their feelings for each other lasted beyond his care.

"This is exactly the sort of inn the Ministry puts people in, when they are on official business. It's somewhere private enough, and comfortable enough, and with decent food, but excellence is not required in any dimension." He gestured. "There must be a dozen of these in different places, all near enough identical except for the details of the bric-a-brac. Father and I used to play games of telling them apart, when I was with him over the summers, in my school years."

"You'd travel with him?" Being away from his room in the Temple seemed to have changed things for him as well. This was more about his family than she'd heard yet, and she could hear his fondness.

"Occasionally. Sometimes there were training exercises, and he thought it was educational for me to see those, when it was a public demonstration or display. My last two years at Schola, I'd act as his aide during hols if he didn't need to bring a proper one. Fetch and carry, take notes, all that."

Elen nodded. They were sitting in Roland's room, at the table and chairs, having finished an early lunch that was indeed unremarkable. Not bad, that would have been notable. Just there. The scone had been promising. "You should have a rest. I gather we're to leave at half-two." It was half-eleven now. "When do you want to change?"

"Two would be fine. I do feel much the better."

"You keep saying that." Elen helped him settle into bed, and went off to her own room, leaving the door cracked between them.

In the end, getting to the presentation turned out to be fairly simple. It was in a Ministry-owned building on the edge of this area of magical London. Roland murmured that like the inn, it was kept for just such meetings. It seemed to soothe him to explain things to her, and she honestly appreciated it. Other than passing through a few train stations during her deployment to the French hospitals, she'd barely had any contact with the non-magical community.

Once they were there, a man younger than Roland took over the arrangements. He made sure Elen had a cup of tea, and a place to observe, well out of the way. It was a sizable room, a long conference table able to fit fifteen or so. Roland was positioned at one end, facing the door. He looked most sharp in his uniform, and he was managing very well with the canes, now. And she at least felt properly dressed, in her uniform dress without the pinafore apron, but with her watch and her own signs of rank properly showing.

People filed in, with an exchange of salutes. A couple of the uniforms were from the magical side, she recognised the special insignia they wore, the single red ring worn on the collar. She could see three of them, and one more she couldn't be certain of, with the angle and the slant of the light.

It was all men, besides Elen, which was one difference. She was used to the Guard, when she saw people in uniform. While they were fewer than half women, she'd never been the only woman in a room like this before. Mind, she'd never been in a room like this, but Roland had been clear that she should stay with him. They had talked through, in their plans for this, about what she could do if his magic flared, and of course she had a handful of emergency potions on hand.

As expected, things began precisely on time. There was a brief reminder that the discussion today was covered under the oaths they had taken, referencing something called the Official Secrets Act. She assumed it must be something similar to their oaths on the Silence, or at least everyone seemed to be nodding and taking it seriously.

Roland was introduced by a person she assumed must be senior by the number of bars on his uniform, whose name she didn't catch. There were a round of introductions, two from their own community, the rest from non-magical units.

Elen didn't have the knowledge to make sense of all of what they did. She knew infantry and artillery, and she knew about the dragoons thanks to Roland. Naval units made sense, too. But she wasn't sure what they meant by airborne units, or engineers. No one bothered to explain, and Roland apparently understood enough of it to be getting on with.

The presentation began by Roland stating what he'd been asked to do. That was to provide a precis of the potential of troops from Albion, fighting alongside the British non-magical ones, based on his experiences. He argued, and quite well, she thought, for the benefit of the magically skilled in carrying and conveying messages, in healing in certain circumstances.

He argued that each soldier's life held value, but that those with magical training should be treated as skilled experts. Anyone who had come out of the Five Schools, certainly anyone who had completed their apprenticeship, had years of exceptional training behind them. He had a particular angle, there, that she'd never asked him about.

He had been speaking for about ten minutes, when an older man with a striking resemblance to Roland came in quietly. He settled without a word in a chair against the wall, like Elen's but on the other end of the room. Roland visibly startled, but then gathered himself, promptly, continuing with almost no hesitation.

It gave Elen a chance to examine the newcomer. He was wearing several medals, and his uniform suggested a rank of major general, or perhaps lieutenant general. She couldn't quite see the insignia fully from where she sat.

About then, the presentation shifted to questions, and Elen needed to pay much closer attention to Roland. She could hear his voice getting rough, and see the slight shake in his hand. She didn't have the authority to stop any of this, but she could see a pitcher of water on the side table, and glasses.

As quietly as she could, she poured a glass, and brought it over. She waited to one side of Roland, until someone asked a question. When he took a breath, she slipped it in front of him. He nodded, briefly, but with a smile at her. "My attending nurse, Therapeutes Morris." She hadn't expected that, usually people wanted them to be invisible.

Eventually, the questions ran down, then there was a general round of thanks and formalities, while Roland smiled and nodded from his chair. He did stand once, to salute properly when his own direct line of command left. The room emptied quickly, except for the man in the corner, the aide who had made the initial arrangements, and Elen.

"Give us the room, please, Thorndike." That was the man in the corner. Thorndike, the aide, blinked and made a quick retreat.

Once it was just the three of them, Roland said,

"Father." He sounded cautious, but not unfriendly. Clearly, he wasn't at all sure what to expect.

"We have a few things to talk about. Perhaps Therapeutes Morris would prefer to take a short break?" It was entirely polite, and also surprisingly not a command. Something about his tone made it clear to Elen, never mind Roland, that his father was leaving the choice up to him.

"Please stay, Elen." Roland's voice was clear and strong. "If you'd come take a seat, here?" That too was a request, and not a command, but of course she would.

His father raised an eyebrow at the first name. When Elen took her seat, Roland nodded. "Elen, my father, Major-General Arthur Gospatrick." Famous heroes, indeed, and he was named in part for his father. It figured. "Father, this is Therapeutes Elen Morris, my nurse."

"The current nurse? I gather there have been a few."

"Once and future." Roland made it a bit of a joke. "She was reassigned elsewhere, and then assigned back to me. I've been improving rapidly since she's been given more free rein in my treatment."

"Ah. About that." Arthur cleared his throat. "First, your mother has a few things for you, they are in my bag, if it is convenient to give them to you now. If it is not, if you would let me know where to send them. You haven't answered our letters, so we weren't sure, and Admantine made it clear she thought very little of your hope for recovery. But then Captain Deschamps mentioned he'd seen you, so it wasn't that you couldn't get in touch."

Roland's expression went through several rapid changes, then settled on a sort of burning need Elen had never seen from him before. "I have not received any of your letters, sir." The last was clearly a comfortable formality they were both used to, rather than a method of distancing. "Nor any package, other than one Treeve sent recently. And I suspect his aide brought that round in person."

Arthur nodded sharply. "Indeed." Elen could see he seemed to be calculating several rows of figures that boded very poorly. "Who are we aiming your mother at then, do you know?"

That broke the tension, and Roland laughed. "That is a good question, though we have recently worked out some pieces of it." He hesitated. "We should not discuss that here."

"No. I need to be back at my office at six, a working supper. Do you have a suggestion?"

"We have rooms at the inn near here. I suspect the tea is the best of their service, honestly. Fake Tudor, metal steins in odd places, and too many flowers on the tea sets, I rather suspect, but otherwise quite reasonable standard from what I've seen so far."

His father nodded, then he took a breath, looking at the canes beside Roland's chair. "How much support do you need, son? Or may I," He hesitated exactly the same way Roland just had. "Therapeutes Morris, if I might ask your professional opinion?"

Elen inclined her head, sharing the briefest of glances with Roland. "That might be better in private as well, sir." She didn't know if it was proper to encourage him to call her Elen. Or even Nurse Morris, in the less formal language.

"Like that, then. Shall I go on ahead and arrange tea to go up to your room?"

Roland nodded slowly. "That might be easier. We won't be long. Elen, if you could get Harry from wherever he's lurking?" He added to his father, "The orderly with us. We're to go back tomorrow morning."

It took a few minutes to sort out getting themselves out the door and down the street. Elen took the chance to ask quietly, "What should I know?"

"Behave as you see fit, it will be good for him. And you, I suspect." That was teasing, but not out of bounds for Harry to overhear. He then added, over his shoulder. "Harry, we'll be having tea with my father, and I'm sure Nurse Morris can arrange for sandwiches or whatever for supper. If you'd like to go out for a drink we can manage once I'm back in my room, I think."

Harry mumbled a "Sir," and kept on with the pushing.

CHAPTER 36

LATER THAT AFTERNOON

"So, the agenda. Who we are aiming your mother at, and Therapeutes Morris's professional evaluation of your recuperation. Perhaps we might take the latter first."

They were settled around the small table in Roland's room, with a tiered cake stand to one side. Elen sat with her hands in her lap, except when she was sipping her tea and Roland suspected she desperately wanted her knitting. He understood the instinct now, but his father wouldn't.

"Elen?" He kept his voice even, deliberately using the informal. He added, "And use whatever name you'd prefer for me."

"Nurse Morris, if you'd rather." Roland's father inclined his head. Elen went on. "I served at a field hospital in France, where I was injured in a building collapse, with lingering headaches that prevented my staying there. I came back to the Temple of Healing to seek an assignment where I might be useful."

She swallowed, then went on. "My background is in long-term care, for those recovering from significant lengthy illness. From the beginning, there were oddities about my assignment to Roland's case. I was not permitted to see his file, nor to recommend any changes to his potions regimen. Normally, I would have coordinated with his attending Healer, regular meetings."

Arthur nodded slowly. Roland knew that expression, the way he was listening intently, to what Elen said and what she did not say. He was pleased she'd chosen to use his first name. His father would pick up on that, certainly, but it was strategically useful to have it become clear now, when his father and mother would be inclined towards anyone who had been of actual help to him. "And what were you permitted?"

"Initially, to sit with him, see he had his meals and to take him out to the garden, in a chair. I got him walking short distances again, but I believe being outside is often as restorative as anything else."

She considered, and Roland could see she was thinking through how to present what had happened. "After a month, I was called in to make a report to a Sister Florinda, one of the administrators. A step down from the Archiater. She could not get me access to his file, but she did tell me who the attending healer was, and gave me permission to taper the potion I felt was causing the most difficulty."

Roland cleared his throat. "Sir, we have since discovered that potion - the evening one - is a mixture of low-cost sedatives, and not what we believe it should contain. Treeve had it analysed just a few days ago, and a friend of Elen's, a full apothecary. We were trying to decide what to do about that information."

"And you could not know that I had arranged to get you away from Trellech for a day." His father sat back, looking briefly gleeful.

Roland couldn't stop his jaw from dropping, he knew his father would crow about that for years, to the right audiences. "Sir." It was an admission of brilliance.

"I didn't know - we didn't know - if you did not wish to speak to us, if you were unable to reply, if you were being prevented from doing so, if you were not getting our messages. The last, as you said, but the others, I do not know about. Only then Captain Deschamps made a point of letting me know he'd met with you, twice. If you did not wish to speak to us, I wanted to hear it directly."

Roland let out a long breath, glancing at Elen for a moment. "You were afraid I didn't wish to speak with you, sir? You and Mother?"

His father nodded, just once, precisely. He said, for Elen's benefit. "I am the commander in charge of the magical troops serving with His Majesty's armies. My rank is complicated, but considered equivalent to a Major-General. I have seen a number of men sent home who were ashamed of their injuries. Or injured in ways that damaged their magic." He let his voice trail off. Of course he wasn't able to ask directly.

Roland coughed once. "Elen, feel free to explain?"

"Sir." Her voice had gotten softer, as if she had fought this particular skirmish before, had a plan, and knew exactly what to do with it. "Your fears are quite common, after a significant injury, especially when you had so little information about what was going on."

She shifted in her chair, to face his father more directly. "We've only been able to discontinue the evening potion in the last week, but the signs so far are promising. Roland was able to call heat - a skill he said you trained him in thoroughly - as well as light."

Roland could see his father relax, as Elen went on. "I

believe the potion was interfering with his magic, there's a fair bit of evidence for it. I anticipate he will be fully returned to strength in a few months, though whether he is best sent back into battle may be a different question. I have complete notes if that would be helpful, during my time with him."

That got a laugh out of his father, despite the seriousness of the situation. "Are you that diligent with all your patients then? Or my son in particular?" Roland noticed, but was not surprised, that his father did not comment on the other part of that, whether Roland might be declared fit again. Or what for.

Roland though some encouragement might be a help here. "Speak freely, Elen, if you're concerned on my account. You know my feelings on the matter."

Elen gathered herself, visibly. "All my patients get my best, sir, of course, but your son and I have discovered a mutual interest beyond that role that we have discussed exploring when he is no longer under my care." The sentence might have come out all prim and tight, but there was a slight bobble of her voice in the middle. Roland reached out his hand instinctively, and she took it, then looked up at his father.

"Who are your people, then?" His father was at least not angry. "I know there is a fair bit that goes into nursing training. You were at Alethorpe?"

Roland knew perfectly well that as soon as his father had five minutes, he would be getting his hands on Elen's complete files, to the extent he could. Elen clearly knew it too. "Alethorpe, yes, sir, then an apprenticeship in the Temple. My father is administrator at the Dolaucothi mines, sir, and my mother was a teacher at the village school. Not fancy people, sir, Fourth Families, but proud of their work."

"And proud of you?" His father said it easily, then must have read something in her expression, because he leaned forward, looking more closely. "No. Not sure what to make of you, I expect. I know enough of the Temple to know you must be quite skilled. They don't generally suffer fools, especially not among the nursing staff." He nodded at Roland. "Do you have theories about the reason for your ineffective potion, beyond the fact of it?"

"We were working on that, sir, when I had to come here. My attending healer was one Ozymandias Cole. Mind, I've only seen him once, I'm aware of. When he sent Elen away, and lectured and prodded me. He dresses suspiciously well."

Elen added, "I only saw him at my reinstatement. It was set up by another senior healer, Healer Rhoe. I am not sure her precise formal title, but she oversees the baths, including the ritual baths." She nodded at Roland. "Roland had one he found helpful and restorative."

"Your particular devotion, Nurse Morris?"

She considered for a moment. "If you would prefer to call me Elen in private, sir, considering everything." Roland squeezed her hand and smiled his approval, and she continued. "Sirona, sir. She has a particular affinity for the longer processes of healing and restoration."

"And what would you prefer as an assignment? Where were you before the War?"

"Before the War, I was at The Temple of Youth. I enjoyed it, it was often very satisfying work. But I'm not sure I want to go back to it, I would rather be taking on a new challenge."

"And your injury, is that still a consideration?"

Elen waited before answering, weighing her answer. "My duties tending to Roland have been very slow paced, and not demanding of stamina, other than long hours. Having a single patient, not having to split my attention, orderlies for the heavy work, plenty of time to sit and read or knit and talk."

She hesitated, and Roland thought this was because she hadn't discussed this with anyone, yet. "I have had a few bad headaches, but not many, and they seem to be improving. I am due for another discussion with the healer in charge of my case next month, but I think the recommendation will be that I not return to the front, or to any battle hospital, but instead find a permanent position elsewhere."

"At the Temple in Trellech or something else?" His father was leaning forward now, tapping his fingers. Roland recognised the sort of plotting that would amuse his mother.

"The Temple of Healing comes with rather a lot of politics, sir, and I am not sure I have handled them well." That sort of frank admission, on the other hand, was exactly the sort of thing that would endear her to both Roland's mother and his father. They both appreciated someone who knew their skills and their lacks.

"We will see if we can improve some of that. I know of Healer Rhoe by reputation, she is no small ally to have. And now that we may more conveniently talk to Roland, we will be glad to assist to the greatest degree he permits."

Roland raised an eyebrow. "I'm scarcely going to decline, sir."

His father laughed. "One should give you the opportunity to, but I am glad that you are not inclined to have a tantrum about doing it yourself. Not that you ever did too much of that when you were two or three."

Roland replied, just as amused. "Mother would have

none of it. Nor Nanny." He added to Elen, "Nanny is a cousin of Mother's from a not very well off line of the family. She still lives there, keeping an eye on things when Mother is away, as she often is." Then he gestured. "You'll need to get back to the portal soon, sir. What else do you need to know now?"

"We have a curious set of behaviours from a senior healer. We have a potion that uses largely cheap ingredients, and they have been requesting a supplement for your care that would suggest, oh, at least three nurses and regular hampers from Lleision and Dyfodwg to cover your meals." That being one of the best fancy hampers in Trellech. "Plus, perhaps, some gold in the daily potions."

Roland winced. "My pardon, sir."

Elen opened her mouth and then closed it. Roland's father raised his eyebrows. "Out with it, we need all the ideas we can get."

"Sir." Elen gathered her thoughts. "I overheard a conversation weeks ago, out in the garden. Two women who handled the forms and paperwork. I didn't hear their last names, but one was Berth, from south Wales, originally, and her friend was Clarice. They were talking about oddities in the paperwork, and they mentioned Healer Cole among others. They didn't have anything concrete they could report, and I think that frustrated them. I mentioned it to Sister Pomona, one of the senior nurses. She couldn't help me much directly, but she might know who else to talk to."

"Ah, now, that should be most useful. What is the best way to get word to you, then, that is reliable? Treeve, or someone else?"

Roland deferred to Elen. "You know the Temple best, though I don't know where the messages were being blocked."

Elen considered. "If you send it to my friend, Mistress Amet Salah. She apprenticed under Master Luther, if you're familiar with his shop?"

"I do know him, though mostly by reputation. That will do quite well, if you would be so kind as to let her know we will be in touch, likely promptly and frequently, until this is resolved." He then stood. "Roland's mother will be interested to meet you, we will see about arranging some sort of suitably neutral territory. She can be a touch intimidating, even with people she likes. I do hope Roland has mentioned."

Elen smiled a little. "He did mention she is impressively competent, sir. I - let me give you a few moments, perhaps, while I step away?"

Roland did not protest, he did want a few words with his father. Once she had retreated into the other room, he looked up. "Sir?"

"We will sort out your treatment. She seems most competent. Plain-spoken, yes, but that is no bad thing in a nurse. You intend to take this seriously, then?"

Roland nodded. "With or without your encouragement, sir, and Mother's. But I would prefer with."

"The circumstances do incline me, at least, to not judge too hastily. You were very badly off, then?"

"Extremely, sir, and barely knowing my own way through it. She has been kind, reliable, and competent, and also quite brave. We didn't mention what brought her back, but that is a story I'd prefer to tell Mother myself."

"I will tell your mother that more is in the offing then. I presume we will be seeing you at the Temple or some such, before too long, but you have only to send a letter if anything untoward happens." The clock chimed, and he shook his head. "I must be off."

At just that point, Elen knocked once, and said, "Sir, oh, yes."

"Elen, I am delighted to know my son has been in good hands, and I am sure his mother will feel the same. We will be speaking more, and soon, I hope. Do write if anything changes, Roland will tell you how to reach me quickly. Take care."

It was rather like a river going through a dam, all that controlled power, restrained for a particular goal. Once his father left, Roland took a deep breath, and felt a relief and security he hadn't felt since he left for France.

CHAPTER 37

THAT EVENING, IN LONDON

O nce Roland's father had left, Elen closed the door behind him. She turned back, to see Roland watching her carefully.

"How much did I complicate things?" She took a breath, taking a step back.

Roland pushed himself upright, and then held out both hands to her. "Come here, if you will?" It was the most cautious, careful request she'd heard. Of course she went. He immediately pulled her into a gentle hug, an embrace like she hadn't had from a man in years, just Amet or one of her other friends. He was steadier on his feet than she'd expected, and sturdier, over all. She did not want to pull away, not one bit.

"I know we cannot, as you say, act on our explorations, yet. But may I, may I kiss you? In hopes of the future?" He sounded wistful, more than anything else, like the promise of the kiss meant a great deal more to him than he was able to say.

She took a breath, trying to do the sums in her head about where her lines were for this. On one hand, he was her patient. On the other hand, unless he had a relapse she did not expect, she didn't think he'd be her patient for long.

A fortnight, a month, before the main need would be rebuilding his strength in whatever energetic mode he preferred. She'd touched him before, of course, but his shoulders under his uniform were broad, even if the muscles needed rebuilding.

None of this was answering him, and she was leaving him hanging. And herself. She nodded, once. "In hopes," she agreed, before her voice cracked.

He got his arm more steadily around her back, giving her enough space to tilt her head up, to meet his, while he bent to her. As their lips met, she could feel his other hand come up to her shoulders. Then the kiss was everything.

She could almost taste his magic mingling with hers, a sort of salty-ocean mixed with something green and fresh like a herb garden caught on the breeze. They both lost themselves in the kissing for longer than she'd expected, and only pulled back when they both mutually ran out of breath.

He straightened a little. "A great many hopes." He coughed, once. "Perhaps, give me a minute to change into something more comfortable? And you might want to do the same?" He shifted his body, and she could feel what he wasn't saying, that he'd found it quite arousing.

She lifted on her toes to kiss his cheek once, fleetingly. "Let me know when you're ready." With that, she retreated into her adjoining room, first slipping on a tea gown in a mid-lavender. It was a frock from last year, and not one she'd wear out in public, with the war on, the colour being a bit too optimistically cheerful. She hadn't been sure tonight would be suitable for it, but she'd wanted something that wasn't all about the War, somehow.

She undid her hair from the tight bun at the back of her head, considered for a moment, and then braided it loosely, letting the weight drape down her back. Soft slippers went on her feet, and it was a relief to get out of her formal shoes, especially after all the travel earlier and standing and waiting. Finally, she took out the knitting project she'd tucked away in her carpet bag, the one she'd told him about but never shown him.

"Come back when you're ready."

Elen opened the door. Roland had changed into a deep burgundy smoking jacket and - well, she knew they were clean pyjama pants, but they looked quite civilised. Before she could say anything, he blinked at her. "My, that's a difference. And a lovely colour on you. Why do they make nurses wear such dark colours?" Then he gestured. "Chair? Bit of the bed? What's your pleasure? I admit I don't want a chair for a bit, my back is aching."

"Dark colours don't show stains." Practical, if depressing. "And I suppose, the bed." It was most forward, but they were both clear on what they were moving toward. And she wanted to be beside him, more than anything. "The jacket?"

"Been tucked away. I don't exactly have somewhere to wear it." He then gestured at the knitting in her hand. "Is that what I think it is?"

"The infamous shawl, yes."

He glanced at it, then at her dress, then back at the deeper purple yarn. "They go together, don't they? Or could. I admit I'm not very good at that, uniforms are very soothing that particular way."

She nodded. "I wouldn't wear this dress out, either. Not now. Too - too cheerful." With that, she took a breath, and settled next to him on the bed, perching for a moment before she gave into her impulses and settled further back, leaving her feet hanging.

"I'm most glad you wore it for me. And brought your shawl. Can I see the lacework, then?"

Elen looked up, trying to decide if he meant it, or if he were just being kind. She found he was leaning forward, his eyes as bright and engaged as he had been talking to his father. She looked down at the shawl, then spread it out, leaving one needle stuck in the ball of yarn she was working from. "Careful of the other end."

"Can't be losing your stitches, no." He let her hold onto it, as she spread the work she'd done so far from her hand over onto his lap.

Looking at her work, she wasn't sure it was showing to best effect, for all she kept it carefully folded up. She was perhaps a third done with it, but it was going to be quite long when it was done, a good seven feet. But the stitches themselves were a bit crumped up, not as open as they would be eventually.

The yarn though, looked grand, a smooth spun fine purple. It had a vibrancy that she loved. More than that, the yarn was soft and easy on her hands, unlike the coarser stuff for the war, that had to stand up to mud and repeated harsh washings.

It was hard to have someone examining her work, even if she knew he was not the most demanding viewer of her knitting. She'd had a few pieces in craft and domestic arts shows in the past, and won the occasional prize, though never first. She always had stitches where things got turned around or bunched up. A casualty, she felt, of the fact she picked up and put down her knitting so often, due to her work. She rather envied the women who had time to sit for an hour with a friend, and do a fair stretch of knitting at once.

"It will look better when it's all washed and shaped properly. The last step, after all the knitting, to make it smooth and even." She knew she was babbling, now, and had to swallow to stop from saying more. Though that made her think, all at once, about the way the water made knitting better, like it made people better. Smoothing and releasing and allowing everything to find its best shape.

Roland ran his finger lightly along the stitches, spreading them very gently. It made her suddenly wonder what his hands would be like doing other things, and she blushed. He, thankfully, didn't notice, or at least didn't ask her. His fingers hesitated where the pattern changed. "Tell me about it? This isn't the ordinary sort of knitting I see people wearing."

"It's from the Shetland Isles." She saw his eyebrow go up, as that was certainly not from where she came from. "Uncle Dewi has a son, a bit older than me, who is an alchemist. He married someone he met at school, from up there, when I was still in school. I don't get to see Mareoun much - she's got plenty to keep busy with - but we write sometimes, and we both knit. The pattern was from her. They don't share them often."

"And you do all this with just the two stitches you showed me, and looping the yarn different ways to do them?"

Elen smiled. "It's magical, isn't it? A few sticks and some yarn, and all the variations. And that's before you get into the colours, or making things to wear that fit you closely, like a jumper or a frock."

He looked up at her, and smiled. "Oh, I knew you were magic, the first time I saw you. You figured out the light was hurting me, right off. And you did all the right things even when I was grumpy and very much a crab."

Elen snorted. "You were my patient, I wasn't going to take offence. At least not unless I was sure you meant it. Even then, my standards for being offended by a patient are rather high." She considered. "There have been a few. Not many."

Roland nodded, then he looked down at the knitting. "I am glad you answered Father as you did. I'm not entirely sure what he thought, and I am quite certain that Mother will have her opinions, she always does. But they are most inclined, right now, to be kind to anyone who has actually helped me."

Elen nodded. "Your father loves you, rather a lot, I think, for all I imagine you've rarely said such things to each other."

Roland blinked several times. "That's what you think of, first?"

Elen shrugged slightly, and found herself leaning a bit more against him. "I know my parents love each other. And they love me, but your father had it right, they don't understand me. I - I was all set not to like your parents. Because they hadn't written, hadn't checked on you, hadn't sent anything. Only, that's not what was going on."

"No." Roland's voice was wry. "My father was hatching a plot to get me on something close to his home territory, without alerting whoever was blocking his letters."

"And your mother?" Elen was curious about that, both what Roland would say, and how he'd say it.

"Mother is very efficiently terrifying. I'm sure Father learned all his debriefing skills from her. She's been out of the country, mostly. And Father's perfectly competent, but Temple politics are not his forte."

"They're your mother's?"

"Oh, no. Ministry, for her, especially the Penelopes and some of the magical research folks." He wriggled his hand. "Mind, they might like having someone in the family with Temple expertise. And connections."

Elen leaned back a little and peered at Roland. "Even after this? And after whatever it is we decide to do?"

He took in a breath, and let it out. "I suppose now's a good time to talk about it? If you meant what you said to Father, about my recovery?"

"I did. I think it will take some time to steady out your magic. But weeks, maybe two months, not forever. Seeing how it's been settling since we stopped the potion."

He almost said something, then refused to get distracted. "They might send me overseas again. To do something dangerous." He shifted his hand to reach for hers, which was still holding the knitting. She gathered it up, and set it carefully, without looking away from him, to the other side. "If they did that, I'd want, I'd want to marry you before I left."

That was rather more than she'd expected him to say, and all she could do for a minute was blink at him. Blessedly, he didn't rush her. Finally, she gave in, and said what had first come to mind. "You barely know me. Or how we might be together."

"I know enough." He shifted to take both her hands, holding them firmly. "You are kind, and clever, and you are stubborn, and there is no one I want more on my side than you. I know you won't give up on me. And you won't let me get away with being less than I could be."

He stopped, as if this mattered more to him than anything else. When he went on, his voice was full of a needy desire. "Every other nurse was content just to dump potions down me, and turn on the lights. You looked at me, and you thought about what I needed. I know you must do that for all your patients, but you also haven't denied this is different."

She nodded, looking at him, then down at their hands. "Would you want me to stop nursing?"

"Goodness, no. I don't know what I'll be doing, but whatever it is will either be in Trellech or near a portal, or somewhere you can't go with me. I'd much rather you do something useful. Though perhaps we could set up in a proper flat, instead of your rooming house with the disapproving landlady."

That made Elen grin despite herself. "I understand one can rent flats, yes, if one has more of an income than I do."

"Money, you may have gathered, is not a particular problem on my end. I have an inheritance and my own salary. And I'll inherit a couple of homes in various places in due course, though I hope very much not for a long time to come. They take rather a lot of upkeep."

Something in his tone amused her. "Not up for the effort?"

"Not any time soon, no. But I could take you to see them, when it's more rehabilitative? If you can get away."

Elen let out a long breath. "I honestly don't know what the future holds. I was so pleased to be back at the Temple. And some of it has been grand. You, of course. And Healer Rhoe. Though she's also a little bit scary?" Roland grinned at her, and Elen went on. "But I don't know now. After all this."

He nodded, more soberly. "I felt the same thing, after seeing the orders we were getting. Like I'd been betrayed. Not me, exactly, not personally. But my ideals. Knowing that there were people above me, people with power, who didn't seem to care what happened to me, to any of us."

"That, yes, that exactly." She inhaled sharply, squeezing his hands. "And I don't know if I want to be around that." She hesitated. "If there's anywhere that isn't like that."

"And I don't know if I want to go back to fighting, even if I can. Even though my family, back generations, has been career military, one way or another. Back to the Pact, near enough. Not always successfully, there were some unfortunate moments in the Jacobin rebellion and the Civil War."

That made her smile again, and look up. "You don't know about the fighting?"

Roland shook his head. "I need to talk to Father, I think. In private, when we know how much I've truly recovered. Certainly about my concerns, since he's in a position to do something about them."

"That, that's something. He'll at least hear you out." Elen then swallowed. "You should have a proper supper. Do you want me to go see about something more than the tea sandwiches?"

"Oh, I can ring. No need to make you fetch and carry. I suspect they do something like a cottage pie here. What would you like?"

The cheerful discussion of what food was likely available, and what she'd prefer, carried them off into other topics. It was only when Elen was falling asleep, much later that night, with the door open between their rooms so she could hear if he needed anything, that she realised she'd never given him a proper answer, if that had in fact been a proposal.

T wo days later, Elen came back from her shift tending the Temple shrines, to hear voices coming from Roland's room. Not just voices, but laughter. She'd thought he'd be reading after his bath.

She knocked once on the door, with a "Hello?"

Perched on the end of the bed was an exceedingly well-dressed woman. Her dress was of the sort of deep radiant blue that made it clear the silk was dyed with charms as well as plants, of a nubbly raw silk that fell in flattering lines. Behind her, over the end of the bed, was a swath of blue-green silk, what might be a coat that would drape and highlight her form, and a matching hat and purse.

Her dark hair was pulled up in a precise smooth chignon, with a single hairstick apparently holding it all in place effortlessly. Her skin was the only odd note, more tanned by the sun than most women in Albion would permit.

She was holding a small box out to Roland, who was sitting on the bed, fully dressed. The woman turned as Elen knocked, and Elen could immediately see the similarity of their faces, at the same angle. This must be his mother.

"Hello, dear. You must be Therapeutes Morris. Candied ginger? I brought Roland a hamper, of course."

Before she could speak, Roland spoke, sounding more amused than anything else. "Close the door, perhaps, Elen? Elen, this is my mother, Melusina Gospatrick. Mother, Elen Morris."

Elen resisted the urge to curtsey. Barely. She took a couple of steps forward, and took a piece of the ginger. "Thank you, Magistra Gospatrick." She glanced around the room, then realised the size of the hamper that had been delivered.

It was of bleached white wicker, and more than big enough to move a moderately large body, if required. It must have taken two people to bring in, at least. She took a deep breath. "Were you expecting to need to smuggle Roland out? He might be a bit cramped, even in that."

His mother threw her head back, and laughed. "Oh, I do like you. I was inclined to, after what Arthur told me." She nodded, once, precisely as if that settled everything. "And Roland, of course, but one has to allow for somewhat more bias in his evaluation."

"Mother." Roland was definitely amused.

She held out her hand, the nails polished to a deep red to match her lips. "Do call me Melusina. And may I be informal with you? I do think that the best plots require a certain amount of informality."

Elen let out a breath. "Elen, please, at least in private. I do have my responsibilities." She glanced at the door.

"Oh, quite. Now, do sit down, please. I shall get out something for a proper elevenses. I told that nice orderly not to bother with lunch, I'm sure I can do rather better."

Melusina stood, every fold of her dress immediately falling into place.

Elen had never wanted to have that kind of command over her clothing, to look that elegant, but she suddenly and rather painfully saw the point. This was not a woman anyone in their right mind would ignore, never mind want to anger. She was so precisely groomed, dressed, and made up, that there was no question that she would not be just as capable at anything else she chose. Elen sat.

Roland reached to offer his hand immediately. "She showed up while I was in the bath, and pointed out that she certainly was aware of where all my birthmarks are. Harry held out long enough for me to get dressed, but it was a near thing."

Elen couldn't help smiling broadly at that, curling her fingers around his as his mother began to unpack a small portion of the hamper, using swift flicks of a wand she had produced seemingly from nowhere, to direct the various components onto Roland's table. Sandwiches, some small things that might be savoury tarts or quiche. "Where does one get hot water around here?"

"Oh, I can get that, it's in the nurse's lounge."

"Nonsense. You must be run off your feet." There was a quick glance at Elen's shoes, then a tsking sound. "Sensible shoes, certainly, but I'm sure we can do a bit better in the way of practicality."

"Practicality, ma... Melusina?"

"I suppose you would need to wear shoes like the other nurses, but there are all sorts of quite practical charms for comfort, better padding, certainly for the most comfortable fit. You're a therapeutes of Sirona, so none of that silly asceticism and suffering for suffering's sake."

She produced several ornately decorated small cakes

from the hamper, frowned delicately, and then added a jar of what was likely potted shrimp and some small toasts. "I mean, I do respect the people who manage it, I certainly couldn't, but there's more than one way to be dedicated to one's arts, don't you think?"

"Yes, um. I suppose so?" Elen was feeling utterly adrift. If it hadn't been for Roland's hand around hers and his amusement, she might have thought she was hallucinating.

"There, that's a start. Now, the water." She moved to the tea pot, sprinkled a handful of tea leaves from a tin in her hand in the bottom, then poured cold water from the pitcher in. She inhaled once, as if testing that everything was proper, then made a few precise gestures with her wand, murmuring something under her breath that sounded almost musical.

"Roland mentioned that your family considers heat, light, and solidness the most practical magics to know well."

"Oh, we do." Melusina turned back, beaming. "We'll just let this steep." She set the pot on the table with the rest of the food. "I am perhaps a little less patient than my husband and son."

Roland snorted. "That is understating it, mother," he pointed out. "You did have a reason for turning up this morning, though?"

"I did. We have been busy untangling exactly what has been going on here, working on it from the angles we can. Roland did explain, Elen, I hope, what I do?"

"Not precisely, but I gather that was somewhat intentional? You're a specialist in complex magics, often abroad dealing with unusual problems, was what I had gathered." Elen kept her voice as even as she could.

"That will do to be going on with. My usual line of work is for the Ministry, or the near equivalent, which means I am also more practised than any sensible person would want to be in unravelling bureaucratic plots. And this certainly seems to be one of those." She tapped the teapot once with her finger. "You, however, have the necessary situational knowledge, as my husband would say."

"It is a rather large topic." Elen managed to cut off the 'ma'am' that kept trying to escape.

Melusina waved her hand. "Explain to me the hierarchy here. From your position up, not the top down. For the moment."

It seemed an odd way to go about things, but Elen was not at all inclined to argue. "This is one of the wards for long-term care. More commonly, several nurses would be assigned to the ward as a whole, but private nurses may be assigned."

"As one has been assigned to Roland, since he arrived, yes? Has there been any particular set of skills beyond what you would expect?"

"No." Elen had considered that before. "I don't know who the others are. Were. But they didn't ask me about anything beyond the skills we all have." She then glanced at the door.

Melusina made a slight gesture with her wand, a sigil of some kind that left a brief glowing trail. Then she repeated it at the window. "No one will overhear us, and we will hear if anyone is coming."

It was that show of magic that convinced Elen of precisely how competent Melusina was. And not just skilled and knowledgeable, but powerful. Most people could not produce a visible show of the magic itself. "You were not permitted to read Roland's records?"

"No, and that is quite unusual. I asked several times, and several different people." Elen swallowed, and continued. "I was assigned here by the Archiater, the chief administrator. I report directly to Sister Almeda, who oversees the long-term care wards."

"Not to a ward sister?"

"No." Elen considered. "I suppose there aren't that many of us here. Or perhaps some of the wards report to someone else. Long-term care usually is a slow process. I normally make weekly reports with a summary, with additional notes for unusual events. Or of course alerting someone immediately if there's a crisis."

"I gather not always." Melusina's voice became dry. "When it might cause problems for my son. Why didn't you report that?"

Elen let out a long breath. "I should have. But by that point, I was no longer certain that reporting it would benefit his care. I hit a wall, every time I tried to get more information, about his treatment, or even his injuries. And it was clear the evening potion was doing him no favours."

Melusina nodded, once. "Tea?" she handed over a cup, to Elen first. It was beautifully fragrant with orange and spices, and a swirl of cream. Elen took a sip, and felt suddenly rejuvenated. Not like it was a potion, but the simple attention, someone giving her something she would enjoy.

Melusina handed the other to Roland, and then settled the table where all three could reach it. "I am supposed to be a stickler for following the rules. In all privacy, and I will deny this in more public settings, I am delighted you did as you did."

Elen ducked her chin. "My oaths are about the well-being of my patients, Melusina. Not about the rules of men. Or women."

Melusina laughed again, at that. "Quite so. Quite. And

who does Sister Almeda report to, before I ask you what happened after that."

"She reports to the chief nurse, and the chief nurse reports to the Archiater. Quite a short chain."

"Very. Much shorter than I'd expected. The chief nurse would be exceedingly busy, of course. And there must be other such chains?"

"Oh, yes. The healers have their own hierarchy. And the healer is considered the one who determines the treatment of a patient. There's a separate structure for tending to the sacred spaces, the garden shrines, the baths, the bathing rooms. And of course, other areas like the cooking and the cleaning and the stores. Healer Rhoe is responsible for the baths. I didn't realise when we first talked to her, how senior she was, comparatively."

"Would that have stopped you?" Melusina had settled to perch on the end of the bed again.

"No." Elen spoke cautiously, and took a sip more of tea to give herself time to think. "It was a thing that Roland needed, to begin healing. And it was a thing I had authority to ask for, one of the few."

"And as you said, you take that most seriously. He mentioned you were reinstated after a particular event, but gave me no details. Nor his father."

Elen glanced at Roland, who had been quiet throughout this, though he had kept holding her hand until the tea was served. He nodded. "Go ahead, Father will probably ask you other questions later, if you're willing?"

Elen took another sip of tea to brace herself, startled to discover she'd somehow drunk two thirds of the cup. Melusina took it silently from her hand to refill from the pot. "Healer Cole came in, for the first time since I'd been assigned, the first time Roland remembered. And he thought he had caught us being improper. About to kiss. We weren't, though I suppose we were both thinking about the possibility."

"I certainly was." Roland's voice was amused. "But I didn't mean to get you in trouble. Of course, I'm fairly sure now that Cole would have taken any chance to get you in trouble."

"What did you think of him, Roland, in that first moment?" Melusina's voice had shifted into something thoughtful, as if much of her mind were processing something in the background.

"He was far too richly dressed. Formal robes, excellent silk. Not quite your quality, Mother, but near that. The other healers we've seen, they have working robes. Usually linen or wool. I'm sure the dye was carmine, and one of the three tailors you'd think for the suit under it."

Roland's voice had turned precise, and his mother nodded. "Thank you, darling. Do go on, Elen."

"He sent me away, and I got a letter later that afternoon suspending me indefinitely. I went to see my friend Amet - Mistress Salah." There was a nod again. "And then a bit later, I got a letter from Healer Rhoe, telling me to meet her on the Temple's front steps at half nine. She had argued that they put me through an ordeal, in order to determine my innocence."

"Nothing damaging, I hope? I presume?"

Elen shook her head quickly. "I didn't know what to expect, but they had a senior priestess of Sirona there. She blessed a cup for me to drink, and I drank it without problems. They all accepted the result, even Healer Cole."

She looked up, to watch Melusina's face. "Though he looked uncomfortable. More than uncomfortable. Maybe like he was afraid, all of a sudden? Like something had become real to him? And the Archiater looked - I don't know. Like he'd started wondering about something being out of order. But it's not as if anyone would tell me any of that."

"Not having the sense the gods gave sheep, apparently." Melusina snorted. "Was that all of it?"

"I didn't know until I got back here that I was glowing, quite noticeably."

The reaction was, frankly, delightful. Melusina's face went blank for a moment, as if that was not information she had expected, as if she were making several dozen new calculations and adjustments. "And being a temple, funda- mentally, they took that very seriously, then. If perhaps finding such an overt display of actual religion a bit unbe- coming. I begin to see why they let you back. You will, I hope, permit me to pester you with questions in the not too distant future? You do not need to answer them, of course, but I am most curious."

Elen nodded. "You may ask," she agreed. "I don't know what sort of answers I'll have."

"Fair, fair. So, that would change the field, certainly. And since then, you have had somewhat more freedom. And you have discovered the... cheapness of the potion provided. What about the morning potion?"

"What it should be, near enough, I gather from the analysis. But that is mostly nutritive, and most of the nutri- tion potions are fairly inexpensive to make. They either rely on readily available plants, or things like alchemically altered beef broth or milk or some such. The magical work doesn't need a journeyman, even, just a trained apprentice, and it can be made in barrels. Not more than twice the cost of the base ingredients, generally."

"And you had no information about what evening

potion he should have been getting. That's thorough. Bluntly done, but thorough." Melusina clearly hated giving credit to whoever had come up with the idea. "So. Between the potion and the requests for support, they have been clearing a significant amount of coin from us. And from the Ministry. Do you think that might be the case for others? And if so, how could we find out?"

"I think Sister Almeda must know. But I suspect they are suborning her, somehow. I mean, it seems ridiculous, to say 'they'. But it would take someone to manage the paper-work, someone to provide the alternate potions, someone to force particular treatments. Possibly someone to deal with families. May I ask, what did they tell you?"

"That Roland was terribly badly hurt, that any visit was out of the question. And of course, we had no reply to any of our letters." Melusina tilted her head. "How much longer would he need to stay here, do you think? First things first, and I admit my own desire to get my only living child out of this place as promptly as possible. Especially if you would be willing to come with him to see to the necessary treatment."

Elen let out a long breath, not asking about that adjec-tive, or exactly how fierce Melusina might be now. "If there's someone to help with bathing and such - Roland said he had a man - quite soon, I think. I might wish to consult Healer Rhoe once more, if she were willing. Perhaps another ritual bath."

"Next week?"

"I believe so."

"I will make the arrangements. And now, dearest, I need to be going, must see a man about a titch of embezzle-ment. Don't wait up." She stood, bending to kiss Roland on the forehead. "A pleasure to meet you, Elen, and I'll be seeing you soon. I needn't ask you to take care of Roland, but please do."

Then she was gathering up her coat and hat, gesturing with her hand and summoning her magic - all the privacy protections she'd cast - with a snap of her fingers. It came back to her hand in a shower of sparkles, like hounds called to heel. Then she was out the door, leaving behind her the remaining food, a whiff of a perfume Elen could not begin to identify, and a rather large silence.

Three days later, Elen again escorted Roland to the baths beneath the temple. This time, he realised, they had something different in mind. He was shown into a space dedicated to Sirona, he could tell by the iconography and by the offerings. Elen had described changing them often enough. Even more to his surprise, it wasn't Healer Rhoe or some stranger who did the invocation.

After he'd been eased into the bath by the orderly, they dimmed the lights. Elen came in, wearing something quite different from her nurse's uniform. Now, she was dressed more like Healer Rhoe, in a Greek shift of a neutral linen with embroidery along the top of the fabric of a long deep green snake. And her hair was up differently, instead of the tight bun, it was pulled into a loosely coiled puff.

He was suddenly glad that the lights were dim, and she almost certainly couldn't see much below the water line. His own reactions were being rather insistent, if also informative about his ongoing recovery.

She had smiled at him, then turned to the shrine,

making the offerings, then chanting. Her voice, in whatever language it was, was fluid. Then she switched into English, though he listened far more to the tone of her voice than the words. He could see something gather around her. It wasn't the glow she'd had, after the ordeal. This was far more ephemeral, like the flickers of fireflies in the summer dark. Like them, though, it was rivetingly beautiful.

As the invocation came to an end, she opened the gate that let the water from the shrine flow down to his bathing pool, and trailed her fingers in it. He could see, or at least felt certain he could, those little flickers of light carried down into his pool, toward him.

He could smell lavender and mint, a strong scent for a brief moment, before it faded out. Then she was turning. She kneeled by him, long enough to kiss him on the top of his head. "I'll be waiting." Just those three words.

He opened his mouth, but before he could figure out what to say, she was gone. He was left alone in the near dark with his own thoughts and the lingering magic. As before, there was no bolt of sudden healing, but he could feel himself renewed. More himself, certainly.

He spent the time lost in thought, letting his mind knit up the choices he knew he needed to make. And he needed to make them sooner than he'd have thought possible just a few weeks ago. It was as if things were settling into place, gently and resolutely.

When his time in the bath was done, Elen was waiting for him once he'd dried off and changed. He hadn't needed the chair to get here, and he didn't need it now. "Back to the room?"

"I thought we might sit in the garden a bit? It's beautiful out. Particularly beautiful, I mean."

"Like you." It slipped out before he could stop himself.

She was back in her uniform, but he thought she still had something of the glow of Sirona around her.

She grinned at him, once, before they came out of the lower passageway, and among people again, and she put on her professional demeanour. He was proud of himself for making it all the way to their usual bench without needing to take a rest. Once they were settled, she offered a flask of tea from her bag, pouring it into the lid for him to drink. He took a long sip, then smiled. "It was different, having you being the one who did the, the prayer?"

"The invocation." She nodded. "I haven't, often. Not like that."

"You said that they'd invited you to the temple." Roland hadn't been sure how to bring this up, but the bath itself had convinced him it was time. "I can do without you for a bit now. Especially if Mother whisks me away, as she will. Though I hope I won't have to do without you for long."

Elen swallowed. "I'd thought." She stopped and tried again. "If you go to your home, your parents, I mean. You wouldn't need me."

"I wouldn't need you, but I would still want you." Roland was very sure of this. He glanced around, and ventured to take her hand, down on the seat, where people couldn't see it.

She was quiet for a worryingly long time. While she was thinking, Roland focused on her, but he couldn't help noticing that there were people moving back and forth in the garden, some of them in Guard uniform. They were out of pace with the rhythm of the place. Nurses hurried, but the patients usually moved slowly, and healers took the time they thought they needed. When she spoke again, though, he immediately thought of nothing else but what she wanted to say.

"Would you make me stop being a nurse? We talked about it, before, but your parents, surely they wouldn't want me working."

"Mother works. Father does too. But while Mother took something of a leave of absence when she was pregnant, from active work, she points out that this is why there are nannies, or governesses. Not that she doesn't love me, but she does important work. And it's meant Nanny's had a safe and comfortable place to live, and that's not a small thing either."

Elen clearly hadn't thought about it from that point of view. "Sharing what you have, then?"

"She likes being a nanny and taking care of people. You'll like her, I'm quite sure, and she'll approve of you. Mother likes - and is exceedingly good at - being a terrifying force of nature. The world probably needs both."

As he'd hoped, it made Elen laugh, and squeeze his hand. "All right. I don't know what they'll want to do, where to assign me."

"Not overseas." He was pretty sure of that. "But possibly not here."

"What about you? They could send you over."

Roland shook his head. "I'll have to figure it out, but I don't think I'm fit. My magic is recovering, but I think I'll always wonder when it might fail me. I'm pretty sure Father can help me find something where I can use my skills, but something more like recommending magical training. I might try teaching some of that, actually, if that's an option. I think I'd like that."

"Sending young men off to..." She stopped. "I mean, we both know what's over there. How bad it is. How much worse it could get."

Roland swallowed. "We do." He squeezed her hand

again. "And I don't know how to solve that. But I imagine Father has some of the same thoughts. On the other hand, what if what I could teach could keep some of them alive?"

"There is that." Elen's voice faded out, and they sat in silence for a good minute or two before she said, "Something's going on. You see, don't you?"

"I do. The last few minutes."

"Do we go and indulge our curiosity, do you think? Or would anyone tell us?"

"This is where being in your room all the time has not been terribly helpful. If you want me to have a gossip network, I have to talk to other people more often." Elen was looking around, though, as if to see if there was someone she recognised. Then she pointed. "That's Sister Almeda, being escorted by that Guard."

"Not under arrest." Roland spotted that at once. "Her hands are free, she's walking beside him, I don't think there's a charm, either. But helping in an investigation, perhaps?" Then he frowned. "That nurse behind her?"

Elen said immediately. "That's Sister Pomona. And my, she looks vindicated, doesn't she?"

It was then that he spotted two figures, coming across the long walkway that ran perpendicular to where the Temple looked out on the gardens. "Ah. We're about to get some answers. See there?"

His father was in mufti, the deep grey robes he favoured when not in uniform, with a flash of royal purple at the handkerchief and waistcoat. His military posture drew the eye despite that. Or it would, except that Roland's mother was wearing a deep emerald green dress. It was nominally sedate, but none of her clothing managed that for long. The dress had a long skirt, that was billowing as they walked. The two were making a beeline directly for their bench.

"Mother promised not to use a location charm on me after I turned thirteen."

His tone - admittedly a bit plaintive - made Elen snort with amusement. "She has some cause. Are we making them come to us?"

"I am still an invalid, ta." Roland grinned. "Besides, this is by far the best bench in the place. Private, shaded, and quite properly the place for a conversation."

Elen smiled a little, and shifted to settle herself a bit better. The facing bench was free, at least, and there was no one near them, either.

When his parents got within easy distance, Roland stood. "Mother, Father. Would you prefer the bench, or somewhere else?"

"Darling, as if we'd make you move." His mother swooped in, kissed him on both cheeks, beamed at Elen, and said, "Elen, dear, so good to see you again. We have a great deal of news, as you may have noticed by the hive being kicked over."

Roland's father nodded smartly at him, and said "Good to see you about. Elen, good afternoon." They both settled on the facing bench, and his mother rustled her skirts into place.

"The Guard are so helpfully bringing in everyone to have a chat about recent events, and the implications. Under proper questioning so there will be no wriggling out of it. That is what took us a couple of days to arrange, suitable evidence. Mind, Healer Rhoe was most helpful. You didn't mention her brother had been at your ordeal, Elen, dear. He's a member of the Council, and that made things vastly simpler."

Elen blinked. "I didn't know." Her voice was a little

shaky. "She didn't say. Actually, I don't think she said anything other than his first name."

"Rhoe is apparently her chosen name, something particular about her healer oath, no one explained it, so, no, I suppose that wouldn't help. And she is married, and that always confuses things unless you've memorised the Golden Book backwards and forwards."

Roland's father leaned forward, to add sotto voce to Elen. "Which she has, don't let her suggest otherwise." Roland was delighted by that, how they were so comfortably including her in the interplay.

"So here we are, I said we'd come find you, I could be vastly more efficient about it than anyone else, blood of my blood."

"I thought we'd agreed you'd not use a finding charm again." Roland squeezed Elen's hand, for reassurance, but he had to admit that bantering with his mother was deeply reassuring in a way he hadn't wanted to admit he needed. She had never been the most maternally inclined person in his life. Nanny beat her by spades with both hands behind her back. But Roland had always been utterly confident his mother was entirely on his side except for those few months of horrible silence.

"I restrained myself until just now. Granted, that's because you were rather out of my quite excellent range until I got back in the country."

"You admitted an imperfection! What's the current score, Father?"

His father snorted. "Seventy-seven you, three thousand, two hundred and three to my lovely wife." He then cleared his throat. "You will both need to come and give your statements, but we have a few minutes, they wanted everyone else under control."

"Do you know what's up?" Roland leaned forward, now very much hoping there would be answers.

It was his mother who answered. "Embezzlement, absolutely, and the sort that will have him up in the Justice Courts promptly."

"Cole?" Roland wasn't exactly surprised.

Melusina shook her head. "Not Cole, as it turns out. Or at least, not Ozymandius Cole. It turns out he's a man named Oscar Cole, a failed businessman born here, living in Africa. The real healer took ill on his way back to Albion, and this Oscar took his place. And then thought he saw a good thing going. Not much work, lots of money, if he did things right."

She waved a hand, her tone shifting to somethign that wasn't approval, but that had some appreciation of the bravado required for the scheme. "He knew enough about the potions trade to know what was cheap to make and what wasn't, and he listened to what the junior healers suggested for options. You, darling, and a dozen others. All from well-off families, he was very careful in his choices."

Roland let out a low whistle. "And you figured that out this fast?"

"Some of it will take longer, to go before the courts. But the Archiater did finally insist on a small private ordeal this morning, and the man thoroughly choked on the cup he was given. Once he could talk again, he was forthcoming enough, though we'll need to see it's all documented. And figure out how he suborned Sister Almeda and several others." She waved a hand. "That may need a titch of restructuring the pensions for nurses. I gather she was trying to put a bit aside for her old age."

Roland glanced at Elen, who was speechless, blinking at his mother. He squeezed her hand, reassuringly. "Is the real

Cole all right? Or I suppose there's been no time to find out."

His father nodded. "We've messages going through the portals to find out, but it will be a week or two at least. They'll want you for the trial, both of you."

He cleared his throat. "That leads to the other necessary conversation, for when this is all dealt with. You had said, Elen, that you thought that might be a reasonable point in Roland's recovery. Does it seem likely he could come back to one of our homes - we thought Wryford, Roland, but if you have another preference, we can fit that up."

Roland said, carefully. "We were just working around to talking through some of that, when you came over. Elen is quite clear she would like to continue her nursing work, but we're not sure yet what the options are. And I'd like to talk to you, Father, about my own options. I would prefer, and I think it might also be necessary, to find me a posting here in Albion."

His father met his eyes, then nodded once. "I will give it some thought, and see what might be a good solution. You were quite persuasive at the meeting, about what would be practical, and what wouldn't be. If you were up for more of that, I haven't seen someone speak to it as clearly."

Roland said, "Mostly, I thought of what Mother would say, toned it down, and left out most of the academic footnotes. Knowing your own line as well as I do, sir."

"As I say, I haven't heard someone speak to it quite as clearly." His father was laughing now, teasing his mother, who looked deeply amused.

She let them have their fun before cutting in. "Elen, I hope at the very least you might come and visit us to get Roland settled in properly. Wryford is our largest country home in terms of land, plenty of excellent walks, a river. If you ride, we have - well, these days, a somewhat diminished stable - but a few good horses too old for the War effort."

Roland held his breath, not wanting to shatter whatever Elen might say. She squeezed his hand again, taking a breath, letting it out, before she answered. "If my assignments permit, I would very much like that, Melusina. I'm afraid my wardrobe might not be up to anything complicated, though."

"We're quite used to the demands of uniform about the place, but I'm sure we can also see about making sure you have something comfortable, too." Melusina eyed her thoughtfully. "I have a few old frocks that might suit you quite well, actually. Especially as we're getting into summer. You'll like the gardens, I'm certain. And whatever you need for your devotions, we'd be glad to provide."

Something about the offer for her devotions shifted things, Roland could feel it before he saw it, a rush of something like that flickering light from the baths.

His mother cheerfully waved her hand and carried blithely on. "I'll be in and out, and Arthur, though we'll see about a few amusements. The portals make that convenient, at least. Such a relief after a long day of convincing other people not to be idiots to be able to go home and see people one actually likes."

"Oh. That. Thank you." She let out a breath. "That makes a difference, I'm sure you realise."

"You are not terribly subtle, dear, but you are charmingly earnest. Don't change that, please, on our account." That was praise from his mother, actually. She liked people to be thoroughly who they were, she found it much more intriguing than the various masks so many people preferred. "That is settled, then. Let us know when you can get free, we'll make sure you can get to us easily."

Elen looked a little overwhelmed, and Roland cleared his throat. "So, we have a plan, for now? Where should we go, to make our report?"

"They should be just about ready. Do you need anything from your room, or your bag, Elen?"

Elen stood up, and bobbed. "Let me run and fetch my knitting. It's very soothing."

As she walked away, his mother watched her. "I wasn't sure what to think when your father explained the situation, Roland. But she is certainly clever and fierce enough for me to approve of. And she knows things I have no idea about, which is delightful."

Roland shook his head. "Mother, you are entirely predictable. And that is grand, thank you. Just what I needed. Now, what should I know that they might ask about?"

That occupied them until it was time to go into the Temple and find the room where the Guard had set up their truth enchantments and oaths.

EPILOGUE

"Love, how are things?"

Elen turned away from the window. She'd been standing there, looking out at the gardens, watching the residents go about their various tasks and amusements. "Roland, you're back early! I didn't see you come up from the portal."

Roland leaned against the doorway to her office, looking amused at something. "I took the train back, and McGowin picked me up from there, he was doing a run for supplies." He brushed his hands off, a little fastidiously. "I'm a bit all over dust, do you mind?"

Elen snorted. "Never." She turned and held out her arms. "How did things go?" She found herself picked up and spun in a circle, until her cap was about to fly off.

Roland set her back on her feet, and grinned broadly at her. "Everything I wanted, and then some. Father's delighted, and he asks can you get away to Trellech for supper in the next couple of days? Tomorrow by preference."

Elen considered. It had been a long slow haul for her to

get the rehabilitation hospital set up, but things were now proceeding smoothly. She could certainly be gone for an evening, without anything falling apart. "Overnight, or just supper?"

"Overnight, if we can manage it, the town house."

"Right. I'll see about packing a bag. I can do tomorrow?" She looked up to see Roland arching his eyebrow at her. "I mean, asking for a bag to be packed." She was still utterly unused to the idea that someone else's job involved doing things like that for her, as well as seeing to any number of tasks.

Roland had been clear when she took this on that it would involve letting other people do things that other people could do. She needed to focus on the things she knew and did best. He wasn't wrong, she knew that. But having other people see to all the cooking and cleaning and tidying and making sure there was food in the pantry still felt decidedly queer. On the other hand, Roland had been backed up by everyone else in this odd little plot of theirs.

Elen took Roland's hand, and tugged him back to the window. "See there? Bartholomew is doing quite well with his illusion work. And there, see Doris with the water? She's got it flowing smoothly and properly." She felt Roland shift to kiss her hair, then settle his arms around her waist loosely.

"Did Gareth get a chance to try the new round of exercises?" he asked. "I know he was worried about that, and you weren't sure how far to push."

"Oh, that." Elen laughed. "Lionel set it up as a challenge, and Gareth rose to it gloriously. He got all three sets today, smooth as can be. Mind, it's repeating it that does the most good, but now he's done it, I think he'll settle to it."

"That's part of what they were so pleased about, this

round." Roland had been in London, coordinating training for those with magical talent posted to particular units. Perhaps more importantly, he was also coordinating what happened to those who had been injured in ways that damaged their magic. Some came to the house here, some went elsewhere. Usually the Temple, to recover physically, but the magical recovery was proving a significant and rewarding professional challenge. For all she wished it weren't necessary at all.

His parents had acquired the house not long before the War. How one acquired a country house, Elen wasn't sure, or why they'd needed another one, since she was fairly sure they'd had at least three already.

In this case, however, it had two points in its favour for this particular project. First, it was in Herefordshire, near enough to Trellech that someone could make the journey by carriage or even automobile, if they couldn't tolerate the portal or train. Not entirely conveniently, but none of this war was convenient.

More usefully, the Gospatricks had been in the process of restoring it after some years of benign neglect when the War began, and had promptly halted the work. Most of the structural repairs had been done, but little of the decorative work, and it had been surprisingly easy to fit it to host a number of recovering soldiers. And more than a few nurses and others who had been injured during the War. They were one of the few places outside the Temple who would accept both men and women.

It was pleasantly situated on rather extensive lands, with plenty of wildlife to observe, and formal gardens for those who wanted something a little less adventurous. A third point in its favour had turned out to be the history. Built in the 15th century, it had the usual odd amalgamation of additions and architecture, and quite a variety of garden spaces. It gave those inclined to visual arts plenty to draw and paint.

Thus far, it had worked out surprisingly well. She leaned back against Roland's shoulder, just looking out. "It's beautiful here. Despite everything. I feel quite guilty."

Roland kissed her hair. "We've both been in the wars, love, and come out the other side. No reason there shouldn't be some beauty there. Mother said there's quite a bit of gossip about your work, that you've managed to help people. Delphine in particular, there's some connection. I can never keep track with Mother, but it helped her with one of her plots."

"Her many plots." Elen shook her head. "Is she going to be pressing me again?"

"I believe," Roland said with some dignity, "That I may finally have persuaded her that you and I will be arranging our wedding. When it suits us, and not before. I did say we will certainly tell her as soon as she can be of assistance." He paused. "But I admit that I'm glad she's going off again, so she can be busy sorting all of that out, and not aiming it at us."

Elen nodded. "It's, you know I will." She hesitated.

"When it's time. And it's not time yet. And we have time, I'm quite sure of that. Now. I wasn't, but then the world changed."

She tilted her head to look at him. "You went by the Temple again." He had that particular tone to his voice.

"The baths, yes. Nothing startling. I didn't expect that. Just knowing that things will be all right. That there's healing and the water flowing, and quiet, and that's a fine thing to have."

Elen shook her head. "I'd never have taken you for a mystic, when I met you."

"To be fair, I wasn't anything of the kind, when you walked into my room and closed the curtains." He kissed her temple again, almost absently. "What did you think of me?"

"I thought you were a man of rather conventional tastes? Given your books and what you asked me to read. But I know rather better now. You just were keeping to what was safe to show."

"And in private?" Roland was teasing her now, but he did enjoy that. And she knew he'd had a long and difficult day.

"And in private, good sir, I am delighted to enjoy your more adventurous and personal side. As you know perfectly well." She glanced down at her watch fob. "We don't have time before supper, though. Twenty minutes, if you want to wash and change."

"If we're to be gone tomorrow, I suppose I'd better put in an appearance."

She turned in his arms, and stood on her toes to kiss him once on the lips. "Much appreciated. Lionel had a question about one bit of the reconstruction, and you're a better person to answer him, or at least put him off." Elen let herself settle on the ground again. "Anything else, before I go wash up?"

"Can you get free to meet Healer Rhoe mid-afternoon? She said if we were going to be handy, there's a patient she'd like to discuss with you. She's not sure this is the right place. Rather a tricky case, I gather, he's having a bad time with hallucinations, and no one's been able to figure out what's going on. Nothing dangerous, he says a lot of them are rather pleasant music unless he's startled, apparently."

"I'll bring my notecase, then." Elen let out a long breath. "We've three rooms spare at the moment, and no other imminent prospects, so it wouldn't be a bad time to take on someone new." They were ideally a house of fifteen or sixteen residents, as well as Elen and her staff. Small enough to be a community, but large enough that people could find their own amusements and friendships without having to deal closely with everyone.

"Excellent. Oh, and she said the actual proper Ozymandius Cole has finally turned up, to take a position for a few years. He's delightful and thoughtful, apparently, and she thinks you should meet him."

Elen tilted her head. "I - I suppose?"

"With me, if you like. She made that face at me, the one that's about necessary healing, you know how she does."

"No use fighting with that, no." Elen was clear about that particular folly, then turned back to the more important part. "If she doesn't think her current patient's ready yet, I might see about going to the country shrine for a few days? If you can do without me?"

Roland grinned. "Never, but I can bear up for a few days, of course. You've not had a chance for months." Then he kissed her forehead. "There. That's all my messages." The bell chimed on the clock, and he grimaced. "I do want to wash up. See you downstairs."

Elen nodded, watching him go out the door. Then she took one last look out at the gardens, seeing everyone beginning to make their way to settle in for the evening meal.

～

If you enjoyed *Carry On* and would like to read more of this series, please sign up for my mailing list to get all the latest news and fun extras. Your reviews (on whatever review site you use) are much appreciated, too!

Read on for more historical details about this book and an excerpt from *The Fossil Door*, the next book in the series.

AUTHOR'S NOTES

Thank you so much for reading *Carry On*. My thanks (as always) to Kiya Nicoll, my inestimable friend and editor. And I owe a lot to my early readers, including Erin and Anne Libby (along with half a dozen others) for making this book much better through their comments and suggestions. I particularly owe my knitting consultants a lot of thanks for this one!

This book has been a chance to dip into two new areas for me: the Temple of Healing (and more broadly how religion works for people in Albion), and a book set during the Great War itself.

The Temple of Healing is the main hospital in Albion, located in Trellech, in southern Wales. Devoted to healing in all its forms, it also has a variety of staff - Healers (functionally equivalent to our doctors, but with more magic), nurses (ditto), and orderlies, as well as the many other people making sure things keep running smoothly through cleaning, laundry, cooking, paperwork, and all the other tasks of any big institution. Each has their own supporting structures and hierarchy - and degree of formality.

Healers and nurses both make formal oaths to some power that they recognise as meaningful. It is possible for someone to swear on their magic, as everyone in the magical community does when they become an adult, but many healers and nurses do have some sort of religious connection they choose to honour instead. (As you can see from Elen's comments on her own oaths, there's a variety, some more common than others.)

Albion itself is, in some ways, more fundamentally Roman influenced than our modern civilisation. When the fundamental shift in the country happened, at the time of the Pact in 1484, many people began to return to family traditions of magic that had been passed down, but not prominent. And in the Great Families, many of these had Roman roots, at least if you went back far enough.

That also affects **religion,** obviously. The various religious upheavals of the Tudors and Stuarts (and the English Civil War) meant that many families who were religious looked at their options, and chose what worked for them in private whatever public gestures they needed to make for political or legal reasons. (For a long time, church attendance was mandatory in the United Kingdom, with significant fines or penalties if you didn't show up on Sunday.)

By the 18th century, things had settled into a wide range of religious practice, including people devoted to a wide range o different deities based on their interests, professions, families, or whatever else seemed relevant. Most of these are not true continuations of Roman practice, but they have kept the tendency of the Roman empire to include whatever interesting bits they found as the empire expanded.

In practice, much of how this works is similar to those groups reconstructing historical religions in the modern Pagan communities, in broad terms.

One of the things I've wanted to do in this series is show a diverse religious community, not just in terms of the types of religions, but the range of personal involvement. Roland is - until this book - not religious at all, nor is he particularly privately spiritual (as we'd put it these days.)

Elen, on the other hand, is actually devout, but not at all public about it, and she comes from a family that is equally religious, if in different ways.

(If you're not familiar with the Welsh Chapel movement her father prefers, it's a nonconformist Protestant movement, intertwined with labour and Welsh political concerns.)

Christianity is certainly in the mix here - Fidelius, in this book, as mentioned. I'm fairly sure several of my other characters in previous books are Christian, it just didn't come up in text. (It may yet in some future shorter works I'm hoping to write.)

Now we come to **the War and its battles**. Figuring out where Roland was injured took a bit of research - especially since I was hoping for him to have been in more than one battle, so that he had a sense of the way the War was rapidly changing everything everyone knew about warfare. I was delighted when I stumbled on the fact that the 2nd Dragoon Guards fought both at the Battle of Mons, and at the first Battle of Ypres.

Also known as the King's Bays (these days, the Queen's Bays) because all of them ride bay horses, the 2nd Dragoon Guards have a long history dating back to 1746. Dragoons were highly mobile infantry who rode fast and nimble horses, and used firearms in battle, often dismounting to shoot and fight once they were in the midst.

The Battle of Mons has a mention in one of my other books (*Outcrossing*) because of folklore. It was, legitimately, a fight against overwhelming odds, and there were resonances with the Battle of Agincourt. (If you've watched the Kenneth Branagh *Henry V*, you know the battle).

Not long after the battle, there was a fictional piece in the papers, describing an angelic warrior or warriors, the ghostly archers who died at Agincourt, coming to save their countrymen with their arrows. It didn't happen in our world, but in the world of Albion, there was definitely something magical going on.

After that, though, the Western Front turned into a long, muddy, awful slog. The **First Battle of Ypres** began in August 1914 and ran through the 22nd of November 1914. Roland was injured badly in early November, so he'd been at the Temple of Healing for about three and a half months when Elen arrives.

As Roland makes clear, this is a horrible way to fight for everyone, and particularly awful for cavalry. Over eight million horses and mules were killed during the War, many early on before everyone realised how futile and awful it was. (I found one statistic which said that Britain lost nearly 500,000 horses, one horse for every two men.)

Roland's concerns about continuing to do the awful

thing the worst possible way unfortunately came true. While many people in 1914 though the war would be over by Christmas, it turned into four years of misery, loss, and destruction.

Last in our war-related topics, before we turn to more cheerful subjects, **shellshock** was truly beginning to be recognised as a significant issue at about this point, though many of the necessary advances in supporting and treating people with what we now call post-traumatic stress syndrome were yet to come. Unfortunately, many people with lingering symptoms (like Roland's depression and other issues) were accused of malingering, trying to get out of going back to the Front.

Healing baths and waters have, historically, been key to many places throughout the British Isles and continental Europe. The most famous of these, likely, is Bath itself, but Baden-Baden in Germany is also well known, as are other sites in Europe.

The Trellech in our world actually does have a healing spring associated with it, including that fascinating tidbit about the water bubbling in different ways to indicate a diagnosis.

There are some theories these days that the healing baths did actually help with physical healing. Not simply through getting people away from often unhealthily crowded cities and smoggy air, or eating too many rich foods - but because the mineral-rich waters helped with a number of circulation and deficiency issues in the diet.

The baths at Trellech have two parts, as Rhoe explains. The shared public baths, in the centre of the temple, but then the smaller bathing rooms, each dedicated to different deities, depending on need and interest.

This brings me to another thing I've wanted to explore. I've been writing a world where characters have agency, the ability to make their own choices. Just as people in Albion have a range of magical skills and abilities (and levels of raw power to work with), I want the **range of religious experiences** to vary. Because, after all, plenty of people have widely different views on religion and what it means for them in our world.

Sometimes what we need is a light in the dark, showing us the way forward, and that helps far more than a miracle would, in the long run.

There are prayers in this book, formal ones. There are also the informal needs, offered up in hope of some small gift. But there's also the moments of going into the dark, and making space for a change, and finding some new path to explore. I wanted a book that has all of those, not in competition with them, but as part of a larger tapestry of what religion and belief might mean - but also what advocating for yourself or the ones you love can look like.

Of course, then we have things like the **corsned**, which is a historical form of ordeal. The term dates to before 1100, and it was originally done with barley and cheese, but it can be done with any food or drink. Other trials by ordeal include trial by combat, by fire, by water, by the cross, or by poison, among others. Many of those end up entirely fatal for the accused, even if they're innocent.

The trick for Elen was figuring out something that would be meaningful proof, without being able to invoke the oaths and mechanisms of justice used by the legal courts (since she has done nothing legally wrong, those don't apply.) Rhoe, of course, is both clever and well-read.

I was delighted when I read the **Official Secrets Act** of the time and realised it easily covered being told that magic existed. The version in this book is the 1911 Act, and basically, so long as you consider "magic exists and as real" as covered, then you can swear by the Official Secrets Act, be sufficiently bound by the Pact (the magical oath that allows the survival of magical society in Great Britain), and get on with the conversation.

Finally, we come to the **knitting** - and much thanks for my early readers who improved this. I am the sort of knitter who loves double-sided knitting, and does not have the patience for complicated lace work. (I'm also lousy at socks, though I can do a good scarf or non-lacework shawl.)

Knitting for the war effort was a huge focus of many women (and not a few men). Keep an eye on my blog for posts with some patterns and history (they'll be in the *Carry On* category.)

It was expected that you'd be busy working on practical items for men in the trenches any time your hands were idle. Besides the smaller more portable items Elen usually knits for this purpose, gloves designed to allow for shooting a gun or caps to be worn under helmets were both common, as well as larger items like warm vests.

By 1916 or 1917, there were a number of patterns

released for knitting, and many women's groups, invalids homes, or other organisations would run knitting gatherings, with the results boxed up and sent overseas as they were done.

They were much appreciated - but as Elen notes, for a skilled knitter, they don't offer a lot of challenge or variety. Items always had to be in an approved colour that wouldn't attract attention.

Her lacework shawl is indeed a Shetland pattern - these started to be published in the early 1900s. While they were traditionally pure white or cream, her love of colour got the better of her.

Many of our modern knitting techniques are, well, modern. Circular needles hadn't been invented yet - and the terms 'tink' or 'frog' for undoing stitches are both much more recent. Figuring out exactly what Elen might reasonably know about knitting and how she'd describe it took a fair bit of research!

≈

Thank you so much for reading *Carry On*. You'll be seeing more of Rhoe (and more of her mysterious brother Cyrus) in future books. The next book in the series is *The Fossil Door*, exploring a misbehaving portal in the Scottish Highlands in 1922.

EXCERPT OF THE FOSSIL DOOR

Spring 1922, London

Rathna knew the bell would ring, a moment before she heard it. She always knew. It gave her enough time to set down whatever she was doing, take a breath, and go see what Morah Avigail needed. This time, she had been sitting in the downstairs office, at her desk. She grabbed the book she'd planned to bring upstairs, and prepared to go up.

Of course, she'd been expecting this. Someone had come from the Ministry just after lunch, asking for her mistress. Whatever else his business had involved, it had included one of the formal letters with the seals that indicated some official communication. She didn't think it was an assignment, Morah Avigail was unlikely to leave the house again for any length of time. It could have been something about a pension, perhaps.

Whatever it was, Sarah, their maid, had shown the man out twenty minutes later, and it had been quiet for the two hours since. Rathna suspected her mistress had had a nap, and would refuse to admit it. That was no bother, Rathna had plenty to keep her busy. She was a fully trained portal keeper, but there was always more to read, and the second stone on the Southwark portal had a resonance that had bothered her when she ran the usual checks this week. A year ago, she'd have asked Morah Avigail to come have a listen and a look. She supposed she'd have to see about getting someone else to come look.

But they were spread thin, these days, the portal keepers. It wasn't just the War, though that hadn't helped. A number of their company had been elderly even before the War, a generation older than Morah Avigail, who was now past ninety. And while tending the portals wasn't a physically strenuous job, it was magically quite challenging. It not only needed a knack for the stones and the waters and the plants, depending on the portal itself, but rather a lot of ability to direct the magic properly. Or coax it, depending on your theory and preference in doing the work.

Rathna paused by the mirror in the entry hall, checking her image. Her dark hair was properly pinned back into a tidy bun. The forest green dress was not the brighter shade some part of her yearned for. But if it didn't highlight her brown skin, it didn't fight with it either, and it was a shade Morah Avigail thought was professional and appropriate.

She had another flash of wishing she looked in the mirror and saw something more like her mother's bright dresses when she was at home, and set it aside. Those wishes had been happening more frequently, the past few months, for reasons she didn't understand. She set it aside, as she always did. The time for that was in her room at night, alone, not any other time. Especially not when she was expected elsewhere.

She then trotted up the stairs. Morah Avigail would

certainly send her down again, on at least one errand, so she'd learned it wasn't worth the bother of bringing up a fresh drink. She got it wrong at least one time out of three, and neither she nor Morah Avigail could abide the waste. At the main bedroom, she knocked, precisely, twice.

"Come, come." The voice inside was as clear as it had been when Rathna began her apprenticeship, but as Rathna opened the door, she was reminded again that the mind and voice were still sharp, but the flesh was not what it had been. Where Morah Avigail had. been hearty and hale until six months ago, she was faded now, into herself. She was wearing a too-pale green bed jacket that did not suit her. It had been made by one of the daughters-in-law, out of yarn sensibly thrifted from someone else's discarded sweater.

One should not complain about the kindnesses shown by others. Or so she'd been taught. Even if they had a very strange idea of colours that flattered.

"Morah Avigail." She preferred the term, for all it wasn't one she'd been familiar with before her apprenticeship. It meant teacher, and she'd much preferred that, once it was offered, to the formal Magistra or Mistress of Avigail's rank.

Technically, being a full member of the Portal Keeper's Guild, Rathna didn't need to use either anymore. She wasn't supposed to, even. But while she would do the proper thing in public, pretend they were all equals, that she didn't need to defer, she'd known since she was eight that claiming equal rights would raise people's hackles.

Morah Avigail knew that lesson too, though for somewhat different reasons. It was why they'd gotten on so well from the start.

"Tsk. Come here, do, sit on the bed." The pale hand patted the bed. "You won't jostle me. I'm sure you're curious, aren't you?" Her voice had the light accent of her original Yiddish, more in the twists of the words than anything more.

Of course Rathna sat, carefully. "I noticed the letter."

Morah Avigail shifted, to pat her hand. "You have an assignment, if you will accept it. And I think you should." She lifted a hand, pointing with the pencil she'd been holding. "You will listen to it, and then you will fetch me a pot of tea. We will discuss it thoroughly, and you will agree with me."

Rathna laughed, she couldn't help it. "And I will be sent to do your bidding, as always."

"No." The word was sharp, this time. "It is time things change. I will not be here so much longer. You must learn to put your own feet on the road, not just carry along as we have."

Rathna wanted to argue. She also knew how futile it was. That didn't change the wanting. Instead, she took a breath, damping down the little flare of her magic that happened at such times. Another breath for good measure, and she nodded. "As you wish, morah."

"I am never going to break you of that, am I?" This time, Morah Avigail's voice was affectionate, and her hand reached to pat again.

"Not in private, no."

Someone else might have argued. The matrons in the orphanage of her late childhood would have suspected something was wrong, and she should be punished for her wrongness. Her teachers at Schola would have been largely unsure what to do with her but they would have left her alone. Morah Avigail, though, she laughed. "As you wish." She glanced at the letter, face down, on the bed tray. "The letter, morah?"

"'There is a portal in Scotland causing some difficulty. Someone must go to see to it."

"A city?" She didn't mind cities. It was not the only reason she was in London, near the Spitalfields portals, but she liked the bustle. The people calling out, the markets she could walk through, the way you heard a dozen different languages walking down some streets near the docks, in a block or two. It wasn't quite like the memories of her childhood, but it was close enough to touch and be real, and remind her she hadn't made it all up in her head.

"No," This time, Morah Avigail sounded sorry. "Quite remote. The western coast, the countryside."

"'That's quite a new portal." Rathna had not particularly studied it, why would she have? But she knew the map as well as any of them did.

"A few years. It has been temperamental for several months, and now it has failed."

"Failed." It came out a bit flat. That was an interesting challenge, but it promised a tediously long trip.

"Failed. You'll have to take the train, I'm afraid."

Rathna permitted herself to make a face at that, grimacing. She hated trains. They were loud and noisy and dirty and metal. Metals were not her strong suit, she did much better with stone and with trees and earth. Worse, trains involved rather a lot of people who would probably not be kind to her. "What kind of portal?"

"Stone. Now, you go away and make me tea, and bring me the proper books when you come back, and we will talk these things through.

Rathna stood, brushing out her skirts, and went. Again, she knew it there was no point in arguing. Morah Avigail had never punished her, she had been a kind and patient mistress in the arts of keeping a portal humming happily along. Her disappointment was a far harsher thing to bear, and it only took a look and perhaps half a sigh. That did not make things easier, just simpler to manage.

Making the tea properly was as soothing as it always was. There were the little rituals of tea leaves, and water, and setting the tray just so. She had fetched the books they'd need to go on the other half of the tray, unbalancing it a bit, and she'd let Sarah know they'd likely be wanting supper upstairs together. By the time she returned, Morah Avigail was dozing, and Rathna set the tray down as silently as she could, before settling into the easy chair by the window with one of the books, about the most recent additions to the portal tree.

Half an hour later, there was a slight cough from the bed. "Tea, please."

The pot had kept itself properly warm. For all Morah Avigail was cautious with her money, she didn't skimp on the tools they used all the time, and that definitely included the tea pot. Their work paid respectably, enough to keep Sarah and have enough food on their table and proper clothes and the various needs for their work that weren't provided by the Ministry, as well as an extensive private library.

But Morah Avigail took her charity seriously. And of course she wanted to make sure she could help her grown children when one of them had a bad spell. That meant that things were used to the edge of their usefulness, and perhaps a bit further. They'd had three weeks of tepid tea, before Rathna had convinced Morah Avigail that they really should replace the teapot now.

Rathna set the tea cup up, and the plate of biscuits, and then put herself firmly on the bed, facing her teacher. "I will go. As you said." Morah Avigail laughed, and Rathna was quite glad to do anything that brought that light to her more times. Every amusement mattered more. "How long do you think I'll need to be there?"

It wasn't just that she disliked the countryside. Or was baffled by it, that might be a better way to put it. But she didn't want to be away if Morah Avigail took a turn for the worse. She knew she'd be shouldered out by Morah Avigail's proper family, she couldn't argue with that. But she wanted to be there to be shouldered aside.

"A month or more, I suspect. And I am fairly sure that is rather less time than I have left. You worry, my dear, rather openly. My condition for accepting, to that nice and somewhat uncertain man from the Ministry, was that there be a quick way to get you home if needed. They are making proper arrangements."

Rathna had never been able to hide either her worry or her relief, and she didn't bother to try to hide the latter now. "Thank you." She didn't say more, she didn't need to. They both knew, for all they rarely talked about it.

"What have they told you about what happened to it? What do we know?"

Morah Avigail snorted. "The report is there. Read it out to me, and we will begin our proper plan." The systematic approach to reviewing the nature of the portal, how it had rooted, whether there were gaps or breaks in the energy, if something nearby had disturbed it, all of their methods. Then, before Rathna could read, Morah Avigail coughed. "You will have company in the work. One of the Penelopes from the Guard. The Ministry man said it was Gabrielle Edgarton. I don't know more than that, yet."

Rathna nodded once. She didn't like the idea much,

someone fussing and jostling her, but she was not the one being consulted here. If the Ministry were being like this, it must be important to someone with power. She picked up the report, and began to read.

Sign up for my newsletter to be the first to hear when *The Fossil Door* is available. Until then, happy reading!